WOLF OF MERCIA

BOOK 2 THE EAGLE OF MERCIA CHRONICLES

M J PORTER

Boldwood

First published in Great Britain in 2022 by Boldwood Books Ltd.

Cover Design by Head Design Ltd

Cover Photography: Shutterstock

A CIP catalogue record for this book is available from the British Library.

Paperback ISBN 978-1-80280-763-9

Large Print ISBN 978-1-80280-762-2

Hardback ISBN 978-1-80280-761-5

Ebook ISBN 978-1-80280-764-6

Kindle ISBN 978-1-80280-765-3

Audio CD ISBN 978-1-80280-756-1

MP3 CD ISBN 978-1-80280-757-8

Digital audio download ISBN 978-1-80280-758-5

Boldwood Books Ltd
23 Bowerdean Street
London SW6 3TN
www.boldwoodbooks.com

For EP. Thank you for always believing, even when I didn't.

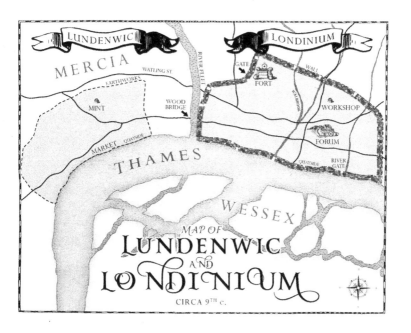

Designed by Flintlock Covers

CAST OF CHARACTERS

Icel, orphaned youth living in Tamworth, his mother was Ceolburh
Brute, Icel's horse
Edwin, Icel's childhood friend, although they have been separated
Cenfrith, Icel's uncle, brother of Ceolburh and one of the Mercian
king's warriors, dies in *Son of Mercia*
Wine, Cenfrith's horse, now Icel's alongside Brute
Wynflæd, an old herbwoman at the Mercian king's court at
Tamworth

The Kings of Mercia
Coelwulf, King of Mercia, r.821–825 (deposed)
Beornwulf, King of Mercia, r.825–826 (killed)
Lady Cynehild, Beornwulf's wife
Wiglaf, King of Mercia, r.827–829 (deposed) r.830–
Lady Cynethryth, Wiglaf's wife
Wigmund, Wiglaf's son
Ecgberht, King of Wessex, r.829 in Mercia as well

The Ealdormen of Mercia

Ælfstan, one of King Wiglaf's supporters, an ally to Icel

Beornoth, one of King Wiglaf's ealdormen

Muca, one of King Wiglaf's ealdormen

Sigered, a long-standing ealdorman, who's survived the troubled years of the 820s

Tidwulf, an old ally of King Wiglaf

Æthelweald, Bishop of Lichfield

Bealdred, Lord of Kent, dead

The Ealdormen of Wessex

Wassa of the South Saxons, holds Londinium for King Ecgberht of Wessex

Eata of Hampshire and Wassa's brother

Wilfhardi, inside Lundenwic

Ælfhere, from Canterbury

Rulers of Other Kingdoms

Athelstan, King of the East Angles

Ecgberht, King of Wessex

Lord Æthelwulf – Ecgberht's son, designated King of Kent by his father after the battle of Ellendun

People of Wessex

Æsc, an ally of Ecgred

Brihtwold, a youth like Icel

Dealwine, Wessex warrior

Ecgred, a healer inside Londinium

Theodore, slave man with a talent for healing

Gaya, slave woman with a talent for healing

Tyrhtil, seasoned Wessex warrior

Æthelred, a warrior

Mercians

Æthelmod, Mercian warrior

Cenred, Mercian warrior

Cuthred, inhabitant of Tamworth

Eahric, commander of the king's household warriors

Frithwine, young Mercian warrior

Garwulf, young Mercian warrior

Goðeman, Mercian warrior

Kyre, Mercian warrior

Landwine, Mercian warrior

Maneca, Mercian warrior

Ordlaf, Mercian warrior

Osmod, Mercian warrior

Oswald, at Kingsholm

Oswy, one of Wiglaf's warriors

Uor, Mercian warrior

Waldhere, Mercian warrior

Wulfgar, Mercian warrior

Wulfheard, a Mercian warrior, Ealdorman Ælfstan's oathsworn man

Bada, Wulfheard's horse

Places

Kingsholm, associated with the ruling family of King Coelwulf, close to Gloucester

Londonia, combining the ruins of Roman Londinium and Saxon Lundenwic

Tamworth, the capital of the Mercian kingdom

Kingdom of the East Angles, part of Mercia at the end of the 700s but reclaimed its freedom under King Beornwulf of Mercia, Athelstan now rules there

Kingdom of Wessex, the area south of the River Thames, including

Kent at this time, but not Dumnonia (Cornwall and Devon)

THE MERCIAN REGISTER

AD830

King Wiglaf of Mercia has reclaimed his capital at Tamworth from the pretensions of King Ecgberht of Wessex and sent his enemy running to the borderland between the two kingdoms. But King Ecgberht is not defeated. He lurks on the southern fringes of Mercia, claiming the twin settlement of Londonia as his own, one wyvern claw in the market settlement, and one in the long-since abandoned, but strategically important, stone-built fort. King Ecgberht guards both closely, his aim to control Mercia's wealth and, in doing so, take command of the lucrative trading centre and mint that supplies so much of Mercia's wealth. King Wiglaf will not allow such matters to stay as they are.

1

AD830

Ahead, I can see the double settlement coming into view. I gasp in surprise. I can make out some huge grey stone walls to the east and smoke billowing from the homes inside the western settlement, the two divided by a wide river glinting sullenly. There's the promise of warmth in the pale blue sky of a very late summer's day, if only we could make our way inside either settlement.

'Aye, lad. It's not exactly small,' Wulfheard offers from bestride his horse, Bada. The beast moves easily, his white-socked legs making it appear as though sunlight flashes with every step he takes.

Beneath me, Brute fights my every instruction. After all we've been through in our ride to defeat King Ecgberht in the borderlands of the Welsh and Mercian kingdoms and to reach my dying uncle, he remains an unwilling accomplice. Still, and as terrible as it sounds, I'd sooner risk Brute than my uncle's horse, Wine. Wine is all I've left of my uncle. I'll not risk his life in the coming attack. For now, Wine is safe in Tamworth, young Cuthred pleased to be asked to tend him for me. Wine seemed just as content to take her ease. Not that Wynflæd had approved of that arrangement.

Wynflæd and I have made an awkward reconciliation at Tamworth. She's not happy with me, and she mourns for my uncle at the same time. The knowledge startles me. I'd never thought she thought much of him. Or rather, I'd never believed she cared for him. It seems I was wrong and now he's missed.

Nothing I can say or do is right. Every time I visit her, there's some new complaint to lay at my door. Cuthred isn't quite who she has in mind as her replacement. She still expects me to do her bidding, despite my oath to King Wiglaf to be his sworn man, and to stand in his shield wall to defend Mercia.

From my vantage point, on the vast length of road that stretches southwards, some of it stone-covered, other parts merely dying tufted grass, I can see Londonia. Wulfheard has explained it all to me on the journey here. It's confusing, to say the least. And now I try to make sense of his words to determine just what I can see.

Lundenwic, to the west, is more or less a huge market, stretched along the banks of the River Thames. I can pick out small craft moving on its forbidding surface bringing with them the goods and people who use Lundenwic to trade and make their living.

Londinium is far older, surrounded by those soaring grey walls, the ancient works of giants, as Wulfheard laughingly told me when I questioned him about the destination of King Wiglaf's warband. I detected the hint of unease in Wulfheard's voice at the words. These giants, as Wulfheard termed them, must indeed have been monstrous men and women to build walls so tall that they're visible even from such a vast distance away. They blot out the River Thames behind them. I see only where the river disappears behind the stone, and then where it appears again, as though two rivers, and not one.

Wulfheard is content to lump both settlements, the abandoned, grey-walled Londinium and the occupied Lundenwic, together and call it Londonia. I think he's right to do so, even with the wide River

Fleet dividing the pair of them so that others might think it two places.

We ride to the east of the River Fleet. There's a bridge to cross by, so I've been informed.

Wulfheard tells me that Londinium might well have tall walls that promise security, but a man and woman can't live on produce grown on the unending layer of stone that covers everything. There's no soil to be found behind those walls. And without soil, there can be no food, and so the walls offer the promise of safety but an empty belly. They're too tall and immovable to allow access to the River Thames apart from in one place. So, Londinium has been all but abandoned. The traders have forged a new settlement and it's built of Mercian wood, Mercian sticks and Mercian shit.

Now I ride towards this many-named place. Like Wulfheard, I decide that Londonia will be the name I choose to describe this twin settlement.

King Wiglaf, fresh from regaining his place as Mercia's king, is eager to have King Ecgberht of Wessex evicted from Londonia. Wiglaf wishes to reclaim the lost mint housed inside the market settlement, and from which Ecgberht mints coins proclaiming himself as king of Mercia. As almost an aside, Wiglaf wants the holy men, and the wealth of taxes that must be paid to allow Mercians and non-Mercians to trade inside the market itself, restored to him.

'We won't find a warm welcome in Londonia,' Wulfheard assures me conversationally. 'They don't care who they pay their taxes to as long as they can trade and live as they want. There's little loyalty to Mercia. They favour making enough coins to purchase the supplies they need to live. And the supplies, of course, can come from Wessex or Mercia, or even, if they must, from the ships that routinely dock at the market, stretched along the market's shoreline.'

I nod, but I don't truly comprehend Wulfheard's explanation.

Yes, I've heard of Londonia. Yes, I know it's Mercian. Or, at least, it was. Now King Ecgberht of Wessex claims it as the last bastion of his failed invasion of Mercia. King Wiglaf means to have it back. It'll be war. I know that. Why else would King Wiglaf have summoned his ealdormen and warriors if not for war? While we're gone, the Welsh kingdoms of Powys or Gwynedd might think to attack, or even that bastard king-slayer, Athelstan of the East Angles, but it's towards Londonia that we're travelling. We must risk everything to rid Mercia of King Ecgberht of Wessex. Like my uncle before me, I fear that in being so single-minded with his purpose, King Wiglaf jeopardises so much more. I know I'm not alone in having such worries.

'What will King Wiglaf do?' I ask, curious. Behind me stretch many warriors on horseback, and to the rear of them, men who run or walk to keep up. They're the king's warriors but have no horse to ride. We're armed, and yet, if the reports from Londonia are to be believed, the warriors of Wessex still vastly overtop those of the Mercians. The Wessex warriors have run from their defeat on the Welsh borderlands, but they've not gone far. They're entrenched on Mercia's southernmost border. King Wiglaf is incensed.

'The king will offer a peace settlement, and when King Ecgberht refuses it, he'll attack.'

'But where will we attack?'

Now Wulfheard smirks at me, reining in his mount so that we can stop and eye the settlement in front of us, rearing up from the lower-lying land close to the vast river stretching moodily along the limits of the Mercian kingdom. 'Where would you suggest, my young friend?'

I eye Londonia in its fullness. My eyes are drawn to the thick grey walls to the east that surround the fort. It seems impossible to gain entry through those enormous walls. I can only imagine how thick they are to support such height. Perhaps Wulfheard is correct.

Maybe the walls were built by giants. And, of course, the wide River Thames precludes an attack from the south, even if there wasn't a wall blocking much of the way. It seems then that an assault must come through the more open area to the west of the River Fleet, on the market settlement.

'There,' and I point towards my chosen location. The land is flat. No walls protect the trading settlement, which lies open so that ships can furnish their trade along the riverbank. Smoke rises into the cold air from the many wooden homes and workshops. It appears it'll be easy to attack.

Wulfheard nods, but there's a knowing smirk on his face. 'I suggest that you leave such matters to your king and his ealdormen. They know much more than you.'

The words sting, as does Wulfheard's abandonment of me, when he encourages Bada onwards to mingle with King Wiglaf and his ealdorman. They ride in front of us, leading the men, beneath a banner portraying Mercia's eagle.

I keep my gaze firmly forward, looking through narrow eyes to hold back the glare of the slanted sun, convinced I've still chosen the best position. And yet, I'm not foolish enough to think I must be right, far from it. I've been a warrior for far less time than all of these men who fight for the king. I've seen one shield wall and hardly fought in it. Still, Wulfheard's dismissal irks. Not for the first time, and despite her angry words meant to wound, I wish myself back to Tamworth and Wynflæd; to my childhood, because one thing is for sure, I'm not a child any more. I ceased to be on my beloved uncle's death. His death remains fresh. I can still smell him on Wine's saddle. Just thinking of him brings unshed tears to my eyes.

I could be angry at Wynflæd that my training was too little to save him, despite my best efforts. But I understand Cenfrith's wounds were mortal. I did what I could to save him. And yet, in the depths of each night, when I wake, expecting him to be beside me, I know it's my fault he's dead and I live. I should have defied King Wiglaf. I should have stayed by his side, protected him from the Wessex enemy, and then he'd yet live. And I wouldn't be alone.

'Ware.' The roar ruptures the air. It comes from the front of the riding men, spread wide over the remains of the ancient road. The summer weeds have been beaten back into submission by the increasingly colder days and nights as men and women scurry to gather in the harvest. I'm riding head down, sullen, the chill of the day making me shiver, even though I've donned my cloak to cover my battle byrnie. For once, I'm grateful for the stinking linen cap I wear inside my helm. It's doing its best to keep my ears warm.

Sleepily, I gaze forward, unsure why the cry has been raised.

'What is it?' I ask of the large man closest to me, but Oswy merely grunts. He and I don't much like one another. I would wish Wulfheard were beside me still and not riding with the ealdorman and the king. Oswy has long been a member of the king's household warriors, and I know him from my time in Tamworth. He once served as Lady Cynethryth's personal guard. Now he fights for the king.

As I ride closer, I realise that not all of the smoke shrouding the market settlement comes from homes. There's an enemy encampment as well. I detect the flashes of weapons, the mass of horses in a picket, the uneven lines of temporary canvas shelters. The wooden stakes angled from the mud to drive into the hearts of man or beast who tries to ride through them. My heart thuds in my chest.

The following command fills my stomach with iron. I swallow, uneasy that the food I ate earlier will reappear in my mouth.

'Shield wall.' It hardly seems the place to have a shield wall, not when we have the horses and the supply waggons stretched out behind us. This isn't planned. Yet, the rest of the mounted warriors are quickly dismounting, handing their horses off to anyone who'll take them, or urging them back to the stable boys at the rear of the procession. Then the warriors run forwards to do as the harsh voice commands, their weapons and shields clattering noisily.

'Hurry up, Icel.' Wulfheard's words ring too loudly as he rushes back my way, Bada easily taking his commands.

As I attempt to dismount, I tangle my leg in my cloak and tumble heavily to the hard ground in a cacophony of hurts and clatters. I'm not a natural rider. I've not trained for this. I'm more lethal with a knife and a bunch of herbs than I am with a shield and seax. My arse still hurts after every day spent in the saddle. My hands as well, from griping seax and shield during my continued training. And Brute isn't an easy beast.

'Come on.' Of course, it's Ealdorman Ælfstan who watches my humiliation. As does Oswy and others of his ilk, their laughter a counterpart to the thrum of the shield wall that faces us in front. The Wessex warriors are keen to begin the slaughter. 'It seems King Ecgberht has news of our arrival.' Ealdorman Ælfstan bends to assist me to my feet with his strong arm. His face shows no sign of humour, his brown beard and moustache covering much of his true feelings on the matter. It's as though he speaks of what he might eat for dinner, and not a fight to the death.

'Are there many of them?' I think to ask. Not that it matters, and, probably, it would be better if I didn't know.

'More than enough,' the ealdorman confirms.

By now, Wulfheard has reappeared before me, his eyes raking me in, no sign of Bada.

'Take your cloak off. You'll be dead three times as quickly if you try to fight in that.' There's disgust in his words.

I'm annoyed. I never meant to join the shield wall wearing it. I just haven't had time to remove it yet.

I bend to remove the mud that stains my knees, wincing at the pain of such a hard impact, even as I reach for my tumbled seax and war axe.

Wulfheard fumbles with my eagle-headed shield on Brute's reins while the cries of laughter quickly fade away. The men have other things to consider than my clumsy dismount.

'Remain at the back,' Wulfheard commands me. 'The last time we faced our enemy, they were weak and numbered far fewer. Stay out of trouble.'

With his words cast over his broad shoulders and his helm wedged in place, the older warrior jogs away from me. I stand, reaching out to Brute, my fear making my chest heave.

Ealdorman Ælfstan spares me a look from casting his eyes over the arrangement of the rest of the king's force, dividing to follow their oathsworn ealdormen. 'The king expects you to fight for him, not to linger at the rear.' His words have no urgency, but they thrum with intensity.

'But...' I stumble.

'Aye, do as Wulfheard says. Now, tie up Brute's reins on your saddle. I don't want him tripping if he gets spooked or has to run.'

I do as ordered, sparing a thought for Brute. The animal eyes me warily. Brute knows better than I do what's about to happen. I don't doubt that he has more experience as a warrior's mount than I have as a warrior.

The men from the back of the procession, those who've walked or run down Watling Street from our muster at Tamworth, hurry past me as I finish my task and prepare to send Brute on his way to the rest of the horses. I watch those men. They have much less equipment than I do. They have no byrnie, perhaps only a spear, and not a seax, and some don't even have a helm. Yet they've fought for Mercia more times than I have. Or, at least, I hope they have. I need to rely on someone other than myself.

'Hurry up.' Ealdorman Ælfstan's voice has lost its sympathetic edge.

With a final rub down Brute's long nose, which is battered aside as though I'm a fly come to annoy him, I amble to a quick run, a slap to Brute's rump sending him to the back.

The last time I faced the enemy, I did so knowing that I could hasten to my uncle once they were dead. There's no such impetus this time. Instead, terror threatens to turn my legs to lead, my arms to dead weights, and I don't believe I'll be as lucky as I was before.

2

I rush past the king and two of Mercia's ealdormen. They remain mounted, King Wiglaf and, of course, Ealdormen Sigered and Muca: the two men who don't like to risk their lives but are happy enough to urge others to the task.

A handful of the king's especial warriors remains to protect them. One holds aloft Mercia's banner of an eagle on a blood-red background.

Ahead and slightly down the slope, I can see where some of the ealdormen have taken command of the shield wall that's forming up. Ealdorman Tidwulf is to the right, Ealdorman Beornoth to the left and, in the middle, Ealdorman Ælfstan has overtaken me and shouts orders to the men that are his to command.

There's no sign of the king's son, Wigmund. He's remained in Tamworth with his mother, Lady Cynethryth. Right now, I think Wigmund's the more intelligent out of the two of us, for all I've been happy to despise him, as have the other warriors, on the journey south.

'Come on, men. Take your places.' Ealdorman Sigered's distinctive voice rises above everyone else's, and I know I'm not alone in turning to glare at him, mounted and showing no inclination of actually entering the coming battle at all. He might be old and lined, but that's no excuse for not taking up his shield and seax.

'Skinny bastard should get off his arse and fight,' one man calls to another just in front of me. The second man tuts loudly enough that everyone can hear. These are the men who have no horses to sit upon.

'He doesn't know his arse from his elbow,' another calls, and they're all laughing. I think it would have been better had Ealdorman Sigered kept his thoughts to himself rather than face such ridicule from men who will stand in the shield wall and risk their lives for the king, and for Mercia.

I wish I knew more of the men who are Wiglaf's warriors or who owe their sword to the king's ealdormen. I'd hoped to come to know them better while we travelled south, along Watling Street, towards Londonia. But Ealdorman Ælfstan has eagerly resumed my training, begun when he assisted me on our journey from Bardney to Tamworth and then to the border with the Welsh kingdoms. He's determined that I should fight as well as anyone, even though my training's being crammed into a short period of time, and some of them have laboured on it since old enough to hold a wooden sword. If I'm to stand in a shield wall, I should know how to use seax, sword and spear. Ealdorman Ælfstan says my uncle should have trained me, although there's no malice in such a complaint. My uncle allowed me to follow my desire to become a healer, not a killer. How times have changed.

During the day, I've been too exhausted to speak, content to allow Brute to have his head, provided that head doesn't take me careering through the fields being harvested by the men and women of Mercia. The damn bugger has helped himself to more than one unearthed turnip, much to the outrage of those who've planted and reaped the crop.

Instead, each night I've slept at the fire Wulfheard has chosen, ensuring I stay close enough that men such as Oswy are content to leave me alone. They resent me for being so unskilled and for winning the grudging regard of their king. Wynflæd would assure me it was all my fault for saving King Wiglaf's life in the borderlands, fighting the Wessex warriors. When King Wiglaf was alone and unprotected, I ran to his aid when no one else saw the danger. Wulfheard lays the blame at the other warriors' feet. Either way, I know I'm not yet enough of a warrior to have earned anyone's respect.

'Oswy's an arse. He's survived so many battles, more by luck than chance. Like Ealdorman Sigered, he's learned which ones to fight in. But, now that King Wiglaf has gathered his ealdormen and their warriors together, he has less chance of keeping out of the thick of it.' Wulfheard's words are meant to reassure.

Not that every warrior has the same story as Oswy. Many of them have little more experience than I do, although they've been training for much of their lives. Unlike me. I've been training to heal and comfort, not to maim and kill. The change has come over me quickly since the summer months. I don't truly welcome such a transformation. Not yet. But there's no going back to who I used to be. I'm to be a warrior of Mercia. Whether I like it or not.

'At least we know our place,' I've heard more than one of them say when Brute has streaked past them and their slower mounts. I hardly think it my fault that the king gifted me such a horse. I think I'd sooner he hadn't. But then, Wulfheard explained to me when I complained to him about it that Wiglaf is the king and he must be seen to recompense his warriors, or why would they lay down their lives for him?

The words are meant to comfort me, but, instead, they remind me of what I did on that fateful day, of my uncle's death and of the new path my life has taken in the short amount of time that has elapsed since then. I never wanted to be a warrior, but the king forced my oath to him, and now there's no choice. I fear I might never reconcile myself to these huge changes that have befallen me.

'Here, boy, get in the shield wall.' Ealdorman Tidwulf thinks to call me to his side of the coming battle.

'Icel, I've a place for you here.' Ealdorman Ælfstan's words flow over those of Tidwulf's, from where he stands ready to enter the shield wall, giving final instructions to his oathsworn men. For a moment, I'm torn, until Wulfheard grabs my shoulder.

'This way, you arse. It's better in the centre. Did no one ever teach you that?' Only, he pauses, flashes me a tight smile of apology. 'I'll teach you more when this is over,' Wulfheard promises and, depositing me between two youths who can be little older than I am, he shoulders his way to the front.

I eye the two youths. They fumble with shields and seaxes, just as I do, only then the one, with little more than a sliver of fur on his top lip, sneers at me.

'It's him. The one they're all talking about,' he announces loudly to his fellow warrior. Both of them look at me as though I'm little better than horseshit on their boots.

'It's the boy who thought to save a king by knocking himself out,' the other jeers, strips of blond hair visible beneath the helm he wears. It's dented. In fact, it's more dent than round, and I can see where it seems to lift from the top of his head.

'You need to get that hammered out,' I inform him. If he takes a blow to the head, that helm isn't going to be any help. It's more likely to pierce him than save him.

'Oh, listen to him. It seems he knows it all.' The two of them both laugh, the sound sharper and deadlier than blades.

I grimace. I don't much want to stand beside the pair of them.

'Get to the rear of the line in front.' Ealdorman Ælfstan's words are gruff as he continues with his instructions.

Ahead of us, we're faced with little more than the broad backs of Mercia's more seasoned warriors. Or if not more seasoned, then at least older than we are. These men have trained all their lives for the honour of serving their king in war.

From in front of the Mercian force, I can hear similar from the Wessex warriors. It always startles me that our enemy shares our tongue. Perhaps, I think, it would be easier if they were Raiders and spoke their harsher words.

Immediately, I move forwards, the smell of the men in front making me appreciate I'm not the only one to fear what's coming.

Of course, the two other lads take their time in following the ealdorman's instructions.

'Frithwine, get in line.' The growl comes from the man in front of me. I don't know his name. 'Garwulf, do the same.'

At least I know their names now. They must be brothers, I decide. They share the same querulous jaw.

I'd sooner be fighting for Ealdorman Tidwulf than stood beside these two jesters.

I wish I could see more of what's happening in front, but it's impossible. Even as tall as I am, I can do little more than see the tightly packed helms of those just before me.

I note that this time the numbers of Mercians are far higher than when last we fought the Wessex enemy. There are four lines of men between me and the curved edges of the shields. They glint in the gentle glow from the sun and I quickly get my head down. I don't want to make myself an obvious target if one of the Wessex warriors should try their luck.

'The Wessex scum will run back to Londonia soon enough,' Frithwine jokes to his ally. Their words are high with excitement. I wish them luck with that.

'Shields.' King Wiglaf shouts the command from behind us all. I'd recognise his voice anywhere.

I place my feet carefully. Ahead of me, the Mercians are doing the same. However, Frithwine and Garwulf aren't beside me. I turn my head, thinking I should say something, but stop myself. I don't want to face any more of their ridicule. They think I don't know what I'm doing. They should take a look at themselves.

From the far side of the shield wall, I hear a harsh cry from one of the Wessex warriors. I doubt it's the king himself, but I might be wrong. King Ecgberht is a man I've never met, although I've seen him from a distance with his iron-grey hair, rigid back and warrior's helm with its proud horsehair crown. I've no respect for him. He abandoned his wounded warriors to face the Mercians. He rode, as fast as his horse could take him, back to the perceived safety of Londonia. I do welcome him being ejected from Mercia. Perhaps, after all, I agree with Wiglaf's decision to bring all of his warriors against the Wessex force maintaining a perilous hold on Londonia. Ecgberht of Wessex is the true enemy, even if Athelstan of the East Angles is the slayer of Mercia's kings.

I just wish I wasn't one of those who had to bear witness to it.

The men in front of me lurch forwards. I'm not expecting to move, and yet it makes sense. The Wessex warriors are defending what they've stolen. The Mercians are the ones who need to claim it back. We must take the fight to them now that they've made it clear there'll be no negotiation.

We walk, or rather run, onwards, the ground threatening to trip, the long strips of summer-ripened wheat waiting to be harvested, ruined by our progress as we've moved aside from the passage of Watling Street.

My breath rasps in my chest, the smell of sweat seeming to bloom from the men before me. I risk looking behind, but I can't see King Wiglaf and the two ealdormen any more. I don't know if he's moved away from his high peak or if we've gone too low to be able to see him. It's impossible to tell as I forge a path through the brown stalks. I've lost sight of Frithwine and Garwulf. I do glimpse Wulfheard at the front of the shield wall through a sudden slit that opens up between the men in front. He's not easy to misplace with his distinctive blackened helm, so unlike the rest of the warriors, whose helms shimmer with the glint of iron.

My eyes focused on where I step, I almost collide with the man in front of me, his byrnie darkened with sweaty streaks beneath his armpits.

'Watch it,' he growls, lips twisted as he glowers. 'You should put your seax away if you don't know how to fight with it.'

The words cut me. I do know how to fight with it. I've saved the king's life with it, but now isn't the time for such a conversation.

I shrug my shoulders at my contrariness. I both do and don't want people to appreciate what I've accomplished on behalf of King Wiglaf.

Bugger it. I'll just have to prove myself one more time and live up to the memory of my warrior uncle, who lived when kings fell beneath the blades of the bastard king-slayer of the East Angles.

3

A thunderous sound, louder even than a Mercian oak being felled to provide sturdy support for a new hall or workshop, reverberates through my body. My heart thuds in my ears, the noise quicker than a herd of horses spurred to the gallop.

The two shield walls have met. I know that, and so do the men in front of me who are ready for whatever might happen next. They're braced, broad backs facing me, the murmur of their prayers or wails of terror a counterpart to the clash of shields and weapons.

But I don't include Frithwine and Garwulf in that. The pair continue to taunt one another where they stand to the rear of the engagement, as though they're about to drink in a tavern, not fight for their lives. They're not battle-ready, even now. Frithwine's shield is upside down on the floor by his feet, the strap entirely out of reach, hidden in the depths of the soil. Garwulf has removed his helm and examines it to ensure it's not as bashed as Frithwine's. His gloved finger pokes at the iron of his helm as though he expects to see it come through the iron.

'Get in position,' I urge them.

To the far side of the pair, there are more seasoned men, eyes forward. Their bodies already ebb and flow as they begin their dance to the death, mirroring the progress of the front-facing line of shields. A sudden retreat or advance won't catch them unawares.

'Bugger off,' Frithwine sneers. 'You're not the bloody battle commander.'

'And neither are you.' This comes from one of the warriors. Blazing eyes settle on the boys. I want to call them men, but they're acting like children. Even I know that. 'Now, get in line. This is going to get bloody quickly.'

Already, I can sense something occurring at the front. My thoughts turn to Wulfheard. I don't want anything to happen to him. Apart from Ealdorman Ælfstan, he's about the only person, other than Wynflæd, who seems to care about me now that my uncle is dead, and I'm alone, with no family to my name.

Before Garwulf can argue with the man, the Mercian warriors surge once more. I'm part of it. I've no one to protect me to the left or right, so I move closer to the man to my left. He turns terror-filled eyes my way that bulge from behind his helm. He takes no comfort in my presence. I don't take it personally.

Looking down, I catch sight of a discarded seax, the sharp edge buried in the crushed wheat of the field, blood glistening on the blade. I follow the handle of the seax higher and grimace. A dripping finger clings to the bone handle, but nothing else.

I think to bend and retrieve the seax, but Frithwine beats me to it. He smirks, forcing me aside in his eagerness to grip it so that I overbalance and fight to stay upright without dropping my shield to the ground.

'Our first battle treasure,' Frithwine gloats to Garwulf, his back to the men of the shield wall, only to shriek, the sound piercing above the duller tones and grunts of the battle. The damn fool hasn't seen the severed finger. The seax flies through the air, just landing shy of my foot. A little closer and I'd be skewered in place as surely as the trampled wheat. 'Did you see that?' Frithwine demands of his ally, pointing to the discarded finger.

But there's no time for a reply. As quickly as the men advanced, they're suddenly retracing those steps – one foot and then another. I wish I'd grabbed the hastily flung seax because someone's going to sever their foot on the upturned blade.

But Frithwine, with his back to the retreat, doesn't realise what's happening.

I watch, my cry of warning too late, as one of the Mercians crashes into Frithwine. The boy has no chance to move, his foot trapped in place by the weight of the Mercian.

Frithwine thuds to the earth. I catch sight of his pale face beneath the dark stalks, fearful, as not one but two men stamp over him. Garwulf throws himself at the two Mercians. They turn, fear making them stab out without thought, and Garwulf earns himself a deep gash on his right arm for his efforts, but Frithwine remains trapped.

Frithwine's screams cover all sound. I can't hear anything from the battle line. I can't make out the echo of any commands from Ealdorman Ælfstan. I know there's only one thing to be done.

Hastily, I shove my shoulders against the men of the shield wall who are crushing Frithwine, forcing them forwards so that they're compressed against those compelled to retreat. I'm aware that, in doing so, the Mercian warriors move uneasily.

'Get him,' I huff to Garwulf, shoulders straining against the weight of not just two men, but every single warrior who thinks to withdraw. I won't be able to halt the men for longer than a moment or two. If Garwulf doesn't hurry, Frithwine will be entirely crushed beneath Mercian boots.

Desperately, Garwulf grabs hold of Frithwine beneath his armpits, pulling him away rather than letting him regain his feet. Angry cries of fear and frustration reach my ears. I'm just waiting for the king or the ealdormen to realise what's happening. Any goodwill I might have earned in my actions that saved the king will evaporate soon enough because I'm putting Frithwine's life above that of Mercia's success.

As soon as Frithwine's free, I stagger clear, allowing the Mercians to take their five steps backwards, for the unstable line of men to reform in almost neat rows.

I don't expect any thanks. I don't get it either. Frithwine continues to wail, prone on the crushed wheat, although at least three horse lengths behind the line of attack. I don't risk looking at him. I know he'll be bruised and muddied. Bloody arsehole. Even I know not to turn my back on the damn shield wall.

'Advance.' No sooner have the uneven lines reformed than the Mercians once more press the advantage. Footprints have churned the ground beneath my feet. There are more and more abandoned weapons, often seaxes knocked from the hands of warriors by shields crashing together or suddenly sundering apart. The crop is entirely ruined, flattened to the earth, just as surely as Frithwine would have been.

I take my place beside my ally once more.

'You should have bloody left the idiot,' he denounces me, but there's no venom in his voice. That's because the intensity of the battle is increasing. One step forward, another back. The men have to stay alert, watchful of what's happening because it's impossible to see around the backs of the Mercians on the front of the shield wall.

The sound of screaming and shrieking fills the air, just as much as the dull thud of weapons hitting the wood of the shields does.

I look down and just avoid standing on the staring eyes of the first of the dead. I don't know his name. He has a seax thrust through one of his open eyes, his helm nowhere to be seen, his tongue greying where it sticks out of his mouth, blood dripping from the corner of his mouth to pool onto the dark earth.

his left hand. With it, the foeman reaches for the feet of the Mercians. More than one stunned man is trying to shake the shock of a fall from his body.

'Wessex scum,' my comrade repeats.

I agree with him, but still, he wears no man's blood. He's good at talking but has done little of note.

Onwards we go, the steps almost a running stride. For a moment, I'm confused. Have the Mercians won the battle already? Only then, the line comes to a juddering halt. I don't quite catch the cry of outrage, but my comrade must.

'They've got a second bloody line,' he complains, disgust in the rigid set of his jaw, which is about all I can see beneath his iron helm.

I risk looking behind me. The Mercians have travelled almost the distance of the sloping wheat field, the wide swathe of destruction attesting to that. The field is filled with nearly as many broken bodies as snapped stems. I don't see King Wiglaf or the two battle-shy ealdormen.

And then I do, more by the fluttering of the eagle battle standard than anything else. The king still observes, but with only one ealdorman at his side, no doubt Sigered. Four of the king's warriors are tasked with guarding his person, beside the bannerman who holds the eagle battle standard of Mercia. Where the other ealdorman has gone, I don't know. I don't have time to consider it either.

'Brace.' I sense the men in front of me stiffen, preparing to hold in place for as long as they must.

The shields of the second row of warriors catch the sun on their rims, almost blinding me, where they hold them in place over the heads of the first row of warriors.

Here and there, the neat lines have become compacted. There aren't as many men as when we started. Yet, I'm still at the back.

I bend and rub my bloodied gloves through some stray green grasses, keen to remove the slickness there. I swallow. My mouth is dry, my lips tingling with lack of water. I couldn't piss myself, even if my life depended on it. I wish I'd drunk more today. It's uncomfortable now that I'm aware of just how thirsty I am.

I feel the two shield walls clash. The repercussions are even louder now I'm closer. I think the Wessex warriors have deceived us. A Wessex reserve must have added their strength to the attack, but there are no more Mercians to come. This is all King Wiglaf can bring to the slaughter field. Too many have lost their lives in the battles the Mercian kings have fought in recent years. A pity we've not killed all the Wessex warriors before encountering this second shield wall.

'Hold.' I think it's Ealdorman Ælfstan who shouts the command, but his voice is muffled by the clamour of battle.

Others take up the cry. I hear the distinctive thud of hooves over the disturbed ground. Has King Wiglaf finally come to join the fray? Not that I get time to find out.

While Ealdorman Ælfstan might direct the shield wall to hold, it bucks and twists. At points, I can see, to my left, where it's forced backwards, or where the centre moves forwards. At other times, I can see nothing but the man to my left and Garwulf to my right. I can do little but add my weight, as slight as it is, to the backs of the men before me.

We trample over the dead and dying, and some of them are Mercians, and too few are Wessex warriors. But I feel as though the ground we travel over sags downwards. We're on bare soil. Maybe the earth wasn't planted this year, or, perhaps, it's already been harvested, even the remaining stalks turned over to make the soil rich for the next crop.

'We're going downhill,' the man to my left bellows. His eyes are wild behind his helm, and still no mark of violence is on his body.

The man who shouted at Frithwine and Garwulf stands on the dead man, his foot crashing through the thickened byrnie and into the man's chest. I taste vomit once more. He kicks his foot clear, perhaps not even realising what he's done. Hastily, I bend to drag the dead man away, hooking my hands beneath his shoulders and pulling with all of my strength. My shoulders, already tested from rescuing Frithwine, scream at this latest outrage. The man's booted feet stick on an outcrop of wheat that hasn't been trampled. I growl deep in my throat.

'Bloody hell,' I grunt, wrestling with the body until it finally comes free and I can drag it once more.

I don't know where Frithwine's gone, but Garwulf stands to the right of me when I retake my place. His eyes are fearful, his helm firmly wedged in place as he watches me reproachfully.

I look down. There's another body, and then a man who yet lives, screaming as he makes his way towards the back of the fighting on hands and knees, his face constantly knocked by the knees and feet of those who yet fight. His helm is missing. His dark hair's slick with sweat or blood, and his eyes are wild.

My gloved hands are slick with the blood of the dead. I bend and wipe them on the still-standing wheat, which caused me all the problems.

The wounded man continues to crawl away. For every time his knee moves, the Mercians travel forwards, revealing more and more of the dead, as though a crop of bodies has replaced that of the ruined wheat. And then I startle.

There are more than just Mercian dead. I can tell from sigils that flash on byrnies and tunics, on the iron amulets that show the Wessex wyvern around necks.

'Make sure the Wessex bastards are dead,' I roar to the man beside me who was so quick to call me a damn fool.

He stares at me, lips open in shock.

I'm already bending low, rushing towards the next man who thinks to escape from the crush. He has no helm or hair, the back of his head stained red. I rotate him to a cry of alarm. I scour him, looking for something that tells me if he's Mercian or from Wessex. Some sign of the Mercian eagle sigil. Some sign of the Wessex one.

'Mercian,' he calls, but his words roll and are thick with a distinctly un-Mercian accent. I've never heard it before.

'Tell me, who's your queen?' I demand, chin high, prepared to give him a chance while I can. Eyes narrowed in thought, his hand bunches at his waist. I thrust my seax through his chest before he can take a swipe at me with his blade. Blood gushes from the wound. I retch at the sharp scent of the slaughterhouse.

The dying man watches me, acceptance on his face. I lower my other hand to pull his eyes shut. It brings me no pleasure to kill my enemy in such a way, but at least he's dead and no longer a threat.

'Wessex scum,' I hear someone shriek, but my eyes are on the next man crawling through the crop. He's on his elbows, using one leg to propel him forward while the other one drags uselessly behind. I narrow my eyes. I'm sure I recognise him. I'm convinced he's a Mercian, even as Garwulf menaces perilously close with his seax.

'Mercian,' the man gasps, his accent evident.

Then I recognise him. It's Oswy, one of the men who thought to ridicule me.

I could allow Garwulf to kill him, but while the man hates me, he's a proud Mercian and one of her warriors.

'Leave him. He's Mercian. I vouch for him,' I call, expecting and receiving a pointed look from where Garwulf stands, ready, seax in hand.

Others have realised the danger. Men bend to check on the dead, nearly dead, and those who yet live. The smell of blood, piss and fear fill my nose. I grimace, grateful to have been left at the rear of the advancing line. There's no time for dread here. I must strike and react, ensure that our enemy is unable to launch a sneak attack on the defenceless backs of the Mercians.

Oswy glowers at me. I meet his gaze evenly, breathing heavily.

'Would you rather be bloody dead?' I demand.

He has a purpling eye, his helm lost somewhere in the melee, but what hobbles him is a deep gash to his lower leg, his trews dark with blood. When he tries to stand, pushing up from the twisted crops, he collapses once more with the thud of his weight and the jangle of his weapons.

'Come here.' I go to his side. The shield wall has stayed immobile for the last few moments. I risk stooping and giving him my shoulder to aid him. He's not alone. There are other wounded too. They all bleed from one wound or another.

A handful of the men and women from the baggage train move amongst them. A roar of triumph or pain ripples through the air every so often. The warriors wince at the sound, but those helping them don't even seem to notice. They don't flinch at the cries or even gaze fearfully at what's happening only so far in front of them. I think they're braver than I am.

I eye them, noting that some do seem to know what they're doing. They clean wounds and bind them. They offer potions to ease the men's suffering and even hold the hands of those who have only moments yet to live. Wynflæd would be proud to see so many of them following the lessons she's taught them in how to save a life on the slaughter field.

I swallow down my unease as I deposit Oswy on the ground.

'Get back,' Oswy grouses at me, but there's half a thanks in the words, more than I received from Frithwine.

I spare Oswy another thought. I hope he lives and I see him once more. The hope is both for my survival, and his. I admit that.

4

I do as Oswy says, trying to catch sight of what's happening at the front of the line of attack. But it's impossible. If I don't keep my eyes on where I'm going, I'll fall to the ground and, no doubt, injure myself.

'Stay in position,' I'm cautioned by a Mercian. His face is covered in sweat.

I note that Frithwine and Garwulf have finally done the same. Garwulf has bound a strip of linen around his wound, but he's not staunched the blood. I open my mouth to tell him, but the shield wall rushes onwards again. I hurry to keep up. I don't want to lose my place.

The cry of 'For Mercia' thunders through the air. I run, eyes half on where I'm going and half on what I run over. The snapped stalks are darkened with blood, the staring eyes of marbled men arresting my gaze, even as I stoop to check they're dead. A Mercian warrior in front of me stumbles and trips.

I stab down into the chest of the Wessex warrior who thinks to take a kill before his last breath. His right hand has been severed, blood cascading from it to drown the churned earth. But he still has

I spit aside a hair from my dry mouth, wishing there was more spittle with which to do so, and notice another warrior on the ground. This man has his head pressed into the mud, a seax protruding from between his shoulder blades. An enemy, then, I assume.

When I focus again on what's happening, I gasp. For the first time, between the rows of men before me, I see the enemy shields, black wyvern on a white background. I can even distinguish the helmed heads of those who think to kill my fellow Mercians. For a heartbeat, I meet cold eyes. Then the gap is closed once more, as the row of Mercians surges onwards.

The men at the front have fallen. Only two lines of warriors remain. Cries and feeble moans reach my ears. As much as I'd like to help these warriors, drag them to safety, I can't. I'm that second line. I discard my shield and force the one in place, up and over the head of the man on the front line.

I don't know what's happened. Why has the shield wall suddenly failed so catastrophically? My thoughts turn to Wulfheard and Ealdorman Ælfstan. Then there's a steadying hand on my back.

'Hold the shield wall.' I know the voice and turn shocked eyes to greet the familiar face of King Wiglaf. 'The bastards know I'm here. They've redoubled their attempts to kill me.'

Given what my uncle said about Wiglaf the last time he encountered the Wessex warriors beside the River Thames, I expect the king to show fear, to quiver with it, maybe even to run away. But Wiglaf holds his place, his standard-bearer just behind me, indicating to those who can see it, Mercians or Wessex warriors, that King Wiglaf has taken his position and will fight with his men, just as they fight for him.

'Stand firm,' Wiglaf instructs, his words stiffening the resolve of others close by, of Frithwine and Garwulf to my right, the one with his bashed helm and the other limping from injuries gained falling over, but who's been urged back to the attack, no doubt by the king.

My arms begin to ache as I endeavour to hold the shield above my head in place, bucking and swaying with the motion of the clash, a constant motion of small steps forwards and back. I'll wear a dip in the soil.

Now I can witness much more than just the emotionless eyes of my enemy. I can see where seaxes thrust through gaps in the rounded shields, where spears are thrown from behind the Wessex line. Where men bleed and shriek, weep and wail, and yet stand firm all the same, even as blood drips into byrnies and onto the churned earth.

'Brace.' Ealdorman Ælfstan's voice is too loud. I'm startled to find the ealdorman only just in front of me – Wulfheard beside him. I can see where blood pools down Wulfheard's wide neck to disappear inside his byrnie. I can't determine the nature of his wound. I hope it's not his blood.

Swords and seaxes flash between the shields. Something heavy hits the shield I hold and I stagger beneath the weight.

'Keep it up,' I'm commanded.

I turn, meet my comrade's startled look, and notice the strain on his face. Whatever has been thrown, it's bloody heavy.

I try tipping the shield forwards standing on my tiptoes and then backwards, bending my elbows, to dislodge the weight. But it does nothing.

'What is it?' I gasp between tight lips. If there were someone behind me, perhaps they could tell me, but King Wiglaf has moved aside, taking his warriors and bannerman with him. I can hear the king emboldening his warriors from elsewhere, the flash of his banner catching the corner of my vision, sweat dripping into my eyes from beneath my helm. My mouth's so dry, I think to lick the sweat, but it'll only make me thirstier in the end.

'I don't know,' the man grunts.

I wish I knew his name. If we're to stand together, fight together and perhaps die together, we should know one another.

Abruptly, the weight disappears, my arms thrusting higher in the air, almost too high. Where before I struggled to keep the shield over the man with the black curls whose back I stand at, now there's too much sky visible, the clouds low, promising rain, and into that small gap, a long spear falls.

Every instinct in my body tells me to step back, to protect myself, but if I do that, I'll be killing another. Instead, I hold my ground, barely breathing as the top-heavy projectile clatters between us, just missing my left foot as it stands proud in the brown earth.

'Bloody bollocks,' I exclaim. The spear risks injuring both of us even now if I don't move it, but to do so, I need to release my grip on the shield. And, at that moment, the shield wall swells once more.

I skip around the still-vibrating wooden pole. But I pause. If I leave it, someone else might injure themselves on it. Hastily, I balance the shield with one hand looped through the leather strap, as I grip the spear with my left. Only the damn thing is firmly wedged, stuck, spear downwards, the shaft disappearing into the dark earth. If that had struck me or a fellow Mercian, we'd be dead.

'Leave it,' a voice huffs at me.

I want to, but I know this battle is far from won. Instead, I lift my leg, kick at the wooden shaft with all my strength, and it shatters.

'Bugger.' That wasn't what I wanted to do. If anything, I've made it worse. The broken shaft flies through the air, hitting the back of the man I'm supposed to be protecting. He turns panicked eyes my way. I rush to close the gap between us. I hope someone will move the remnants of the spear, but I can't see that anyone will.

Perhaps they don't need to do so, after all. The shield wall keeps advancing, passing over the dead and dying. I quickly realise that more and more of them are Wessex warriors, the black and white of their emblem easy to pick out on byrnies, tunics and sleeves now I know where to seek it.

'Hold.' The single word issues from the rear. Once more, King Wiglaf thinks to direct the battle.

I realise why. The centre of the shield wall has got ahead of itself. It moves too quickly, too fast. We're at the point where we can see the Wessex warriors as they battle against the Mercians to the left and the right, under the commands of Ealdormen Tidwulf and Beornoth. If this continues, the shield wall will disintegrate into three pitched battles. I'll be on the wrong side of it. The Mercians under Ealdorman Ælfstan, in their eagerness, risk being lost to the Wessex warriors if only one of their commanders is quick-witted enough to change tactics.

'Move back.' Ealdorman Ælfstan's words thrum with authority, but his fellow warriors are unable to obey them. They're too focused on beating their foemen because it seems that they can't but win now. The eyes of the front row of the shield wall focus only on their enemy. They don't know what I've realised.

The orders of Ealdorman Beornoth can be heard, urging the men under his command on, trying to get them to follow the successes of the centre of the line of Mercian shields. Only there's no more time for me to think. The man before me grows still, his movements arrested, before abruptly turning and falling at the same time. Blood gushes from a slit throat, hands clawing at it, turning black with the rapid flow, fear and terror in his brown eyes.

'Fill the bloody gap,' a warrior from the front row implores me in a breathless voice.

I tremble. Swallow, try and spit. I take a breath, inhale more than just air, and step over the bucking body of the dying Mercian.

'Hold firm,' I'm ordered.

I slip my hands through the orphaned shield, feeling the slick sweat of another on the leather cord even through my gloves. The smell is intense. I try to hold my stance, as Ealdorman Ælfstan has advised me to do, but my right foot slips on something foul-smelling and sticky. I slide and catch myself, the shield in front of me crashing to the floor so that I'm faced with the black and white shield of my enemy. Behind the shield, I can see smoke billowing into the sky. I can hear the shrieks of the Wessex injured, and then my shield is back in place.

'Hold firm,' my right-hand shield brother urges me.

I can feel nothing but the air above my helm. There's no one to protect my head, not in the battle line.

Another spear sneaks between my shield and the man to my right, while another waves over my head. They mean to skewer me. I'm glad then that I have no water with which to piss myself.

I grip my seax tightly, thoughts suddenly clear. I need to batter aside the spear that comes at me from in front. And I need to pull down on the one that comes from above, have it slip from the hand of the man who thinks to hold it. His hold will be poor from so far away.

With my seax, I thrust upwards. I can't see the man's hand, but it must be there, somewhere. Without the shield to protect my head, the dull afternoon sun glints in my eyes, temporarily blinding me. When I can see once more, the blackened tip of the spear is even closer. I duck aside and into the path of the spear that comes at me from in front. The shield wall warps once more, and I'm moving backwards, the Wessex warriors finding a means of advancing against us.

'Back,' Ealdorman Ælfstan directs curtly. His words are shock-ingly easy to hear.

The retreat knocks the head-high spear aside, the Wessex warrior perhaps stumbling or simply failing to keep up with the quick advance. That leaves me with only one weapon to counter while trying to stay upright. There's a dead man behind me. There's blood and piss and shit on the ground that can trip me. I can't even risk looking to ensure I keep clear of it all.

The second man to my left abruptly disappears from view, the shield of our enemy pressing tightly into our shield wall. I feel it in the strain on my hands, hear it in the grunts of the warrior directly next to me. And then the Mercian is once more on his feet, hands through the leather strap.

'Back again,' the ealdorman demands, his words rich with authority.

With another step, the spear before me jabs close to my eye. It makes a soft dinging noise as it hits my helm. I recoil in horror. Without thought, my seax jabs upwards, following the line of the spear, seeking the hand that wields it. Through the gap between my shield and the warrior to my right, it slides, and then beneath its questing edge, I detect something solid but not metal. With all my strength, I stab, and then jab, and then stab again. The movement is unnatural, my enemy too far away, but it's my best chance.

I hear a gurgling sound, something wet dripping to the ground as though it's started raining, and the shield wall advances one step. I'm standing on the man who thought to kill me. His eyes are wild with pain, his lower right arm a blooming mass of burgundy, even the white of bone visible through his jagged sleeve. I kick him, hard, in the bollocks, and he bucks upwards, unable to prevent the recoil, and dies on my blade.

Another of the bastard Wessex warriors is dead. Now, I need to kill those who still fight against Mercia's might.

5

We retreat two steps. We need to regain the advantage. I can no longer see around me. All that's visible is the shield I hold in front of me, the men to my left and right. Above my head, flickering sunlight assures me that someone protects my back.

My chest heaves as I suck in much-needed air, but I'm not terrified any more. Neither am I convinced that the Mercians will prevail, even though I will it with every bone in my body.

A thin blade appears above my shield. I eye it coldly. It's not long enough to reach me, not with the shield before me. I watch it, waiting for something to happen, only to feel a jabbing at my feet. Hastily, I move my feet to spread my legs. The enemy spear threads through them. Damn the Wessex warrior. He thought to distract me with the seax. But, I consider, if he holds the seax, and the shield, then who's in command of the spear?

I don't have a spear. I've not yet mastered the art, and in all honesty there was little expectation that I'd find myself at the front of the shield wall. But others do have spears with which to poke at the enemy.

'Hold still,' a gruff voice calls from behind me.

I do as I'm told. Once more something moves close to my feet, but this time, it's a Mercian who thinks to impale a Wessex warrior. I prefer it that way.

I'm straining to hold the shield. Our foe is strong and fearless. Everywhere I look along the shield wall, I can see spears, seaxes and swords trying to cut my fellow Mercians.

The man to my right grimaces at me. I recognise him from Tamworth. Cearl bleeds from a deep cut to his chin. His eyes are wild, glowing with the fire of pain and revenge combined. He shifts his shoulder against the shield to enable him to reach for a seax from his weapons belt. With it, he batters aside the probing weapon working its way quickly between the guard and that of the man next to him.

I risk a glance and meet the leering face of Wulfheard.

He startles on seeing me, his mouth opening as though to berate me for not heeding his words to stay at the back, but once more the shield wall shifts. And it does so suddenly that I fall, the weight against my shield disappearing between one breath and the next.

Refusing to release my hold on the Mercian shield, it crashes to the floor with me, taking my weight, while all around me my comrades surge onwards. I bend my head low, seeking out the enemy through the legs of the rampaging Mercians, but they've run off into the distance, to where the menacing walls of ancient Londinium are so much closer than before. In their wake, the Mercians sense victory.

I get kicked, knocked into, pushed over, and still, I sit, huddled on the shield with my knees beneath me. My seax is stuck in the ground, driven there by my weight. I grip it when I see no one else means to run me down, but my weapon is stuck firmly in the solid brown earth.

'Leave it,' a voice commands.

I turn to meet the eyes of Ealdorman Sigered. I'm staggered to find him in the midst of the slaughter field, but it only makes me aware just how far the Mercian warriors have run.

'Get up and join the rest of the warriors.' There's no kindness in the voice. It brokers no argument. I'm tempted to ignore it. After all, surely he should be in the thick of the fighting. But the ealdorman speaks to me from the back of his black horse, forelock a shimmering silver, and I scramble to my knees, picking up the shield at the same time.

I run on. My knees and feet pump beneath me, while my eyes scour the battlefield. There are dead and dying men spread out on the earth or huddled around their injuries, pitiable moans filling the air. There's an abandoned cart, and then another two, and I take it that we're racing through the line that the Wessex warriors thought to hold against our advance.

My eyes flash from the ground to the ongoing confrontation in front of us and then to the wall that's coming ever closer – the towering walls of the ancient settlement.

There's a mass of swelling men ahead, the sound of hooves behind me getting nearer.

I struggle to keep going. My arms shake with the exertions of holding my shield. My breath is harsh because there's no moisture to be found in my throat. To my untrained eye, it also seems as though the fighting has become evermore frantic and bloody.

'Damn bastards,' I hear Ealdorman Sigered call to another rider, the thud of hooves driving me onwards. There are more and more abandoned pieces of equipment to fall over. No doubt items deemed too weak for war against the Mercians. And all of them could trip me if I don't keep looking.

'Surround the shield wall.' The cry comes from far behind. I only just hear the words. I doubt any of the Mercians in front of me hear them, let alone heed them.

'That way, damn you.' Ealdorman Sigered is beside me, tapping me on the shoulder with his spear and indicating where he wants me to go with its point. It's hard to tell where he's directing me. The sun is too bright overhead, as though shards stab at my vision. My eyes tear, and I can hardly bear to look where he indicates. All the same, head down, I change my trajectory, hoping that I'll be able to see soon enough.

I cut through the edge of the warring men. I can hear Mercians calling to one another, demanding more room, while others rumble to let them through. I squint into the distance. I have an idea of where Ealdorman Sigered is sending me. And, indeed, others are following my lead. Ahead, too far in the distance for me to hope to catch, some of the Wessex warriors are scuttling towards a huge gateway in the stone wall of Londinium. I know then that our foe thinks to hide behind the fastness of stone built up high. I understand why Ealdorman Sigered is keen to have me rush this way and prevent the Wessex warriors from retreating behind the walls that will prove impenetrable for the Mercians.

Yet, he, with his horse, might stand a chance of reaching the gateway. I don't. And neither do many of the Mercians, although those under the command of Ealdorman Beornoth are already much, much closer.

I hurry my steps. Sweat flows freely down my back. I can feel my slick feet slipping inside my boots. The ground rises and then lowers, my knees jolting with the abrupt change.

A bellow comes from where the majority of the Mercians have attempted to stop our opponents. I risk a look, only to misstep. Arms cartwheeling in the air, I keep my feet and power forward even faster.

I've lost sight of Frithwine and Garwulf, of Wulfheard and

Ealdorman Ælfstan, but Ealdorman Sigered rides behind me. Does he think to claim a victory for himself, even after all this time?

But now there are more hooves, and I hear a familiar voice.

'To the fort,' King Wiglaf orders, his words louder than a winter deluge.

I redouble my efforts. Ahead, the wall is getting ready to jut outwards once more. Above my head, I can see where the wyvern standard of Wessex flies from the top of a buttress, and men are watching from behind the perceived safety of those walls.

I don't know what to think of what I'm seeing. Perhaps it's a fort. Maybe it's merely where the warriors keep a half-arsed watch over Londinium. Certainly, I think it won't be easy to crest the walls and pour inside Londinium itself.

To the right of me, where the River Fleet cuts the land between Londinium and Lundenwic, the market settlement stretches out, devoid of walls and with little means to protect itself. It's no surprise the Wessex warriors scurry towards the walls.

And yet, I'm perplexed. If Mercia's opponent locks itself up inside the fort, how do they plan on escaping? Or profiting from the taxes from the trading centre?

I'm forced to consider whether King Wiglaf has the numbers to attack such a vast wall.

'To the fort,' once more echoes over the heads of the warring men. I perceive more and more Mercians realising just what their king is telling them.

I watch as the Mercians under Ealdorman Beornoth finally meet the fleeing Wessex warriors. Guttural shrieks and cries fill the air, men limping onwards, others clutching at bloody innards as they sense that much-needed protection is so close.

The imposing Ealdorman Beornoth, leading from the front, is relentless. His shield hits men on their backs. His seax stabs down when they fall to the ground. He strides steadily onwards as though a behemoth.

The number of Wessex warriors grows ever smaller, but then more rush from the fort's gateway, called to arms by a strident voice from inside. These men carry more shields, spears visible between them. And still, Ealdorman Beornoth advances, gouging as he goes. At least thirty Mercians surround him. They mirror his actions, and there can be only fifty Wessex warriors in the new shield wall. They allow the majority of their fallen comrades access to their protection and then begin their retreat as another barked order issues from inside the fort.

I can see more of the gateway. It holds a substantial double wooden gate built from fine Mercian oak. If that slams shut on us, it'll be all but impossible to gain access.

I feel that Ealdorman Sigered's advance has slowed now he realises there might be some fighting. I shake my head, hurrying to catch the rear of Ealdorman Beornoth's men before they face the enemy, only to hear my name being called.

'Icel, get your arse over here.'

I stop abruptly, the man behind me almost colliding with me, to stare, open-mouthed, at Wulfheard.

'Stay by my side,' he orders me. He's bleeding from more places. His helm's lost somewhere so that I can see the streaks of blood running through his hair. I still don't believe it's his blood.

Wulfheard lopes onwards, not seeming to tire, even though exhaustion threatens to drag me to the ground. If I could just have a drink or close my eyes, I'm sure I'd feel reinvigorated. But there's no time for that. The Wessex warriors, well, some of them, have made it behind the solid protection of the grey walls. The Mercians howl to reach the gateway before it can slam shut, while those from Wessex inside Londinium shower them with anything they can get their hands on from the bastion above our heads.

The number of remaining foemen diminishes the closer I get to the gaping gateway. They're going to escape. They're going to live to fight another day, and I could howl with the fury of it all. So many men are dead or dying, and still, the victory isn't assured.

Ealdorman Beornoth rears up before the gateway, the closest Mercian of all, using his shield against the Wessex warriors. But two of the relieving force hold him stationary with their attack so that others can make good their escape. If only I could run that little bit quicker, but I can't. I'm almost entirely spent. Yet, somehow, the gateway into Londinium remains open, just one half of it.

Wulfheard is battling his way through the enemy shield wall that protects the retreating foemen and bars entry to the gate. His seax sends streaks of blood high into the air. He grunts softly with every impact, but it's nothing compared to the cries of our opponents who bleed and fall because of his advance. So close, and yet these Wessex warriors who encounter him will not be saved. I watch on, shocked by his ferocity, by the uselessness of it all. Wulfheard and Ealdorman Beornoth will not make it in time to stop the gate from being closed to us.

Abruptly, Wulfheard's behind me, his hands on my back, his breath fierce down my neck. He's pushing me through the closing gap of the other half of the gate where Ealdorman Beornoth fights only one man now. Others are screaming for the Wessex warrior to run, while, overhead, a piece of masonry thuds to the floor, just missing the ealdorman's head.

'What?' I gasp in horror as Wulfheard pulls my hand free and forces something else into it.

'Get inside, lay low, find a way to open the gates for us.' And I'm swallowed up as the remnants of the Wessex shield wall collapse around me. I'm left with no choice but to go with them or face being crushed by the Mercians howling for blood as they run ever faster, as though they can beat the inevitability of the oak doors' final closure.

I seek out Wulfheard's face in the mass of Mercians trying to kill me, but I don't see him, and then I'm swept along in the rush of men desperate to find some respite at their back. The wooden doorway slams shut with such force I feel it reverberating up and down my back.

6

I suck in much-needed air to still my rapidly beating heart. I finally look down at my shield hand, seeing that Wulfheard has taken my Mercian shield and replaced it with a hated Wessex one of white and black. I fumble for my seax, and realise it too has been taken from me. The blade at my belt is unfamiliar to me. I swallow, terror almost making me piss myself, as I stagger out of the way of the few remaining retreating men as others rush to place the bars in place to keep the double gateway closed against the Mercians outrage.

All is chaos. There are shrieks and moans of pain and fear, and, above it all, no one voice rises to take command.

I eye the gateway. It's firmly closed, two pieces of wood already slid into place across it to ensure the Mercians can't force it open, although they hammer on it. To either side, the stone wall extends upwards at least the height of four men. There's no hope that I can escape that way.

I can't believe what Wulfheard has done to me. Tears of terror threaten to run down my bloodied and bruised cheeks as I lift my helm from my head, snatching the stinking linen cap away as well.

The wind rustles my hair, bringing with it the smell of sweat and other less pleasant aromas.

I'm not alone in seeming to be stunned by what's happening. A man lies spread out before me, his face bleaching white, his black beard and red lips gleaming too brightly. Further down his body, a significant slash through his byrnie reveals his slit belly. His eyes are almost rolled back into his head. I know he stands little chance of surviving, especially when there's no one rushing to his aid.

Beside him, a youth no older than I sits and sobs, blood pouring through his fingers where he holds them tight at the top of his left arm. That, I think, is a wound he might live through if he's lucky.

And there are more and more wounded and dying. The scene is so pitiful, it horrifies me, and I hate the Wessex bastards.

'Help me.' The cry from the youth rouses me from my stupor.

I stagger to his side when it seems no one is coming to aid him. Those men who are hale are moving away from the secure gateway. From the far side, I can hear the frustrated cries of the Mercians. I don't recognise any one voice, but I would certainly sooner be with them than here, inside a Wessex enclave.

I bend to meet the youth's eyes. They're green but flecked with pain, snot smearing with blood that he must have rubbed over his face from his wound. I can see where his skin turns even paler. He's losing too much blood.

'You need to staunch the bleeding,' I advise him, my words soft so that he doesn't seem to hear them, not above his moaning and weeping.

I sigh heavily and bend to rip a piece of cloth from the tunic of a man lying dead closer to the gateway. I can see where boots have left an imprint on his face, even as he lies facing upwards, his eyes forever open but seeing nothing – poor sod.

A clatter against the gateway has me jumping aside, my heart pounding, even though the men out there are my allies.

'Here, let me help you.' I hasten back to the youth, keen to provide support before he too tumbles to lie in the churned mud of the roadway.

'What?' he asks, not seeming to note me. His single word sounds different to the way the Mercians speak, similar to the way the Wessex warrior spoke who tried to pretend he was a Mercian. I note it but can do nothing to mask the way I speak. I know no other way.

'Let me help you,' I say more loudly. 'If we stop the bleeding and bind your wound, you should survive, but we need to do it immediately.'

He continues to misunderstand what I'm saying to him. I imagine he's in shock from his wound and Wessex's catastrophic failure to beat back the Mercians.

With practised ease, I thread the linen around the top of his arm and then tie it tightly, binding the two strands, end over end, so that they won't come loose, and the flow of blood immediately turns to a trickle.

'That hurts.' Sullen words greet my action.

'Better that than bleeding to death,' I retort, already reaching for my knife to cut aside what remains of his tunic lower down his arm. It's sodden with blood. The rest of the tunic is a dull red, but it's almost black below his wound.

'What are you doing?' His elongated words are edged with fear.

'Cutting your tunic. The wound needs to be cleaned and bound. It might even need stitches.' At my words, his eyes narrow, and he licks his lips. I can smell how much he needs to drink just from his breath on my face. But I have no water, and I don't know where to get any. I've never visited the fort before.

'How do you know that?' he asks.

I shrug my shoulders. 'I know how to heal better than I know how to kill.' I speak without thought and silently curse my loose tongue. I need to be careful what I say and to whom I say it.

'I've not seen you before,' he presses, eyes narrowed with pain and suspicion.

'I've not seen you either,' I snap. 'Now, do you want my assistance or not? I'm happy to help that poor sod there,' and I indicate the man with the slit belly.

'Sorry, sorry. Please, help me. I don't want to die. I didn't even want to be here, but as one of the king's warriors, I had no choice. Those Mercians are proper bastards, aren't they? The ealdorman said it would be easy to kill 'em all. He said they didn't know how to fight.' Guiltily, my patient looks around to see if he's been overheard. I recognise his worry.

'They were lethal,' I admit, unsure what else I can say. I'm wary of stating something that'll give me away as a Mercian. With the bottom of his sleeve cut away, I purse my lips and eye the wound. It's deep, but not long. It's bled a lot, and yet, it should be easy enough to sew together, only I don't have anything with me to do that.

'Will it heal?' the lad asks me, trying not to look at it.

'Yes, if I can stitch it, and the wound-rot stays away.'

'We need to go to old Ecgred,' the lad states.

I nod because I don't know who Ecgred is or even where he might be.

He makes to stand, only to tumble backwards. I jump to stop him from falling on the dead man. He looks down when I've righted him, and a thin wail leaves his lips.

'Dealwine.' And he crashes to the ground beside the dead man. I would pull him away, but he's in no danger for the time being. The blood flowing from his wound has slowed to a dribble. Provided we get him to this Ecgred soon, he'll live.

I eye the belly-slit man with mild interest, then gaze all around

me. The wooden gate is set into the two sides of the wall, extending into the fort itself. These same walls form a section of the walls. I turn in a slow circle, head tilted back so that I can see as much as possible, noting that the wall runs as far as I can see, no doubt, as Wulfheard told me, all the way to the River Thames. My heart beats too loudly in my chest, and for a moment, I struggle to find enough air to breathe.

Wulfheard has thrust me into the heart of an enemy encampment, and I have no idea how to escape from somewhere with such impressive walls and such a huge gate.

The belly-slit man grunts and comes awake, howling with the pain of his wound. I meet his dull eyes, and he attempts to sit upright, only to crash back to the slick ground.

'Will I die?' he demands from me, the words edged with fury, his accent similar to the lad I've already helped.

'If you lie there and no one aids you, then yes.' There's no kindness to my words. Sometimes, it's a kindness to be honest, and not promise false hope.

'Get me to Ecgred,' he demands.

Again, I don't know who this Ecgred is, and I certainly don't know where to find him.

The lad continues to sob over the still body of Dealwine. Few people linger beside the wooden gateway. There are a handful of Wessex warriors, the men looking as though they've not fought in the battle. I assume they must be the gate wardens, but I don't know for sure. They look nervous enough as the Mercians crash against the gateway from the far side. The Mercians don't have a ram, I know that, and so they won't make any progress. But the battle fury must have a hold of them, and they won't give up, even with such an insurmountable obstacle. I hope Wulfheard doesn't expect me to take on the seven Wessex warriors alone. I can't think that was what he meant.

Then the lad looks at me, just before his gaze slips to the slit-bellied man.

'Tyrhtil,' he gasps. 'Dealwine is dead,' he moans to the dying man.

'Aye, and I'll be soon if you don't get me to Ecgred.'

Only now does the youth notice Tyrhtil's wounds.

'Help him, as you did me,' he demands angrily, facing me once more from where he still kneels on the floor.

I shake my head. 'I can't. Not here. There's nothing to clean the wound or pack it.' I indicate the space in which we stand. There's little to be seen other than the dead and dying and the few remaining guardsmen.

'Then get him to Ecgred.'

The repetition of the words frustrates me. I don't know who Ecgred is, and even if I did, do I want to help the belly-slit wounded Wessex warrior? He looks like a fierce man, one used to winning his battles. If he does live, it'll only be to fight another battle against the Mercians. In those battles, he might well cause the death of those about whom I care.

'How?' I ask instead of denying the request, hoping such will end the demands.

'He needs carrying. Get some of the garrison. They'll have access to something to carry him on.'

'You go,' I immediately retort. I don't know where to go.

'Hurry up, Brihtwold,' Tyrhtil commands him, although his voice wavers on the final word.

And Brihtwold does just that. Although he's still weak from blood loss, Brihtwold veers along the wall and disappears from sight where the wall seems to buckle in on itself.

I remain standing, unsure what to do with myself. In all honesty, I can't help the wounded Tyrhtil. Anything I do now will merely become undone when he's moved to wherever Ecgred might be.

'I don't recognise you,' Tyrhtil wheezes through hollow cheeks. Sweat beads his face.

'I don't recognise you either,' I snap once more, wishing I could think of a better reply, but I know almost nothing about Wessex. I know the king's name and that Winchester is his capital, but I don't know the names of places, of the ealdormen, or even of the bishops, not even the Archbishop of Canterbury. I'm sure I've heard Bishop Æthelweald mention him before now, but when did I need to concern myself with such matters?

'Well, King Ecgberht called on his ealdormen to bring their warriors together for the defence of Londonia. I imagine there are others here I don't know. We've got to work together to ensure that bastard Mercian upstart doesn't take it back. We'll all be rich from the proceeds of trade from the market.'

I open my mouth to speak but clamp it shut again. I'm not going to argue with him. I won't say that Wulfheard told me all of Londonia's trading takes place along the Strand and that the Strand is in the market settlement, on the other side of the River Fleet.

Perhaps Wulfheard's wrong, although I doubt it. He knows a great deal about Londonia. He told me he was born there before moving further north to serve Mercia's kings. He spoke of a childhood spent on the foreshore of a contrary river, likely to flood at a moment's notice. His words weren't fond as he spoke of the smell and stink of a tidal river that routinely revealed a grisly past.

'But I suppose it makes strangers of good Wessex men.' Tyrhtil sneers at me before gasping in pain and clutching once more at his belly wound.

'Don't put your hands on it,' I instruct him harshly. 'Your fingers are filthy and carry no end of corruption. It won't heal if you infect it.'

'You know a lot for such a young 'un,' he retorts, although I notice his hand does move away from his wound as though burned.

'Someone taught me,' I offer.

'Aye, and how to fight as well?' he asks.

I just nod to this, biting down on my lip. I can't think that Wulf-heard thrust me inside the fort to make idle conversation with two wounded Wessex warriors. What does he expect me to do? And how quickly does he expect me to do it? Is he, even now, waiting for me on the other side of the enormous gate?

I can still hear the Mercians, but they're shouting words of disdain at the Wessex warriors, because their weapons won't reach. Has Wulfheard told them what he's done? Do they all wait for me?

And then a group of four men appear, all of them dressed for war, although they show no sign of having just fought against the Mercians. Their byrnies are clean, and their weapons bear none of the stains that mine do.

'What you done to yourself?' the first man directs at Tyrhtil, chin jutted out.

'A little scratch,' Tyrhtil counters, his words strong despite how much pain he must be feeling.

'A little scratch?' the man replies, eyeing his bloodied tunic with unease. 'It looks like you're for it. You know no one heals from a belly wound like that?'

'It's not caught his innards.' I speak without thought. 'If they're not cut, he stands a chance, just like any other wound.'

The warrior rears up before me, his heavily eyebrowed face twisted in fury at being contradicted.

'Who the hell are you?' His eyes rake me from my boots to my disarrayed black hair, freed from the confines of the helm.

'Icel,' I retort. 'A warrior, with some healing knowledge,' I'm stung into explaining.

'Well, I've never seen you before, so I can't see that Ecgred will appreciate you interfering or suggesting he can repair this man's injury. Tyrhtil, you're as good as dead. I'm telling you.'

I go to argue once more, but Brihtwold speaks instead, his words flecked with rage so that his bloodless face suffuses with crimson.

'He's going to live. He just needs Ecgred. Anyway, you're not in control of who Ecgred treats and who he leaves to die. Take Tyrhtil to Ecgred, or I'm going straight to Ealdorman Wassa.'

'And what do you think Ealdorman Wassa will do? He'll probably demand that Tyrhtil is fed to the pigs if he even speaks with you. He's trying to work out how the damn Mercians managed to drive us back inside the fort. Half of Wessex's warriors are in bloody Lundenwic, and we're stuck here, with no chance of getting to them because the Mercians have taken the bloody bridge across the River Fleet.'

'He won't. And I know it.' Brihtwold, despite his slight shakiness, bristles before the man who casts doubt on my words. I notice that the two are the same height; for all, Brihtwold is half as wide as the other man.

'Fine. It's not like we won't have to move him away from here anyway when he's dead. Come on, lads, let's shift this useless hunk of meat and then we can clear the rest of the dead away as well.'

There's a feeble cry of terror at the words. I turn towards the sound. It seems that the collection of men I took to be dead aren't. Not quite yet. Although, the man who cried out has a huge wound, half of his head caved in so that one eye meets mine while the other is lifeless. Such a sight makes me want to vomit to see so much grey, white and maroon on display.

'So tell me, fool, will he live or die?'

I don't want to have to say, but my silence answers for the spokesman, and he cackles.

'Daft git.' But by now, Tyrhtil is held between the four men, using two rounded shields to carry him, and I'm grateful that he and Brihtwold will soon be gone. As soon as they are, I'll sit with

the dying man. I'll probably end his suffering. It would be the kindest thing to do.

'Icel, you have to come with us. Tell Ecgred what you said about Tyrhtil,' Brihtwold urges me.

'I'll be along in a moment,' I promise instead. There's more than one bobbing head amongst the twenty or so who lie dead and dying, forgotten about by everyone. I even see a Mercian warrior amongst them. I recognise him from the battle on the borderlands. He watches me with the cold gaze of the dead. I want to close his eyes, remove the eagle shield that lies at the tip of his outstretched hand, or the Wessex warriors will do worse things to him, even though he's beyond caring.

'Come on,' Brihtwold presses me. He needs to sit down, or he'll fall.

'I'll find you,' I confirm. I'm far from convinced that it'll be the right thing for me to do, to follow the wounded. Perhaps I should stay here and work out how to open the gate. Although, well, it's a bloody big gate with two barriers across it. I won't be able to open it alone. I need to find another means of allowing the Mercians inside.

'Hurry,' Brihtwold urges me.

I stand and wait for the carping men and the groaning Tyrhtil to move aside. Only then do I go to the dying man. I kneel before him. He's surrounded by the slickness of his body, the scent of piss and blood combining. His skin is already translucent, yet he doesn't seem to notice how wounded he is.

'Help me,' he demands, his voice gruff from beneath a thick black moustache and beard, which reaches to his thin shoulders.

'I can't,' I offer, sympathy in my words despite the fact he's my enemy.

'I just need to get to my feet,' he argues, confused by my words.

'You're wounded,' I say gently. 'Your head.'

His left hand reaches upwards, as though not believing me. His fingers probe the wound, going deeper and deeper until he trembles. His one eye cries, his other one looking down at his nose, useless. The man's hand comes away covered in blood and gore. He holds it before his eye and stares at it as though disbelieving what he sees.

'What's that?' he demands to know, his words slow and elongated.

I swallow down my revulsion at the wound on display.

'The matter inside your head,' I answer truthfully.

He shivers at my words and grows belligerent.

'I know who you are, you little Mercian whelp. I saw what that warrior did. I'm going to tell 'em who you really are, and then you'll be just as dead as I am.'

His words make me gasp, but I'm reaching for my seax, even as I check that no one has heard what he's said. But, with the gate shut, the Wessex warriors seem to think the battle entirely lost, even though they feel safe enough behind the stone and wood. I know what needs to be done. I was going to do it anyway.

Far too easily, for a blade as dull as the one I now carry, I slide it beneath his armpit, forcing it upwards. He doesn't so much as notice what I'm doing as he tries to raise his voice loud enough that one of the guards will hear. But no one is coming, and he dies with a whimper. The Wessex warriors don't even look my way to see what's happening.

I reach over, close his one eye, and then try to do the same with the useless one, but it refuses to shut until I place a small piece of grey stone on it.

I sit back on my knees then, trembling from head to toe. I slide my seax back into my weapons belt, noting the trickle of dark fluid that drips onto the dead man's outstretched arm. Perhaps I should

follow Brihtwold and see this Ecgred, but I can't help thinking it will place me in even greater danger.

I feel vulnerable and terrified. If Wulfheard were here, I'd kill him for the position he's placed me in. And yet. If what the Wessex warriors said is accurate, that their numbers have been split between the two parts of Londonia, then King Ecgberht's force is already halved. If the Mercians can just get inside the fort, then they can win, I know it, and the market settlement lies open and unprotected anyway.

On trembling legs, I make my way to the side of the dead Mercian. Although I don't know his name, I recognise him as one of Oswy's cronies. He was a slight man, quick on his feet. It's no surprise that he made it inside the walls before the Wessex warriors managed to close the gates.

I reach out and thrust the eagle emblem shield aside from him. It rolls away, clattering against the thick stone wall. Sunlight glints off the iron rim. I almost reclaim it, but no, I need to take the Wessex shield that Wulfheard gave me and discover the secrets of the fort. At least, I hope it has some secrets. Otherwise, I don't know how I'll ever escape.

7

Taking my battered Wessex shield, with its wyvern on it, I follow Brihtwold's path inside the fort. Before me, more walls reach high above my head, but there's also a smaller door, much smaller than the gateway that led inside the walls. A Wessex warrior is on guard. He bleeds from a scratch on his pale, narrow face and leans heavily on his spear, as though he might fall at any moment. On seeing the wyvern shield, he merely raises his chin and allows me inside without even asking who I am.

Beyond the small aged wooden door, that can no doubt be more easily defended than the huge gateway if it comes to a fight, I feel the confines of a building with more than one floor above my head. Immediately, I enter what looks like a large hall, with a fire raging at the centre of the hearth, despite the heat of the day. There are abandoned tables with jugs and cups, and I eagerly walk towards one, desperate to slake my raging thirst. My tongue feels drier than Wynflæd's desiccated mushrooms. I keep expecting someone to call out a caution to me, but nothing happens. My feet move over the much-buckled wooden floorboards noisily. I drop the enemy shield

to the floor with a loud bang, slosh water into a wooden beaker and swill it around my parched mouth.

It hardly has any impact, so I hoist the entire jug and greedily drink directly from it. I feel water run down my beardless chin, but I don't stop drinking, even though it's not very cold or even particularly fresh. It has the hint of mud about it, but I don't care.

I'm unsure what this room is and why there's no one inside it. What was the guard at the door guarding? Uncertain of what to do, I move towards a door to my right. I pass into another small room, but at least it's easy to determine its use, for shields and spears are stacked up inside the wall. There aren't that many weapons and shields in there, not now. No doubt, it was full before the battle. Those that remain are in poor condition, streaked with old rust. I can see why they were left behind.

Through the next door, the ancient hinges making the door jump unevenly, I enter yet another room. I feel a gust of wind disturb the stale air and make my way outside. Here, I seem to be in the middle of the fort. There are stone walls all around me, reaching far above my head. They look strong and hale, although lichen and moss cover them in some places. The scent of damp is overwhelming. There are places inside the fort where the sun must never touch the ground. At its centre there are a collection of tangled weeds with only a splash of once-green grass.

Finally, I encounter some other people, a great deal of them. The Wessex warriors stand high on the defences built on top of the walls. There's a flurry of activity directly in front of me. Men and young lads rush that way, while someone shouts orders with the crack of authority. Perhaps, my opponents haven't given up on defeating Mercia just yet.

Curiosity guides my steps. I forge a path up the many stone steps leading to the precipice. Puffing with the effort, my calves complaining at the unfamiliar movement of lifting first one foot

high and then another, I alight on the viewing platform. I can finally look out over the slaughter field. And it's a slaughter field.

The ravens and crows have already descended to feast on the dead and dying. Without much success, I see a feeble arm batting aside a jet-black raven. The arm falls lifelessly to the floor as the raven jumps on the body, gorging on the grey and pink flesh that's all that's left of the man's neck. I hope he was a Wessex warrior. I shouldn't like to think of a Mercian dying in such a way.

But it's what's happening amongst the Mercian forces that intrigues me. I expect to see them preparing to attack the gateway that would give access inside the fort. To see them forming up with their shield wall once more, perhaps even hacking down some of the few trees close by that could serve as rams to batter through the aged wood of the gateway, but I'm entirely wrong.

In the distance, where I left my horse when this battle began, a collection of bodies lies prone on the exposed field where crops once grew. The Mercians tasked with caring for the horses and feeding the warriors bend to check the fallen are indeed slain. Some small distance away, others work to erect tents and canvases for the Mercians to shelter beneath. The horses are out of sight, perhaps held to the far side of the slope we ventured down during the battle. Others stand in what I take to be a war council, the king's banner fluttering above their heads.

I take comfort from seeing the familiar emblem of Mercia's eagle flapping in the breeze. I could only wish I was there, and not here, surrounded by my enemy, should I say or do the wrong thing. Despite the fact I breathe easier now that I've recovered from the steep climb up the steps, my heart still thuds too loudly in my chest. If the air wasn't so clear up here, I might struggle to suck in enough to breathe.

'What they doin'?' an aged man asks the people around him, his Wessex accent pronounced. I notice then that the Wessex warriors, all of them, are focused, not on the Mercian camp, but on what the Mercian warriors are doing.

I turn and watch them with intrigue. They've moved aside from the high walls of the fort, out of reach of anyone who might think to throw spears or stones at their heads. Now they're heading towards a slit in the landscape. I can tell that it's somewhat boggy, men walking with exaggerated care towards a surging river and a thin slither of a wooden bridge that crests it, pieces of stone at either end of its length. Behind that river, I can see the market settlement. It's not quiet there, but no one rushes from between the collection of wattle and daub buildings to stop the Mercians. That surprises me as I see a Wessex banner flying.

'They're cutting us off from Lundenwic,' a brisk voice informs, his words bringing a groan of dismay from those who watch the events unfolding. Not that they deny his words. It's almost as though there's a collective acceptance.

'But the king's inside Lundenwic,' another announces eventually. His voice ripples with concern. He didn't need to say that. The sight of the Wessex king's banner is enough to know that these warriors are separated from their king.

I catch sight of the earlier encampment. It's not overrun just yet, but it has been mostly abandoned.

'And what are we doing?' a mocking voice adds to the general unease.

'Watching 'em,' the brisk voice continues.

I'm bending forward, looking along the almost silent line of men, trying to get a look at who speaks. I've a feeling it must be whoever commands here. And in that case, it's the man who ordered the wooden gateway sealed against the Mercians.

'We should be out there, hunting the buggers down,' a derisive voice chastises.

Now the brisk-voiced man turns. He's a grey beard, straggles of silver and white hair showing beneath his elaborate helm. His byrnie is bedecked with Wessex's wyvern, and it looks to be twice as thick as any other byrnie I've seen. Yet, the man hasn't watched the battle from this lofty station. That much is obvious. No, he's been in the middle of the fight. His trews are sheeted in maroon, and there's a rip above the left knee, from which a trickle of blood can be seen.

'So, you suggest that I open the gate and allow the Mercians inside?' he demands to know. His words are edged with fury. 'They outnumber us, and King Ecgberht and his warriors can't get to us from inside Lundenwic with the Mercians taking the bridge over the River Fleet. We have half their number, maybe less than that. We're lucky to have made it inside the fort.'

'We should be attacking them from here then, using the advantage of height to kill them all.'

'And you can throw a spear that far, can you? We don't have enough archers or arrows. But you can waste our good spears if you want. But you'll be helping the enemy if you do that.'

'We can't just stand here and watch!' There's a shriek of outrage from someone else.

The Mercians continue to check the dead and nearly dead on the elongated slaughter field, I see, as one man is stabbed through the chest when he tries to attack a Mercian. At the roar of outrage that greets the action, the Mercian stands, drops his trews and shows his naked arse to the Wessex warriors.

I admire the stones of the man, but then, he's out of danger where he is. And so are his stones.

Before relacing his trews, the Mercian adds further insult by pissing on the dead Wessex warrior. I shiver with unease as, inside the fort, the men howl as though wolves on a full moon. I hate our opponents, but I'm not sure the Mercian warrior does the right thing with his actions.

'We need to get out there,' an outraged voice demands, and

others take up the cry as well. Seaxes flash beneath the glowing sun, and more than one yelp greets the actions. The damn fools are wounding their allies with their thoughtless actions.

'We can't do anything. Not at the moment. King Ecgberht will come to our aid. I'm sure of it.' But the ealdorman, I assume he's an ealdorman, sounds far from sure. From the way the men react, I don't think they believe it either. And still, they stand and watch the Mercians as they take control of the bridge that both divides and joins the twin parts of Londonia together.

In the distance, my attention is once more drawn to King Wiglaf's maroon banner flashing in the intermittent breeze. I consider whether he knows what Wulfheard has done. I ponder whether he'd even care about what Wulfheard has done, and then I look towards the market settlement.

From here, I can see how exposed it is. It lacks the walls of the fort, even if those walls have seen better days. It's exposed to the north, to the east as well. I can also see the glittering menace of the River Thames to the south, but I can't imagine Wiglaf ordering an attack from there. Wulfheard made it clear that the river is always an enemy and never an ally, promising safety along the water's edge, even as sucking mud tries to claim the lives of unwary inhabitants of the settlement.

But the Mercians haven't begun an attack on Lundenwic, despite its evident weaknesses. From here, the size of Mercia's forces appears enormous. I can see men and horses spread over a vast distance back up the hill we descended. Looking around, it doesn't feel as though the fort could contain that many Wessex warriors, and so I think they must be right. They're outnumbered and cut off from their king.

Yet Wulfheard made it clear that the Mercians want to get inside the fort, not the market settlement. How I'm supposed to bring that about, I have no idea. Not alone. Who can I turn to for aid? While the Wessex warriors might howl like a wolf pack, I'm the opposite. I'm alone. A lone wolf. The thought chills me. I must do everything for myself.

Slowly, some men begin to drift away from the vantage point. It's clear the Mercians have stopped their attack for the day. I suppose I could find Brihtwold and ensure Tyrhtil has been tended to, but I can see my Mercian allies from here. I might not be with them, but just knowing they're there fills me with much-needed confidence.

Slowly, the sun begins to slide from the sky in a welter of yellows and pinks, and still, I stand and watch. Campfires spring up, the Mercian dead are pulled aside from the Wessex corpses. They're piled onto carts, and horses begin the slow task of taking them away for burial. And still, I watch. I don't know what to do with myself. The fort is imposingly huge, and I've not even turned to gaze at the vastness contained by the massive walls that constitute Londinium. While the Wessex warriors might think themselves outnumbered by the Mercians, I'm overwhelmed by the number of my enemy who could kill me at any moment if they realise what I am. The pack of them could easily overwhelm a solitary figure.

Only as full darkness coats the view do I turn aside from my high point. I've not realised, but there are only a few men there, and they wear cloaks in preparation of standing the night watch. The rest of the warriors have taken themselves away, perhaps to eat, sleep, or mourn. But what should I do?

'Ah, there you are.' Brihtwold appears before me, his words breathless and his face pale in the deepening gloom. 'I've been looking for you. You said you'd help Tyrhtil.'

'Hasn't Ecgred tended to him?' I speak irritably. My situation is becoming more and more evident to me. I'm stuck in an enemy encampment, all alone. Perhaps I should just fling myself from this high wall and have done with it. At least my death would be at my hand then.

'No, Ealdorman Wassa takes up all his efforts. I think Tyrhtil will die if you don't help him.' His words are filled with urgency.

I sigh. This isn't what I planned on doing, but then, I didn't expect to be inside a fort filled with Wessex warriors while my few allies are on the opposite side of the enormous stone walls.

'Take me to him,' I concede. 'I'll do what I can, but I make no guarantee. How's your arm?'

'It still needs stitching,' Brihtwold informs me.

I shake my head at the actions of this Ecgred. He's not a very good healer, to judge by what I'm hearing. Wynflæd wouldn't accept him inside her workshop as an equal. She'd dismiss him until he could prove his worth to her, by actually tending to the wounded. The thought reminds me of my home at Tamworth and the smell of her workshop. I'd wish myself there, if only wishes could make it possible. It would be better than being here, alone, inside a Wessex stronghold.

Brihtwold leads me down the steep steps and back into the building attached to the fort, and I assume towards the room with the hearth. But no, immediately, I'm taken outside again and along a path paved with pieces of stone. It's surprisingly flat beneath my tired feet. I appreciate that this must be an old road, made by the men who ruled this land before Wiglaf was king, in fact before even the legendary Penda was king of Mercia. The men and women who built these walls must also have constructed roads. I wish there were more light with which to see.

Smoke drifts into the air, tinged with something that makes me cough. Then Brihtwold stops abruptly, bowing his head deferentially. I hasten to follow suit as a man strides past us, his face smeared with blood, his eyes white and reddened. I take him to be the ealdorman who was commanding from the walls earlier, but I can't ask. To do so would give away the fact that I don't know who anyone is within the fort. That would mark me as a Mercian more quickly than carrying an eagle-headed banner.

'Bloody arsehole,' Brihtwold mutters when he's walking once more.

In front of us, I spy a squat stone-built building, which has men lying all around it. They're in various stages of alertness, only visible in the dancing flames of fire leaking from inside the building and by brands which have been lit outside it. I take this to be where Ecgred practises his craft. I almost gasp. It's a magnificent hall compared to the wattle and daub workshop where Wynflæd tends to the sick and wounded inside Tamworth. It has stone walls and a half-decent roof that only seems to sag in the far-left corner.

Brihtwold marches onwards, but I pause, eyeing the men before me. They all carry one wound or another, although most have an ally with them, bringing water to those who can drink, while others are delirious. Dirty bandages attempt to stem the bleeding from arms and legs. One man is already dead, abandoned amongst the still living, the smell of him ripe as flies flock to rest on his bloodied nostrils and inside his mouth where his tongue is no longer pink. I almost gag at the vision.

Tyrhtil is lying, still on the upturned shields, holding his belly and whimpering softly. But his eyes are alert, the pain keeping him sharp. He just needs stitching together. I consider my options. Wynflæd doesn't believe in leaving someone in pain, not if she can help. I have a choice to make, but really, it doesn't feel like I do.

'Can you get gut, a needle and some hot water,' I demand of Brihtwold.

He nods, determination in the set of his lips, and then marches into the squat building. I can hear voices coming from inside, some grumbling, others arguing. I risk standing and making my way to the door. What I see inside makes me furious.

There's a thin man in there, his hands bloodied up to his elbows, attempting to treat someone lying on a high-up table or bed. The wood of the structure is darkened with blood close to the dying man's belly, and the smell of his ruptured gut hangs in the air, despite the herbs burning on the fire. The man is all but dead, and yet Ecgred, I take him to be Ecgred, still treats him, his hands busy with reddened bandages and bits of abandoned gut and needle.

But it's Ecgred's words that boil me.

'The coin,' he argues with another of the warriors, who gesticulates towards a bleeding figure bent double on the floor. 'The ealdorman gave me the coin, and so I must treat the man he bids me save. You have less than half of the coin, and so your man must wait twice as long.'

I shake my head, moving aside quickly as Brihtwold rears up before me. He carries the items I requested in his hand, which surprises me. He knows his way around Ecgred's workshop well if he knows where the pig's gut is stored.

'Here, I'll get some boiling water.' He thrusts the items into my lifeless hands. I've left my Wessex shield beside Tyrhtil.

I look down at the things Brihtwold has given me. The pig's gut is good quality; that much is evident from the smooth feel of it in my hands, the thin needle almost sharper than my seax. It'll be easy to knit together Tyrhtil's belly. The biggest problem will be ensuring he keeps the wound clean and doesn't overexert himself while he heals. But then, that's not exactly a new problem. Warriors make the worst patients. Wynflæd's always firm on that.

'Does he always charge?' I mutter to Tyrhtil when I'm back beside him, kneeling to get a closer look at what I need to do. I hope he won't think it strange that I don't know this.

'Yes. The highest bidder always wins, whether or not he's likely to live. The men try to ensure they keep some coins by should they ever require him. I have the coins.' And Tyrhtil opens his hand to show me five dull pennies, that are only a little bent, or flat on the edges. He does have the coins, but it seems not enough of them for Ecgred to tend him.

I gaze into the near distance, using the half-light to try to get a feel for the place. It doesn't seem to me as though there's a lack of people inside Londinium. I can see people going about their usual business, heads bent in conversation, while the smell of cooking food is rich in the air. Perhaps they're relieved that the fighting has come to an end, for now.

'Is there no one else who has the knowledge to heal?' I can't see that a settlement of this size has only one healer.

'The women have no skills for battle wounds. Only for healing the sick and tending to pregnant women and those too frail to walk far.' Tyrhtil gasps as he tells me this, his forehead slick with sweat. He's in agony. 'And they remain at home to do that. There are no breeding women here in the stronghold.'

'There's really no difference,' I mutter to myself, bending to examine his injury one more time, angling myself so that the light from the workshop and the brands illuminate what I need to see. I'm not about to argue with a wounded man.

The edges of Tyrhtil's skin are jagged. The wound wasn't made with a sharp enough blade. It was meant to cause the most amount of torment and be the most difficult to heal. But I've seen Wynflæd draw together two pieces of sundered skin like this. I'll just need to be careful. I curse the brutality of the Mercian who forged the wound even while understanding that, in war, whatever it takes to win is a necessity. I know that. I've killed men with no thought for them, only for my survival.

Brihtwold returns with a beaker of scalding water, a cloth over his arm as he tries not to spill it on his feet. His eyes are furtive. It would be better if Tyrhtil weren't in such open sight of the doorway that leads into the workshop from which arguments rumble, but there's nothing to be done about that now. Between us, we won't be able to move Tyrhtil. He has the build of a seasoned warrior – thick with muscle, and he'll be no help.

'My thanks,' I offer Brihtwold.

He thrusts two pieces of fine linen into my hand with the slightest glance over his shoulder. Brihtwold shouldn't have the items, but then Ecgred should be healing those who might actually live. The man with the slit guts who already stinks of the slaughter-house would be sooner left to die in peace or hurried along with some of the more deadly herbs about which Wynflæd has taught me. They're for desperate times and to bring much-needed ease-ment. There's a time and a place for everything, so Wynflæd was fond of telling me.

'This will hurt, and then I can find something to dull the pain,' I advise Tyrhtil.

His eyes are fixed on my hands. I know what I'd be giving him in Tamworth, but I'm unsure here. Perhaps some ale to swill for the pain will suffice if nothing else. I can't see that Brihtwold will be able to find herbs I need for something stronger. Maybe I could find them. But no, I'm not going into the workshop.

I dip one of the two cloths into the scalding water and move aside the filth and muck that's adhered to the two lips of ripped skin. My fingers tingle with the heat of the water, my gloves discarded.

I also place the pig's gut in hot water. It'll glide more easily if it's warm and supple.

With deft fingers, I begin my work. Brihtwold makes it evident that he's not going to watch, instead talking to Tyrhtil, his back firmly to what I'm doing, although it also serves to shield us from the scrutiny of any who should emerge from Ecgred's workshop.

It's an effort, after all the time in the shield wall. My arms throb, and moving the needle between the skin is difficult, despite its sharpness and the pig's gut being warm. By the time I finish, Tyrhtil has fallen silent, and even Brihtwold has run out of things to say. His low mumble has been a counterpart to my actions, allowing me to focus on them and not just on the terror I feel at having to tend such a vicious wound.

Once more, I wipe the sealed wound with the now cool water and sit upright, keen to straighten my back and ease the ache in it. Only then do I realise someone is bending over, watching me, his rank breath filling the air.

'What are you doing, boy?' There's both unease and scorn in his voice.

I have an idea who observes me, but I don't jump aside. I do catch sight of Brihtwold's fearful face as he finally turns to look at me. I take a breath, consider what to say. I could meet my death here, tending to a dying Wessex warrior. The thought turns my stomach sour.

8

———

'He'll live,' I announce instead, using the remaining linen as a bandage against the wound. Ideally, I'd like to add a poultice of moss, honey and vinegar to the injury to ensure it stays free from the wound-rot.

'Who gave you permission to treat him? To use my supplies of pig's gut?' There's more than mockery in the words; there's fury as well. Ecgred speaks with petulance. It's not a good sound to hear from the lips of a grown man.

I lumber to my feet, noticing I tower over the smaller man with his blood-splattered tunic and petty eyes, his arms darkened below the elbows, no doubt with the same blood I observed earlier. He's a man used to close work. That much is obvious. It's impossible to determine his age. His hair is thick, brown curls running down to his neck, although he has no beard or moustache. I'd think him little older than me, apart from the lines around his eyes and the deep welts surrounding his lips. He looks furious.

He rears back, one step and then another, and I look down. I'm covered in the gore of the battlefield and wearing my byrnie and weapons belt. Even though I don't hold any of my weapons, I must look fearsome as I tower over him. I notice then that there's someone close by, holding a flame so that Ecgred can see what I'm doing. I focus on the flame and then close my eyes tightly, seeing its brightness against the back of my eyelids.

'I took what was needed to heal a wounded warrior,' I announce, unprepared to make the reply sound like an apology, opening my eyes to glare at him. 'You were busy with the dying man when you should have been tending those who might yet live.' I'm aware that my accent marks me as a Mercian, but Ecgred doesn't seem to notice. I hope no one else does.

'What?' The word is barked.

'The man on the table with the split guts. I take it he's dead, or nearly so?'

'Now, boy,' and the word is elongated and filled with contempt, 'you might know how to sew a wound, but the matter of whether a man will live or die is not for you to decide.'

'So, he isn't dead yet, then?' I'm aware that our conversation has aroused the interest of more and more people, the dying and the not dying. Despite the darkness, I sense the scrutiny of others. I should simply bow my head and have done with this matter, but the pride in my skills won't allow it.

'Is he dead?' A stern voice roars over the heads of those absorbed by this strange spectacle. 'You assured me that twenty Mercian silver coins would ensure he lived?'

'Now, my Lord Wassa.' Ecgred turns all deferential in the blink of an eye, his words as sweet as honey. 'These things take time, and I did advise prayer as well, which I note you're not conducting?'

'Dying doesn't take time,' I mutter. I sense the tension in Ecgred's shoulders. What is he doing, promising to ensure someone lives when the situation is so bleak? Does he intend to lever more coins from the ealdorman? And why, I consider, must they be Mercian coins?

Now that I look more closely, the ealdorman's face is bruised and bloodied. His left eye is almost entirely closed. When he speaks, I can see where one of his front teeth hangs by a thread, blood on his lips. He should just yank the tooth out. There's no saving that. I sense his scrutiny and glance at him before returning my gaze to Ecgred's shoulders.

'So, Ecgred, will he live or die?' the ealdorman demands once more.

'My lord. You must allow me time for my potions to work.'

I feel my eyebrows rise on my face at the outrageous statement. Potions is it, now? I shake my head in disgust. So far, all I know about Ecgred is that he takes payment for his services, and his services always fall to the warrior who can pay the most. I've not seen him heal anyone yet.

'Boy, examine Eata for me. Tell me if he'll live.' It's not so much a question as a command.

I hear Brihtwold gasp from behind me, but I don't meet his eyes or take notice of Tyrhtil's weak restraining hand on my arm. Instead, I nod.

'Very well, my lord. I'll do just that.' I try to pitch my voice to roll, as the ealdorman's does. I don't know if I'm at all successful.

I move around Ecgred, mindful that he purposefully blocks my path towards the workshop, although the man with him doesn't. Only then am I assaulted by the stench of a man who's dying in terrible pain, the light from the fire blinding me all over again. I almost stumble on the uneven stone floor, but manage to stay upright.

Eata lies stretched on the blood-strewn table. His belly wound lies open and bleeds. I can see the greyness of his innards, the twisted gut ropes which have been shoved back inside the cavity, in no sort of order. They twist and turn over one another. If the man should ever wake from his stupor, he'll never be able to shit again.

His injury isn't even covered to keep away the flies that are drawn to the smell. I shoe them off with my hand.

But Eata's not going to wake. Already his skin is turning yellow. I lift one of his eyelids and see the buttery shade there as well. If Wynflæd were here, she might have been able to cure the yellow disease, but the slit belly and trailing innards make it impossible for Eata to wake again.

I'm mindful that Ealdorman Wassa is inside the workshop. His warrior's bulk fills the doorway, while Ecgred has been excluded by his choice of position. I'm also aware that Ecgred doesn't work alone. He has two slaves, both of them shackled around naked feet, one of them a man, the other a woman.

The man was outside, holding the flame to light the way for Ecgred. Now they both labour in front of the fire and beside a table, where small shoots are cut into smaller pieces and fed into the pots hanging over the flames. I amble over to look at them, unsurprised when both shy away from my interest. They carry the bruises and welts of a wicked owner on their skin, their clothes ragged for all they're not dirty. I pity them, even as I appreciate that the man, with skin the colour of Ecgred's hair, might know what he's doing.

The pieces of wild carrot are certainly well prepared, and the garlic is separated so that the higher potency leaves are cut even smaller than the milder parts of the leaves. I offer a smile but am rewarded with nothing but a flash of terror from warm green eyes.

Into one of the pots, the female slave places a random collection of objects. Some I know have healing qualities, some I know that don't. And why, I think, have four small stones been added to the mixture? They won't be edible.

'Well?' the ealdorman demands, recalling me to my task, his voice rough, even as his tongue plays with the loose tooth.

'He'll die. I'm sorry. There's nothing that can be done. The wound has pierced his gut. It won't heal, and if he wakes and eats, the shit will simply stay inside him. That'll kill him if the wound-rot doesn't.'

'Now, my lord...' Ecgred is all puffed-up wounded pride once more as he forces his way into the workshop, eyes flashing with dark malice. 'Would you sooner believe this... this "child" or me?'

'This "child" as you call him has stood in our shield wall, defending Londinium from the bastard Mercians. He saves the life of a good Wessex warrior without payment while you haggle and extract the best price from those who can afford more than they should. You promise false hope.' Ealdorman Wassa's eyes are fixed on the prone figure, whose chest rises and falls, but slowly, and laboured. The smell of the dying man is noxious, the herbs in the cauldron doing little to drive the stench away. His voice is filled with barely suppressed rage.

I try to make my escape. I've drawn more than enough attention to myself, and Ealdorman Wassa has reminded me that in healing Tyrhtil, all I've done is ensure a man who should have died on the slaughter field will live to fight my Mercians again. What will Wulf-heard say when he hears of this? What will my oathsworn lord, King Wiglaf, say?

'Stay there,' the ealdorman instructs me, even though he's not moved his scrutiny away from the dying man.

I pause in the act of escaping. In the doorway, Brihtwold waits for me, his head constantly turning from what's happening inside to what's occurring outside. I meet the eyes of the slave who cuts the roots. His eyes are hard. There's no sympathy to be found there for my current predicament.

'You'll stay here. Treat those who can be saved. Ecgred and I need to have a conversation. For now, you have complete command of the resources in this workshop. Ecgred?' The ealdorman strides away once more but pauses at the doorway and looks at me. 'Ensure my man has a good death. I'd not have my brother suffer unduly from his injury. He's a good Wessex man. He should have died on the battlefield, not here, in this hovel.'

A heavy silence fills the space left behind by the ealdorman's departure. I think that Ecgred will begin to scold me. But his name drifts back through the black doorway, and he hurries to follow the ealdorman, cold eyes appraising me with disgust, as he shouts instructions in a language I don't understand to the two slaves.

Both of them immediately stop what they're doing, shuffling away with the soft clunk of their chains and then out of the workshop as well. The ealdorman didn't demand the slaves help me, and Ecgred has instructed them not to do so. Not that I mind. If I can't speak to them in their tongue, they can hardly help me.

When the four of them are gone, Brihtwold enters the workshop, eyes wild with fear and confusion both.

'Sorry,' he whispers.

I shake my head. It's not his fault. If Ecgred had been any sort of healer, it wouldn't have mattered that he'd taken the pig's gut and the linens. Wynflæd wouldn't have objected. She'd probably have been pleased to have some help. Although, well, she would have been critical when the task was completed. She's never happy unless everything is done the way she wants it done, and no one can perform even the simplest of tasks as well as she can.

'Right.' I breathe in deeply. This wasn't what Wulfheard intended for me to do. There are at least thirty wounded warriors outside the door in the darkness, and I have to heal them as best I can to enable them to battle the Mercians once more. Of that, I'm sure. 'Can you help me?' I ask Brihtwold.

'With what?' His eyes are fearful.

'With fetching water, feeding the fire and just by being here?' I explain. I can't do all of this alone. Just as I can't win the fort for Mercia alone. At least here, I stand half a chance of knowing what to do.

'Yes, I suppose. I know where the well is.'

'Good, I need as much water as you can bring me. While you're doing that, I'll examine the wounded, see who needs assistance first.'

My eyes are taking in the shelves. I'm perplexed. There are jars and jars filled with the roots and dried leaves of healing herbs, yet Ecgred hasn't even begun making a poultice to keep the wound-rot away for Eata. Doesn't he know what he's doing?

'How's your arm?' I ask.

Brihtwold grimaces. 'It hurts.'

'Right, sit. You can't help me if you're in pain. Show me.'

Brihtwold reveals his arm. The deep wound greets me, but it is one that stopped bleeding a long time ago. It seems the bandage I tied above the injury has at least prevented him from dying of blood loss.

'This'll hurt, as I need to clean it and pack it with moss and honey. But then it should knit together.'

Brihtwold licks his cracked lips as I speak, but nods. I appreciate how young he is. He doesn't have the build of Tyhrtil, and not even of my childhood friend Edwin when I last saw him. But Brihtwold's stood in the shield wall and watched men he knows breathe their last. His black hair is thick and shaggy, the pretence of a moustache playing above his lips. I can imagine he sees something similar when he looks at me. We're both youths playing at being men.

Quickly, I walk to the shelves and stores, finding the items I need by lifting lids, sniffing jars and generally making a mess of the tidy workbench. I don't detect the work of Ecgred here. If he can't be bothered to wash the blood away from his hands, he's not going to take the time to prepare and correctly store a selection of herbs. This is the work of the slaves.

'This will hurt,' I remind Brihtwold when I'm content I have what I need. Holding a cloth to the wound, I carefully wipe away the mud and grime that's intermingled with the congealing blood. Brihtwold hisses through his lips but doesn't shudder away and I'm satisfied that I've done what I can for him, the sharp smell of vinegar making my eyes water. It's good stuff. A pity Ecgred doesn't seem to know its purpose. 'Do you mainly use your left or right hand?' I ask.

'Right,' Brihtwold answers quickly, looking at where I tie a piece of cloth in place around the honey and vinegar-soaked moss.

'Good, then don't use your left for anything for the time being, certainly not for carrying anything heavy. I'll recheck it tomorrow.'

Happy, Brihtwold ambles away, taking a bucket in his right hand. I watch him and then clear the worktop where the one slave had been cutting the herbs, being careful to return the correct leaves to the correct brown jar. Then I stir the mixture in the blackened pot and raise a full ladle to my lips. It's a grey and murky brew and smells of nothing I recognise. I lift the entire pot, unsurprised it weighs so much when it has stones in it, and take it outside. I pause then, looking for somewhere to leave the fluid. I pour it away into the open sewer that I think has been used for such things for many long years and which runs along the side of the building, cut into the stone-lined ground and, itself, lined with flat stones. This, like the walls and the bits of road I can see, is ancient, but has endured.

In the distance, the hulking menace of the walls can be felt. I shiver at the realisation of where I am and what I'm doing.

When I return to the workshop, Brihtwold has already brought me two full buckets of water. I slosh some of one into the empty pot. It sizzles, and I sniff, inhaling a strange scent.

I need boiling water to treat the wounds. 'Take this outside, and empty it again,' I ask Brihtwold. He moves to do as I ask without questioning me as I find another cauldron and pour all the remaining water in it.

When Brihtwold returns, I add more water and, satisfied it no longer stinks of something I don't recognise, I begin to add the herbs I need to make a healing salve – dandelion, wild carrot, yarrow and woodruff, while I hunt for agrimony amongst the other jars.

'Can you get me some more water?' I ask Brihtwold when I alight on agrimony and betony.

Again, he does as I ask without questioning me and despite how late it must be by now. The stars are out, the moon offering more light than the fires and brands that flicker outside. My thoughts turn to the Mercian camp. Does Wulfheard worry about me? I doubt it. But I can't imagine he thinks I'm employing myself in such a way.

I eye the well-stocked shelves, the cobweb threads hanging down from one of the shelves, and the jar of precious honey beside it. I can smell the sweetness. Next, I look for more pig's gut and, having found it, I lay it to one side, searching for a smaller bowl. I place the pig's gut into that and then spoon some boiling water into it. I eye the fire. It's not as warm as it should be, but Brihtwold has already returned with more water and now he works to add wood and pieces of dried dung to the flames. They leap high, blue and hot, and I smirk at him.

'Thank you.'

'Who do you want first?'

'I don't know. I should see how badly wounded the men are.'

He nods as I wash my hands and arms with the too hot water, making my fingers glow pinkly. I hiss at the pain, but better to have clean hands than filthy ones.

Outside, hopeful eyes meet my appearance. I know I'm far from done with my duties. But I don't have any choice, having given away my skills at healing. Once more, I consider King Wiglaf and Wulfheard and what they'd say to me about my current actions. It wouldn't please them.

I move through the men, noting cuts and deeper wounds, eyeing warriors who can hardly focus on me when I bend before them and others who can't even sit up. Brihtwold follows with a brand to light my path. Three of the men are dead. I can do nothing for them. It's evident where they've bled to death, the skin bleached white. I shake my head. Surely, someone knew to staunch the wound, to cut off the blood supply, but it seems not.

'I'll take him first,' and I point to a man with his hand clamped over his shoulder. A spearhead is wedged there, the wooden pole long since broken off. He's done well to keep the missile where it is.

Brihtwold helps the slight man inside, offering him a shoulder on the other side of the wound. I move ahead of them, already thinking about what I need to do. And then there's a loud chink, of metal on the uneven stone floor, and I meet the eyes of the brown-skinned slave. He eyes me, licks his lips, and begins to move around the workshop as though I'm not there. I watch him, unsure what he means to do, but he collects linens and small wooden bowls, and by the time my patient is lying down, I appreciate he means to help me.

I think I've probably found the reason for Ecgred's skills, and it's not his knowledge. No, Ecgred can do nothing without the aid of his slave.

Between the two of us, and without words, with Brihtwold to hand to keep the fire blazing, we work to ease the missile free from the man's shoulder, to staunch the bleeding and to sew the wound tightly closed. I wish I knew the slave man's name. Then, I begin to make a poultice, only to have one handed to me. I sniff it, detecting the sweetness of honey, and smile my thanks. He nods and points towards the body of our patient. The man stinks of the battlefield but is bright and alert. He's hardly complained about how painful it must have been to have the spear removed and the heat of a blade applied to his skin to cauterise the wound.

'You'll need to keep this clean and dry,' I inform our patient. 'If it bleeds more than a trickle, come back here. If it begins to smell of shit, come back here. But come back every day for a new binding.'

'My thanks,' he mumbles. I can tell from the state of his boots and trews that he's not a wealthy man. If it had come down to payment, he'd have been last on Ecgred's list, which is nonsense, as he'll heal quickly from such a wound.

'I'll take the man with the slit calf,' I say to Brihtwold as he helps the spear-free man outside.

'Aye, I'll get him.' Brihtwold disappears into the darkness.

I'm startled when I see the female slave beside the fire, carefully feeding small slithers of wood to the heart of the flames, stirring a pot as she does so. I take note of her shackled ankles, anger replacing my exhaustion. She meets my eyes defiantly from a slender face, hair obscured by a serviceable piece of cloth, so that I can't tell whether it's long or short. Beneath her dress, I can visualise the sharp angles of her hips. I feel that she should be eating the roots she prepares, not using them to heal others.

The male slave has also found some good candles to light the workspace, better ones than the stinking ones that I've unearthed.

'Thank you,' I offer them both in the stillness between one warrior and another. I'm grateful for their support. 'My name's Icel.'

Neither of them speaks, the man's cheeks lift a little, and I think he might speak, or smile, but he does neither.

'Icel,' I try once more, but when they don't offer me their names and the woman continues to glower at me, I turn aside, preparing for the next man I need to stitch up.

And so it goes throughout the long night. Of the thirty men waiting outside the workshop while Ecgred did nothing to aid them, three are already dead. A further three are so mortally wounded, I worry they won't survive to the morning, but I do all I can for those who waited for Ecgred to heal them, the two slaves assisting me with competence but no words, other than the occasional sibilant sentence they share with one another.

Brihtwold falls asleep at some point, his snores soft, head back against the wall, as the busy nameless slaves and I tend to the wounded and dying. We never share a word, even though I often talk so that there's something above the silence and soft whimpers of the wounded. The brown-skinned man knows far more than I do, that much is evident when he sometimes waits for me to move aside to examine wounds and apply poultices. Yet he also stands back on more than one occasion, watching me as I work. Perhaps, I hope, I know things he doesn't. I confess, I allow a tendril of pride to suffuse me. It keeps me going through the long, long night when I want nothing more than to curl up and sleep. Certainly, it stops me considering my predicament.

I'm yawning when a once-more awake Brihtwold tells me there's no one waiting for my services, although Tyrhtil is calling for my aid. He's slept outside, a cloak flung over him to keep away the chill of a later summer dawn, and he moans softly.

'It hurts,' he informs me.

'It's going to,' is my less than sympathetic reply, tempered with exhaustion. 'You've been slit from side to side across your belly. Even the smallest cut on a finger would be hurting you as it heals, let alone a bloody long thing like that. But,' I hold up my hand to forestall his next argument, 'I can offer you something to help you and to make you feel strong again.'

The younger slave woman has been tending to a thickening pottage all through the night. I've watched as she's added item after item, perplexed on occasion, and understanding on another that the pottage is filled with items that should make the weakened men strong. Again, I worry about what Wulfheard and King Wiglaf would say to me for helping the Wessex warriors. But these are just men, not ealdormen or king's thegns. These aren't the men to call others to arms. They're merely the blunt weapons.

Before I can return inside, a trail of men appears, led by Ealdorman Wassa, and I step aside. His man is dead, his brother. He never woke, and as the sun rose with the coming of a new day, his last breath left his body. Ealdorman Wassa, head bowed, with the aid of his warriors, carries the dead man away. No doubt he'll be buried, but where, I don't know because all I can see is stone layered upon stone. Indeed, as the sun begins to shade the day from grey to brightness, I gaze around me. Other than the workshop and the latrine ditch or drain, or whatever it is, I've not explored the settlement. I don't know where anything is, other than the fort, which looms in front of me, where the sun will set, not rise.

As I eye the fort uneasily, I hear the rumble of warriors on the move from somewhere close by but outside the grey-tinged walls, covered with creeping vines and dying weeds that might well be undermining how they're held together. I quickly appreciate that the Mercians haven't given up their prize of gaining entry to the walled settlement. No doubt, Wulfheard has told the king that I'll ensure they're admitted, but I have no idea how to do that. I've not spent the night seeking a means to open the huge gates. No, I've been saving the lives of my enemy.

I look down at my nails, noting the grime that's stuck beneath them, seeing the blood that streaks my hands, and I know I've done precisely the opposite of what Wulfheard would have wanted me to do.

I stifle a yawn. I'm weary, yet I won't get time to rest, not any time soon, as those I sent away to sleep are slowly moving back towards the workshop. They come, as Tyrhtil does, to complain of pain and tell me of fresh bleeding, even as the Mercians renew their attack on the fort.

I sigh heavily. What have I done, and what am I to do?

9

I sleep like the dead of Mercia, which I soon might be if my deceit is discovered. I'm exhausted, and I simply stop between treating one man and another. I'm aware of activity around me, of the two slaves tending to the ills of the warriors, but that fades away to nothing. Even the drumming of seax and shield from beyond the walls doesn't wake me. Nothing does, until I startle awake at some point, much, much later.

The sound of a knife cutting something into small pieces on a wooden board, and the crackle of the fire, makes me believe I'm sleeping in Wynflæd's workshop. It's still daylight outside. I can tell from the light streaming in through the open doorway.

'What happened?' I ask, recalled to where I am.

It's Tyrhtil who answers. He's standing in the doorway, blocking out the natural light. 'The Mercians are attacking the market settlement. They have the gateway surrounded at the fort. The other four entrances through the walls are blocked up and have been for much longer than we've held the fort. We're trapped apart from where the River Thames flows past the settlement, and that gate only gives out on to the river.'

I strain to hear now, and I can, just faintly, the sound of seax beating shield, but it's coming from much further away than before.

'The gate held, the walls as well, although for how long, I can't say.' Tyrhtil sounds neither worried nor pleased by the revelation.

I'm surprised to see him standing. I expected him to be lying down, allowing his wounds time to heal, but perhaps the slaves have given him something to numb the pain so much he feels hale although he's not.

'Ealdorman Wassa mourns the death of his brother. The Wessex warriors haven't even stirred from their beds today.'

I can't tell whether that's a criticism or not. I don't know Tyrhtil well enough to say either way.

'The ealdorman wants to see you,' Brihtwold informs me next.

I rub my eyes, yawn, pat my empty belly, and dread fills me. I don't know what to say to the ealdorman.

The two slaves have finally stilled their labours. The woman sleeps in the back room while the male one keeps a guard. I sense that this is often necessary from their poses. The male slave carries a lethal-looking wooden stick, the end weighted with iron. The thought upsets me, even as I realise that Ecgred hasn't been seen since the ealdorman spoke to me last night.

'Where's Ecgred?' I ask, even while Brihtwold attempts to hurry me. He seems much restored, and I note his bandage has been changed. There's no sign of blood leaking from it.

'With the ealdorman.'

'Huh.' I'm not sure what I think of that. It can't be good that Ecgred is with the ealdorman and that the ealdorman has summoned me.

Having swilled water into my parched mouth and thrust my hands into warm water to slide some of the residual muck from them, I follow Brihtwold through the abandoned settlement, but not towards the fort in the north. It all seems quite orderly, even as I appreciate how much stone is missing from the old buildings and how turf roofs have been placed over long-standing walls by the Wessex warriors or others who've thought to find safety behind the steep walls.

I know Londinium is ancient. Wulfheard told me as much. He also said that, once, the local settlement of Wall, where Cenfrith, Edwin and I spent the night when fleeing from Tamworth, would have looked like Londinium because the same people built it. I know he must have been exaggerating. Wall is little more than a handful of abandoned buildings on the side of a road, a pile of hastily collected pieces of masonry. It can never have looked like Londinium. But Wulfheard refused to confirm it was teasing. That makes me think he might have been right.

Brihtwold is quiet as we walk. I'm too busy trying not to gawp to speak. This place isn't at all like Tamworth; although it shares similarities – the wide river in the distance is one of them. Although, well, Tamworth has not one river, but two, the Anker and the Tame, running around it to the south. Londinium has the River Thames in the distance. Yet, I can also hear the sound of water moving more closely. I must assume there's another river, or stream, running through the settlement. And, of course, although I can't see it from here, there's the River Fleet that divides the fort from the market settlement, a river wide enough to need a wooden bridge to crest it.

And then we come to a stop. In front of me, there's a structure I can hardly comprehend. All around it are smaller piles of stones, no doubt the remains of other buildings. Beneath my feet, I walk on gravel and tufted grasses. Lifting my feet to peer down, I question whether the whole place was once laid with stone upon which to walk? I pause, gaze around me. In the distance, almost further than the entire settlement of Tamworth, are hints of more walls, more random pieces of white stone, discarded and abandoned. I don't see any crops or greenery, only shrivelled weeds and little else. If I were to live here, where would I grow my food? Where would Wynflæd harvest her herbs from? The place is dusty and barren, just as Wulfheard told me.

The ealdorman has decided to set his camp inside the remains of a vast building, consisting of more than one level, although little of the upper floor remains. It must once have formed some ceremonial purpose for the giants who roamed this land, although what it might have been used for is beyond me. Why would anyone need a building so vast if not for ceremony, like the king's hall or the wooden church in Tamworth? It might well accommodate everyone who lives in Tamworth, Repton and Lichfield, and there'd still be room for more people.

There's a forest of stone plinths guiding us towards the smell of campfires, with some immobile figures on them, all missing arms, or legs, or feet or even heads, their whiteness attesting to being made from some sort of priceless stone. To me, they look so similar to the bodies of the dead that, for a moment, I can't quite decipher the intent behind them. And Brihtwold is no help. I can hardly ask what this place is because I should already know.

I expected the ealdorman to be inside the fort, but he's not. The smell of good wood being burnt drifts from inside the building, and I shudder, fear temporarily making me want to bolt in the opposite direction.

Finally, Brihtwold stops and looks back at me, where I stand, trying not to be overawed by all I'm being shown. Brihtwold's expression surprises me. It's as though he sees me for the first time, perhaps realising I can be no older than him.

'The ealdorman isn't alone,' he admits hesitantly. I'm unsure why.

He says nothing further, moving slowly up five wide stone steps, where he nods to the two door wardens standing with their spears and shields, and walks inside the open maw of the building. I feel my forehead furrow and then rush to join him. I don't want to anger the ealdorman any further.

Once inside, I stop and peer around. I feel on more familiar ground here. This is little more than an ealdorman's hall, with his warriors sitting or standing, talking or sleeping, servants rushing to feed people and a small raised dais at the end where Ealdormen Wassa sits talking with another man. I can see that the wood of the dais is fresh. This is a new addition. The only real difference I note is that the roof of this building isn't made of thatch and wooden struts but, instead, of the same stone, blackened in places by years of fires being lit beneath it. I appreciate then why the door to the building remains open. It's smoky inside. The stone ceiling offers no means for the dancing smoke to escape.

No one watches me as I pass through the collection of eating and drinking men. Although the sight of the black and white wyvern shields worries me, I hold out hope that this is merely an opportunity for the ealdorman to thank me for saving his warriors.

Of course, I'm entirely wrong.

'It's the king's son,' Brihtwold eventually informs me as I see the other man watching me from the dais. He's younger than the ealdorman. His clothes are some of the finest I've ever seen, and his weapons belt carries not just a seax but two of them. On his tunic, I can see the emblem of the wyvern, depicted in glittering stones in the candlelight. He has a full head of dirty-blond hair and the traces of a beard and moustache on cheek and chin. A long nose dominates his face, almost too long, and when he turns to the side, it extends far beyond his chin. Behind him, in the shadows from the fire and candles, his shadow is all nose and little else.

'What does he want?' I demand. Suddenly, I'm aware once more of what I am. I'm a Mercian, in the heart of a Wessex encampment. One wrong word and I could be put to death for being a traitor. I swallow. My tongue tastes foul, and my eyes itch with exhaustion. I wish I'd thought to bring my gloves with me. I'm all too conscious of the mark on my hand from where I healed my uncle using my heated blade. If someone looked at it, they might well determine it carries the sigil of Mercia's eagle. It's either easier or more challenging to decipher depending on the light. I can only hope no one will recognise it in the smoke-filled hall.

'Icel.' Ealdorman Wassa's greeting is warm enough as Brihtwold and I stand before the dais, for all his words are slurred. I would suggest he's spent much of his time drinking to dull his sorrow at the death of his brother. And, perhaps, at the amount of Mercian coin he paid to Ecgred to cure a man who was already more than half dead.

'My lord.' I bow low, and so does Brihtwold, although an impatient hand bids us rise.

'I wished to thank you for your labours with the wounded.'

'My lord.' I'm conscious that my words don't sound the same as Ealdorman Wassa's, and so I don't want to risk saying too much. I'm just waiting for him to realise my true heritage.

'The ætheling, Lord Æthelwulf, the king of Kent, also wishes to know you. It seems that Ecgred has been making some complaints.'

Ah, I think, now he gets to the heart of the matter.

'My lord?' The words are all the response I make as I again bow to Lord Æthelwulf. I'm curious to see what sort of man Æthelwulf is. I imagine he has his father's fierceness.

'Ecgred says you don't know what you're doing, and equally, that you've stolen his slaves.'

I don't think this a matter for the ealdorman and the king's son, but what do I know?

'His slaves assisted me, yes. I couldn't steal them, for I don't speak their tongue.' Only now do I realise that Ecgred sits beside Lord Æthelwulf, half in the shadows. He gives himself away by gasping with fury at my words. 'I'll tend no others if that's your wish. Ecgred is welcome to return to his workshop. I would, however, suggest that he not accept payment in Mercian coin from the men.' I speak coolly, surprising myself with the ferocity of my wrath.

I feel Brihtwold startle beside me. Perhaps I do a poor job, or perhaps, in my anger, I betray my Mercian accent. I've no doubt already said too much. Why, I consider, did I think to stress Ecgred's demand that the coins must be Mercian? Only then do I realise a fundamental reason why King Ecgberht holds Londonia's mint. Does the Wessex king not have moneyers of his own? Is the Mercian coinage still prized above his, even now? Or is it merely about the trade undertaken in Lundenwic?

'Very well,' Lord Æthelwulf concedes after a brief pause, in which he flashes a perplexed look at Ecgred. Maybe he too has realised there's something strange happening. Lord Æthelwulf turns to watch me intently, but there's no flicker of anger on his face. 'Ecgred, return to your workshop, treat the men, and don't take Mercian coins from them. I'll ensure you're recompensed for your labours.' The stress on Mercian isn't missed by any of us there.

I bow again, thinking the matter done with, but it seems not.

'And you, tell me, from where do you hail? Someone as skilled as you should have come to my attention before now.'

This is what I've been dreading. I know Wessex poorly. There's only one option available to me.

'From the kingdom of Kent, my lord.' I keep my head as low as possible. I don't want Lord Æthelwulf to get too close a look at me. I fear he'll see my Mercian heritage written into every line of my face, as though having a scruffy black beard makes me Mercian. I know it's foolish, and yet, I can't help but think it. After all, Brihtwold has a black beard and moustache as well, and he's undoubtedly from Wessex.

'From where, exactly?' Æthelwulf presses me. I can see his eyes gleaming. Of course, he's been named the king of Kent by his father. No doubt he thinks to know everyone in that kingdom and doesn't recognise me.

'From a small settlement a day's ride south of Canterbury.' I offer half a smile, although it's an effort. Wulfheard had told me of Canterbury when it belonged to Mercia. I'm once more grateful to him, even though most of the time I think he tells me facts I'll never need to know. I think he does it to bore me, not assist me. I'm not about to say to Wulfheard he might have saved my life. Not when he's the one that's placed it in such a perilous situation. If not for him, I wouldn't be here, so I wouldn't be relying on his unwanted teachings to ensure I know as much about Mercia as he does.

'And who taught you such skills?'

'An old woman in our settlement.' I don't want to name Wynflæd because I'm aware she and King Ecgberht were known to one another, but all of a sudden, I can't think of a single woman's name. I know I'm being too vague. Yet, Lord Æthelwulf doesn't press the point, although a silence hangs between us for just a moment too long.

'And you came to Londonia?'

'With the warriors of Kent,' I reply quickly. I wish I'd thought to ask Brihtwold from where he came. Or really, any of the men, but I didn't, and now I can feel my legs trembling. I'm sure they must know that I lie. I don't even know the name of the ealdorman there, if there even is one now that Lord Æthelwulf rules Kent for his father.

'And you'll continue to fight for the kingdom of Wessex against the Mercian scourge?'

'Of course, my lord,' I reply to the ealdorman this time, as he asks the question. He flicks his fingers at me, and I bow once more and move aside, grateful to be dismissed even as Ecgred glares at me from beside the ætheling. I have an overwhelming urge to run from this place, to be away from the knowing gaze of all three men. I rub my hands, one inside the other, and feel the edges of the scar seared into my skin. I must keep the palm of my hand away from the sight of anyone. I need to reclaim my gloves.

My legs are still shaking, and my mouth is dry, but I walk from the grand building, now turned into an ealdorman's hall, desperate to be away from the ætheling and the ealdorman. I need to leave this place. As soon as possible. I shouldn't have allowed myself to become distracted from Wulfheard's set task.

Just as I'm about to take a deep breath of the smoky air from outside the hall, I feel a hand on my shoulder and turn quickly, hand already reaching for my seax.

But I spin and clap eyes on Ecgred, his small eyes piercing me as he rears back from the sharp edge of my blade.

'So, a warrior as well as a healer,' he hisses at me, hatred on his weaselly face, standing too close, no doubt because his eyes are weak from working in the dark and on delicate tasks all the time. Or at least, from pretending to while his slaves really do the hard work. He's smaller than I am, and there's no strength to him. It would be too easy to slice his fingers from the hand that touches me, and yet I don't.

Pulling the blade away, I wait for him to say more.

'You've done me out of a great deal of coin, boy.' He speaks the final word dismissively. I might be a 'boy' as he calls me, but I'm proud of that.

I find a smirk on my face. 'You call yourself a "healer", but I know your secret.'

'What?' And now terror flashes in his shadow-darkened eyes.

I almost give myself away then because I don't honestly know anything about his secrets. Or maybe I do.

'The slaves can't talk your language,' he hisses at me, stepping aside as a limping warrior enters the hall through the door we stand beside. I don't recognise him from my healing work. Perhaps it's little more than a twisted ankle or an old wound. The scent of him is terrible. He needs to drink more and bathe more. He stinks of the charnel house.

'The slaves don't need to be able to talk to tell me all I need to know,' I crow over him, going with it because I genuinely know nothing other than the fact that Ecgred is no healer. Of that, I'm sure. He relies entirely on the knowledge his slaves possess. And we're already enemies, so what does it matter if he hates me more than he already does?

'Watch yourself, boy,' he leers at me.

'And you, *healer*,' I deride, and he rushes from me, through the door and off into the deepening dusk, back towards the corner of the settlement where the fort lurks and where he'll find his workshop.

I follow, more slowly, legs still unsteady, heart beating too fast in my chest. Ecgred is a worm, but he's a powerful one, and I'm a Mercian inside a Wessex stronghold.

I don't turn to Brihtwold, who mirrored me in being dismissed by Ealdorman Wassa, but I can well imagine the look on his face. Instead, I stamp onwards and then pause. I don't know my way around Londinium. I don't know anything about this place other than the River Thames is to the south of me, and my home, Tamworth, is to the north and, for the time being, out of reach.

Brihtwold lets out a huge sigh. 'Well, you've made a good enemy there. Ecgred isn't a man to cross,' he cautions me. 'What with all his potions and poultices. They say that he can poison a man or woman if the coin is sufficient to take the risk.'

'He can't do anything.' I dismiss the thought. Yes, some herbs will poison if given in the wrong quantities, but I don't think Ecgred will want to take any such risk. Even if he knows which they are and can prevail upon his slave to provide the concoction. Which I doubt.

'He can,' Brihtwold answers hotly.

'Who would pay the Mercian coin?' I demand from him, noticing that his face is pale in the lowering light. I imagine he's as terrified as I am to be summoned before the ealdorman and the king's son. 'I've upset no one but him. He won't want to do it if there's no profit to be made.'

Brihtwold's eyes narrow at my words, and then he shrugs his shoulders.

'You might be right,' he confirms. 'Right, we need something to eat and to get back to Tyrhtil. I wouldn't put it beyond Ecgred to undo all the healing you've done.'

I wait. Brihtwold needs to lead the way because every road looks the same to me now that there's less light by which to see.

'This way,' and he strides out in front.

This time, I eye my surroundings more carefully as we pass them. It might be growing darker, but the walls are ubiquitous in the distance. They surround Londinium, menacing me with their sturdiness. Tyrhtil spoke of other gates to the one at the fort, but he also said they were all blocked up, apart from the river gate. I need to find another means of escaping. And, of course, now that I've calmed down, I'm remembering that my purpose here is to help the Mercians get inside. It's all well and good for me wanting to escape, but that's not what I need to do.

I stumble on a loose stone, tripping and landing heavily on my feet, although at least upright. If such a simple thing can fell me, then how I'm supposed to aid Wulfheard and the rest of the Mercians, I really don't know. And, in the meantime, I need a friend to assist me, even if he should be an enemy. I hurry to follow Briht-wold. Without him, I'll quickly become lost.

10

Brihtwold leads me back towards the fort without further mishap. I can hear nothing of any battle taking place between the Mercians and the Wessex warriors outside the walls. No doubt, it's too dark to continue. I can smell smoke. To my mind, it comes from more than just the hearth fires inside the walls and those from the Mercian encampment outside. Maybe the market settlement burns. Maybe the Mercians have raised the bridge that provides the only access between Lundenwic and Londinium. I wish I knew, but that would mean going inside the fort once more and climbing the steep steps to look out over the surrounding countryside. I'm too tired for such as that.

Men spill all over the free ground before the fort, with the grey stone walls at their backs. Some of them laugh, some drink, some snore, and yet more are still weak with pain. Their friends help them, yet I know more could be done for them. There's no need for them to suffer when a simple remedy could be given to them.

I cast an eye in the direction where I know Ecgred's workshop is, but I'm not going anywhere near it. Not when the vindictive little man is likely to be there, lauding over all who seek his aid. I hope that at least the two slaves are not badly punished by him for helping me. For them, I am sorrowful. We didn't speak, and yet I believe we worked well together. Certainly, Wynflæd would be pleased to know the two slaves. They would have much to share. I almost wish I'd not given up my hold on the workshop so easily. I should have refused the summons to attend the ealdorman and the king's son. But then, Ecgred would have found another means of claiming back his possessions.

'Here.' Brihtwold thrusts a wooden bowl of food into my lifeless hands. I only just grip it in time. I'd not even realised he'd left my side and gone inside the building that makes up one wall of the fort.

I sniff, smelling the vegetables in the pottage as my belly rumbles angrily.

He also holds a further bowl, and I follow him to a small area beside a tumbled-down wall that will provide some shelter from the night air thanks to the piece of stained canvas stretched over the top of it. The day is growing colder. It's not the only such structure. The Mercians might have their tents, but here, over the hard ground, more of it stone than not, there's nowhere to pin the ropes and canvas in place and the Wessex warriors have been forced to improvise.

Already, I can sense the end of the day coming, and with so few clouds overhead, it might become even colder. I'd be happier with a hearth to warm me.

I'm surprised to spy Tyrhtil already inside the temporary structure. He's lying on his back but not asleep. He shuffles upwards on his arse when he sees Brihtwold.

'That git Ecgred is back,' he snarls, as though answering my question as to how he's made his way so far from the workshop alone with such a wound. His snippy tone leads me to believe he's been denied the aid of the slaves and their healing potion. I can barely imagine the pain in which he must be. I might have been less than sympathetic earlier, but, honestly, he must be in agony. 'Here, I retrieved your gloves for you.' He nods down to the ground, and I see them close to his knee.

I reach out and take them. I need to find a way of pulling them back on that won't arouse too much suspicion. I need to cover my hand before Brihtwold sees my scar.

'Lord Æthelwulf commanded it,' Brihtwold explains through hungry mouthfuls, having handed Tyrhtil his bowl.

I sit beside the two, although I eye Tyrhtil uneasily in the flickering flames of a nearby fire. The fire casts his face into shade and shadow, and it's impossible to know how he fares just from looking.

'Bloody fool,' Tyrhtil continues to complain, although he's sitting now and taking tentative mouthfuls. I don't think he should be sitting quite so upright, but I hold my tongue. He needs to eat, and that's never easy when you're prone. Tyrhtil eyes me over his bowl of pottage. The food is hot enough to burn. I don't know how Brihtwold manages to eat it. I need to wait, even though I'm ravenous. 'He came marching back in, ordered his slaves around in the strange gabbled tongue they must understand, sending men hither and thither as though he'd cured them all, and not you. For what did the ealdorman want you? Just to tell you that you shouldn't be healing people?'

I nod, giving in to my need to eat and trying not to burn my tongue, even though it's impossible. I should have waited.

'Hardly seems like the sort of thing the ealdorman needs to deal with?'

'Lord Æthelwulf said he'd pay Ecgred for his services,' Brihtwold adds, already looking hungrily at my food.

'Really? About bloody time it was easier for the warriors to get some healing, as opposed to it just being for the ealdormen, king's thegns and thegns.' Tyrhtil speaks with some respect in his voice for the king's son.

'You told Lord Æthelwulf you were from Canterbury,' Brihtwold says next. I'd been hoping not to be asked any more about that. 'But, if you're from Canterbury, you should have been with Ealdorman Ælfhere.' There's suspicion in Brihtwold's voice.

'Got separated from them,' I try, holding my voice steady.

'Ah, who cares from where he comes? If it weren't for him, I'd be dead, and we wouldn't be having this nice little chat anyway.' Tyrhtil dismisses the interrogation quickly. But, I realise, I need to be wary of Brihtwold.

'Where are you from, anyway?' I ask, eager to have the attention on either of the other two.

'I'm from good old Winchester way,' Tyrhtil says quickly. 'Born and raised there. Been a member of the king's warband for the last ten years. And young Brihtwold isn't from far away either. First time fighting for the king, though.'

I nod. I know where I am when they talk of Winchester. That's where the Wessex kings have their primary residence and their royal treasury, where they build their churches and bury their dead. It's not unlike Tamworth, for all the Mercian kings could go anywhere within the kingdom.

'Everyone here is from Winchester way,' Tyrhtil continues. 'Those from the south-west are in the market settlement, under Ealdorman Wilfhardi's command. Poor sods. He's an old man and should be leaving such to his sons and grandsons. He's about as dynamic as the wide trunk of an oak tree. Ealdorman Ælfhere is the more forceful there. Not like here, under Lord Æthelwulf and Ealdorman Wassa of the South Saxons. Wassa's brother was an ealdorman as well, of Hampshire. Poor git. We'll need a new one now. Especially as we're at war against the damn Mercians.'

'Doesn't Wassa have another brother?' Brihtwold queries. I'm pleased that Tyrhtil has managed to distract him from asking me more questions.

'No idea. Don't keep track of those toforans. If they can fight well and command better, I might know who they are. But what happens at King Ecgberht's court is beyond me. I'm just a warrior, not a politician.' The two of them laugh at Tyrhtil's words. I sense a camaraderie between them, even though the two warriors are so far apart in age.

I've finally managed to finish my bowl of pottage and only burned my tongue a little. Brihtwold stands easily and takes the three bowls back to where the food has been handed out to the warriors inside the fort. So it seems the abandoned hall I entered yesterday does have a use, after all, that of providing food for the Wessex warriors. A brief silence falls between Tyrhtil and me. I'm thirsty, but I don't know where to get water from, and I don't want to ask either and give the lie to everything I've been saying about hailing from near Canterbury and being a Wessex warrior.

'You've made a powerful enemy in Ecgred.' Tyrhtil's revelation hardly surprises me, but the fact he tells me does startle me. 'He's got a reputation, you know, and not a good one.'

'Brihtwold told me he's a poisoner.'

'And the rest. A proper little worm, but in with King Ecgberht, for some reason.'

By now, Brihtwold has returned, his face alight with worry.

'They say the Mercians have made an encampment inside Lundenwic and that King Ecgberht is threatened.'

'Do they now?' Tyrhtil mutters. I can see he's furious at the news. 'With his force split, as it is, King Ecgberht might be in real trouble,' he muses. 'The king should have retreated inside the protection of the fort, not into the chaotic mess of the market settlement. There's nowt in there for him to hide behind, and certainly not the precious mint.'

'His forces were cut off. The Mercians pressed them hard,' Briht-wold counters, shrugging his shoulders as he does so, the action making him wince. He covers it by pulling an old seax from his even older weapons belt and reaching for some stray dry grasses with which to clean it. I can see that he's already thinking of the Mercians he'll kill. The thought makes me shiver with fear. Even though we talk of King Ecgberht and the Mercians, I've forgotten that I'm on the opposite side of this war to Brihtwold and Tyrhtil. The pair of them seem like good company. I almost wish I wasn't their enemy.

I watch Brihtwold's nimble fingers as they clear the rust from his blade, and swallow heavily as I realise that blood is from a Mercian.

I should do the same with the seax that Wulfheard thrust into my hand alongside the shield, but will it also be Mercian blood? The thought sickens me.

I appreciate then that I don't even know if I can fight with it. I've only used it by instinct to threaten Ecgred.

'Then we'll need to come at them from behind, trap them in Lundenwic between our forces and those of King Ecgberht's.'

'No chance,' Tyrhtil counters. 'There are no walls to ensnare them on that side of the river. They'll just escape into the fields or the rivers and rally to come back at us once more.'

'But at least all the Wessex warriors would be in one place,' Brihtwold acknowledges.

'We would, yes, but it wouldn't be behind the walls of this fort. No, I think King Ecgberht is more likely to try to reach us here. Either that or escape over the River Thames and come to the fort via another route. Being split like this is no good for the king. And he's wise enough to know that.'

'No.' Brihtwold shakes his head vigorously, his hair rising from his shoulders with the movement. 'Lord Æthelwulf and Ealdorman Wassa will want to make a name for themselves, show the Mercians the Wessex force can't be beaten that easily. You mark my words; we'll be fighting the backs of the Mercians tomorrow.'

11

Brihtwold's wrong.

We sleep where we eat. In the morning, with fog shimmering in the air, we're roused from our hard beds by a loud argument coming from the fort.

I'm stiff and sore, all sorts of pains making themselves known as I stagger upright from my stone bed. I've not even had a cloak to wrap around myself. More than once during the night, I wish I'd taken a cloak from one of the dead men.

Brihtwold is in no better state than I am, for all he does have a threadbare cloak held tightly to him by an iron brooch that's seen better days. Poor Tyrhtil can't even sit, let alone stand.

Concerned, I drop to my knees and eye him.

'Show me your wound,' I demand.

He lifts his cloak and ripped tunic clear from his belly with no eagerness. In the dull grey light of early morning, I touch the skin around the injury and then remove the linen bandage and poultice.

My forehead furrows. 'It's healing well,' I advise him, surprised at the revelation. The skin is pink and puckered, but the stitches are holding together, and if anything, his skin is cold, not warm as it should be if he had a fever.

'It's not that,' Tyrhtil admits, attempting to stand. Brihtwold is quickly to his other side. I support his weight from the left. 'I need to piss and drink. My gut feels churned up. I need to shit as well, but I can't.'

I nod. I had considered it might be a problem, but I'd hoped that his guts would have escaped the ravages of his wound. It seems I've been too optimistic.

Between Brihtwold and I, we get Tyrhtil to the latrine pit and wait for him. It stinks. The smell is foetid, rising above everything else, even clearing the fog that sticks persistently in other places. I can see the ground begins to dip down from where we stand. The stream I heard yesterday must be at the bottom of the dip. The ground looks boggy as well, with the stone covering tipped at odd angles, lending more credence to my thoughts.

'Can you fight? How many Mercians did you kill?' Brihtwold eyes me uneasily from beside Tyrhtil, who sits to empty his bladder. He groans as he does so, and an even more foul odour makes itself known.

'Yes. I can fight. And enough men fell below my blade to make me a warrior. Can you fight?' I ask, stung into retorting. I've not thought of myself as proficient in killing men and protecting Mercia, but I don't appreciate Brihtwold's questioning of me. I wish I could tell him of saving King Wiglaf's life in the borderlands, but he wouldn't thank me for that, and I'd give away my affiliation as well. I can tell him of the Wessex lives I took. How many men have I killed? I wish the number wasn't imprinted on my mind. But I remember the men I killed fighting for Mercia on the borderlands. I remember how I killed all three and now I've doubled that number fighting at Londonia. I can only see the number will continue to increase.

'Yes, I can fight.' His words are flecked with just as much bile as mine. I can't help it, I grin.

'Good, then we can both bloody fight.' I arch an eyebrow at him, and his unease slides from his face. He returns my grin.

'It's just, your seax is shit,' and he points at my warrior's belt, smirking.

I know it's not a good weapon. I tried out the weight in my hand last night when everyone else slept. It's top-heavy, the handle too long, the blade too short. But what can I do? 'And you think yours is any better?' I demand.

'I suggest we both find ourselves good Mercian blades when we face our enemy.' His words are filled with bluff. We might doubt one another's abilities and hate each other for doing so, but we relish the coming battle, should it come, with little enthusiasm.

As Tyrhtil staggers back to his feet and we rush to his side, I sense some movement amongst the rest of the men.

'Any success?' I ask Tyrhtil.

'No, not yet. I pissed, but not the other.'

'Drink a great deal,' I instruct him. 'And if we can find you some garlic, that'll aid you as well.'

Only as I'm talking, we all become aware of another noise. The banging of weapons against shields from beyond the walls alerts me that the Mercians are once more on the attack. I curse myself. I've not yet found a way to allow the Mercians easy access inside the fort. I should have done something by now. Wulfheard will be growing impatient with me.

Lord Æthelwulf strides from the rising sun, encased in shadows and the promise of light. 'We fight the Mercians today,' he commands the Wessex warriors. 'Now, on your feet.'

My knees quiver at the thought of willingly facing my fellow Mercians. Yet, the melee in front of me doesn't immediately resolve itself into a force of men eager to leave the safety of the fort.

'You can't fight,' I inform Tyrhtil, as his pale face flashes with sweat. 'Not until you've emptied yourself, fully,' I caution him. He can barely stand upright. If I had access to Ecgred's vast store of herbs, I'd make him a potion of garlic, mustard and pennyroyal. It would ease him. I smirk at the thought, reminded of the horse I tried to aid in just such a way at Kingsholm. It seems that man and beast can't live with a belly filled with the foulness of the body.

'I must,' Tyrhtil hisses through tight lips.

Between us, Brihtwold and I return him to where we slept the night before. Men are waking slowly, grumbling, moving towards the latrine, and generally ignoring the instructions of their king's son. That surprises me. King Wiglaf wouldn't allow such as this, for all I detected unease in the warriors I fought beside before banishing King Ecgberht from Mercia. King Wiglaf would have the men on their feet quickly. Or, rather, Ealdorman Ælfstan would. He's a man who likes to be obeyed before the instructions are even uttered.

'If you fight like this, you'll be dead without felling a single one of your enemies,' I caution Tyrhtil. I don't know why that shouldn't be what I wish for, but having tried to save his life, I'm reluctant to have him throw it away once more when I know it'll be folly.

'My lord demands it.'

'Your lord demands healthy men in the shield wall, if that's what it will be. You'll fall and leave it sundered.' Brihtwold has taken up my argument now.

'It's not to be a shield wall,' another Wessex warrior grouches, walking towards the latrine. 'He wants his warriors to rush across the River Fleet at its narrowest point, to join the king's warriors inside Lundenwic. He'll be leaving as few people inside the fort as possible.'

The news astounds me. I've not been back atop the walls of the fort to see where the Mercians are, but I would anticipate they've already considered the possibility of such an attack. I also don't understand why Lord Æthelwulf would abandon such a strategic location – well, not abandon, but leave it weakened. Unless, of course, it won't be weakened.

I turn slowly, eyeing the walls that surround me, some close, some much further away. Does Lord Æthelwulf believe the walls will hold against the Mercians? Does he genuinely think that just keeping the one gateway closed will be enough? Perhaps he's correct in his belief. After all, I've found no other means of escape.

'Hurry up.' Ealdorman Wassa rears up amongst the ramshackle collection of warriors trying to rouse themselves to full wakefulness. They moan with all the aches and pains of a good night's sleep after a hard-fought battle. 'Your Lord gave you an order. I mean to see it's followed.' Ealdorman Wassa's face carries the ravages of his grief for his brother. It's aged him overnight. I think there's vomit in his beard and wince to see a man brought so low by too much ale. I can tell that rage drives him onwards. He intends to exact his revenge against the Mercians. I wish him luck with that. 'And don't think you're not required to join your fellow warriors. Ecgred is the only healer the Wessex warriors need. You can fight. He can't.'

I recoil at his harsh words as he stands before me, finger jabbing into my chest. I feel as though I've been unduly singled out just because I told him his brother would die. The words of yesterday are entirely forgotten.

'My lord.' I bow my head low and hope that Wassa doesn't catch sight of Tyrhtil, but he does.

'You're no good to me in that state,' Wassa announces, glaring at Tyrhtil. 'You can throw missiles from the walls.'

As the ealdorman strides away, his echoing cries bring stragglers to their feet. I'm almost grateful that Wassa has banished Tyrhtil from the coming attack. But Tyrhtil isn't. His tired face is furious, his eyes flashing brightly even in the dim daylight.

'And how am I supposed to get up there?' he all but wails, pointing to the bastion atop Londinium's wall.

'On your backside, if need be,' I inform him. 'And take a latrine pot with you. When your belly lets up on the filth inside you, you'll not want to have to travel far.' I offer this as though it's a given that his belly will empty itself, which it isn't.

'Here.' Tyrhtil reaches to his discarded weapons belt and hands me the seax handle-first. I can see how sharp the blade is just by looking at it. 'I don't want you to die out there. If you make it to Lundenwic, then that's good; if not, you can come back here and heal my guts.' His lips twist in pain once more.

'Drink as much water as you can,' I repeat, taking the blade, although my gloved hand trembles to do so. It's a fine weapon, much better than the crap one Wulfheard thrust into my hand. He honours me, and yet he's a Wessex warrior, and I'm a Mercian, and we should be enemies if only he knew my true identity. I go to give him mine in return.

'You can keep that,' he dismisses me. 'You couldn't cut a bleeding finger with that,' and I chuckle. He's right. It's a crap blade.

Now I look all around me. I have no idea where my shield is, but Brihtwold does. His face is inscrutable. He still has his terrible blade. I would wish he had a sharper one as well, but Tyrhtil has only one seax to offer.

'This way.' Brihtwold sighs uneasily. His face looks wraithlike in the greyness of dawn. He's terrified, and I should be, but I'm not. This, I hope, will be my chance to escape; even if I haven't brought the Mercians the victory they need, I'm sure Wulfheard would rather I didn't attempt to kill Mercians. Surely?

As soon as I'm outside the walls, I can run towards the Mercian line. I'll abandon Brihtwold and his allies to their fate. There's no other choice.

12

Lord Æthelwulf has more men than I can count. At least fifty of them line up behind the mass of us before the still-closed gate of the fort. They're in position to ensure no Mercian rushes inside the fort. I smirk. They already have a Mercian inside their fort. They just don't know it. But then I sober. I don't want to fight for the Wessex force, and I certainly don't want to injure any of my fellow Mercians. I need to make my escape.

At my side, Brihtwold is quiet. I can see his pulse fluttering on his neck. He's terrified, and I can't think of any reassuring words. When we once more step onto the slaughter field, there'll be no one to ensure either of us lives to see the sunset. It's a sobering thought and one I try to banish. When I've fought before, Wulfheard or Ealdorman Ælfstan were never far away. Now I'm more likely to be trying to kill them than be saved by them.

Not only do I have to stay alive, but I also need to try to make my way to the Mercian force. I can't see that it'll be easy.

In front of us all, Ealdorman Wassa stands, ready to lead the force away. Lord Æthelwulf, much to my disgust, has decided to follow along behind the majority of the force. He has at least twenty sworn men who protect him. He doesn't mean to lose his life today in this effort to reach his father.

Around me, men talk, or fall silent, whisper prayers to their Lord God, or merely sob quietly. I think no less of them for their fear or bravery. The Mercians are an evil lot. They have vengeance on their mind, just as Ealdorman Wassa does. The Mercians will happily slaughter every single man here. I can only hope if we're overrun, that someone recognises me before they try to stab me with seax, spear or sword.

I have my Wessex shield in my hand now. It's heavy and unwieldy. Already, it tugs my shoulder down. I don't have a spear. There were none left when Brihtwold led us to the weapons store of men who were already dead. I have no skill with a spear anyway. Brihtwold has managed to lay his hands on a sharper seax. That pleases me. Sending him to fight with a blunt blade is no better than sending him knowingly to his death. I swallow against the knowledge that once the gate opens, we'll be enemies. I hardly know him, and yet he's aided me. Maybe I'll be able to ensure he lives when the Mercians overwhelm the Wessex force. Not, I think, that he'll welcome my intervention. He is a proud warrior of Wessex.

Above my head, the sun finally climbs high enough to be able to see everything surrounding me. As though that's the signal, the two wooden planks reinforcing the gate are removed, and half of the gate squeaks open on ancient hinges. It's a miracle the whole thing doesn't just fall over. I expect to hear the roar of the Mercians at this, but any sound they're making is coming from far away.

I wish then that I'd thought to take a vantage look at the way the Mercians are arranged, but, of course, there was no time for that. I must assume that they're still harrying King Ecgberht in the market settlement because there's no cry from Ealdorman Wassa to warn that we're under immediate attack.

We begin to move forwards. It's a slow shuffle, not a quick sprint, as I pass outside of the fort, the smell of ripe bodies assaulting my nostrils despite the unseasonable coldness of the previous night. The Mercians have left the Wessex dead to rot.

The men in front of me lumber to a run in a crash of iron and wood. I do the same. Brihtwold, beside me, is muttering beneath his breath, a mantra of some sort, but I can't hear the words. I look down, jump aside to avoid a decaying corpse, and then I'm running.

The ground moves beneath my feet, alarmingly quickly. I breathe deeply, in and out, keen for the air to freshen, but the filth of stagnant water merely replaces the scent of the dead.

The Wessex warriors remain tightly packed. I can't see where I'm going or risk stopping to determine my location, for those behind me will collide into me. Brihtwold and I manage to remain close together, more by chance than an effort to do so.

The ground abruptly clears of the dead, the churned earth telling me that we might be getting close to the river. I remember eyeing it from some distance away, a thin stretch of dirty grey water that splits the two disparate parts of Londonia.

Only now do those ahead of me falter. I bump into the man in front of me, who's suddenly stopped, as I feared to do. Together, we crash to the floor in a tangle of shields, arms and legs, his angry cry and mine mingling, while around us I can hear the same happening amongst the rest of the force.

The Mercians have realised what's happening.

'Shields.' The cry comes from someone in front. It's roared so loudly that I can't tell who speaks. It could be Ealdorman Wassa of Wessex. It could be Ealdorman Ælfstan of the Mercians. I just don't know. And neither can I join either shield wall because I have a mouthful of stinking, dirty-blond hair and a foot in my belly, while the man I've crashed into turns to strike me, only for another foot to knock his hand aside, as it also kicks my chin.

I try to pull my body together, dragging my feet and legs up to my chest, my arms as well. I've let go of the Wessex shield and now offer my back to whoever means to run over me next. A boot hits between my shoulder blades, another kicks me up the arse, grazing my rear end and making me wish I still had hold of the shield to cover my tender parts.

Battle cries and roars, and some whimpers, reach my ears. I hold myself in place because more Wessex warriors think to run over me. We were too tightly packed together. No one could tell what was happening. Then I hear a voice I recognise, and it drips with contempt.

'Bloody fools,' Lord Æthelwulf cries with frustration from behind me.

Only then do I risk raising my head. It's entirely the wrong thing to do because the Wessex warriors who've kept to their feet are retreating, chased by the Mercians, and I'm in their way.

'Get up.' There's a shriek of outrage. A hand touches my shoulder. I clamp eyes on one of Lord Æthelwulf's mounted warriors. He holds out his hand, and I grip it, trying to untangle my legs, arms and head so that I can escape this fresh stampede.

His horse's breath steams in the cool air, eagerness in the tense muscles of the animal's hind legs, and suddenly, I'm not only standing but being hauled up behind the man as well. He's not alone. I can see others being pulled upright, and all the time, the bellows of the retreating Wessex warriors are loud in my ears.

The horse, a chestnut animal, seems to turn on its back legs and leaps clear just as a host of men reaches the place where I was crumpled. My eyes take in the site. I'm one of the lucky ones. Others are bent and twisted, backs caved in, blood and stark white bone visible for all to see. And still, the Wessex warriors rampage.

'Hold on,' the unknown man says to me. I do just that.

I have no idea where Brihtwold is. I hope he lives.

The gallop jolts me over rough ground. Despite the fort being the one place I was desperate to escape from, I'm grateful to pass through the open gate, to feel the weight of stone above my head and to be helped down to the ground. Only then can I breathe in deeply around the ache in my chest and the pain of my back.

Blood drips down my nose when I remove my dented helm, the sweat-laced linen cap as well, now rimmed with the pink of a winter's sunrise. I become aware of my surroundings. I'm inside Londinium, yes, but I'm not in the fort. The rider has taken me into the heart of the settlement, not far from where I was led to meet the ealdorman and Lord Æthelwulf.

I can hear the roar as the tide recedes for the remaining Wessex warriors, no doubt leaving them floundering on the ground, but hopefully, inside the fort.

I spit, and my saliva is flecked with blood as well. I reach up, touch my lips, and feel the swelling there. Checking with my tongue, I sense the bitter sharpness of a cut lip. I can only hope my teeth remain in one piece, but I can't see for myself.

The horse, his brown tail high in the air, his white socks a counter to the rest of his coat, has left me, his rider turning in a tight circle. Other mounted men have joined the rider and horse, although I don't see Lord Æthelwulf amongst them.

My ears throb with the sound of my heartbeat, and I'm unable to move. My legs are too weak, and the taste of vomit sours my throat. I spit again, but it doesn't help.

'Here.' A skin of water is thrust beneath my nose. I take it, swallowing deeply, eager to drive the nausea away.

All is chaos. It was bad enough when I arrived inside the fort when Wulfheard thrust me behind the enemy shield wall. This is so much worse.

I watch, trying to focus on what's happening. Lord Æthelwulf appears, his face puce with rage, as he expertly guides his black horse with its single white stocking on its rear leg through the press of bodies. I can't hear what Lord Æthelwulf shouts. My heart still beats too loudly, all sound muffled. I must have taken a blow to my head when I was overrun.

I reach for my metal helm, run my fingers around the curve and immediately find a dent. I hold it close to my eyes, trying to determine which part of my head has been hit. Only a wave of nausea hits me. I turn aside quickly to cover the rough cobbles of the road with the bile from my stomach.

My belly heaves with the action, sending a fresh surge of pain along my back. For a moment, I can't catch my breath. I'm sucking in air, but nothing gets past my throat, and panic makes my legs weak. I'm already buckled in pain, and now I can't breathe either. I think of Wynflæd, of how she's brought others from such a trance with practised ease, and I seek the calmness I've seen in her, hearing her words in my head.

Imperceptibly, almost so slowly I don't notice, I find myself breathing again, the pain receding. I turn, slump again on the ground, hoping no one has seen me, but I have been seen. Ecgred, with his malicious eyes and haughty face, watches me from close to Lord Æthelwulf's mount. I can see the pleasure my current state gives him, and if I could, I'd march to his side and wipe the smile from his face.

Only, I don't need to. As though sensing what's happening, I feel Lord Æthelwulf's gaze settle on me. He looks to Ecgred, and fury still painting him maroon, he reaches out and thuds the handle of his seax onto Ecgred's head. I hope the action hurts, but I have no way of knowing other than to see the hastily removed gloating turn to fury on Ecgred's face as he jerks away from the unexpected attack. The man hates me even more. Then someone crouches down before me, concern on his face, and I eye Brihtwold with joy.

His helm has come loose, his dark hair tousled and blood-stained, clumps of it sticking together. He's talking to me, but I can't hear him, only see his lips move.

I open my mouth. Words form there to tell him that I can't hear, but I don't heed them either. The sound of my words vibrates against my throat, and I cough.

He nods, understanding on his face.

'Come,' and he bids me rise with his hands. I can tell that single word from how his lips form their shape.

I stagger upright and follow him. I imagine I know where we're going. My first step jolts my body. I gasp against the sharp pain in my chest. I pause, and Brihtwold doesn't notice, moving on without me. Lights flash behind my eyes. And then he's beside me, offering me his shoulder for all he looks little better than I do.

We walk through the mass of Wessex warriors. Lord Æthelwulf catches my eye as he wildly gesticulates to others who form a circle around him. His mouth opens and shuts, but I don't know whether he shouts or speaks. I still can't hear, and I have to keep my eyes on where I'm going, fearing time and time again that the ground will rush up to greet my bloodied lips and cause even more damage.

When Brihtwold finally stops walking, we're in front a tumbled-down building, half a roof covering it. Tyrhtil eyes me with unease from where he sits, close to a small hearth fire, flames licking hungrily at the dry wood and even drier horse dung he's managed to find to combat the cold.

'What happened to you?' he asks, yawning. Although they sound echoey, the words reach me, and I shake my head as though that will help.

'Don't you know what's happened?' Brihtwold demands angrily.

'I've been asleep,' Tyrhtil retorts, anger flecking his words. It seems he didn't make it to the bastion. I'm not surprised. 'What did happen?' Now his curiosity gets the better of him as I stumble to the ground. I sit but jolt my back in the process. I hiss at the fresh pain.

'We did as commanded,' Brihtwold shouts. I can tell he shouts because I can hear him easily. I'm also eager to listen because I don't really know what occurred. 'But the Mercians were waiting for us. They must have expected us to try to reach King Ecgberht via the narrowest crossing on the River Fleet. Our force bunched together, and people fell, Icel amongst them. And now we've all retreated, and Lord Æthelwulf's furious. More Wessex warriors lie dead from the stupid stampede.' Brihtwold paces the small space as he rails. He's enraged. His shoulders are hunched, almost touching his ears. He's been wounded on his head and leg and his arm isn't fully repaired from the first attack on the Mercians

'What happened to you?' Tyrhtil asks, raising his voice so that I can hear him.

'Crushed in the stampede and rescued by one of Lord Æthelwulf's mounted warriors.' Tyrhtil's mouth opens in surprise at the revelation, as I wince to hear my voice so echoey in my ears. I swallow down, hoping to clear my ears, but it makes no difference.

'It was a bloody mess.' Brihtwold finally flounces to a spot on the floor and glares around him, as though a Mercian might appear at any moment. 'We were hardly gone for a morning, and you've found yourself a nice place here.'

'I needed somewhere to hide from the king's thegns. They were calling everyone to join the attack, even the wounded, and I couldn't make it up the bloody steps. My gut was on fire.'

'They were too eager,' Brihtwold complains, his hands raised in frustration. 'And now there are even less of us, and the Mercians have killed without even doing a great deal.'

I stay silent at Brihtwold's tirade. I can't help but be pleased that the Mercians were once more triumphant. And yet, I owe my life to a Wessex warrior and a man sworn to the king's son. If I could do it without my ears ringing once more, I'd shake my head in confusion at my mixed thoughts.

'What will happen now?' Tyrhtil says aloud.

'How would I know?' Brihtwold hunkers down, his legs drawn tight to his belly, and he holds them there. I envy him the movement. If I did the same, I wouldn't be able to breathe.

'You don't look so good.' Tyrhtil turns his attention to me.

'Winded,' I expel. 'And my head.' I rest my right hand on my head, wincing at the movement. My voice still sounds strange to me, although I can hear a little better.

'You need someone to tend to you?' Tyrhtil asks.

I almost shake my head again, but remember in time.

'No. I need coriander in boiled water. It'll ease the pain of my mouth.'

'We don't have any coriander,' Tyrhtil says regretfully.

'I know. I'd go to Ecgred, but he's just been crowing over my wounds. Lord Æthelwulf noted it, but, of course, Lord Æthelwulf isn't in Ecgred's workshop to oversee everything. I'll be fine. Some sleep.'

'Then sleep, and I'll keep a guard.' Tyrhtil half-smiles. 'And what of you?' he asks Brihtwold.

'Sleep as well, and then something to eat.'

'What of your head?' I ask him.

Unconsciously, Brihtwold lifts his hand to his hair, and it comes away bloody once more. I try to rise to my knees, but my legs ache too much.

'Head wounds always bleed a great deal.' Now I beckon him closer, and he shuffles towards me. I lift his pink-rimmed hair and carefully examine his scalp. I find a slice at the top of his neck, shallow but wide. 'Your helm,' I advise him. 'It cut you. As I said, head wounds bleed a great deal. You'll be fine to sleep, and I'll tend to it when we wake.'

He nods, his eyes fierce at my words.

'Wake us if you need to,' Brihtwold informs Tyrhtil.

The other man grunts and winces as he does so.

Now it seems we're all injured in some way or another. If I had access to the stores that Ecgred has command over, I could ease our suffering, but I need to sleep for now. My head pounds, my hearing keeps coming and going, and I'm exhausted. Just breathing is an effort.

Brihtwold pulls a cloak towards me from a small pile of supplies that Tyrhtil protects like a dragon over his gold. I take it eagerly. I'm cold, despite the heat from the fire. My teeth chatter, making my gums ache, and I lie down as a hundred new ills make themselves known. I appreciate when I wake that it'll be a torment. But sleep drags me down, and I'm powerless to fight against it.

I close my eyes, the sound of the busy fort a dull throb in the distance. It's far from reassuring. I need to make my way back to the Mercians before anything else befalls me.

13

I wake to the sharp stink of vomit and know it's mine.

'You're awake. Thank the Lord,' Tyrhtil announces on seeing my eyes in the shadowed greyness of another dawn.

I ache. All over. Not one part of me doesn't hurt. Not even my toes.

'Urgh.' I raise myself on my elbows, feeling the world lurch around me. I swallow, desperate not to vomit again.

'Hold it in, please,' Tyrhtil begs me.

I swallow. My tongue feels like it's too large for my mouth, and it probes my split lip even though I know not to do so.

'Where's Brihtwold?' I gasp.

'The latrine pit. He's had a rough night, but not as bad as you. I've never known anyone vomit in their sleep.'

I haven't either. I force myself upright, the pain in my chest and back making lights flash in my vision once more, but at least I can hear properly.

'My apologies.' Tyrhtil nods and offers me a skin of water.

I swill a small amount into my mouth, aware that I have a raging thirst, but drinking too much now will only make me sick.

'Take it easy,' he cautions me. I do as he says.

'I stink,' I complain.

'You do, yes. That Ecgred came looking for you some time ago. Well, not Ecgred. The two slaves. They left you this.' He hands me a bowl, and I smell the concoction suspiciously only to recognise the herbs I need to heal. I shouldn't be so fearful of what they've brought me. I know that Ecgred wouldn't know how to create this potion.

'My thanks.' But I'm perplexed. 'They came together?'

'Yes, the man was keen, the woman much less so. They hurried here and back. They pointed at you, so I knew it was for you.'

'Did they look well?'

'Better than you,' Tyrhtil offers, a wry smirk on his lips, and then he sobers. 'They were both bruised. The woman had an almost closed eye; the other limped heavily.' That was what I feared to hear.

'I should have spoken for them in front of Lord Æthelwulf.'

'Perhaps, but what are they to you? They aren't your slaves.'

I find the argument far from reassuring.

Eagerly, I swallow the potion made for me. It's not as thick as I'd like it to be. The coriander is thinly sliced, milk, no doubt from a cow and not a breeding woman, used to give it some thickness. If not enough.

'I can't believe they found me and knew of my injuries,' I muse.

'They brought me a new poultice as well.' Tyrhtil lifts his tunic to show me the green strip of cloth that he holds against his wound.

'How does it feel?'

'Good, all things considered. I even managed to empty myself earlier.' He grins. Such simple delight in taking a shit when he's been unable to for the last day. I've seen men and women skip with the joy of being free from such pain and weight inside.

'Why are they looking after us?' I consider.

'Maybe they hope you'll free them.'

'How would I do that? Lord Æthelwulf has removed me from the workshop, and I have no influence with anyone here.'

'I don't know, but still, it's a thought. That might be why they sought us out.'

I shake my head, swallowing quickly to ensure I keep down what I've consumed. I desperately need to piss, but that involves standing. I don't yet know if I can do that.

'Perhaps it was a kindness,' I begin, but lapse into silence. The slaves and I have not exchanged any words between us. How could we when I can't speak their tongue?

And then Brihtwold appears in the doorway. He smirks on seeing me. I notice that he's washed his hair and blood no longer clumps amongst his dark curls.

'You're awake then? The whole encampment is in an uproar.'

'Why?' Tyrhtil demands to know.

'Lord Æthelwulf and Ealdorman Wassa have been arguing about how to reach King Ecgberht, and Lord Æthelwulf has determined the only way to do it is via the River Thames. Ealdorman Wassa says it'll never work. The Mercians will see the ships.'

'And?' Tyrhtil presses when Brihtwold says nothing further.

'Lord Æthelwulf has commanded Ealdorman Wassa to lead the force, and he's refused. He says the death of his brother is all the payment he'll offer to the Mercians. He hasn't said that King Ecgberht has overextended himself, but he may as well have.'

'And?' Again Tyrhtil presses when Brihtwold's words grind to a halt.

'Lord Æthelwulf says he'll pay five hundred silver pennies to any man who takes the risk.'

'Five hundred?' Tyrhtil isn't alone in having his mouth drop open in shock. I think of what could be bought with five hundred silver pennies. A warrior could buy a horse, sword and byrnie, as well as a slave to clean his equipment for him. A farmer could buy all the animals he might need, as well as the farm buildings themselves. A trader could outfit half a ship. It's not a small sum. I wonder how the Wessex lord can afford to offer such a rich prize. And then I realise that they mean to take it from the Mercian traders and from Mercia's mint. They don't plan on paying it themselves. They'll take the money as payment when Mercia is defeated.

'Yes. And I've said I'll go,' Brihtwold confirms, puffing up his chest as though such an act makes him more manly. I notice his grimace as he does so.

'You've never even been on a ship,' Tyrhtil laughs. 'You'll be sick and fall overboard, and I bet you can't swim. The Mercians will have access to ships, you know,' he further cautions.

'I'm doing it. I can leave the king's force and return home with five hundred silver pennies. I could live forever on five hundred silver pennies.'

'Well, not quite forever,' I caution him. I don't want him to take such a risk. It would be certain death, and Lord Æthelwulf knows it. Why else is he offering such a vast sum? If it succeeds, the Mercian traders will pay the bill; if it fails, it will cost the Wessex lord nothing but the death of men on his conscience.

'We should use the ships to return to Kent and Wessex,' Tyrhtil states abruptly. 'The Mercians will leave us be if we go home. King Ecgberht has already lost the kingship of Mercia. Their capital is firmly back under King Wiglaf's command. This is desperation.'

'You would leave our Lord King in Lundenwic? Lose Lundenwic to the Mercians?' Brihtwold decries. His words are flecked with anger.

'Our Lord King can do the same. He could take a ship from the traders and go back to Wessex. It would be easy for him to leave. He just won't because of his hatred of the Mercians.'

'You have no loyalty.' Brihtwold's words are hot, his face flushed.

'I wish to live. This,' and Tyrhtil points to his belly wound, 'has shown me how weak one man is against sharp iron and blades.'

'You have no honour,' Brihtwold tries again, his lips drawn together tightly. He looks terrified to my eyes but is also determined to do as he boasts. A heady combination. I thought him like my childhood friend Edwin from Tamworth. But at this moment, I think not. Edwin wouldn't have sworn to do something that scared him so much.

'I have more than enough honour, you young scroat. I've fought for our Lord King all my life. If anyone could live on five hundred silver pennies and never fight again, it would be me.'

'Then you should do it,' Brihtwold flings at him.

'Then perhaps I will. At least I can bloody swim, and I know the way to the far side of the River Thames as well, back to the realm of Wessex.'

I expect Brihtwold to continue his argument, but he falls silent instead, chest heaving with his frustration and, I imagine, fear.

'I'll go,' Tyrhtil says more softly this time.

Something passes between the two, but I don't understand it.

'Good,' Brihtwold eventually announces. This argument has been about something more than who can swim, of that I'm sure.

'When will the ship leave?'

But before Brihtwold can answer Tyrhtil, I have to ask the question.

'Why didn't they use the ship in the first place?' I've not yet made it back to the pinnacle of the fort. I don't honestly know where the Mercians are or what they've achieved. Do they surround the walls? Do they still have command of the bridge over the River Fleet? Do they have a foothold inside the market settlement itself? Where, exactly, is King Ecgberht of Wessex? I can but hope that my question doesn't arouse too much suspicion. Wulfheard didn't tell me much about the River Thames. His concern was with the settlement of Londonia.

'The river is tidal and deadly. The Mercians living along the Strand's shoreline have built defences against the Wessex forces. It'll be impossible for the king to retreat with his warriors that way. He must go forwards.'

'So, how can you get to him?' My forehead furrows in consternation.

'Lord Æthelwulf has thought of that,' Brihtwold confirms confidently. 'We'll travel at night and make it there before they can stop us.'

I open my mouth to argue once more, but then I shake my head. It's better if the Wessex warriors fail. That the brave Mercians kill them as they attempt to sneak past them. Not that all of the traders in Lundenwic are Mercians, but the Frisians will fight for King Wiglaf because the Mercian kings tax them lightly and provide well for them. The Wessex king has so far treated them poorly, raising their taxes and disrupting the river trade by sending his reeves to examine every little detail of who brings what and from where. King Ecgberht has made enemies of the traders.

I decide not to argue further, even though the idea is folly if the Mercians have such defences in place.

'So, King Ecgberht is trapped inside Lundenwic,' I summarise. 'The Mercian inhabitants will not let him gain access to the ships on the River Thames, and he can't get past the Mercian forces encamped outside Lundenwic.'

Brihtwold nods earnestly. It seems he doesn't sense the difficulty, but Tyrhtil is quiet now, his eyes far away. I know he feels that the coming endeavour is foolhardy.

I sigh. I'm coming to like Tyrhtil, despite the fact he should be my sworn enemy. If he dies trying to seek entry into the market settlement when he should just go home by rights, it'll be a waste.

The Wessex king is trapped. His forces are split. And yet, I know only too well the madness of kings. King Ecgberht ought to approach King Wiglaf and forge a peace, but both men hate one another. They'd sooner kill all of their warriors than admit that either of them were wrong.

14

Voices from beyond our shelter have me turning to look towards where the door should be if there were one, but there isn't. The far end of the shelter is open to the elements.

'Icel.' The word is barked, and I eye the man before me. He's small and squat, his legs widely spaced, as he glares at me. 'Come with me. Ecgred demands an account from you for the mess in his workshop.'

'What?' I ask. I left no mess. I know I didn't.

'Get on your feet and come with me.' He's beside me now, his hands reaching towards me. It's clear he means to force me upright, even though I stink of vomit and I'm still suffering from my head wound.

'Leave him be, Æsc,' Tyrhtil hisses, giving a name to the unknown man.

'You can either come with me, or Lord Æthelwulf will send his warriors to retrieve you.' The squat man is determined. His face is riddled with long-healed cuts, his lips slightly upturned in the right-hand corner of his mouth.

'I hardly think...' Tyrhtil starts, his voice filled with coldness, but I stagger upright.

'It's fine. I'll go and see what the fuss is about.' I pause then, trying not to vomit again, and the stupid fool stretches towards me and yanks my arm. The room spins, and the next thing I know, I'm on my hands and knees, yellow bile staining Æsc's boots.

He kicks me – the damn arse. My nose explodes, and now I'm choking as well, blood streaming into my mouth. I taste the sharp bite of iron and expect to retch once more. Only it has the opposite effect on me. My vision clears, and I can see more clearly than since the Wessex warriors crushed me.

'Give me a moment,' I urge Æsc. I watch his foot tapping, the yellow bile slowly working its way onto the ground. Only then do I stand.

While forced to wait, Tyrhtil's done nothing but berate Æsc for being an arse. An arse of everything, from pig to cow to horse and even a goat. If I didn't want to worsen the situation, I'd be laughing in Æsc's face.

Outside, the sun is closer to setting than rising. I've slept away much of the day. No doubt I needed it, but all the same, I don't like to have my daily routine disturbed in such a way.

I expect to see the Wessex warriors huddled together in groups, or practising their training, or even just sleeping, but it seems that Tyrhtil isn't the only one who thought it wise to find some shelter following the cold night we all experienced. I can smell smoke and even hear people, but I don't see anyone as I follow Æsc back towards the workshop, along the uneven stone roads.

I'm unsure what I expect to find when I get there. I made no mess in the workshop. With the aid of the slaves, I produced salves and lotions and treated the wounded. What then, I think, is Ecgred blowing steam about?

But then I hear Ecgred's voice, raised in a fury. Æsc abruptly veers away from me, assured I'll face Ecgred rather than him.

I duck my head inside the low building, quickly noting that everything is in the same orderliness as when I left at Lord Æthelwulf's command, apart from the sick and injured. One or two wounded lie on beds of straw, groaning softly, although they watch what's happening eagerly enough.

'At last.' Ecgred eyes me. Hatred spills from his eyes as he threatens with his fists.

Quickly, I begin to suspect the problem.

'What have you done to them?' he challenges, indicating the source of his fury.

'Done to them?' I decide to pretend I don't understand.

'Yes, done to them. Look.' I do look, and a slight smirk plays around my lips. I'm pleased that the night is beginning to draw in and that Ecgred can't see my delight in seeing his two slaves sitting together, one beside the other, on a small wooden bench before the fire.

Ecgred lectures them, spittle flying with the words. I don't understand the tongue he speaks, but now I doubt the slaves do either because the words merge together too quickly. I don't think he's taken one breath since he began to rebuke them.

It's not my fault, far from it, but Ecgred's slaves have evidently realised that they don't need to share their knowledge with their master. No, they can hoard it to themselves, and there's nothing that Ecgred, or I, can do about it. Even as Ecgred waves his thin hands before them, pointing to his shelves of supplies, to the wounded with their hands clutching Mercian coins, the two ignore him. The slaves have made their feelings clear to their master. I'm pleased by their defiance, even when Ecgred has tried to force them with his fists. As I was told, the female slave has a swollen eye. I'm disgusted that he's tried to force the man by attacking the woman. What a worm he is.

'You've stopped them from obeying me.' Ecgred eventually turns his gaze back to me.

I shrug my shoulders, wincing with the movement. 'I can't even speak to them. How could I have done that?'

At this, Ecgred's mouth snaps shut, a wildness in his eyes assuring me that he's not far from hitting me. Equally, he can't deny the truth of my words. That much is obvious. Silence falls in the workshop. I move slightly, trying to catch the eye of the brown-skinned man and his female companion. Their expressions are stoic. They've made their decision, even though they don't meet my gaze.

'Then why aren't they fulfilling their tasks?' Ecgred eventually questions, making an effort at calmness.

I look at him, trying not to show the disdain that I feel for this wild man who thinks to profit from the skills of others. 'Have you asked them?' is all I can think to say.

'Asked them? *Asked them*? They're my slaves. They should do as I want when I order it.'

But I shake my head. 'Slaves only do as they're commanded. You give specific commands to them.' I can't see that my words will help him. The slaves have determined to disobey him, no matter what.

A trickle of words spills from Ecgred's lips. I see the shoulders on the female slave tense. But nothing happens.

'What did you ask them?' I enquire.

'To treat the wounded?' Ecgred's growing furious once more.

'Then you must tell them what to do. Which herbs to use, which potion to make. They're enslaved. They must be instructed in every little detail.'

Again, Ecgred's mouth falls open in shock as he comprehends my words.

'But,' he manages to squeak.

I nod at him, encouraging him.

'But they know what to do. They've done it many times in the past.'

'Then you should also know what to tell them to do,' I counter.

Ecgred has moved to his shelves and pulled down two jars. He opens the lids and sniffs one and then the other. The smell of coriander wafts close to me. He looks into the stone jars and then at his slaves, but they don't move.

'What are you treating with that?' I ask him conversationally. I can't deny that I'm relishing this. For the first time in my life, I understand that Wynflæd, with her sharp words and edged silences, might have enjoyed watching my pathetic attempts at mirroring her actions.

'A poultice, to protect against wound-rot,' Ecgred whines.

I shake my head. 'That won't work. Those aren't the ingredients that you need.'

I'm distracted from Ecgred's response by a groan of pain from one of the warriors. His face is bleached white, stark in the half-light of the flickering fire and advancing night.

I move to him. 'Where are you injured?' I enquire.

His eyes half close, and then he lifts his right arm. I see where he's been impaled on something, almost cutting him from beneath his armpit up through his shoulder, but the weapon's stuck lower down because of the sharp angle. Dirty, bloody rags try to suppress the blood flow.

'You'll need stitching together,' I inform him.

He moans once more, as though the words wound just as much as the blade.

I head to where I know the pig's guts are kept and quickly place them in a bowl of hot water to soften, the water taken from a boiling pot over the hearth. I feel the eyes of both slaves on me. I nod and offer them a smile. I hope they understand my regard for what they're doing, even though I'm helping the warrior. Ecgred hovers behind me, watching what I'm doing, and I ignore his presence.

I also reach for the herbs I need to make a poultice and a remedy for the wounded man to drink. My hands and nose easily find the ingredients I need, the honey and moss, the garlic, nettles and oats. I obscure the jars as best I can so that Ecgred will learn nothing from me.

'What's your name?' I ask the man over my shoulder.

'What does it matter?' he growls.

I rear backwards. I didn't expect such anger, but then, he's been lying in pain for some considerable time. While I've slept, have the Wessex warriors attempted another strike against the Mercians? I didn't think to ask.

'Well, my name's Icel,' I inform him, holding his arm out from his body to closely examine the wound. He stinks of sweat and pain, of blood, and his skin is too dry. I'm glad my nausea has passed, or I'd be no good to him. I'd be the one vomiting, as opposed to my body merely aching with every movement I make.

I turn aside, find a jug and splash water into a waiting wooden bowl.

'Drink this,' I urge him.

He drinks it thirstily, only to scowl at me again. His forehead is a welter of blackening bruises, a long gash running beneath his thinning hairline.

'What happened to you?' I ask, taking the bowl from him and returning to my initial task. I have another bowl of hot water. I dip a rag into it and begin to clean away the muck and filth. I also cut aside his tunic. He glowers at me, in silence, as I do so.

It seems I'm to get no answer from him. It's not going to stop me from helping him. Wynflæd never turned aside an arrogant

sod, although she always managed to bend them to her will.
Eventually.

I work quickly. The silence in the workshop should be oppres-
sive, with Ecgred dividing his time between berating his slaves and
observing me. He should watch. Then he might know what to do in
the future. I expect him to run to Ealdorman Wassa or Lord Æthelwulf at my intervention, but he does neither of those things.
Perhaps, like the rest of the encampment, he's aware of the barely
contained resentment between the two men and unprepared to
exacerbate it further. Maybe he genuinely hopes to learn something. The fact he allows me such free rein does surprise me.

When I'm done, I eye the warrior once more. His face is sheeted
in sweat. He doesn't look well.

'You need rest and good food,' I inform him.

He heaves himself upright, left hand teasing out the work I've
done beneath his right arm.

'I'm going in the ships,' he informs me, the first true words he's
spoken. The warrior seems to bounce off the table, sending the
water jug tumbling over the side. I leap to catch it, and water covers
my hands. 'I'll earn my five hundred silver pennies.' With that, he
staggers from the workshop, weaving a path that sees him kick a
bucket of water all over Ecgred's feet, much to Ecgred's disgust.

My hands are smeared with blood, and my nails are black with
dirt. I eye them with a grimace before plunging them into another
bucket of warm water deposited close to the fire.

'Right then.' The male slave catches my eye as I turn to the next
waiting warrior. He's been quiet all this time, hunched around
himself where he sits. I don't know what the slave tries to tell me,
but I offer another smile. 'What's wrong with you then?'

Reddened eyes greet mine, but it's the lip that has me staggering
backwards. It looks to me as though the man's been bitten or
gnawed his lip. Now the skin lies jagged, exposing the stumps of his

yellow teeth and the redness of his gums, the paleness of his jaw, shown against the backdrop of a dirty-blond beard and moustache. I already think I'll have to shave him to repair the lips. Only then does he pull his hand aside. I see he has more than one injury. His left hand is as jagged as his lip.

'What happened?' I demand to know.

'A dog,' he grumbles, standing with a wince. 'It went wild because a group of arseholes decided to use it for target practice.' His voice is filled with disgust.

'And the dog?'

'Dead. The bastards killed it when it turned on me,' he answers remorsefully.

'Any other wounds?' I query, my thoughts turning to the poor, dead dog. One of the Wessex warriors must have brought it with them to Londinium. A strange decision to make.

'Only bruises and small cuts.'

'Then I'll tend your lip first and then your hand. It'll be nasty.'

'Aye. It'll teach me to get involved where I shouldn't.' I can't place his accent, but his words don't roll as so many others of the Wessex warriors do.

'I need to shave your chin,' I inform him.

'Do whatever you must. I don't shave because it's too much effort. I hate the damn beard.'

Carefully, I use a small cutting knife to shear away as much of the beard as I can. The hair falls to the floor, exposing more of the wound. I wince in sympathy as its extent becomes clearer.

'I would suggest you might never want to shave again,' I caution. My fresh bowl of warm water is a murky brown, more like mud than blood. There are big lumps of dark black congealed blood from his chin and mixed in the tufts of beard that remain. I don't want to pull them apart because I imagine it'll hurt, but neither can I sew the wound until I do.

'This'll be painful,' I advise him.

I see his red-rimmed eyes harden as I begin the process. It takes a long time. I'm unaware of just how long until a candle appears beside me. I eye the brown-skinned slave with surprise. I look around and can see that Ecgred has become tired of his tirade and, feeling useless, has left me to my work.

In his absence, both of the slaves are busy in the workshop.

The male slave shoos me aside, and I step away. He takes my place immediately. I watch his more delicate work as he begins to help the bitten man. I stay silent, occasionally handing over bowls of warm water and threads of pig's gut. The flames from the fire leap higher, and water is replenished by the female slave, and still, there's silence. The wounded man can't speak while the delicate work of reconnecting the flesh is taking place.

Eventually, the slave nods and gives a little grunt; I take it to be of happiness and he turns his attention to the ripped hand. I watch him, as does the warrior.

'Where are you from?' the warrior asks me, the words muffled by his fattened lip. The wound looks even worse now, but it does stand a good chance of healing, of that I'm sure.

'Kent.' I remember my lie.

'So, more than half a Mercian then?' His fair eyebrows disappear into the welter of blackened bruises.

'No, a good Wessex warrior,' I reply quickly.

But he's shaking his head.

'I'm from Kent,' he informs me. 'I'm much more than half a Mercian, but I fight for Lord Æthelwulf now. I remained behind to ensure Lord Bealdred escaped from Lord Æthelwulf. At some point, and I'm far from sure how, I ended up fighting for the Wessex lords.' There's no anger in his voice. It's as though he speaks of how to make a pottage and not of for whom he risks his life.

'And would you return to Mercia now?'

The man stills, as though unsure whether to say more. His eyes meet mine, and I think I've forgotten how to breathe. So much rests on his answer. And then he shakes his head.

'I'm a Wessex warrior now. After all, it's two Wessex healers who'll ensure I live.' I think he tries to smile, but with his chin all exposed as it is, it's more of a grimace and not a pretty sight at all.

I drag my eyes from his face and breathe in deeply. I should have liked an ally amongst the Wessex warriors. In truth, I should be determining how to help King Wiglaf and not saving a man who's changed his allegiance to another.

Then I turn. Æsc has returned. His eyes blaze angrily, even as the Kent warrior gets to his feet and quickly escapes from the workshop, his face and hand repaired as much as possible.

'Where's Ecgred?'

'How should I know?' I taunt him.

'I'm telling him of this,' he cautions me. Only then do I realise Æsc glares at the two slaves.

I open my mouth, but before I can argue with him, he's gone, lurching through the workshop and out into the darkness of night. I shiver. It's another cold night. The brown-skinned slave shrugs at me, no hint of fear in his eyes. He says something to the other slave, and she nods, biting her lip and hurrying to tidy away the herbs he's been using. She shows more concern than him. I wish I knew their names.

'My apologies,' I say, tone regretful.

The man grins at me. It seems he doesn't care. I eye where his feet are chained together, and I shudder. This man shouldn't be here. He should be free to heal with the extensive skills he possesses. If Wynflæd knew of him, she'd wish him freed. And then he surprises me by speaking.

'Theodore.' His voice is rich.

'Icel,' I reply, and he nods, a sharp tongue licking at his lips. He grips my hand when I'm not expecting it and turns it over. I gasp as his fingers probe at the scar there. Even in the weaving shadows of the fire and candle, I can see the image clearly. It marks me as what I am, a Mercian.

I go to snatch my hand back, but he holds me tight. I expect to see a threat in his hard eyes, but, instead, he points at my scar and nods. I swallow heavily. I don't know what to say to him, even if I thought he could understand me. I nod slowly. He does the same, the hint of triumph in the curve of his thin lips.

He releases my hand and steps aside, just as Ecgred appears, a thick cloak covering his scrawny legs and hands. His face is purple with fury, his eyes only just visible as two dots of white.

'You Mercian bastard,' he curses, leaping towards me. I don't see what he carries, but it's evident he means me harm. I startle that he calls me a Mercian. How can he know that?

I've faced enough people trying to kill me to interpret the signs. Yet, my feet don't move, and I'm held in place as though they weigh a hundred times more than usual. I close my eyes, anticipating the blow, swaying slightly as though my nausea has returned. Only there's a loud thud, as though a body hitting the ground. My eyes snap open, and it takes me time to make sense of it all, and then I gasp.

The female slave stands, menacing the prone body of Ecgred with a heavy jug, which she strains to keep hold of, her arms shaking with the weight. Ecgred's eyes flicker once, behind his closed eyelids, and then fall still, and I tumble to my knees.

'No, no, no,' I mutter under my breath, reaching out to touch Ecgred where his pulse should beat at his neck, but there's nothing. I notice the sliver of blood that pools from beneath his head, and I sit back, knees beneath me, my feet useless.

He's dead.

15

Theodore stands beside the woman slave and gently extracts her fingers from around the jug. He places the jug carefully back on the table, far from the prone body of Ecgred. I can see that she's shaking, but whether with terror or from the sudden cold wind that's blowing through the room, I'm unsure.

I don't know what to do.

I can imagine the punishment the slave might endure for causing the death of her owner, and yet, I can't help thinking that she did it to protect me. Did she, like Theodore, realise I was a Mercian, just as Ecgred had clearly done? How, I don't know, but looking at my hand, I must assume he saw my burn mark. I've not done a good enough job of keeping the visible scar hidden. I keep removing my gloves when I tend to the wounded.

I wish I could speak to them both to determine what we should do next. I can only hope that Æsc doesn't follow Ecgred into the workshop before we can work out what's to be done.

Abruptly, I stand, keen to be as far away from Ecgred as possible. Theodore nods at me, his expression blank, as he remains close to the woman. If only I knew her name, but Theodore didn't think to tell me it.

Once more, he nods at me and moves towards Ecgred. I don't want to see what he's doing, but my curiosity is rampant. I watch him check the pulse that no longer thuds at Ecgred's neck and then hold his ear close to where air should pass in and out of Ecgred's body at his mouth. But there's nothing. Theodore grunts as though satisfied the man is dead and moves into the shadowed area of the workshop. He emerges carrying two blankets. I know what he means to do with them, even as my heart beats too loudly in my ears.

The female slave rushes to join Theodore, and between them, they quickly have Ecgred covered. I pretend not to notice that Theodore takes the weighty coin bag from the dead man's waist. In all honesty, it should have been their money and not Ecgred's at all. Ecgred knew nothing. He was entirely reliant on Theodore and the woman for what he managed to accomplish. It makes me consider how the two slaves came to belong to Ecgred.

When the pair bend to lift the body, I know they won't be able to move him without my help. Yet, I shy away from assisting them. Should the death not be reported to Lord Æthelwulf? After all, it was an accident. She didn't mean to kill her owner. Not, I imagine, that the Wessex lord will believe that. And what if Lord Æthelwulf determines I caused Ecgred's death?

No. The death needs to be concealed. As Theodore cloaks the knowledge that I'm a Mercian. I need to help him and his comrade. I cover the distance between us quickly and hook the ankles of Ecgred with a grimace, all of my aches and pains making themselves felt all over again. I could do with a healing potion, but there's no time for that now.

The woman moves aside eagerly, going to aid Theodore with Ecgred's head. Only then do we begin to make our way, not towards the open doorway, but, instead, to the shadowed part of the workshop, where I suspect the two slaves have lived while Ecgred made Londinium his home. I can't imagine Ecgred lived here all the time. I must assume he came here with the Wessex force and took command of this dwelling.

I can hardly see anything as I follow the pair of them into the darkness of the rear of the workshop. Ecgred's body is surprisingly light, but then, he isn't a tall man, or a fat one. Perhaps I could carry him alone, but I hardly wish to be found with the body of the imposter. What excuse would I have? Not that the two slaves can help me if we're caught. No one else speaks their language, and if someone catches sight of my hand, as Theodore has, they'll realise that I'm a Mercian and kill me.

The slaves lead on, shuffling backwards with their heavy load, their chains clinking with each step, and quickly I realise there's a further door to the outside world. Theodore and the woman go first, and I duck because it's not a tall doorway.

Outside, it's fully dark, the wind blowing strongly, chilling me immediately, as I continue to lug the body. I can see well enough, the sky crystalline, the moon bright in a sky that shimmers with stars.

I risk looking around, expecting to see Æsc or even Lord Æthelwulf eyeing me with fury, but the night is quiet. It must be late enough that everyone sleeps.

'Where are we going?' I hiss before realising I'll get no reply. My arms start to scream from the weight, which grows heavier with every step. I know I won't be able to go much further, not without resting my arms. Ahead, I can sense the shadow of the ancient wall coming into view. It promises protection from those outside, but it bars my way to escape. I know my true enemies come from inside Londinium; I need to escape.

So focused on the wall and the problem of my enclosing inside it, I don't realise that Theodore and the female slave have stopped until I almost fall over Ecgred's prone body, dropping his feet in the process. They land noisily on the stone-lined ground. Do they mean to leave him here? I look around. It hardly seems like it's a good hiding place. And then Theodore disappears from view. An involuntary shriek leaves my mouth. I clamp my hand over it, even as the woman watches me, finger to her lips, as the moon provides enough light to see her clearly.

Her skin isn't the brown of Theodore's, but it's certainly a warmer tone than Ecgred's. I want to know more about her. About how she came to be here, and why she must wear chains around her ankles.

I shuffle forwards and meet the white eyes of Theodore. He's standing on much lower ground, and then I understand his intentions – such clear thinking on his part. I hope there haven't been more occasions than this one where he's had to hide a body quickly.

Looking down, I can see what appear to be turrets of stone sticking up from a stone-lined floor and supporting another layer of thinner stone above it. It looks to me as though there are two floors, one above the other. Why that would be, I don't know.

Theodore makes 'hurry up' movements with his hands, making his intention clear. I grip Ecgred's feet one more time and pull him towards where Theodore waits. He steps back as one of Ecgred's feet comes free from the covering of the blanket. I grip Ecgred's shoulders to thrust him over the side to where Theodore stands.

The body lands wetly and with a harsh crack that seems to split the silence of the night. Hastily, Theodore pulls on Ecgred's legs, manoeuvring the dead man so I can't see him, sliding him beneath the top layer of stone. I think it's a good place to hide a body, but for how long? Surely it'll start to stink soon enough, and more than just Æsc will come looking for the missing Ecgred. I realise what it means only as the body disappears entirely from view.

As I offer my hand to help Theodore up from the lowered floor, I appreciate that not only do I need to escape from Londinium now, I also need to take the two slaves with me and somehow find a way to undermine the Wessex forces. Although, that part might be the easiest of the tasks I've been set, especially with Lord Æthelwulf's desperate bid to get inside the market settlement.

'Do you know a way to escape?' I whisper to Theodore when he stands beside me, but he shakes his head. I don't know if that means he doesn't, or if he doesn't understand me. And then the woman speaks, her words shocking me.

'You'll help us?' she asks, her eyes meeting mine, determination showing in the line of her slight jaw and cheekbone.

'If I can,' I offer, hardly words of comfort, but it's all I have for now. I can't believe that she can speak my tongue, having pretended to be unable to understand anything I've said until now. 'Do you know a way to escape?' I ask again, but she shakes her head, walking back the way we've just come.

I don't know how long it'll take someone to realise Ecgred is missing, but however long that time is, I don't think it'll be enough for me to work out a way to escape the high walls, and the peril has just increased. Æsc will accuse me of killing Ecgred, of that I'm sure, and if not me, then the slaves. While the woman might be responsible for his death, I can't believe it was an intentional act. It was done to protect my identity. It was in her and Theodore's interests that Ecgred didn't announce my Mercian loyalties.

Returning to the workshop, I expect Æsc to be there already, Lord Æthelwulf as well, but all is silent. Apart from a thin trickle of blood amongst the rush-covered floor, there's nothing to show what happened here. I look down at it, considering what to do next. I stifle a yawn. I need to sleep once more and probably eat.

Movement out of the corner of my eye has me reaching for my seax, but it's merely Theodore and the woman moving into their part of the workshop. It's evident they too mean to sleep. I meet Theodore's eyes and stride from the workshop. My mind is buzzing with this new problem to solve, but I can't do anything right now.

My steps drag with exhaustion, and when I stumble into the dwelling where Tyrhtil and Brihtwold already snore so loudly, it's as though thunder rumbles overhead, they don't even notice I've returned. I make myself as comfortable as possible on the hard floor, and between one breath and the next, I'm asleep.

* * *

When I wake, Tyrhtil is shaking my shoulder as I crack open one eye.

'I'm leaving,' he informs me. 'Wish me luck.'

'Leaving?' I demand, too sleep-muddled to remember where he's going.

'Yes, to join the ships. The tide is right. We'll sneak into Lunden-wic.' He grimaces as he speaks, his hand reaching towards his wound. He shouldn't be going anywhere. If he couldn't climb the steps of the fort, then how does he expect to fight today?

'You need to rest,' I caution him, sitting upright now, the events of yesterday slowly reasserting themselves. Perhaps I should go with Tyrhtil. I might be able to sneak away from the rest of the Wessex warriors once I'm inside the market settlement. But what of Theodore and the woman? I know I can't leave them. And, I've not yet fulfilled Wulfheard's task. I need to accomplish both of those duties and sooner rather than later.

'I need five hundred silver pennies.' Tyrhtil attempts to grin, making his way to the entrance of the shelter.

There's no sign of Brihtwold. He was here when I returned earlier. I don't know where he's gone now.

I follow Tyrhtil outside. It's perishingly cold, a reminder that the good weather of the long summer is coming to an end. I imagine it might be warmer tomorrow, but for today, a cold breeze blows from the river, bringing with it the distinctive smell of damp and wet. I shiver, staring up at the crystalline sky.

Where there's water lying on the ground, in dips, I can see it shimmering beneath the sun, turned solid and slippery by how cold it's been overnight. That's two cold nights in a row. With the weather on the turn, the Mercians and the Wessex warriors will soon be thinking of returning home. There's only so much war that can be waged when men can't feel their fingers or toes.

I follow Tyrhtil as he makes his way towards one of the roads that leads downhill and, I assume, towards the river. It takes him past the place where I met the ealdorman and Lord Æthelwulf, and further east, to the far corner of the settlement. I can just glimpse what I take to be ships from here.

I see then that he's not alone. More and more men join the snaking line. There's nothing like the promise of payment to make men eager for such a dangerous attempt. I follow on behind, as do many others, curiosity on their faces, fear on others. Everyone looks pale and cold beneath the too-bright sun. They also look scared.

I just can't see that Lord Æthelwulf's attempt will succeed, and it feels as though I'm watching men walking to their death. That makes me even colder, reminding me of the body we hid the night before. I blink grit from my eyes. I thought the war against Wessex would be bad enough, but my current situation is so much more dangerous than that, I hardly know what I'm doing or why I'm doing it.

Further ahead, I catch sight of Lord Æthelwulf, mounted once more and overseeing the warriors on the way to their doom. I can think of it in no other way. His breath plumes in the air, his horse standing firm, eyes watching the men with as much eagerness as his rider. And Lord Æthelwulf isn't alone. Beside him sits Ealdorman

Wassa, his face creased into a scowl. His breath comes too fast. I can tell that he's trying to hold on to his patience.

There's no sign of Brihtwold. I expected him to come and say goodbye to Tyrhtil, to wish him luck for the coming endeavour. But it seems not.

Just before I lose sight of Tyrhtil, I rush through the crowd of warriors to his side. He stops walking forward, and men part around us like we're an upturned stone in a river. He turns to glance at me, surprise on his face when I tug on his arm.

'Take this. You'll need it,' and I hand him back the seax he lent me. He takes it without complaint, but still I hesitate. 'You don't have to do this,' I remind him. He might be a Wessex warrior, but he's still a man, someone I might have considered a friend in another time or place.

For a moment, his face flashes with fury, and then a broad grin breaks out, showing his missing teeth and yellowed gums. Even if he's managed to open his bowels and piss since I stitched him back together, he's quite unwell.

'I know, lad, but five hundred silver pennies and the chance of eternal glory, no man can turn such down.' His grin spreads wider, and then he shakes his head. 'Look after yourself,' he cautions me, beginning to move away. But he pauses, turns back and meets my eyes. 'You need to get better at lying if you're going to survive here.' And he's gone, swallowed up by the other warriors walking to the ships I can see, low in the water, filling with warriors beneath the harsh glare of the sunlight. The river doesn't carry the same sheen as the icy patches underfoot. Instead, it flashes grey and foreboding, even black in places. For a heartbeat, as I gaze at them, I see not men, but rather the bones of men, standing upright, sightless, hairless, without skin or muscle, and I turn aside, cuffing the unbidden tears from my eyes.

I'll not see Tyrhtil alive again. Of that, I'm sure.

I make my way back through the watching crowd, eager to stay away from the eyes of Lord Æthelwulf and Ealdorman Wassa. If they ask me about Ecgred, what should I say? Will they realise, as soon as I speak, that I know his fate? I've never considered myself skilled at telling falsehoods and Tyrhtil has just confirmed those suspicions. But the eyes of the lord and the ealdorman, and the warriors who surround the pair, are fixed firmly on the two ships. They must leave the shore, oars pulling with the flow of the River Thames. It's evident they don't see the future quite as clearly as I do.

Kicking aside my dark thoughts, I appreciate that now is the perfect opportunity to find a way to undermine the walls. With the focus of the Wessex warriors on the ships and the hope of success, few of them have followed me away from the river's edge.

I pause, retracing my steps to where two roads meet and divide the settlement into smaller segments. I turn slowly, eyeing the grey walls all around me.

Yes, they're above head height in most places, the greyness of the stone promising protection, and yet, in the distance, I can see the landscape. The walls might be high, but the land beyond them is much higher in places. I wish I understood the layout of the area better. If I were inside Tamworth, I'd know where all the weaknesses in the wall lay, where there might be the chance of finding loose stones or even drainage ditches cut beneath the wall to allow water and shit to pour away from the homes and workshops of the inhabitants.

But this isn't Tamworth, and I've spent most of my time either in Ecgred's workshop, unconscious or being crushed in the battle against the Mercian warriors.

I revolve slowly, eyeing up all the possibilities from here. Should I go left, right, north or south? Well, north will take me back to the fort. I know it's not impregnable, but, equally, I can't move the huge gates alone, not with the substantial wooden bars in place. And such an act would be far too visible, even in the darkness of a cloudy night.

If I turn south, I'll once more be by the river, but it has its own walls as well. The people who built this colossal citadel didn't consider the river their ally. And, if I make it through the walls and to the riverfront, how will I assist the Mercians in getting inside Londinium? I've no ship for them, and they have no access to a boat because all the Mercian ships are at the market settlement, and it's not yet restored to Mercian hands.

So that leaves left and right. Right will take me to the further reaches of Londinium and far from the Mercian warriors. Left will take me to where the Mercian warriors are closest. I can feel my face twisting in thought, and then I walk right.

I keep careful watch, turning every so often as though admiring the jagged teeth of the ruined buildings and the places where the roadway just seems to disappear. But really, I'm keen to ensure that no one's following me. I don't want awkward questions. As I said, I'm not the best at being less than forthcoming with the truth.

The road goes on much further than I anticipated. Londinium is vast compared to the complex at Tamworth. The day grows cooler, not warmer, the bite of the wind forcing my cloak aside and getting through all the small gaps in my clothing. My body continues to ache, although my headache hasn't returned, which pleases me. My resolve quickly fails me. Yet I push myself onwards. I've not endured all this just to achieve nothing for Mercia and my friends.

My thoughts turn to Tamworth, Wynflæd, even young Cuthred. I would far sooner be with them as the summer finally gives way to winter than here, in the middle of a battle between Mercia and Wessex. Or rather, here, in Mercian territory, currently held by Wessex when I'm a Mercian.

I consider Tyrhtil's final words to me. Does he suspect me of being a Mercian, or does he mean something else? Does he know about Ecgred's death? For a fleeting moment, I wish him dead if he does suspect the truth about Ecgred. But then I don't. I didn't kill Ecgred. Neither did the slave woman, not really. Ecgred's own malice brought him an early death. If I've involved myself in hiding what's happened to him, it's only to protect the three of us: the two slaves and myself.

Finally, I reach the outskirts. Here, the ground dips lower than elsewhere, and I can see where clogged drainage ditches try to dispel the muck of the settlement beyond its confines, only they're mostly blocked. Wrinkling my nose at the stench that not even the bite of the cold weather can keep at bay, I bend low, close to the wall. I've an idea of how I can escape and get the Mercians inside, but it relies on a bit of luck and a few fallen pieces of masonry.

I attempt to kick aside the compacted leaves of more than one summer and some other objects that might or might not contain small bones, but the sudden dip in temperature for the last two nights has done its work and the mass is both frozen together and frozen to the deep ditch of the drainage system.

But, before I give up on this location, I test the stones at the base of the wall. I can see that there should be a gap, if not for the clotted mass of items, but it doesn't matter. The stones stand firm. Rearing back, I gaze upwards and think that here, of all places, the wall stands taller than elsewhere. The Wessex warriors trust the height of the walls to keep them safe. No doubt that accounts for why there's no one watching this particular location.

I stand, brush down my hands, and begin to make my way northwards, trailing the wall. If I glance along the rows of broken buildings, I can see that there was once a tidy street plan, even though clumps of grasses and dying weeds push through them. There's yet another drainage ditch leading towards the walls to the rear of those long-dead workshops and homes. In fact, if not for the trenches, which have survived far better than the roads, I could be forgiven for thinking that the collection of stones was little more than there by happenstance. There's not a roof to be seen.

This gives me hope that I might yet find a way to escape. But the next two ditches that run below the height of the wall are as filled with rubbish as the first. I quickly begin to doubt my idea. It's time to think of something else, but I don't know what else there might be. Are there, I consider, areas of the wall that aren't free-standing, where a ladder might allow entry? Perhaps, I hope, there's even another gateway that hasn't been blocked up, although Tyrhtil told me the remaining four gateways have been obstructed.

With the sun bright in my eyes, even though it offers no warmth, I continue walking, eyes alert, occasionally stopping as though to admire the view or bending to examine something that's further away from the walls. I'm aware that people might see me and wonder what I'm doing.

I see now where a banner flaps from the top of the fort. The black wyvern on a white background is too indistinct to make out from where I stand, but I know what it is, all the same. The vast stone complex in which I met the ealdorman and Lord Æthelwulf dominates my view as well, but I've finally walked beyond its extent. The view to the fort is unbroken.

I've heard little noise while on my journey. It's as though those who watched the warriors leave by ship have returned to sleep, or perhaps they huddle inside, beside warm fires. My feet ache with the cold wind, and my toes are already numb. I can only feel my fingers because I've stuffed them inside my gloves, eager that no one sees my scarred hand again.

Yet another drainage ditch comes into view, this one slightly wider than the others I've seen, if not quite as deep. Water runs sluggishly along it, skirting areas where there's frozen water, but it's mostly empty of leaves and dead animals. I follow it, eyes down, to see if this will perhaps be suitable. In my heart, I already suspect it will be because it's so much shallower than the others I've seen. It'll be a struggle for me to fit between the stone-lined channel of the ditch and the towering wall and even harder for the Mercians to get inside. And it's much closer to Ecgred's workshop. It couldn't be more fraught with danger if it tried.

I curse when, suspending my legs over the ditch, I even manage to turn one of the pieces of stone at the base of the wall. It yields under my kick, not coming entirely loose, but rather making the gap wide enough for me to fit through. The kick makes me gasp with pain, forgetting how cold my feet are. This is the place, I know it is, but I'm not happy with it. I bend low, peering through the gap, and see the grassy landscape that's beyond my reach.

Maybe, it'll be enough just to escape from Londinium with the knowledge that I have of how desperate the Wessex lords are to reach King Ecgberht, where he protects the mint and all the wealth that stems from that.

Unhappily, I stand and begin to make my slow way back towards the workshop, having used my hands to force the stone back into place. I don't want anyone to see it and make a more concerted effort to block it. I want to ensure that Theodore and the woman are well. I'm also hungry and cold. I hope they have a fire going against the bitter wind that whips my cloak around my face.

I purposefully walk away from where I suspect we left Ecgred's body during the night. I don't want to be seen anywhere near it, should someone find him there. They might recall my interest, and I know Æsc would quickly condemn me.

As I near the workshop, the scent of woodsmoke fills my nostrils, and I'm just about to dip inside the squat building when I hear angry voices coming from inside. I'm pleased then that I've approached the little-known back entrance that Theodore uses. It means no one will see me.

I edge forward, ears straining, keen to know what's happening.

In the gloom, I meet the startled eyes of the female slave, and she holds a shaking finger to her lips.

I recognise the voice then. It's Æsc. I'd half hoped he might have gone on the ships with the others.

'Where are you, Ecgred?' His words are slurred. I imagine he's enjoyed too much of the ale being offered by Lord Æthelwulf to ensure the warriors will fight when called upon to do so. 'Ecgred.'

I can hear him moving through the workshop. A sharp bang and a smash assure me he's collided with one of the many clay jars and sent it tumbling to the hard-packed earth floor.

'Tell me where he is,' Æsc roars, no doubt to Theodore.

That there's no response from the slave only serves to infuriate Æsc further.

'Where are you, little swine? You owe me money, and I need it to escape this place.'

My ears prick at hearing this. Does Æsc have an escape plan in place? Could I find out how he means to do it?

'Ecgred.' The cry is short and sharp, filled with aggravation at being so ineffectual.

I shake my head to hear him.

'Fine, suit yourself, but if you don't pay up, I'll tell everyone you're a bloody fraud and then where will you be, you turd?' Heavy footsteps make a less than direct path outside.

'What's your name?' I ask the woman.

Her terrified eyes meet mine, and I think she'll keep her silence, but then she speaks.

'Gaya,' she offers. Her voice is soft, laden with the same sibilant roll as Theodore's.

I can hear someone moving inside the workshop and assume it's Theodore, tidying away the mess Æsc has made.

Gaya hesitates and then joins him. I follow her. Theodore glances up from where he pulls cut herbs from the broken shards of the pot. He nods at me in greeting. His eyes reflect neither fear nor triumph. Everything else in the workshop is undisturbed and looks the same as last night, which surprises me. I can't even see the splash of blood that ran from Ecgred's head when he fell to the floor. There's no sign of what happened here.

'We leave?' Theodore asks me.

I'm surprised that, like Gaya, he speaks my tongue. I need to stop underestimating these healers and their great skills.

I shake my head. 'Soon,' I offer, noting that Theodore looks unhappy. I'm still considering Æsc's words. Does he truly have a means of escape, or is he merely drunk and looking for a fight with Ecgred? I should have liked to follow him and find out where he went, but Theodore touches my arm, his grip tight.

'Soon?' he demands, and I nod.

'Yes, soon. I have a plan.'

16

Darkness falls early, and there are few fires lit inside the walls. I quickly understand why when Lord Æthelwulf appears, once more sitting on his horse, his eyes looking towards Lundenwic from a high point behind the walls, close to the building that's become his temporary home. They're seeking out flames in the other settlement. They're hoping for a victory in fire.

I watch as well, hardly daring to breathe. I don't want them to be successful against the inhabitants of Mercia. The men and women who use the settlement as a trading base spend their winters here, sheltering under the watchful gaze of whoever is the king of Mercia. Not, I suppose, that they've enjoyed much of that of late. For a moment, I consider whether they're still loyal to Mercia. Might they, perhaps, just allow the Wessex warriors into the heart of Lundenwic to reinforce King Ecgberht, where he claims the lucrative mint?

While the sky remains clear overhead, the stars shining brightly, the moon as well, I stand, huddled inside my cloak, wishing for a second, or even a third one to cover my shivering body; I hold my hopes tight to my chest. The men and few women discuss how long it'll be until they see flames and know there's about to be a victory for Wessex, but I keep my wishes quiet.

I don't see Brihtwold, and I haven't seen him since before Tyrhtil left. Tyrhtil is trying to sneak into Lundenwic from the River Thames, despite his unhealed wound and realisation that it's an endeavour doomed to fail from the beginning. And Brihtwold is elsewhere. Having shared some secret with Tyrhtil, I'm fearful of what Brihtwold is doing. I dread that he's followed Tyrhtil on to the ships. None of the other wounded men has remained behind either. All of them have gone to fulfil the task set them by Lord Æthelwulf, the lure of five hundred silver Mercian pennies too much for them to ignore.

While there might be no fire to warm us as we stand our guard outside, some of the Wessex warriors standing proud on the fort, Lord Æthelwulf remains mounted.

I glance at him more than once, noting his expressionless face. He holds his jaw firm, his hands steady on the reins, the horse moving only slightly forward and backwards. He's not ordered the remaining warriors to be ready to leave the fort should the infiltration of the market settlement be successful. I anticipate the order coming, as do other warriors. They wear byrnies beneath their cloaks, weapons belts chinking around waists. Some even wear their helms, but I think it's more as a means of keeping warm than because they'll run through the darkness of night, crossing the river, to attack the Mercians.

I've left Theodore and Gaya inside the workshop. She's anxious, I can tell, but I think she often is, regardless of whether she's just killed a man or not. Perhaps, like Wynflæd, her skills and knowledge are sometimes more of a curse.

More than once, I've turned back to look at the faint glow coming from where I know the workshop is located. I can't help considering that we should leave now, while everyone is so distracted. It's not as though I'll be able to help the wounded warriors if there are any, because I doubt they'll ever make it back to the ship, let alone Londinium. The tide might be in their favour, but defeating the Mercians isn't assured.

I stand and stare, and when boredom takes me and curiosity, I make my way inside the fort and climb the stone steps to gaze out over the shimmering landscape. It's another cold night, and the grasses look like sharpened stakes, the lights from the Mercian encampment promising warmth and safety that's missing, even behind the vast grey stone walls.

The conversation between the Wessex warriors starts buoyantly and is filled with hope but quickly fades away to nothing but the plume of breath in the cold air.

No one even speaks to me when I shoulder past them to, firstly, stare out at the Mercians, and secondly, when I retrace my steps.

Time is moving on, the dark expanse above my head seeming to shift, and I realise that now is the time to leave. No one looks away from the market settlement, and they won't, not until dawn tinges the sky with the cool pinks and purples of a new day.

I consider returning to the dwelling I sheltered within to retrieve my borrowed shield, but I don't believe it'll fit through the gap I've found between the drainage ditch and the ancient wall. And, if I take it, the Mercians might think me a Wessex warrior and cut me down before I can announce who I am.

Instead, I go to Theodore and Gaya in the workshop, lit only by a hearth filled with glowing embers. I think they're expecting me because they eye me warily. I don't even have to tell them to follow me, bringing with them what small trophies they might hope to retain.

I pause to allow Theodore time to remove the shackles from their ankles. The key moves slowly in the lock, and I think it'll stick, but it finally comes free. How long, I think, has Theodore known where the key was? Still, it will make our escape much quieter.

I eye the workshop, and all the clay jars, with a hint of sorrow. There's so much wealth here, but I can't take it with me. Perhaps it'll still be here when I return. And then I think, where did it all come from? Was there a Mercian living here before the Wessex force arrived? Was it Theodore and Gaya? Did Ecgred enslave them? There's no time for such questions. I should have asked them sooner but I don't know how well Gaya and Theodore understand me. Maybe I'll ask them when we're free of this place.

I lead the two slaves out of the rear entrance of the workshop, first pausing to ensure no one's watching us. For a moment, I think Gaya won't come, fear on her face. But with a final backwards glance, she steps free from the workshop and I know there's no turning back now.

I don't dart through the jagged remains of the buildings, some with uneven floors, others with gaping holes in them as though raised high from the ground, similar to the place we hid Ecgred's body. Hesitating to emerge from behind the abandoned wall of one of the ruins, I look behind me, towards the market settlement, seeking out any sign of flame, but there's still nothing. What light there is comes from sporadic fires shimmering silver and cold, and emanating from the moon and the stars. I shiver inside my cloak and continue on my path.

Behind me, I hear the clatter of a kicked stone and hold in place. Carefully, I peer backwards and catch sight of Gaya, hopping and biting her lip. It seems she's responsible for the noise. Or is she? I swivel quickly, scouring the distance we've travelled. I'm sure I've seen something that shouldn't be there, a flash of cloth, perhaps. But there's nothing now, and impatience wars with my desire to remain hidden from view. I must trust to the distraction of the Wessex warriors and the cloak of greyness that shrouds our passage.

Quickly, I continue. The way looks very different at night, even in the monochrome colours of a bright moon, but I counted the drainage ditches as I made my way back to the workshop. I know where I need to go.

I hold my dull seax steady on my weapons belt, the original one that Wulfheard pressed into my hand when he thrust me inside the closing gates. Theodore also handed me a war axe before we left the workshop and it hangs beside it. I'm terrified that the two weapons will collide and make the unmistakable noise of iron over iron.

Theodore moves swiftly, encouraging Gaya to keep up with us, and then we're where I stood during the daylight, the narrow drainage ditch beckoning to me. With another glance to ensure I'm not being observed, I step down into the stone-lined channel, aware the trickle of water is starting to turn glassy as the temperature plummets. I bend to once more dislodge the enormous stone that I managed to move with my cold feet earlier.

Again, it slides easily with my weight against it, but it doesn't come entirely free. Neither do I want that to happen. If this stone gives, then the entire wall could tumble onto me. I wouldn't welcome such a death.

Theodore encourages Gaya to crouch down first and then to spread herself on her front, pulling herself through the gap while I hold the stone aside, my arms aching with the weight of it, while my back screams with having to bend so low. Gaya's slight, not much taller than Wynflæd, and without even the extra flesh that Wynflæd can claim. With only the briefest of fearful looks, she disappears beneath the wall.

Theodore and I both pause to listen. I don't know what lies to the other side of the wall, other than the grass I saw earlier. Then a small hand reappears in the channel, encouraging us onwards.

I look to Theodore, but he shakes his head, indicating that he'll hold the stone while I escape. I shake my head, but he shakes his head even more vehemently. He does make a good argument with his silence. Gaya could have slipped through without me moving the stone aside. Theodore can do the same, but I can't, not with my broader shoulders and taller body.

In the distance, I suddenly hear a murmur of something and release the piece of stone to stand upright. Immediately, my eyes alight on a flicker of flame coming from the western horizon. I swallow heavily. I don't know if it means a victory for Wessex or Mercia inside the trading settlement, but, certainly, I don't wish to remain inside Londinium any longer.

Only as I move to duck into the drainage ditch, wary of jamming myself inside it, does a glint of movement coming from close by startle me. This time, I know I don't imagine it. The next moment, I hear hurried footsteps and realise we've been discovered. I crouch down once more and hold the stone, while Theodore struggles to grip it. I move it aside with my greater strength and turn to him. I don't know if he can hold it for me, but he attempts to take my place all the same. His eyes are wide in the moonlight, there's no fear there, but his jaw is set tight with determination. As slowly as I dare, I let go of the whole weight, watching his slighter body tremble with the effort of it all. I can hear footsteps coming closer, kicking aside pieces of stone unseen in the colourless light, and I know I need to move quickly.

Theodore grunts at me, 'Go.'

I shuffle into the channel, head forwards, feet behind me, looking up. I don't pause to look upwards at the towering edifice. If it all falls, I'll be trapped here, forever. I know of other cases of bodies found encased in old walls. I don't wish to add myself to their number.

Using my hands to pull me forwards, my feet and toes to brace against the uneven stones sticking up from the drainage ditch, I begin to advance. I'm too wide, really, for the space, but I can just wriggle my way from side to side until I have to pause because my head is going beneath the stone wall.

I swallow, close my eyes, and press on. Two much smaller hands slip into mine from the other side, pulling with all the force they have, although it's not much. I feel my body move in one lurch, only to hold in place. My feet scrabble on the ground, heels digging in. The hands pull me, but I release them, blindly feeling for an edge to the tunnel to grip hold of and lever myself free. It's dark, even with my eyes closed, and it smells of fat and rancid cooking, of piss and also blood. I try not to breathe too deeply, the scent cloying and threatening to clog my throat.

My fingers slip and slide over the grimy dampness of the stones, and my right hand grips something. It's hard and firm, just wide enough to get my hand around, and I pull with all my might, ankles propelling me at the same time.

I move, but not much further forwards, and now I can hear someone shouting at Theodore. My heart pounds too loudly, my blood rushing in my ears. Gaya has her hands on my arm, pulling it with all her strength. It feels as though a baby grips my finger. But my left hand has found a similar rock to the right. I pull myself again. It's narrow and confined, and there's little room to bend my elbows outwards, so I bring them inwards, inching forwards. Abruptly, I feel fresh, cold air over the top of my head and redouble my efforts.

The space my body is confined in suddenly widens and I'm able to slide down the side of the wall, mindful that out here, on the far side of Londinium's wall, the ground is much lower than on the inside. I land in a tangle of dying nettles, the smell of garlic scenting the air, as the air threatens to leave my body with the distance of the fall. There's also an unpleasant squelching noise, but I try not to think what that implies as I stagger to my feet.

'Hurry,' I whisper to Theodore, hoping he can make it outside as well and that I've not placed him in greater peril by allowing him to stay behind when we're being chased.

I see his hands appear before his head almost immediately and reach to grip them. Only for them to disappear with a strangled shriek. I startle forwards, almost pulling myself back through the gap. Now his feet appear instead of his hands. Is he using his hands to fight off someone? I grip both of his feet, Gaya attempting to do the same. I shake my head at her. I need the room, and she doesn't have the strength to be of any great assistance.

Theodore's ankles are scrawny, his feet long and elongated. My hands are slick, but with his ankles acting as a catch, I pull on him. There's some resistance. For a fleeting moment, I fear I might have pulled only half of him through, perhaps his head sliced from his body. But Theodore's entire body follows his feet, and we both fall back into the squelching muck of the drainage outpoint.

I can hear an outraged cry from inside Londinium. I recognise the voice of Æsc.

Into the hole we've escaped through, a spear thrusts. It sparkles ferociously in the bright moonlight. I rush to my feet, hand on my seax, waiting for someone to follow us. The spear jabs and jabs, as Theodore staggers backwards, and then I leap forwards, grip the weapon around the shaft and tug it.

The entire weapon comes loose from whoever holds it. I only just manage not to skewer myself as I fall back, once more landing heavily, the breath gushing from my open mouth so that I feel as though I can't breathe.

The spear is embedded in the ground, just to the left side of my head. I watch it, shadowed against the brightness of the moon, and think how bloody close I came to killing myself.

I stagger up on my elbows, eyeing the gap with unease, as though expecting another weapon or someone else to follow us through, but there's nothing.

Grateful, I sag back on my elbows, wrinkling my nose as I do.

I stink as fiercely as the ditch. I turn aside and vomit noisily into the undergrowth.

I only give myself a few moments to recover. Whoever tried to kill us might simply be getting more warriors to follow us as we attempt to escape.

'This way,' I advise Theodore and Gaya, pointing where I mean. We need to make it to the Mercian camp as soon as possible. I'm still uneasy that we might be followed. I'm far from confident that I'll be able to protect all three of us if the Wessex warriors come at us with spears, seaxes and war axes. They won't bring shields. It would be impossible to fit one through the small gap we escaped through.

Although the terrain is uneven, in places seeming to rise to meet the top of the wall, and at others to fall away so that the wall extends much lower than I might expect, it feels as though we make good time beneath the silver of the moon.

Theodore and Gaya occasionally mutter something to one another in their own tongue, but other than that, we move as silently as it's possible when we need to breathe and sometimes bend or reach beyond our capabilities.

I feel relieved to be outside the walls. I appreciate what Wulfheard wished to do, forcing me inside to open the gates for the Mercians, but it left me exposed and liable to make a mistake. It left me a lone wolf against a pack of snapping hounds. I just about managed not to expose myself as a Mercian, although, evidently, some people have realised I wasn't what I seemed.

Now, I'm pleased to be making my way back to Wulfheard and the rest of the Mercians, even if that means I'll have to fight again.

At least I'll face my enemy alongside my fellow warriors. And I carry the news of what the Wessex king and his son hope to achieve. That should help King Wiglaf and his ealdormen direct their efforts towards the correct target inside Lundenwic.

Eventually, almost dropping with exhaustion, and with the streak of dawn behind us, we round the far end of the walls, and the height of the stone-built fort with its bastion comes into view. I can't yet see the market settlement, but I spare a thought for Tyrhtil, and for what those flames meant. I hope Tyrhtil still lives. I hope Brihtwold does as well.

Just as I'm beginning to think we'll reach the Mercians without incident, something lands close to my foot. I peer down and then rush to put the stone wall at my back.

'Move,' I urge Theodore and Gaya, beckoning for them to join me. Wide, tired eyes greet mine, but they hasten to do what I ask. There's a heavy stone on the ground. I don't know if it's fallen from the top of the fort or been thrown down at me.

I strain to hear if someone is shouting derisively at me, but it's impossible to hear anything above the rapid thudding of my heart.

'Bugger,' I exclaim. It is possible that whoever witnessed our escape has been tracking our passage around the fort.

Fearfully, I step away from the wall. I can't see the top of the fort. It's too sheer. I don't know what to do. Should I risk moving or will that merely see something else flung down at me?

I step back again.

Theodore looks at me in confusion. I point to the stone, shimmering whitely in the growing daylight. He shrugs his narrow shoulders at me and points upwards.

'Was it by chance?' I ask him.

He doesn't say anything in response.

'Right,' I decide when more time passes and nothing else

happens. It's beyond time we were away from the walls of the fort. 'We run,' I inform them both.

'Run?' Theodore parrots, and I nod. I hope he knows what it means.

'Now,' and I rush away from the wall. I've got my eye on a strip of land some distance away. I'm hoping it'll be too far away for any warrior to throw a spear or stone at me or at Theodore and Gaya.

I keep expecting to hear the whisper of something coming towards me or the cry from someone who spots our movements. But there's nothing, and I jump onto lower land and crouch down, waiting for Theodore and Gaya to reach me. They do so quickly with perplexed expressions on their faces. I'm just about to laugh at myself for scaring us all, but then I feel a blade at my throat, and Theodore gasps in shock.

I can't move. I daren't even breathe.

'Who the hell are you?' a voice I recognise grumbles.

I sag against the weight of Wulfheard.

'It's me, you daft sod. It's Icel.'

The blade moves immediately. The hands on my shoulders turn me.

'Where the bloody hell have you been?' Wulfheard demands, but in the half-light I can see that he's just as relieved to see me as I am him.

17

Together, we make our way back to the main Mercian encampment. Wulfheard doesn't ask who my allies are, nor do I ask how the offensive is going. There'll be time for that. I turn and gaze at the formidable stone fort and grey walls every so often. Now I've been inside them, I'm seeing everything in an entirely new light. I don't believe the fort is as impregnable as when I first saw it. Mind, it looks as though it should be. The giants who built it, if they were indeed giants, knew how to impress.

As we walk, I can hear Theodore and Gaya talking to one another in their soft tongue. Wulfheard glares at them more than once but seems content to leave them alone. He doesn't ask me for any sort of explanation. I think he's as relieved as I am not to have sliced open my neck, thinking me one of the Wessex warriors. I also think he's happy I've returned in one piece. Perhaps.

It takes almost no time to reach the Mercian encampment. The bleached canvas of the tents appears grey and gloomy in the dim early-morning light, and there are men on guard duty, yawning. I imagine they've kept watch all through the long night. There's the scent of horseshit and fires, and somewhere, someone is cooking something that mostly seems to consist of onions. Unless, of course, that's the stench of the predominately male encampment, which it could be. Warriors don't tend to worry about bathing when they're fighting for their lives.

But one of the warriors on guard duty is alert. I recognise him as Oswy. He sneers, his pronounced nose seeming to meet his forehead as he eyes me. His swollen eye is now green, and he stands heavily on one leg. No doubt his wounds from the first battle have been tended to and are healing well, otherwise he wouldn't be on guard duty.

'Who the bloody hell are these two?' Oswy demands, pointing to my two allies with his chin.

Theodore startles, pushing Gaya behind him in a move I think too well-practised to be the first time it's happened.

'They're with Icel,' Wulfheard says quickly, his voice booming in the stillness of a camp mostly asleep. 'And so they're coming in.'

'They might be Wessex scum?' Oswy retorts. He holds his spear menacingly as though desperate to skewer Theodore with it.

'They don't fully speak our tongue,' I counter. 'No one could speak to them other than their master, and that piece of horseshit is dead and lying cold.' I put a great deal of emphasis on the fact that Theodore isn't fluent in our language. I'm concerned about how we'll talk to him. I know that Gaya knows some words, but I doubt enough to hold a conversation.

'That doesn't mean they haven't come to harm our king or our cause.' Oswy is belligerent.

I sense Wulfheard hesitate, expelling his argument without uttering it. Wulfheard doesn't look at me. I think he'll take the easier option of abandoning Theodore and Gaya here so that I can stand as surety for my two allies. That's not what I want to do, especially not when Oswy looks as pissed as he does.

Again, I'm aware of Theodore speaking to his companion. Oswy listens, his gaze fixed on them, eyes narrowed. Their words are lyrical, almost bewitching in their soft lilt. Oswy hates it, and even Wulfheard's shoulders are tense now.

'Then I'm not entering the encampment either,' I announce. 'They aided me in my escape from the fort. I'll not abandon them.'

Wulfheard sighs. 'I'll seek out Ealdorman Ælfstan,' he concedes and forces his way past Oswy, who continues to leer at me. I want nothing more than to punch him in the face for making my return so awkward. I'm exhausted, almost beyond endurance.

I turn aside, slump to the ground to the far side of the small ditch and bank that the Mercians have laboured to create in my absence. It's pitiful compared to the huge walls they face.

Theodore looks from me to Oswy and then to Wulfheard's disappearing back and does the same. Gaya sits between the pair of us and, moodily, I stare out at Londonia. My thoughts centre on Tyrhtil and Brihtwold, but more Tyrhtil. I hope he's survived whatever happened the day before. I hope Brihtwold wasn't foolish enough to join the expedition, although his absence suggests he was.

The Mercian encampment is to the eastern side of the River Fleet, but as day breaks and the amount of light grows, I can see that Mercians are positioned to either side of the wood-and-stone bridge that straddles that river. Yet, the fact that the main encampment is on this side makes me believe their main focus is on the fort. I know it should be on the market settlement. I store the information away. When I manage to speak to Ealdorman Ælfstan or King Wiglaf, I'll share with them all that I know.

I stifle a yawn. In the distance, on the western side of the River Fleet, I can see a dull glow close to the River Thames.

'Tell me, Oswy.' I lean back and look at the other man.

He glowers at me as he too stifles a yawn. 'What?' he demands. His eyes are like slits in the thin light of a new dawn.

'Was there an attack on the market settlement, close to the river, yesterday?'

'We weren't involved in an attack, but there was an almighty fire,' Oswy grudgingly admits. 'A ship was burned as well. We could see it while it blackened and sank.'

'Just the one ship?' I clarify, my heart sinking at the news. I doubt Tyrhtil still lives. Although, well, two ships left the river gate. Maybe there's a chance he does.

'As far as we could tell from here,' Oswy confirms. I can see he wants to ask more but refuses to do so.

I lapse into silence. Behind me, I can hear men and horses waking, going about their morning business. I shiver. Now I've stopped moving, the coldness of the dawn is starting to seep into me. I'd welcome a warm fire and something hot to eat. I imagine that Theodore and Gaya would as well. It's hardly a fitting reward for the risk we took in escaping from the Wessex force.

'Why do you ask?' Oswy eventually concedes, startling me. I've started to nod, my eyes opening and closing, my chin resting on my chest.

'Lord Æthelwulf believes the only way to reach his father in Lundenwic is to use the River Thames.'

'What, so King Ecgberht isn't inside the fort?'

'No, just Lord Æthelwulf and Ealdorman Wassa.'

'Bollocks,' Oswy rumbles.

I want to ask him about his reaction, but there's a commotion, and I jump to my feet on seeing Ealdorman Ælfstan, clearly roused from his bed, accompanying Wulfheard. Ealdorman Tidwulf is also a member of the small group, and that confuses me. Ealdorman Ælfstan has sleep-tussled hair. Ealdorman Tidwulf looks as though he's just stepped from the king's hall. His clothes aren't wrinkled, and he even looks as though he's found time to shave, his black skin shimmering with whatever ointment he's thought to oil himself with.

'So, boy, the gates of the fort aren't exactly open to allow Mercia's warriors inside,' Ealdorman Ælfstan queries, although there's no fury in his words. He looks surprised to see me and, I hope, also a little relieved.

'No, my lord.' I offer him a quick bow and then repeat what I've told Oswy. 'King Ecgberht is inside the market settlement and cut off from his son and reinforcements.'

'Is he now?' Ælfstan demands, his eyes narrowing as he gazes between Londonia's two halves in the near distance. I can almost see his thoughts.

I'm distracted by a heated discussion between Theodore and Ealdorman Tidwulf. Now I understand why Wulfheard thought to bring him along.

Theodore babbles, his hands gesticulating wildly, while Gaya interjects from time to time, her comments making Tidwulf grimace and shake his head, only occasionally nodding as well. Ealdorman Tidwulf asks many questions, and the conversation is long and complex. I listen to the lyrical words, marvelling that Tidwulf can understand them all. Slowly, and much to my surprise, a grin spreads over Tidwulf's black face, his eyes alight with some knowledge he's garnered from Theodore and Gaya.

In the end, I'm not the only one listening. Even Oswy, although he should have gone to his bed when relieved by a Mercian I don't know, lingers. We'd all like to know what Tidwulf learns.

But he doesn't tell us.

Instead, Tidwulf turns to me, a hint of a smirk on his face. 'Well done, boy, well done.' And he marches off into the campsite, Theodore and Gaya hurrying to keep up with him. Theodore looks at me as he rushes past but indicates nothing further. I find myself lifting my hand to acknowledge him, only to drop it back by my side when he doesn't reciprocate. I allow a niggle of frustration. I brought Theodore and Gaya here. Am I to be entirely ignored?

'Well,' Wulfheard overrides my thoughts, 'that solves that, then. I take it, Oswy, that Icel may now enter the interior of the camp?'

Oswy does me the courtesy of grimacing. I almost think he might apologise, but he doesn't, instead following the retreating backs of Theodore, Gaya and the ealdorman.

'Come on, lad. Let's get you some food.' Ealdorman Ælfstan breaks the silence. 'And then you can tell me all about the Wessex forces.'

'Of course,' I begin.

'But not until I've had a few quiet words with Wulfheard, here, for throwing you into the heart of our enemy encampment on his own initiative. It wasn't well done.'

I open my mouth to defend Wulfheard, but Wulfheard fixes me with a stern gaze, the promise of laughter in the lines around his mouth.

'We were training him up. We still are training him up,' Wulfheard retorts to Ealdorman Ælfstan's back. 'I make no apology for that.'

Belatedly, I realise I'm all alone, apart from the Mercian who watches me with sleepy eyes.

'Morning,' I call to him, and with a final look at the imposing fort, and the more ramshackle arrangement of the trading settlement, I hurry after them all.

* * *

I hope to be allowed to eat and sleep, but I don't get my wish. It feels as though I've only just closed my eyes inside one of the tents when Wulfheard wakes me once more. Ealdorman Ælfstan's harsh words to Wulfheard for what he did to me were little more than a gentle scolding. I know Wulfheard would do it again without even considering the consequences. I vow there and then to never stand behind the tall man in battle again. I won't take the chance.

'Get up.' His words aren't friendly.

I've fallen asleep in Wulfheard's tent, seemingly on his bed of furs. 'Sorry,' I begin. I struggle upright.

'You needed to sleep. It doesn't matter where that occurred,' he rumbles at me. It appears he doesn't mind. I stifle a yawn. 'Anyway, it'll do you good for when we leave tonight.'

'Leave for where?' I demand to know, entirely alert now.

'You'll lead us back inside the fort.'

'What?' I gasp.

'You'll lead a group of Mercians into the fort. We'll take control of it and, if possible, Lord Æthelwulf and the warriors there.'

'But King Ecgberht is inside the market settlement?' What I'm being told doesn't make sense to me.

'King Ecgberht is the concern of Ealdorman Tidwulf and King Wiglaf. We're going after Lord Æthelwulf.'

'But I can't be sure that we'll even be able to get inside the way I escaped.'

'Then you better hope that we can.' Wulfheard is far from reassuring as he fixes me with his steady gaze. 'King Wiglaf demands this of you. If I didn't know better, I'd say he was aggrieved you survived your ordeal. That man is an ungrateful sod.'

I gasp to hear Wulfheard criticise the king, yet I more than half agree with him.

'What of the slaves I brought with me?' I've not seen Theodore and Gaya since they left my side, following Ealdorman Tidwulf.

'They're Tidwulf's now. He's taken control of their destiny.'

'They're both healers,' I state. This means something to me.

'Ah, lad. Whatever they are, they're valuable because of what they know. Don't concern yourself with them.' But that's easy enough for Wulfheard to say. He doesn't know them, and I do.

'Is he at least ensuring they're kept warm and given food?'

Wulfheard chuckles at the reproach in my voice. 'They have better accommodation than you do and more than enough food. I wouldn't worry about them. Ealdorman Tidwulf seems only too eager to have someone to speak of his homeland with.'

Grudgingly, I accept that might be pleasant for all three of them.

'Who's joining us?' I demand to know.

'You'll see, in good time,' and I understand that the warriors the ealdorman will command are not men who've taken kindly to me. I imagine that Oswy will be amongst their number. I can hardly wait.

18

It's dark when I follow Wulfheard to the edge of the encampment once more. Heavy-looking clouds shadow the moon, and while it's not as cold as the previous night, I can't help fearing the downpour that it portends.

'We'll need to get there before the rain, or the drain will be full.'

Wulfheard doesn't glance at me as I run to keep up with him. He walks with great purpose.

'We'll get there when we get there, and if it's pissing it down, we'll still make it inside.'

I wish I shared his confidence, but Wulfheard is a broader man than I am, as too are the other men, when we finally draw level with them close to the edge of the encampment. They carry shields and wear thick cloaks, the scent of animal fat assuring me that the cloaks are greased to keep the impending deluge away.

'You won't need shields,' I begin before I've fully come to a stop.

'What?' Oswy's eyes are cold as he glares at me. Thanks to the crackling flames of a sentry post, I'm able to see.

'The shields won't fit through the gap,' I explain quickly.

'If the bloody shields won't, then how will we?' Oswy demands.

I shrug my shoulders. I don't think he will. Maybe Ealdorman Ælfstan and Wulfheard won't either. The other men are equally well built. I meet Ealdorman Ælfstan's eyes evenly. He watches me, considering what I'm saying.

'Stand beside me,' he asks.

I do as he requests.

'I'm much wider than you are,' he confirms thoughtfully.

'And I had to wriggle to get through the gap. It was easier for my companions because they're of a much slighter build.'

'I hadn't considered that,' the ealdorman admits, his eyes flickering with annoyance. 'Wulfheard, go and find me some men who are as narrow, if not narrower, than Icel at the shoulders.'

'And make sure they have small bellies as well,' I add, just to reinforce the point.

Wulfheard huffs and thuds back into the camp, while the other men deemed too broad and too fat glare at me. I won't apologise. If they get wedged in the small gap, then they'll die, and we won't be able to get beneath the wall.

'The gap was truly so small?' Ealdorman Ælfstan reiterates, feeling the heat of the same stares. The other men mutter to one another. I refuse to hear what they say.

'Yes. It's a drainage channel. I had to manoeuvre a loose stone even to find the gap.'

'But the stone is loose?' The ealdorman jumps on my words.

'Yes, but someone needs to be inside to move it.'

'The wall is what, two hands thick?'

'More like three or even five,' I confirm, looking at my long hands as I say it.

'But someone followed you to the gap?'

'Yes, someone tried to skewer me with a spear. I would have informed you if you'd asked me.' I feel annoyed to have not had the opportunity to state this before I was asked to steal my way back beneath the walls.

'Ealdorman Tidwulf had Theodore explain it all, and he advised the king and the other ealdormen. Ealdorman Sigered pressed for the king to abandon the fort, but I argued against it. After all, it's Lord Æthelwulf who rules in Kent. It would be good to restore Kent to the rest of Mercia by killing the king's son.'

The explanation surprises me. It seems that Ealdorman Ælfstan is incredibly ambitious. I spare a thought for King Ecgberht's arrogance that has brought him to this catastrophe. Some would say he has eyes bigger than his belly. I'd say he has ambitions that far exceed his capacity and the abilities of the Wessex warriors.

'What do we do once we're inside? If we make it back inside?'

'Taking the fort would be a good start, but so would killing the Wessex warriors one by one, so slowly that it might not be perceptible to Lord Æthelwulf until he's left with no one to protect him.'

'There must be nearly two hundred warriors inside Londinium?' I interject. I should have taken a count, but it was impossible when I was so busy healing the sick. There were many more than that, but the vast majority went on the ships. I can't see that many of them returned, not if Oswy was right in saying they watched a ship burn down during the night.

'And?' Ealdorman Ælfstan eyes me as though testing my resolve.

'They can't all be Mercia's enemies?' I'm thinking of the men I helped and Tyrhtil if he still lives.

'They fight for their king, against Mercia, and so they're enemies.' Ealdorman Ælfstan is firm on that point. His surety reminds me of my uncle. Cenfrith always knew who the enemy and the allies were. Thinking of him makes me remember his painful death. What would he think of me? Healing Mercia's enemies?

I've not given much thought to who Wulfheard will recruit to join our small collection of warriors while he's been searching the encampment, but I really should have done.

The querulous voices of Frithwine and Garwulf make themselves heard before I can see them.

Wulfheard stomps into the firelight, his face shadowed and unreadable.

'Everyone is too wide or too damn fat,' he complains. I notice that he's sucking in his stomach as he speaks. 'These two, even with their wounds, are the best I can do.' He risks looking at me, almost daring me to argue, one eyebrow arched high into his hairline, and I decline to do so. He's furious. That much is evident.

'What do you want us for?' Frithwine demands. He's not yet seen me. When he does, he'll be even more unhappy.

'For an important matter.' Ealdorman Ælfstan's voice ripples with his authority.

I witness Frithwine visibly swallow back his arrogance.

I duck my head and allow half a smirk at such a response. I'm trying to see how Frithwine fares since I last saw him in battle. Has he recovered from being trampled? Now that it's happened to me, I have more sympathy for him, but I'm not expecting any thanks from him for saving his life.

'Were there really no others?' Ealdorman Ælfstan directs to Wulfheard, his words betraying his frustration.

'No, my lord, there bloody weren't. We need to ensure our men are kept in better physical condition, and we need to give them much less food and wine. It doesn't help that Ealdorman Tidwulf has also gathered his men together to attack the trading settlement,' Wulfheard concedes.

Frithwine looks from Ealdorman Ælfstan to Wulfheard, his mouth slightly open. I take that to mean he's not been invited to join Tidwulf's endeavour. Mind, before I can enjoy that sense of achievement for long, I'm reminded that I haven't either.

'We take our shields,' the ealdorman confirms, despite my advice to the contrary. He's not sent any of the men away. I can't see that all of them will make it through the small gap. 'We might need them yet. But we move quietly, and no one is to talk. Muffle your weapons, but ensure you have them close to hand should they be needed.'

The contradictory advice has Frithwine once more looking confused.

I've not yet had a clear sight of Garwulf. I try to remember what wounds he carried. I recall he had a deep gash on his right arm. I hope it's not caught the wound-rot. That would be an unpleasant way to die. I also hope that Frithwine has beaten the dent out of his helm.

'Lead on, Icel,' Ealdorman Ælfstan announces, and I've the pleasure of watching Frithwine huff in shock at hearing my name.

'But he's a bloody traitor,' Garwulf gasps, his voice a harsh croak.

No one answers, and then Wulfheard can be heard muttering. 'And that's why we leave the little shits to polish their seaxes. A fat lot they know about war.'

I grin and check my weapons belt holds all the blades I might need. That includes my eagle-marked seax, which Wulfheard kept safe for me.

I slip through the defences the Mercians have built, down the slight slope and into the ditch, facing towards where I know the fort of Londinium is, and its walls, which promise safety but, in reality, provide very little.

* * *

Despite the advancing darkness, it's easy to find the walls. The Wessex warriors have small fires burning on top of the bastion,

unlike last night when there was no light other than that of the
moon and stars. The fire blazes fiercely in the concealing darkness.
But I'm reminded of when I thought we were under attack, so I lead
the troop of Mercians at an angle, aiming to meet the wall some
distance away from the fort and its defences. I'd like to know who
threw that stone at me. I hope it was Æsc, but he could have told
anyone by now. We might be walking into a trap.

I'm trying not to consider how, in the dark, I'll find the drainage
channel I used when I took no accurate accounting of my surroundings. I simply wanted to escape. Never in all my thoughts did I
consider that I might be forced to return. It might have helped if
that had been made more evident to me, but then, I'm beginning to
suspect that Wulfheard didn't honestly know what he was doing
when he thrust me into the Wessex shield wall. He saw an opportunity and took it, without any thought.

For a time, I can hear the murmur of conversation from the men
on guard duty on the fort's high walkways, but it quickly falls silent
as we make the turn around the wall that eventually leads down
towards the River Thames. It's impossible to see the river from
where I stand. I can't hear it either. It's as though the river has
ceased to exist. The dark encompasses everything, and no dancing
flames startle me from the far side of the wall. The Wessex force is
tiny compared to the length of the walls. Even if they suspected
someone might try to gain unauthorised entry into Londinium,
where would they think to look other than where I escaped with
Theodore and Gaya? That concerns me, but Ealdorman Ælfstan
knows of this, and still he bids me lead his warriors on. I can only
hope that no one waits for us there, or this attempt will be over
before it's begun.

The dreaded rain promised by the thick clouds overhead
suddenly begins to fall, a torrent that soaks me in an instant, no
matter how closely I try to get to the stone wall. The rain falls from

the east, great gusting sheets of it that sound as loud as a contingent of the king's mounted warriors. I flick my cloak over my head, but it's too late. Rain drips from my helm, and down my neck. I grimace at the cold fingers that slither down the bone of my back, only to pool around my weapons belt.

I don't welcome having to polish my weapons back to sharpness. It's as though I can feel them growing less sharp as the rain increases. The shield thrust into my hand by Wulfheard as we began walking grows heavier and heavier. No doubt, the thin wood tries to buckle with the moisture.

And still, I keep on walking. I remember it took me longer than I thought it would to reach the Mercian encampment when I was going the other way. But, all the same, I feel as though I've been walking for half of the night. I've tripped and slid, and even waded, almost knee-deep, in pools that have formed with the rain. The ground here is just as boggy, and I don't like to think what I might be walking in as the water falls from the narrower drainage channels and to the exterior of the walls.

No one speaks, but I can sense the frustration of those who follow me. I can't do anything about the rain, but, no doubt, they do expect me to find the place where we can gain access as soon as possible. I only wish I could be confident in my abilities to do so.

Only then something does catch my eye. It's just the briefest glance, but there's a shimmer of something before the rain falls once more. I move forwards eagerly. My hands reach out and find the spearhead that tried to impale me. Hurriedly, I gaze at the wall in front of me and let out a short-lived strangled cry of triumph.

I've found it. I run my hands over where the gap should be, but there's something in the way.

'They've blocked it,' I whisper to Wulfheard because he's closest to me. I realise then that he's been tasked with ensuring I'm protected while the rest of the Mercians trail behind. I don't see

Ealdorman Ælfstan, but I know he's one of the number. He's not merely ordered his warriors to do this; he's taking part as well. I was grateful for that, but now I fear I've let him down. The thought of going back to the Mercian encampment unsuccessful fills me with more unease than if I'd not managed to find the place at all.

'We can move it,' Wulfheard informs me, his words firm. He's perhaps correct, because around whatever they've pushed through the hole, water is streaming into a deepening puddle on the ground. The rain might just aid us yet. 'Here.' Wulfheard has reached his hand through the gap in the stonework. I watch his rain-drenched face in the shaft of moonlight that illuminates the pool of water at our feet. 'I can feel it. It's not stonework.' And then he steps back, horrified, looking down at his hand. I can't see what's spooked him, but he spits and gags, so I know it's something disgusting. Perhaps a dead deer or just a small animal. It's not exactly what I'd have used to block a hole, but each to his own.

'What is it?' I whisper to him, but he still doesn't speak, and the rest of the men are silent.

I curse my curiosity then as I thrust my hand through the gap. I feel forwards with it, and then I encounter what feels like a rag tied around something that might once have been alive. I grimace, feeling the slipperiness of the texture. I can see why Wulfheard didn't appreciate this. But I persist. If this is the only thing preventing us from getting inside, then I'm happy to force it loose.

Only then the smell reaches me, and it's worse even than the clogged drains that have been dispersing their waters into the ditches that surround the walls, and through which we've been walking.

I try not to breathe, gritting my teeth, desperate to succeed. I feel something come loose, a malleable part of the body pulled to one side, and I leap back as the blockage works itself free. I'm quick, but not fast enough. As I splash back to Wulfheard's side, through the puddle that now reaches my knees, I know what I'm going to glance at, and I'm not disappointed.

It can only be the body of Ecgred.

Whoever put it there knows what happened to Ecgred and knew where to find him after we hid him. But does that mean that they're waiting for me on the other side of the wall?

19

'What is it?' Wulfheard demands. I thought he knew, but it seems he wants confirmation.

'The body of a dead man.' I'm trying not to breathe too deeply. The stink is revolting. I would have expected a body to take longer to rot, but then, if they dumped it in the drainage ditch as soon as I left, that might just account for the putrid smell.

'Bloody bollocks,' Wulfheard exclaims, but his words are barely above a whisper. He already appreciates what this might mean.

'So, they know the killer escaped, and how?' Ealdorman Ælfstan is standing right behind me.

I startle at his words. I hadn't realised he was so close.

'It seems so.' This leaves us with a real problem.

'It doesn't matter,' Ealdorman Ælfstan quickly decides. 'We've come this far, and I'll deliver the fort to King Wiglaf. After all, no one has tried to stab us yet.'

'I'll go first,' I announce, although I don't want to.

I wait, hoping Wulfheard will protest and go in my place, but I'm the one who escaped this way. I must be the one to retrace my steps.

'I'll have four of the men stand far enough back from the wall that they can throw their spears if we hear you cry,' Ælfstan offers. I think it's supposed to reassure but it really doesn't. I could be dead by the time a spear hits our enemy.

I nod, swallow, and almost turn to add my vomit to the soggy remains of Ecgred.

'I'll need you to help me. Give me a leg-up.' I've dropped my shield to one side. I can't take it with me, as I cautioned the ealdorman. It would get well and truly wedged, and then no one would be able to get in or out. Mind, the drainage ditch would fill as well, which might mean all of Londinium would be underwater. I can't see that the Wessex warriors would appreciate swimming with their own shit.

'Show me, and go carefully.' Wulfheard stands close to the wall. The water must be nearly to his knees, just as it is for me.

'I need to go on my back and have my hands free to manipulate the stone out of the way, if it's still there.'

'You won't have a weapon then.'

'No, I won't, but I can't do anything about that. I'll have my weapons belt should I be successful at getting inside.' I'm impressed that my voice sounds firm. No doubt Wulfheard will realise that my legs are shaking in his hands.

I spare a thought for the clouds far overhead, the blackness of the sky and the lack of a moon. It seems I'm to face this task with heavy rain thudding into my eyes and mouth and without the ability to see much beyond my nose. I almost welcome the sensation of my body passing beneath the wall.

Carefully, I use Wulfheard's cupped hands to angle myself correctly. I need to lie down and use my hands to pull me through the space, arms above my head. I'll be entirely exposed should I be able to force the stone aside. If someone is waiting with a spear, seax or war axe, they'll be able to stab me before I can do anything to protect myself.

The lingering stench of Ecgred's body fills my nose, as does the scent of rank water and rancid shit. Then I'm pushing my arms through the hole, my back banging against a channel worn smooth by the passage of water over more years than I can comprehend.

I gasp and bite my lip, trying not to cry out. I walk my hands back over the stones above my head, seeking out a means of forcing myself through the gap. I manage to get so far, my feet still in Wulfheard's hands, only to feel something blocking my path.

It's hard and firm. I can just about slip my hands and arms beneath its weight. The dislodged stone is firmly in place. I need to force it aloft. But it's impossible. My hands aren't strong enough, and I can't position my arms in the right way to move the stone upwards. There's just not enough room. I can't help thinking that even if I did manage it, I'd still need to get the rest of my body through the small space as well without dropping the stone and crushing my chest.

Water runs over my hands, flowing freely through the ditch. The rain drums so loudly that I can't hear if anyone stands and waits for my arrival. Not that I'm ever going to emerge from the channel. I push and shove the stone, feeling my legs kick out and hoping I don't kick either Wulfheard or Ealdorman Ælfstan in the process. I twist my body, my arms straining with the effort. I know it's hopeless. I could get out through the walls, but I can't get back inside.

Only then, the stone gives, allowing me access. With a final kick and push from Wulfheard, my belly is beneath the towering edifice. My head emerges, my hands gripping the side of the stone. I look straight into the eyes of a leering Wessex warrior, and one I know only too well.

'You Mercian scum,' he screams at me, stabbing down with a

glinting blade, from which water drips onto my face. I turn my face aside, thinking to evade him, forgetting I'm trapped, on my back, with my feet still possibly kicking Wulfheard's nose.

I should have realised that Æsc would have seen everything I did. No doubt, he was suspicious when Ecgred disappeared.

With fumbling hands, I reach for my weapons belt, even as I force myself backwards; Wulfheard alert to what might be happening, as he adds his heft to push my feet once more.

Somehow, and I don't know how, Æsc's blow misses me. It gives me the vital time I need to fully emerge once more on the inside of the grey walls. Æsc continues to scream at me, his words incoherent as he capers in the rain, his seax missing me every time. It's as though he's too frightened to get close enough to engage in the battle now that I'm no longer helpless.

I slip my eagle-seax from my weapons belt as I surge to my feet. I glimpse my surroundings, rain drenching me from head to toe, but Æsc is alone. For now, at least.

'Why did you come back?' he leers, scampering closer, only to veer away even before I attempt to slash open his inviting forearm.

'I have unfinished business,' I inform him through tight lips. The stone has slanted once more to cover much of the gap, which means I'm entirely alone against Æsc. I don't much relish the thought of killing him. But I need to so that the rest of my fellow Mercians can get inside. 'Why did you expect me to come back?' I ask him when there's no reply.

'I told them you would,' Æsc counters. 'But they didn't believe me. They said I was a damn fool and should make my way to the trading settlement in the ship, but I knew better. There's no point trying to break into Lundenwic when the Mercians are coming for Londinium, I told 'em.' This surprises me. I don't know Æsc, but I'd dismissed him as unable to determine my intentions. It seems he knew King Wiglaf's mind long before I did.

Æsc rushes me then, seax flashing in the deluge. I waver, still standing in the channel, which is slick with water. Æsc prevents me from finding a flatter surface. I can just make out the cry of Wulf-heard from beyond the wall, but I can't do anything to help. Not yet. And then I see a hand and know that Frithwine or Garwulf has been sent to follow me. They're the only two who could still make it inside even with the stone slanted once more over the gap.

Damn. I need to get rid of Æsc, and quickly.

'Help me.' A pale hand emerges from the narrow hole with the words, but Æsc doesn't notice it. Perhaps he's not quite as far-thinking as I've determined he must be. Æsc seems to believe there's only me.

I step backwards then, not onto the stone path that Æsc stands on, but instead the one to the other side of the channel. He's not expecting my movement. For once, the reach with his seax is good, but he overbalances, trying to slice me. Quickly, I land a blow to the back of his head with the hilt of my seax. He tumbles, lifeless, into the flowing water.

I use my toe to prod him, but he doesn't move. I'm glad he's dead, alongside Ecgred. The two of them were the only ones to suspect me for who I am.

I rush to the slanted piece of stone and force it upright.

'Come on then,' I hiss to Frithwine. I can tell it's him now.

'What took you?' he moans, rolling from one shoulder to another as he shuffles fully into view.

'Someone was waiting for me,' I grunt. I've got my hands beneath the stone, but it's painful work. It's bloody heavy and my arms are starting to tremble. 'Come and help me,' I whisper to Frithwine, but he ignores me, slowly getting to his feet and moving to nudge the prone body with his toe as well.

'It doesn't look like there was much of a fight,' he mutters, peering into the watery gloom inside the walls.

'Will you help me?' I hiss. Garwulf is following his brother, but if I'm not careful, he'll be crushed by the stone, and I'll be stuck inside the walls with Frithwine.

'You can do it,' he calls, striding up and down, hand on his seax, as though daring one of the Wessex warriors to fight him. He's almost strutting like a peacock.

'Get back here,' I cry louder this time, hoping the heavy rain will drown out our conversation for anyone else who might be listening.

'Why? Can't little Icel manage on his own?' Frithwine mocks.

'Do you want your brother to die?' I retort quickly. My legs are starting to shake. As well as my arms. I don't remember the stone being this heavy when I made my escape. Perhaps a different part of the wall has fallen, or it's moved position. Maybe even the rain makes it feel heavier. I don't know, but I do need help.

'If he dies, I'll kill you,' Frithwine grandly announces.

'If he dies, you'll be inside the walls with no one but me to help you. You already know I've survived the experience once. I don't think you'll be quite so lucky.'

'So now you threaten me.' Frithwine rears up before me. I see his teeth shimmer in the reflection from his blade. Damn the fool.

'Help him,' his brother gasps from between where my legs are spread, one on each side of the ditch.

'You help him,' Frithwine jeers.

My left hand slips off the stone. It falls heavily, and both Garwulf and Frithwine cry out, the one with more fear than the other because he now has a face full of stone.

'Help me,' I command through gritted teeth. 'Or you'll have your brother's death laid at your door. I'll ensure everyone knows it wasn't inevitable.'

'Move over then,' Frithwine mumbles, finally seeing the problem.

With our arms straining, Garwulf emerges with grunts and groans. Now I've two others to help me. Hopefully, Wulfheard and the rest of the men will be able to get inside when we've moved the stone. But I can also hear male voices, calling to one another. I think the Wessex warriors might just have decided to come and see whether Æsc was correct or not with his assertions.

'We need to hurry,' I whisper harshly.

Garwulf is standing but bent over, hands on knees as he breathes deeply. I'm unsurprised. It feels like a weight is crushing you even without a face full of stone at the end.

Frithwine hasn't moved. He and I continue to hold the stone, but it won't come entirely free, although we can wiggle it from side to side with grating sounds.

'Help us,' Frithwine commands his brother, but it's as though Garwulf doesn't hear.

Damn the fool. They're both as bad as one another.

A spear thrusts through the gap, its shimmering blade catching what little light there is. I imagine it's Wulfheard, trying to determine if it's safe for him to come through yet. And it isn't.

Water pools down my back, merging with the sweat there, and still, the stone won't move. Together, Frithwine and I are simply not strong enough. It's hard to get a good grip on the rain-slick stone.

I can still hear voices. I don't know if they come from without or within the walls.

'Garwulf, get your bloody arse over here,' Frithwine growls. Between us, we're trying to work the stone loose, shifting it towards Frithwine and then towards me. At the same time, it needs to be held straight. When it hangs low into the channel, it won't budge at all. It's bastard heavy.

'Now.' I fill my voice with as much resolve as my uncle would once have done, and Garwulf finally heeds it. He stands upright, blinks, and then moves as though I control his arms and legs. Legs splayed over the ditch, he dips down on his knees and uses his shoulder to keep the stone level. Finally, I feel some give in the stubborn piece of masonry. 'Keep going,' I huff through tight lips. My eyes are focused only on the stone. I almost don't want to turn to face the interior to be greeted with the glinting iron of our enemy.

The spear remains, and now I can hear someone grunting, and two hairy hands appear.

'Get back,' I order, hoping they'll hear me. If the stone should fall now, they'll have broken fingers and probably wrists as well. 'Get back,' I urge once more as the stone lurches.

Garwulf leaps away, mindful of his feet. But in doing so, he lets go. Once more, the stone grinds to a stop in its slow passage.

'Get back here,' I'm now begging Garwulf.

He comes, but warily. I think he's right to be concerned. The stone is massive. If it does fall on him, just like the hairy hands, which have thankfully disappeared, he'll be crushed – toes, ankle, foot, he might even break his leg. I'm not cruel. I don't want Garwulf to be maimed, but Frithwine and I can't do this without his aid.

'It's coming,' I quickly confirm once we're working together again. 'As soon as I feel it start to give, jump away.'

There's a sudden lull in the sheeting rain. Again I detect conversation from nearby, but I suspect it's merely the Mercians, desperate to join us inside the walls.

'One more heave,' Frithwine mouths through his exertions.

I put all my effort into it. My hands are agony, my arms and shoulders shrieking with the effort of it all, and then it slips and slides.

'Move,' I bellow to Garwulf.

He staggers backwards, only to lose his balance and place one foot in the water-filled channel where the spear once more probes to see if the obstruction has been cleared.

'Move,' I repeat.

Everything happens both too slowly and too fast. The colossal piece of grey masonry thuds to the side of the drainage ditch, but it veers alarmingly towards where Garwulf's right foot remains outside the trench.

I almost can't bear to watch, knowing he'll either be trapped or sliced by the spear. At the last moment, Garwulf lurches clear, falling heavily to the left, the knock of his knee on the hard surface making me wince.

I can see the glint of the Mercians when I bend low enough to peer through the wall, even if I can't determine their features in the poor light.

'Now,' I urge them. There's still one place where the space is too small for them, but I can't move an entire wall. They'll need to work their way through the gap. And as I said, there's no way that a rounded shield will come through. If they want them, they'll have to rig up a system to pull them over the top of the wall.

I slump down, agony coursing along my back and down the back of my thighs. Only then, I hear another noise, and appreciate that we've been discovered when we're still not a full force.

Frithwine helps Garwulf back to his feet. He's bitten his lip in the fall, and blood runs down his chin, mingling with his weak effort of a beard. But he surprises me by grinning.

'Bloody hell,' he crows, 'we did it.'

'Yes, but we've been discovered.' I point into the darkness.

From somewhere close by, I can hear running footsteps. I don't know how many have detected us, but if it's more than three, we're in trouble.

'We need to protect the channel,' I inform the two brothers, speaking without appreciating that I'm commanding the two of them.

Frithwine bends down and pulls the spear from the ditch. It's been thrust through and left there, while the scrape of someone coming through the tunnel can also be heard.

I reach for my seax, wishing I had a spear as well, but the grunts from the tunnel tell me that whoever is coming is doing so very slowly. They might even be wedged in place. This isn't going to plan.

'We have no shields,' Garwulf moans.

'No, but we don't need them.' I speak with far more confidence than I feel, especially as the gleam of metal draws my eye to whoever is about to face us. They still haven't spoken, whoever they are. With Æsc already dead, I'm concerned with how many people suspect the Mercians are trying to burrow their way inside the imposing, if neglected, walls.

Frithwine stands to my left, Garwulf beside him. I'm drenched, and just moving my arms around the tight, sodden material is an effort.

And then, I can see who rushes towards me. I almost sag with relief, for there are only two men. Two against three should be easy enough for us.

'Æsc,' a guttural voice calls. 'Stop pissing about and get back to the main encampment. Ealdorman Wassa is looking for you.'

Ah. I realise the men aren't actually seeking me.

'Hurry up, it's bloody wet,' the second man complains.

I appreciate then that the flicker of iron I've seen is from byrnies and weapons belts, not from weapons held in their hands.

'Who else have you got out here?' the first man mutters, finally appreciating that there's more than one man and that they face him as though ready for battle.

'Stop pissing around, Æsc,' the second man complains.

Whoever is coming through the tunnel has managed to free themselves. The sound of their advance is audible. Metal scraping over stone is one of the loudest noises imaginable, even with the thundering rain all around us.

'Now,' I urge Frithwine and Garwulf. We need to silence these men before bringing more to this place.

Without waiting for them, I spring forward, seax in my hand, eyeing the pale neck of the man before me, the first one to speak. He doesn't anticipate my movement. It's too easy to stab downwards into his exposed neck because I'm so much taller than he is.

With a soft whimper, he slips from the blade, and I catch him. I don't need him to fall like a stone weight.

Frithwine and Garwulf are slower. The man they face is more alert. As I silence his companion, he has a seax in one hand and a war axe in the other. He aims carefully with the weapon in his left hand, the seax going for Frithwine, while with the war axe he makes a wild swing towards Garwulf. Both of them startle back, Frithwine managing to tangle his legs in the drainage ditch, seeming to forget he has a spear in his hand. He could have skewered the man quickly enough.

Garwulf thrusts his seax between him and the war axe, and now I'm turning. It feels unfair, three men against one. Well, two really, for Frithwine is useless to me. I bend, snag the spear from Frithwine's weak grip and plunge it into the man's exposed back.

He shrieks, the sound like an eagle deprived of its prey. I rush to clamp my hand over his mouth as he bucks against the pain. I palm my seax, pull it up to his throat and silence him with a splatter of hot blood that covers Garwulf.

The man would fall, but I gently lower him to the ground, breathing heavily.

'Well done.' A voice I know well sounds filled with praise. Wulfheard watches me with an appraising eye. 'You fight well when you have to,' he confirms, one hand reaching down to pull Frithwine free from the drainage ditch. 'You might yet prove to be as valuable as your uncle to the king. You, on the other hand,' and he turns to Garwulf and Frithwine, 'need more practice. Don't forget you have weapons to protect yourself with.' His words aren't filled with condescension but rather the keen eye of a teacher. 'And be wary of what your damn feet are doing.'

I sag to the stone floor, mindful of the growing pool of blood, pleased to hear that more of the Mercians are forcing their way through the tunnel.

'We'll push the bodies back through the tunnel when we're all through,' Wulfheard offers as though it's nothing to be disposing of men in such a way. 'Three of them!' he exclaims, noting Æsc as well now.

'Aye. This one here must have seen me leave. The other two came looking for him. Which means that, in no time, someone will come looking for them as well.'

'When we're all through, we'll head north.' Wulfheard is peering into the rain-sodden landscape around him. 'It looks bloody different in the dark,' he confirms.

I've forgotten that many of the warriors have no doubt been inside Londinium before. The place might be largely abandoned, but the fort is worth keeping hold of, even if it's only because it looks impressive to the enemy.

'Well, the fort is that way,' I indicate, pointing where I know it looms in the darkness. 'And if we keep close to the wall on the inside, we shouldn't run into any of the Wessex warriors because they're in the centre.'

Ealdorman Ælfstan has made his way through the narrow drainage ditch. He eyes the dead men, nods at me, a sign of praise, and bends to encourage the rest of the men to hurry up.

Frithwine and Garwulf have taken themselves closer to the wall. I imagine they would happily exit through the way they've come in, but under the watchful eye of the ealdorman, they dare not.

Garwulf indicates his clothes, and I'm sure he must complain about the blood that covers him.

Eventually, much of the small party is inside Londinium, the shields, as I cautioned, abandoned on the far side. We'll have to fight with what we've got, and as I examine the rest of the Mercians, I appreciate that they're all fighters, not just warriors. Oswy, I know, is good with his fists, and he's not alone. Cenred is a mean bastard, Waldhere vicious. The others all look fearless as well. For a moment, I pity the Wessex warriors we'll come into contact with, and then I shake my head.

If they didn't want a fight, they should never have taken Mercia's stronghold of Londinium.

20

All but two of the Mercians make it through the gap to stand, wet and uncomfortable, inside the walls. I eye those I don't know: Maneca, Kyre, Æthelmod, Goðeman, Osmod and Landwine. They gleam with fury and blades. They're mean fighters, all of them.

'You're too damn fat,' Wulfheard calls to the stranded men, his voice showing his amusement and frustration. 'Don't get bloody stuck,' he then cautions angrily, as, once more, two hairy arms appear, trying to pull themselves through. I can see the strain in the hands. 'Stay where you are,' Wulfheard hisses.

Ealdorman Ælfstan bends low, calling back through the tunnel in a low voice. I just pick out the words.

'Go back to the main encampment. Ensure the king knows of our success. And take as many shields with you as you can carry. But do it quietly. If you're discovered, we'll all be in peril.'

There are outraged grumbles from the two men, and Oswy's face twists at the news.

'They're two of the finest warriors. We should try again.'

'We've wasted enough time. They're too bloody fat, and they'll never fit through such a small space.' It's the ealdorman who speaks.

Everyone is grimy with the muck of the tunnel. I'm actually grateful for the heavy rain which seeks to drive it from my body.

'Now, we need to get the Wessex bodies through so that they're not found, and the stone needs moving in such a way that it covers what we've done.'

But here, there's a problem, because the hands in the tunnel belong to Wulfgar, who's well and truly wedged in place. I remember that his belly overhangs his weapons belt. It's good that he was one of the last two to make his attempt.

'Pull him,' Wulfheard instructs Uor, the remaining man on the far side of the wall.

'I am,' comes the heated response, muffled by the weight of centuries-old stone.

'Push him,' Wulfheard orders Oswy at the same time, and yet even with Oswy lying flat in the foetid channel, Wulfgar won't move.

The night has moved swiftly, and there's a lightening in the distant east. If we're not careful, we'll still be standing here when the sun rises, even if the clouds overhead assure me it'll be a dank day.

'You need something to make him slick,' I offer. I'm unsure what. I know I'm stating the obvious, as becomes apparent when Wulfheard glowers at me.

'I'm afraid, Icel, that I don't have a barrel of butter to assist me in such a task.' The words bite.

I hear either Frithwine or Garwulf snigger where they stand, waiting impatiently with the rest of the men.

'I don't see you offering any solution,' Wulfheard snaps at them, his irritation immediately transferred from me to them.

'Can he at least try to wriggle himself into a different position?'

Ealdorman Ælfstan barks. All of the warriors have moaned and grimaced about how they made it inside the walled settlement.

'It's very bloody tight,' Wulfgar complains. His voice is filled with a tendril of fear. It echoes from beneath the grey expanse. I'm not surprised. He must be looking up at the immovable stone above his head and considering what sort of death it'll be if he can't be moved.

'Then bloody breathe in, and try removing your weapons belt or something,' I suggest.

'It's snagged.' Wulfgar's words emerge with a strange echo.

'Bloody hell,' Ealdorman Ælfstan huffs. This would be funny if it weren't so damn important.

'If he can't be shifted, then you'll have to go and get some help from the encampment,' Wulfheard eventually announces when nothing seems to be working. 'And we'll have to hope we don't need to escape the way we came in.'

While all this has been going on, Frithwine has climbed to the top of the wall and peered down. His head is shaking when he returns.

'It's too high to risk jumping from it,' he confirms. Not what we needed to hear.

'We need to get on,' Ealdorman Ælfstan announces. 'Oswy, you can stay here and protect Wulfgar, or you can come with us.'

It's not really a choice, but Oswy wavers all the same. I'm surprised he'll abandon his comrade.

'And pile the bodies up over there.' Ealdorman Ælfstan points to a section of the wall where stones have fallen from the top, but not enough to lower it a great deal. But, it's a handy place to hide the three bodies.

The waiting warriors leap to grab hands and feet and carry the three dead men away, which we couldn't force through the drainage ditch.

'We're staying close to the wall, weapons muffled,' Ealdorman Ælfstan confirms, his words drowning out Wulfgar's echoing complaint. I catch sight of the two hairy hands still gripping the stone tightly, but no matter how much he strains, Wulgar's well and truly stuck. No doubt, his legs are waving in the air on the far side of the wall. I feel sorry for him then. 'You know the plan, so let's get on with it before it's too late.'

'Are we really leaving him?' I ask Wulfheard.

He nods. 'For now, yes. Hopefully, Uor will get some aid, or the damn fat git will fart or something and then he'll come loose. Now, lead on,' Wulfheard informs me, and I make my way to the front of the line of thirteen warriors. I thought it bad enough when we tried to sneak inside the settlement, but now there are just a few of us against the Wessex might. I swallow, my mouth abruptly dry, and almost wish I was the one stuck in the drainage ditch.

* * *

Slowly, the smell of smouldering fires and poorly cooked food reaches my nostrils. The rain doesn't stop, and that's good because it falls so heavily it drowns out the sound of our passage. In the half-light, it's too easy to slip on cracked stones, and more than once, I hear stifled cries from the men behind me.

I keep my eyes focused forward, following the wall's path across other ditches filled with just as much muck as the one we've used and now flooded with water as well.

And then I pause. Ahead, lights flicker into life on the drab day. There's someone inside Ecgred's workshop. I'd not expected that, but then, it's filled with the means to heal the wounded, and even the most unskilled can throw a few herbs together and hope it's enough to cure an ailing comrade.

A murmur of moaning reaches my ears. Who's wounded now? I

realise it must be men returning from the raid on the trading settlement. I spare a thought for Tyrhtil. I hope he yet lives. And Brihtwold. I wish I knew what had happened to him.

'It's not far.' I risk turning to inform Wulfheard.

'Then hurry up and get us there,' he hisses at me, his words sharp with tension.

I bend to do as he asks, eyes narrowing as I try to peer into the gloom towards the fort.

A building blocks my path, and I scamper beneath the mouldering thatch, grateful for its slight protection as the rain no longer blinds me. Out of the half-cocked doorway, I can see the entrance to the fort. It feels as though half a lifetime has passed since I was last here. But it's merely been a day.

Wulfheard forces his way into my line of sight and beckons Ealdorman Ælfstan close. I shuffle backwards, jostling with Frithwine, who glowers at me. Despite everything we've accomplished this morning, it seems he still thinks me little more than a traitor.

Wulfheard and Ealdorman Ælfstan bow their heads together, whispering one to another, while the rest of us take what ease we can in the cramped conditions, grateful to be out of the rain.

Eventually, Ealdorman Ælfstan turns to speak to us.

'We go now. It's not night any more, but it's dismal out there, perhaps a better time to capture the fort than when it's dark. Do as we discussed.'

This leaves me looking perplexed. I've no idea what I'm supposed to do.

'Icel, you stay with Wulfheard. Frithwine and Garwulf, you're with me. Oswy, you know what to do.' Ealdorman Ælfstan holds Oswy's gaze for a moment. I consider just what it is that Oswy needs to do.

Wulfheard, Godeman, Æthelmod and Cenred scamper through the half-missing doorway first. I rush to keep up with them.

Emerging into the downpour once more, I note the road that leads from the fort into the interior of the settlement and the fact that no one stands on it. Everyone is staying out of the rain.

Wulfheard moves slowly along the deserted road, shoulders hunched, cloak over his head, as though one of the Wessex warriors. I bend to pull my cloak over my head when I notice the other three do the same. I wish I knew what we were doing, as Wulfheard beckons me to join him.

Wulfheard turns just once, his pale face flashing in the gloom, to ensure he has the warriors he needs, and continues on his path to the fort.

Ahead, the looming gates of Londinium make themselves known as sodden masses of brown etched against a sky that glints sullenly of unpolished blades. I can't see if Wessex warriors guard them. But I imagine not. Why would they need to stand a guard on this side of the gate? Their enemy is outside Londinium.

But it's not towards those gates that we go, instead we head towards the door of the fort. Here, at last, we finally encounter some of the Wessex warriors. They huddle around two braziers, and all four men turn miserable-looking faces towards us. I imagine they think we've come to relieve them from the tedious duty and a flicker of hope touches noses that are so red with cold, they glow brighter than the fires they stand around.

'What took you?' one of the men calls, his words flecked with angry spittle.

It quickly turns to confusion as Wulfheard hurries his pace, rather than slowing it. I can't see but understand well enough that Wulfheard has skewered the man with a seax held tightly in his right hand.

The dying Wessex warrior gags, his tongue flailing as he

attempts to shout a caution to his three comrades, but Goðeman, Æthelmod and Cenred are too quick. All four men die with soft whimpers and confusion on their faces. I stand, dazed by how quickly these men have gone from noisy life to soundless death.

'Help me.' Wulfheard breaks the spell. I grab the dead warrior's feet and together we carry him to what seems to be the remains of an abandoned cart and leave him behind it. Wulfheard releases him with a dull thud. I allow his feet to fall. First one and then another, wincing at the wetness of a limp body.

Next, Wulfheard rushes to assist Goðeman, and I help Cenred, leaving only Æthelmod standing with a dead man held in his arms. The two could be embracing.

We add the bodies to that of the first man. Cenred assists Æthelmod to do the same. Hastily, Wulfheard stands beside the braziers, pretending to warm his hands over their heat. Overhead, the weight of the fort presses on me, and I'm aware of all the Wessex warriors who might be inside the building.

I look to Wulfheard. He's breathing heavily, his eyes alert to everything around him, hand not straying from his seax. I notice then that the other Mercians slide through the open doorway. Our task, it seems, was to ensure the path was clear for them. Oswy and Ealdorman Ælfstan labour to ensure it remains so. I catch the eye of Frithwine, but we don't exchange words. I become aware of noises. There are a few grunts, compressed by the dampness of the air, and even a strangled cry that quickly becomes a gurgle. And then silence falls once more, as we stand, and pretend to guard the door to the fort.

'We should hold the fort now,' Wulfheard informs me when no further noises are heard for a moment or two. 'We've taken it from the Wessex warriors, and now we can keep it.'

I feel my forehead furrow.

'Why?' I ask him. It makes little sense to me. Have we merely become those under siege? 'I thought we were to attack the king's son?'

'Where will he go from here?' Wulfheard demands from me. 'We've taken back the bastion that Lord Æthelwulf thought would protect the Wessex warriors.'

'But they're still inside Londinium?' I counter.

'For now, yes. But how will the Wessex warriors escape? There's the gateway by the River Thames, but no other way for them to abscond unless they risk falling from the walls. From here, if we need to, we can pick them off one at a time if they try and make it to the gateway here.'

'They might find a ditch, as we did?' I suggest. I confess I don't understand why we've captured the fort. It doesn't seem to make it any easier for the Mercians to take Lord Æthelwulf.

'We have the fort itself. That's what's important. When King Wiglaf's banner flies from the top of the fort, King Ecgberht will fear his son is lost. And he'll know not to expect any further reinforcements.'

When Wulfheard speaks, it all seems to make sense, but I'm still not convinced.

'Now the fort is secure, we'll move into Londinium itself and kill any Wessex warriors that we encounter. It'll cause panic.'

'So, we won't put the banner up yet then?' I ask, just to be sure.

'No, Icel, we won't.' Wulfheard grins at me, while Æthelmod watches me as though unsure what to make of me.

'You survived, in here, all alone?' he demands. Æthelmod is not the tallest of men. Certainly, I can see the top of his helm from where I stand, but he has the athletic build of a warrior. His breathing is hardly laboured despite our exertions during the night and in the last few moments.

'Yes, they took me to be one of their number,' I assure him.

'And you could pretend to be one of them?' he presses me.

'I wasn't asked. I had no shield or seax to mark me as a Mercian.'

'I'm impressed.' His voice is rich with regard.

I shrug. 'It was nothing. I was lucky.'

'That's it,' Ealdorman Ælfstan calls to us from across the open expanse. 'We're in command of the fort.' It all seems far too easy to me. 'Now, for the more difficult task.'

I'm unsure why Ealdorman Ælfstan watches me, but then he speaks once more, and all becomes clear.

'Now, Icel, you'll lead us to the building where Lord Æthelwulf can be found. Until then, we're to continue as though we're men of Wessex. We don't want them to realise that they've had the linchpin of their defence stolen from beneath them. We'll each be allowed some time to rest, before striking out into the heart of the camp once night has fallen.'

The rest of the Mercians have appeared. They all seem hale, although Frithwine drips blood down his chin, whereas Garwulf is limping heavily.

'Don't we open the gates of Londinium to allow the Mercians in?' I ask. I'm thoroughly confused by what's happening. I'm aware the gates are outside the fort, but not far away. If we open them, and the Mercians flood inside, then Lord Æthelwulf will be captured anyway.

'Not yet. We can't do anything that gives a lie to the illusion that the Wessex warriors still hold the fort. Only when Lord Æthelwulf is dead do we open the gates to Londinium.'

I open my mouth to argue, but Wulfheard interjects.

'Leave the planning to the king and his ealdormen. We're merely here to do as they command,' Wulfheard informs me harshly.

'Half of you get some sleep in the main hall,' Ealdorman Ælfstan states, giving me no opportunity to argue further. 'The other half will stand a watch on the battlements, and two of you will protect the doorway into the interior of Londinium. Don't allow anyone inside the fort, no matter what they say.'

This stage of the plan makes me uneasy. I think we've done well to survive as long as we have without being discovered, but now we're to do much more. I only hope Ealdorman Ælfstan hasn't overextended himself with his far-fetched idea for Lord Æthelwulf and the fort while the king's focus is on capturing King Ecgberht.

21

I manage to sleep close to the hearth, rolled up inside my cloak, but with my seax nearby. Frithwine and Garwulf do the same, although where the others sleep, I'm unsure. The smell of my damp clothing is unpleasant.

When I wake, I'm called upon by a grumpy Wulfheard, who tries in vain to stifle a huge yawn, to stand on the bastion. I can hear the driving rain thudding against the roof and walls as soon as I'm awake.

'Stay alert,' Wulfheard cautions me as I march from the room. I'm still uneasy after the way he spoke to me earlier. Perhaps, if he'd informed me of what was to happen, I wouldn't have been quite so shocked when we didn't immediately open the gates to the rest of the Mercians. I didn't much appreciate being reminded of my indebtedness to the king either. Is he truly in control of my life now? Do I have no choices unless he makes them? Is this how my uncle felt? Not for the first time, I wish I'd known more of my uncle.

I groan, pulling my cloak over my head as I make my way outside to peer into the gloom beyond. I grimace at the low-hanging clouds. I can't imagine that they've lifted all day, the greyness that particular shade that speaks of a gloomy day when it's best to stay by the hearth and do as little as possible. How quickly has the season slipped from late summer to the advent of winter.

It's slippery underfoot as I carefully make my way up the steep stone steps, pitted and misshapen by years of use. I can't even see the Mercian encampment when I finally crest the last step and stare out to where I know the Mercians are sheltered against the weather. To the east, Lundenwic doesn't seem to exist at all, although I can hear the gurgling of the River Fleet. I imagine it threatens to break its banks and flood both Londinium and Lundenwic and that where it meets the River Thames there's a torrent.

When I turn southwards to gaze over the walled settlement and the hint of the grey River Thames in the near distance, I feel a prickle of unease. Smoke lingers in the air from the many campfires beneath the half-ruined buildings, trapped low by the rain and making the fog from the rivers appear more pronounced, but it all seems too quiet. Surely, someone must have noticed what's happening inside the fort? It's ridiculous to think that the Wessex warriors haven't realised there's no hot food for them, and nowhere to store their weapons. Unless, of course, they did all go to Lundenwic, chasing five hundred silver pennies, and their dead bodies are now floating away with the flooded river. Perhaps, Æsc and the two men we killed at the wall were the only men left alive, other than the four who guarded the fort. Maybe Lord Æthelwulf and Ealdorman Wassa cower in their hall, or have attempted to escape via the river gate.

My unease grows because, no matter what, I know that when true darkness falls, I'll need to lead the Mercians to where Lord Æthelwulf has been managing the affairs of the fort, in the heart of the complex. And what if the Wessex warriors know we're coming for them?

My belly grumbles, and my mouth is dry, but I don't descend

the steps, not yet. Instead, I stand and stare, willing back the lingering cloud, hoping for a sight of the Wessex lord and his warriors. But, of course, I can't command the weather, and eventually, cold and aware that darkness is beginning to fall, I trundle down the stairs and eagerly spoon the waiting pottage into my mouth. It tastes of little more than mushrooms and onions, but it satisfies my hunger all the same, even if others complain.

'We're in a bloody enemy camp,' Wulfheard growls at Oswy when his words are bitter and twisted as he glares at the unappetising spoonful of food, allowing it to drip back into the bowl. 'Be grateful you're not eating the bloody rats that infest this place.' Wulfheard scratches his arm as he speaks, and suddenly, I'm itchy as well. That's all we need, to be as riddled by fleas as the rats.

Frithwine and Garwulf look uneasy at the argument, and I realise they've been tasked with preparing the food. At least they'll have been in the dry to do so, and not sodden once more, as I am.

Apart from two men still on guard duty, everyone else has gathered within the room, with the hearth at its centre. Even Ealdorman Ælfstan shares our meal. He eats with relish. No doubt, he's as hungry as I am.

'When we leave here with Icel, Maneca, Kyre, Landwine, Osmod and Æthelmod will remain under Godeman. Carry on as normal. Don't allow the Wessex warriors in, not that they seem to want to be inside the fort. No one has demanded admittance all day long. I admit, it's strange. If the worst should happen, and our enemy attacks, two of you should make your way to the gates and open them. Hold them until more Mercians can assist you. Whatever the rest of you do, hold the fort. No matter how few of you there are, hold the fort. I'm sure King Wiglaf will see sense and come to assist you all.'

The ealdorman's words surprise me, and I turn to Wulfheard, mouth open. He shrugs his massive shoulders, no hint of apology there for implying this was the king's decision. It seems I'm here on the ealdorman's command, and not the king's at all. It's far from reassuring. Now I understand why the gate hasn't been opened.

Godeman grunts and nods sharply. I realise with dismay that if Godeman is to hold the fort, then Oswy is to journey with the ealdorman and myself to kill Lord Æthelwulf. I'm hoping Wulfheard will also be included in the group. I'm not expecting it also to comprise Frithwine and Garwulf.

'If this all goes wrong, and we can't make it back to the fort, then we escape the same way we came in. That's why it needs to be you youngsters.'

'It's to be hoped that fat Wulfgar has finally managed to free himself,' I mutter, unhappy at this new risk that must be taken.

'He has,' Wulfheard rumbles, a smirk on his face as he once more sucks in his belly, reminded that he's far from svelte. 'He and Uor journeyed back to the gate and made themselves known. Mind, it took them a long time.' Wulfheard's eyes glint with malice as he speaks. It's easy to see what he's thinking.

I know a moment of pity for the man with the large belly. Wulfheard didn't exactly slip through the opening easily either, so he's a fine one to be complaining, and he knows it.

Under Ealdorman Ælfstan's watchful gaze, I take note of the small party who'll once more venture inside Londinium itself. Other than the ealdorman, Wulfheard, Frithwine and Garwulf, there's also Oswy, Cenred and Waldhere. The two are firm friends. They're not pleased at being put with three of the younger warriors. I can hear them muttering about how untried in battle we are, but, equally, those with more experience have the build to go with them. If we're forced to flee through the wall the way we made it inside, they'll cause problems. Oswy and Waldhere, whether they realise it or not, will have to ensure the rest of us get away before they attempt the same.

Wulfheard glowers at them, but they don't seem to notice or appreciate the honour of being asked to escort Ealdorman Ælfstan.

'Now, Icel, tell us how we reach Lord Æthelwulf and Ealdorman Wassa?'

'They're in the centre of the settlement, in a stone-built building, one of the few that still stands to two levels. We head towards the east, and it's in the centre. It's difficult to miss it during the daytime, what with the ruined columns that still stand, and the statues that guide our steps towards it, but in the darkness of night, it might be a little more tricky.'

'But you know the way?' Oswy glowers at me from beneath his thick eyebrows.

'I know the way. During the day,' I retort, not appreciating the disbelief in his voice.

'Wonderful,' he rejoins flinging his arms into the air in disgust, causing his weapons belt to jingle at the same time. 'This won't bloody work,' he jabs at Ealdorman Ælfstan, his voice entirely lacking respect.

'Then we'll die on the edge of Wessex blades,' the ealdorman replies calmly. 'And I don't know about you, but I don't much fancy that.'

* * *

The door to the fort building creaks open, and I step once more into Londinium itself. It's dark and gloomy, no longer raining, but damp enough that I can feel moisture on my skin even without the rain.

I gaze into the heart of Londinium, trying to pick out the way I want to go. Whereas when the Wessex warriors first retreated behind the closed gates, they didn't venture far from the fort in the northern tip, those temporary camps have moved away now. There's a faint glow of firelight coming from Ecgred's workshop, but nothing else. I must assume that everyone is close to the massive building the ealdorman has claimed or at the quayside, waiting for news of the men who journeyed to the market settlement along the River Thames.

'This way.' I turn to Wulfheard, his eyes just about visible, although the rest of him isn't.

'Stay close,' I caution as I move away from the door. I hear it close with grim finality. It seems this is it, then.

I walk like I belong, for all I don't. I feel the same fear as when I first arrived, although having Wulfheard with me alleviates some of the worry, if not all of it. Should a Wessex warrior appear from out of the gloomy ruins, they mustn't question my being here. We've heard no outcry about the men we killed when we gained admittance beneath the wall early this morning. Hopefully, that means our presence here remains unknown. For now.

Beneath my feet, the stones and gravel below the tufts of grass are uneven. I walk close to the side. It's easier to stay on track with the drainage ditches to guide me. I sniff the air. But only when I can see some hazy lights ahead do I smell the smoke of the fires and the food that's being cooked. The stink of men who've not washed for too many days drifts on the air alongside the festering wounds that need treating, or men will die of the wound-rot. We've reached the place where I first met Lord Æthelwulf. Any moment now, I expect the twin lines of broken statues to appear before me.

A hand on my shoulder startles me. Wulfheard's eyes gleam in the darkness.

'We're not going to just march up there,' he huffs, jutting his chin towards the lights, as though I'm going to do just that.

'You did sort of imply we would,' I snap, ensuring my words are only loud enough for him to hear.

'Lead us around the back of the place,' he orders.

I bite back all of my complaints and veer away to the left. So much for looking like Wessex warriors. If we skulk through the ruins, we're sure to be discovered.

Besides us, there's the ruined outline of a dilapidated building that allows access to another pathway. The colossal building and stone complex can be seen ahead thanks to firelight.

'Watch your feet,' I hiss to Wulfheard. I hear stones being kicked and someone's outraged complaint of pain when they kick a piece of the original building that still stands.

The voices of the Wessex men can be discerned, little more than soft murmurs, one to another. They don't sound victorious. I'm not sure they sound like anything other than men trying to keep warm on a cold night.

My thoughts turn to Tyrhtil and Brihtwold. I hope Tyrhtil still lives, even if he is a Wessex warrior. And then someone cries out ahead.

'Who the hell are you?' The voice is rough, edged with pain. It's as though I've summoned Tyrhtil to my side merely by thinking about him.

'Tyrhtil?' I call, for the moment forgetting what I'm doing here.

'Icel?' he gasps.

I rush forward, unheeding of Wulfheard's hiss of denial before I do so. I feel his hands just miss my shoulder as I forge onwards.

'You survived?' I find Tyrhtil sitting, spear in one hand, on a piece of masonry that must have once formed steps into the building that's our destination, only from the side, not the front. In the distance, there's a brazier, and it makes him appear wraithlike. In the time I've been gone, he's shrunk in on himself.

'Barely,' he comments. He's trying to find out who follows me, peering over my shoulders, but the rest of the Mercians have faded into the background.

'Are you wounded?' I demand. I can smell the stench of dried blood on him.

'Yes, but at least I escaped. The bastard Mercians burnt us. Less than a quarter of the men made it back alive. And those the Mercians didn't burn drowned in the ship that sank.'

'But you were one of them who lived,' I offer with warmth in my voice. I detect someone's objections being stifled from the rear and know that it's Oswy.

'Not that it's going to do me a lot of good. I should have died there. It would have been better than the pain. Ecgred is dead. I'm sure you know. And his slaves gone. There's no one to treat the rest of the men or me.'

I feel torn. In a leap of flames, I can see the blistering that's shorn away half of Tyrhtil's black beard, his skin as well.

'Where have you been?' Tyrhtil demands, recalled to the fact that I could tend his wounds.

I open my mouth to speak, but no words gush forth. What can I say?

And then I detect a flicker of movement. Wulfheard stands behind Tyrhtil, seax held at the other man's throat.

'Do it,' Tyrhtil whispers.

I can see his anguish. I can also hear the hope in his voice. Tyrhtil wants to die.

'Don't do it,' I say at the same time. 'He helped me.' I fill my voice with calm. One false move and Tyrhtil could alert the Wessex warriors of our presence, another and he could be dead.

'Do it,' Tyrhtil demands, his eyes filled with my betrayal, even as he lifts his hand to wrap it around Wulfheard's hilt as well, pressing it even tighter. Now Wulfheard has to not let his seax slip against the man's throat. 'It seems that Æsc and Brihtwold were correct when they denounced you as a Mercian.' Tyrhtil glowers at me. His eyes are slits of pain. What wound does he carry now?

'I can help you,' I pronounce, trying to ignore the knowledge that Brihtwold suspected me just as much as Æsc did. 'I know where the slaves are, Theodore and Gaya. I can get them to you. All you need to do is stay quiet, and let us do what needs to be done to return Londinium to Mercian control.'

Tyrhtil gurgles, and I don't know whether he's laughing or sobbing.

'You expect to find Lord Æthelwulf here?' There's incredulity in his voice. 'He's gone, taken the one remaining river-worthy ship across the River Thames back to the safety of Wessex. Bloody coward. He's abandoned his father and his warriors,' Tyrhtil spits, his words sharper than the seax at his neck.

'But Ealdorman Wassa remains?' I query, shocked by the news of what Lord Æthelwulf has done. Will Ealdorman Ælfstan change his mind about attacking Wassa now? I know he wanted the Wessex king's son, but he's beyond our reach now.

'Yes, he does. Unhappily.'

'And he's inside that building?' I press, pointing to our destination.

'I'm guarding him.'

'From who?'

'From rumours, and now, it seems, from the fact there are bloody Mercians inside the walls.' He's furious.

'You're not doing a very good job,' Wulfheard mutters.

Tyrhtil startles as though he'll turn his head, only to remember he has a blade at his throat.

'I'm doing what I can.' He's finally removed his hand from the hilt of Wulfheard's seax. 'I'm doing more than those men too terrified to leave the safety of Ealdorman Wassa's stone-built hall. They're all snivelling babes.'

'Help us, and I'll help you,' I suggest.

'But you're Mercians.'

'And Londinium is Mercian.' Ealdorman Ælfstan has joined the debate, stepping into the semi-light from the distant brazier.

'Aye, it is,' Tyrhtil agrees, eyeing the man before him. Ealdorman Ælfstan wears nothing to mark him as an ealdorman, and yet, Tyrhtil senses it all the same. His next words are more deferential. 'And welcome to it as well. The Mercians living in Lundenwic are a fearsome group. I hardly know how King Ecgberht took it from them.'

'He didn't, not really. He holds the mint and little else.' I didn't know this, but I trust Ealdorman Ælfstan to tell the truth.

'If I help you, what will you do? Kill 'em all? There's over a hundred men still living, half of them sitting at table with the ealdorman, all of them trying to find their courage at the bottom of their ale.'

'We'll kill our enemy, yes,' Ealdorman Ælfstan is honest enough to admit.

Tyrhtil closes his eyes as he considers the options available to him.

'If I asked you to kill me, here and now, would you do it?' This is directed at Ealdorman Ælfstan.

'Yes.' The ealdorman doesn't even take the time to consider his answer.

'Then I'll help you. The sooner this is over, and King Ecgberht is back in Wessex, the better. Never again should he attempt to take so much and claim it as his own to rule. And if the bastard Ealdorman Wassa dies in the process, then so much the better. The ealdorman is inside the building. It'll be impossible to approach him from the main entrance. He's doubled the guard since some of his men went missing, Æsc amongst them. But there's another one, to the rear. It's smaller and filled with rubble, but you can get through with some effort. No one guards it.'

'Icel, you stay here, with your friend.' Wulfheard stumbles over the word he must apply to the Wessex warrior.

'You have my word. I'll do nothing to endanger you. I can hardly stand,' Tyrhtil counters. It seems he doesn't want me to stay with him. Perhaps he knows the time left to him is short, and he doesn't want anyone to witness his death, should it come before I can help him.

'If you can hardly stand, then how will you escape?' Oswy barks, his words so loud all of us look around in horror, hands reaching for seaxes, dreading the arrival of the Wessex men.

'We'll aid him in return for him helping us.' Wulfheard surprises me by defending Tyrhtil.

'Fine, but if you raise the alarm, I'll slice your tongue from your mouth and then peel the rest of your skin from your face.'

I grimace at Oswy's graphic depiction as he leers at Tyrhtil.

Tyrhtil is forced backwards, and I think he scowls, but it's difficult to see in the dim light.

'I'll do as I said. You have my word. All I ask is that Icel help me, as he promised.'

'Then we have an agreement,' Wulfheard confirms, his voice pitched low so that the sound won't travel. 'Now, tell us how to find the second entrance to the building.'

I listen with only half an ear as Tyrhtil shares all he knows. I feel terrible for involving him in this, but he hardly seems to show any remorse for betraying his fellow warriors. I can't decide if I hate him for being so weak or admire him for being so brave.

'We'll come back for you,' Wulfheard promises the Wessex warrior. 'And if we don't, we're either dead or can't come here. In that case, make your way to the fort, if you can, and inform the men who answer your banging that you're an ally of Icel, and on the word of Wulfheard, you're to be admitted. They'll do so.' I consider why Wulfheard doesn't say the ealdorman's name, but then realise that even the Wessex warriors might have heard of one of Mercia's ealdormen. They won't know there's a Wulfheard in the group.

Tyrhtil nods, but his gaze is focused on me. I consider that he tries to decide where my loyalties genuinely lie, if I'm to be trusted, and if I can do what I promise to do. I try to offer a smile of reassurance, but my cheeks are too tight, and it comes out as more of a scowl.

Wulfheard leads the men away, but Tyrhtil grabs my arm and holds me in place.

'If you come across Brihtwold, please don't harm him. He won't thank you for sparing him, but I will.'

I swallow heavily. My spark of delight at knowing Brihtwold still lives disappears quickly. In the press of what's to come, how am I to ensure Brihtwold stays safe?

'I'll do all I can,' I assure him, and Tyrhtil releases my arm quickly.

'Catch them, or you'll become lost,' he whispers, and I leave him to scamper over the rest of the ragged road to where the final figure of Frithwine is just about visible. I don't pause to look back. I don't want to know if Tyrhtil is true to his oath or not. It doesn't matter. There's no choice now but to try to kill the Wessex ealdorman.

22

Wulfheard finds the entrance and beckons all of us close to him, and then Ealdorman Ælfstan speaks.

'We move quickly and stealthily. The primary task is to silence as many Wessex warriors as possible, including the ealdorman. If we're overwhelmed, we retreat to where we entered Londinium, or, if we can't, towards the fort. There are at least fifty of them, and we number much less. Keep alert.'

I can hardly see him, just the glimmer of his unsheathed iron seax and the whites of his eyes. I can hear him, though, and now the true nature of what we're about to do threatens to hold me stationary.

I had no choice when I was abandoned inside Londinium but to survive as best I could. To willingly make my feet carry me into the centre of Wessex power might just prove to be impossible.

'The youngsters stay at the rear, but there are few enough of us as it is. You'll be called upon to kill and to stay alive.'

This last is growled. It's as though the ealdorman thinks it's entirely in our hands. Which it isn't. I frown. The words are hardly reassuring.

'I know all three of you have the ability and the talent. Don't let older men overwhelm you. Remember, they're older and fatter than you are. They'll rely on that and will just expect to win. And that'll be your advantage over them.' As he speaks, I feel my rapidly beating heart begin to slow, and I focus not on what I can't achieve but what I can. I stayed alive alone inside the walls of the settlement. I was a lone wolf, and still I led the rest of my pack to the prey. I protected King Wiglaf on the borders. I can, as the ealdorman assures me, do this. I just need to believe myself capable.

I hear Oswy rumble with frustration, but this time Wulfheard speaks.

'You were a young fool once, Oswy, remember that. I know stories about how you used to fight. It's a wonder you're still alive. Give them a chance, or I'll share what I know and then who'll look the bloody fool.'

I detect the flash of Ælfstan's teeth as he grins at Wulfheard's threat.

'Right, enough of this. Let's begin,' and without pausing, Wulfheard turns his back on the small group and crouches beneath the crumbled ruins of what must once have been a vast doorway. He disappears, and the rest of the men hurry to catch him. I don't want to be last, but Frithwine and Garwulf elbow me aside, and Oswy has followed Wulfheard, while Ealdorman Ælfstan is the next to go. I expect Waldhere to shoulder me aside as well, but he doesn't.

'I'll go last. Watch your backs,' Waldhere mutters, clearly unhappy about it.

I dip my head low and feel the weight of fallen stone above my head. It smells of shit and dead animals, the scent so noxious, I almost gag. But ahead, there's a flickering shadow that promises I won't feel trapped for long. I hurry to keep up. I try to watch where I place my feet, but I kick a piece of stone, cursing as pain stabs my toe. The noise echoes ominously. I hear the clink of weapons and know that everyone has turned to see who's made the noise. It's only a momentary pause, and when no one speaks, we quickly resume.

We emerge from beneath the stones. Only, the ceiling gets even lower. I'm forced to my hands and knees, not even able to bend double, to progress forward. I grimace as my hand touches something slippery and slimy. Tyrhtil didn't mention this, but perhaps we should have realised. An abandoned doorway is likely to fill with detritus.

Ahead, the shadow dies away. I fear we might have been led into a trap, only the ceiling suddenly surges upwards. I'm grateful to stand upright, wipe my hands on my trews, and take stock of where we are.

The sound of voices reaches us. It's not the cry of men celebrating a great victory. If anything, the sound is sullen and filled with suppressed fury. Wulfheard listens and then continues down a long stone-lined corridor, although it's open above our heads. I reach for my seax, wanting that feeling of iron in my hand before we encounter our enemy.

A scuffing sound ricochets down the corridor. Wulfheard presses his body against the wall. We all follow suit, able to see what he's doing in the light from a dancing fire in a room up ahead.

Someone staggers into the corridor. I hold myself as still and silent as I can as the stranger releases his foul-smelling stream onto the broken pieces of stone on the floor, only to shamble away again. He bounces from one side of the corridor to the other, seemingly insensible.

'Blind drunk,' Waldhere mutters in my ear, and I nod. I can hardly believe we've not been discovered. 'If they're all that drunk, this'll be easy.' There's a hint of hope in his voice.

We inch our way closer and closer. Now, I can pick out single words, the thread of a conversation taking place between disgruntled men. I know how that feels to be let down by your king or lord. And it's Lord Æthelwulf who's taking much of the abuse.

'Damn bloody coward,' a loud voice shrieks. 'We hold Londinium's fort. What does he think will happen to us? The Mercians can't get inside. The gate's shut. The river entrance heavily guarded as well.'

A chorus of jeers greets the words. I take it to mean they're agreeing with the speaker.

Wulfheard is close enough to risk glancing into the room the men occupy. He does so, and then he furiously beckons us on. I hurry to get closer to avoid the splash of piss against the wall, but still, Wulfheard and Oswy emerge into the room before I'm entirely ready.

I expect a cry of dismay, the grind of iron being lifted from scabbards, but it doesn't come, not straight away. Not until I round the doorway do I catch sight of what's happening, and then fear stills me, driving all thought from my mind.

It's one thing to hear someone say fifty men. It's quite another to be faced with that number.

Two rows of backs face us, looking to where Ealdorman Wassa stands in front of them all. He has his mouth open as though to add his opinions to those of the man proclaiming Lord Æthelwulf a deserter. But the words perish on his lips, and the men at the rear of the hall wither with the same strangled exhalation, a hearth fire providing a patch of light by which to see. The five men die with barely a whimper; Wulfheard and Oswy quick to take advantage, Ælfstan a little slower. Wulfheard kills two men in the time it takes me to make sense of what's happening.

Ealdorman Wassa struggles to release his seax from his weapons belt to offer the words of alarm needed to rouse his men. In that time, I slide my seax into the exposed neck of a man slumped in sleep on his forearms, a board before him with two candles burning on it.

As he slumps forward, one of the candles shakes itself to the edge of the table, and I hastily extinguish it with my foot. Fire is everyone's enemy. I don't want to start a fire that'll be as deadly for us as it will the Wessex warriors.

And then the Wessex ealdorman manages to shout an alarm.

'Attack,' he roars, the words rumbling through the room.

But men, sodden with ale, and cold with fright, don't respond well to a sudden demand for weapons. The warriors to either side of me struggle to stand, let alone draw forth their weapons. Instead, the one man, a shiny pate flashing thanks to the flames of the hearth fire, grabs for his eating knife and turns to jab me with it. I knock downwards with my seax handle, impacting his hand and sending the weapon tumbling to the floor.

The second man, long blond hair tightly braided, lurches at me, trying to offer me a smack on my nose, for he's a similar height to me. All he gets for his pains is my elbow in his face. He howls, grabbing his nose as blood pours from it. I stab him through where his heart should be, and the sharp tang of blood and piss taints the air.

This gives the first man, the bald one, the opportunity to escape from the bench still tangled around his legs. He jumps upwards, landing on the bench, only for it to shudder with his weight. One leg falls to the floor, his other knee staying in place, and he all but hits himself in the face with that knee as his balance gives way.

I shove him, using my bloodied gloves, which leave two imprints on his dirty-white linen tunic. He reels backwards, arms flying, and smacks one of his fellow Wessex warriors behind his head. The movement jars the other man forwards, and Frithwine is there to take advantage of his shock, and he dies with a blade through his neck.

But the bald-headed man isn't done yet. His fingers fumble over the table behind him, and he grips a heavy drinking jug, similar in design to an ale cask, the metal rings around it look menacing in the poor light. I move aside, duck low, but all the same, I feel the glancing blow on my left arm, and a strange sensation shimmers over it, as though I've knocked my funny bone.

And he's not finished. He tries again, aiming for my lowered head as I dash beneath his arm. He doesn't have the means to hit me, not now. I stab upwards with my seax, clenching my teeth as my blade struggles against the tight muscles of his belly, where his knee doesn't protect him, but eventually, his hot, stinking breath in my face, he sags.

'Bastard,' he heaves at me, and his guts drip to the floor even as he empties his belly by vomiting all over me.

'Bloody hell,' I exclaim, trying to rush back to avoid the foul-smelling fluid.

He smiles, blood pooling from his mouth, and dies like that. One leg up, one leg down, his lifeblood splattering the floor tiles as though a rich wine from the south.

But I don't have time to examine my work, for the Wessex warriors are getting themselves in some sort of order. The men have little more than their eating knives to defend themselves with, but some of the more enterprising have lifted silver platters to use as shields or byrnies. The ealdorman has also managed to summon his door wardens, who come running, their hands filled with the discarded seaxes and blades of the Wessex men, while the few servants there are scream and rush the other way. They collide, a clatter of weapons hitting the hard stone floor.

Ealdorman Ælfstan fights with the skill I witnessed my uncle use. His movements are quick, concise, always intended, almost a step ahead of his foemen. Oswy uses his bulk to batter aside his opponents, while Wulfheard is more careful, trying to determine his opponent's skills first. Garwulf lingers behind me, but Frithwine screams at the top of his voice as he launches himself at a wiry foeman.

Not that I've time to watch him. I surge forwards, my eyes on an enemy to the right of Wulfheard, only to be brought up short by a man who scurries beneath the table and the bench before leaping to his feet in front of me, war axe in one hand.

'Bastard,' he hollers, his drooping moustache moving aside from his bulbous lips by the passing of his air. The blow lands on my byrnie, just below my left arm, and it hurts. Oh yes, it does, but I can feel no rupturing of my skin for now. Perhaps, I hope, the blow wasn't as decisive as it should have been. Or maybe, the blade wasn't sharp enough, dulled by the blood of others.

I face him, licking my lips and determining how to attack him. I overtop him by a good head, but those around us jostle as they fight, and I don't think being taller is the advantage it could be. If anything, it just leaves more of me exposed to him.

Thinking of how my uncle fought and the lessons Wulfheard has taught me, I jab with my seax, aiming for his weaponless hand. He has no silver platter for protection and no byrnie either. He dances aside from the blow, but my left hand is already bunching. As he moves to veer aside, I punch him.

It's not my strongest hand, and it doesn't land where I want it to but instead close to his neck. Nonetheless, he jerks backwards, gasping for breath. I redirect my seax beneath his underarm, and as he gargles and gesticulates, as though trying to speak with his hands, I thrust the blade as high up as I can get it, releasing the tang of sweat from his armpit.

Blood fountains over my gloved hand, and once more, I dart aside, only to knock into the back of a Wessex warrior who doesn't even break stride. I know he's one of the Wessex warriors because he advances against Frithwine, who fights with wild strikes and stabs, seax in one hand and a war axe in the other. I can see Frithwine's eyes, and they're wide and fear-filled beneath his bashed warrior's helm. He screams at the top of his voice, and I don't even think he's aware of it.

The foeman laughs as he easily evades each and every strike of the younger man, even as blood jettisons from a cut on Frithwine's chin and another to the base of his neck. This hulk of a warrior knows where all the weaknesses are on a man who fights with a byrnie to protect him. Any moment now, I expect him to stab beneath Frithwine's armpit as Frithwine lifts his arms higher and higher.

'Remember your training,' I roar at Frithwine. The damn fool is doing half the job for his opponent.

To help him will mean turning my back on the enemy, but I can't leave Frithwine to die like this, even if he and I are far from allies.

Only, I've been too slow, and now Frithwine is wedged in place, with the first table against his back, his opponent sensing victory. I glance at the fighting, but everyone is battling with someone else. There's no one but me to help Frithwine.

'Keep your arms down,' I shout to him. I think he hears me, but it's impossible to tell above the shrieking of wooden tables and benches being forced over the stone floor.

I jab out with my seax, a welter of blood immediately oozing from the diagonal cut I score across the man's back. But even though it must hurt, he doesn't stop attacking Frithwine. No doubt he's drunk too much to feel any pain. And now Frithwine's cries are becoming more and more frantic.

Again, I slash across the foeman's back, my blade moving the other way, but it doesn't earn me the attention of the Wessex warrior.

I aim at where his trews meet his tunic. When he lashes out at Frithwine, he reveals a welter of snail-trail scars on his back.

Putting all my weight behind the movement, I stab into the exposed flesh, meeting resistance immediately. I push and push.

'Get him away from me,' Frithwine roars.

'I'm bloody trying,' I grunt. If this is all the thanks I'm going to get, I'm not sure why I'm bothering and now my seax is wedged in the man's back. I can't retrieve it, and neither can I force it deeper.

Another shriek from Frithwine grants him a look from Ealdorman Ælfstan, where he fights to the right of me, but even that slight lack of attention earns the ealdorman a slice down his arm.

'Use your seax,' the ealdorman admonishes, but his attention is immediately taken up with his own foeman.

Hastily, I bend because something has caught my eye, a knife that one of my opponents has dropped to the ground. I have an idea.

The man might be a strong bastard, but we all have weaknesses.

I test the edge of the knife and find it woefully inadequate.

'Hold him,' I direct Frithwine and, from my place on the ground, I shuffle forwards. I stab upwards, into the softness of the foeman's leg, to the side of where his stones should rest. Ideally, I need something to slash with, but the knife is too blunt for that. So I hack and hack, aware that, at some point, the man must move to defend himself and that I'm scrunched on the floor, my knees tight to the tiles. It'll be a struggle to get out of his way.

I expect the enemy to buckle, to tumble to the floor, but he's a strong man. Once more, Frithwine whimpers, trying to defend himself from the wild strikes of his opponent.

'Bugger,' I exclaim, shuffling back, so I have the room to swing my war axe. I aim for the giant's knee. The blow lands with force, and his leg finally gives, impacting the floor so forcefully I expect the stone to shatter.

Although he's on one knee, it doesn't stop him from fighting on.

'Will you just bloody die,' I huff to myself. I aim the axe at his other knee, and now he drops to the floor. I catch sight of Frithwine's terrified and bleeding face. 'Finish him or bloody move,' I order him.

I've finally got the attention of the enemy warrior, and he swings his body at me, even as I can hear the sound of his blood pouring to the floor.

'You're dead,' I spit at him.

'And so are you,' he rumbles, showing me his bloodied teeth, as he directs his seax at me.

Frithwine is finally able to step back, the entire table giving with a tortured shriek of wood over the stone. He's surprisingly quick to leap clear, a sideways look as he staggers backwards and backwards again. There's a space between him and the enemy now. I harbour the thought that he might run for it, perhaps find somewhere to hide, leaving me to contend with the dying man alone.

A blade flashes beneath my nose. I swerve my neck to avoid it. I'm missing my seax now. I know how to fight well with it, but it's still embedded in the man's back. But we're level now. I can see the cords on his neck that run beneath his tunic. I see, too, his bent nose, his scar-filled face, the emblem of Wessex's wyvern which flashes in iron around his neck. I realise that this man has fought many, many times before. No doubt, he's gorged his blade on Mercian blood time and time again.

I swing my war axe, aiming for his nose, but it cracks into his jaw, shattering teeth so that they tumble to the ground, mixing with his blood. And my war axe stays there. It will not budge, even when I try to swing it away from the gaping hole of his cheek.

His eyes flash dangerously. His seax arm aimed to strike at me. I brace for the impact because I might have freed Frithwine, but in doing so, I've merely trapped myself.

But the attack doesn't come.

I open my eyes, peering at the man, and then grin. At last, the huge giant is dead, his seax arm slowly falling to his side, his eyes wide but seeing nothing. I kick him with my foot, and he falls backwards, my war axe coming free with the movement. Beneath him, it's no longer possible to see the tiles because they're smeared in blood so dark it's almost black.

I suck in a much-needed breath.

'Duck,' Wulfheard roars.

I do so, feeling the sensation of disturbed air over my head.

'My thanks,' I mutter, reaching down to pull my seax loose, the force of so much blood pouring on the ground, finally releasing it.

With two blades in my hand once more, I shuffle aside from Wulfheard's fight with a Wessex warrior who already bleeds from a cut below his left eye and his chin. Somehow, Wulfheard has become turned around. Now he fights as though one of the foemen, while the foeman labours as though he's a Mercian.

And it's the same for others as well. The first table, and the benches from either side, have been forced backwards and backwards so that they meet the wall that delineates the room from the passage we used to gain access.

Frithwine hasn't run but has joined his brother. Both of them trade blows with a man of medium height who has a seax in either hand and seems to be just as capable with both of them.

Men lie on the floor, unmoving or groaning feebly, while Ealdorman Ælfstan stands back from his latest victim, who twitches in his death throes. I look for the Wessex ealdorman, but I don't see him amongst those who fight or lie dying on the floor. Has he escaped? I hope not.

I gasp in much-needed air, looking around to see where the

fighting is fiercest. For all the men we've killed, many of the Wessex warriors still seem to stand. I know I've killed five of the enemy. If the others have done the same, then we should be close to winning. But instead there are more and more of them pouring into the room, wild with their rage. The killing is far from done.

23

I thrust my seax against a younger man, who glowers at me, a bandage peeking out from beneath his torn and bloodied tunic. The wounded have been called upon now. At least the Wessex ealdorman must be running short of men to protect him.

And then I catch sight of Ealdorman Wassa. He's close to the door, urging more and more of his warriors to join the battle. I can't see he's having the desired success as he pulls men to his side, tunics ripping with the movement, only to push them in the direction of the fight.

The man I battle tries to stab me in the upper arm, but I avoid the blow and instead plant one into where his wound must lie, at the top of his shoulder. He howls with pain. I twist the seax tighter and tighter, feeling the linen bandage grow tauter as his muscles protest the movement before giving way. He goes down heavily, and I lift my knee to hit his nose so that the sound of his gurgling is loud in my ears.

'Wulfheard.' I'm desperate to get his attention as I shout his name. Someone needs to get to Ealdorman Wassa to stop him from adding more kindling to the growing contagion. But Wulfheard doesn't heed me. I quickly realise that he, Oswy and Ealdorman Ælfstan are embroiled in their own battles.

'Garwulf,' I urge him, as he's the only one not currently fighting. His face is pale beneath the splotches of blood that have landed there.

'What?' He focuses on me, but I think it's difficult for him.

'The bloody door?' I call to him.

I don't think he understands me.

'Get to the door where the Wessex ealdorman is,' I reiterate, already turning to force my way through. The Wessex warriors are in all sorts of pain and confusion, some of them I even recognise from Ecgred's workshop. It distresses me to stab and lash out at them, knowing only too well where their injuries are.

I hurry my steps, forcing a bewildered-looking man aside, blood oozing from an open wound on his head. Garwulf might follow me, I'm not sure, and then I'm before the ealdorman.

'You,' he hisses at me, now recognising me. 'Brihtwold told me you were a traitor.' He's fumbling with his weapons belt, no doubt seeking another weapon. Sweat drips from his forehead, but he has no wound that I can see. While he speaks to me, he forgets the Wessex warriors at the door. I notice more than one of them slip away into the darkness of night. No doubt they'll hide until the attack is done and then attempt to escape through the river gate.

'Not a traitor. A Mercian,' I correct Wassa, jabbing forwards with my seax while my war axe menaces on the other side of his body. He wears no byrnie, and only the thinnest of tunics, heavily decorated with the Wessex wyvern for all it's filthy and stained.

'You'll die,' he snarls at me, spittle flying from his mouth. I notice then that his front two teeth are missing. He must have pulled the loose tooth free. All the same, he faces my coming attack with confidence.

'Perhaps,' I retort, swinging wide with my war axe so that I can aim for his left side. It's a wild stroke, but his eyes watch it. While he's distracted, I stab forwards with my seax, hoping to catch a blow on his chest or upper arm. For the time being, I can't get to a part of his body where the first strike will be mortal unless I slash upwards into his chin and through his mouth, and my grip is all wrong to do that.

His back is up against one of the standing stone walls. 'Help me,' he bellows to the men wavering beyond the remains of the massive wooden door. I imagine half of it has been used for firewood.

Any moment, I expect to feel the edge of a blade at my throat, but it doesn't come.

'Weak bastards,' the ealdorman glowers. I hear footsteps running away. Wassa has lost his support.

I open a line of blood just below his neck, scything from left to right, but he has his seax held firmly in front of him, blocking the passage of my axe.

'To your lord,' the ealdorman tries now, perhaps hoping some of the warring men will come to his aid. I believe the fighting is too intense for any one man to risk exposing himself by heading towards him.

With the flight of my seax completed, I snatch my elbow close to my body, determined to kill the ealdorman if I can. If he's dead, the remaining Wessex warriors will have no one to command them. They'll surrender, or at least I hope they will.

Again, I rip his tunic, leaving it to hang in tatters from his shoulders. His hairy chest is exposed in lines, beneath which I see nothing to show he's been wounded there before.

'To your lord.' His cry rings hoarsely once more.

I'm getting closer and closer. My war axe arm might be compromised, but I can stab and slash with my seax, provided I don't drop it. I begin to think I can win this, kill the ealdorman and bring the fighting to an end. I thrust my elbow upwards, but it misses his chin altogether, even as my seax stabs into his chest. The blade slices deeply, cleanly, and I pull it back, sure that this must be it, only for someone to crash into my seax arm. The blade, slick with blood, tumbles from my gloved hands. I glower at the man who's stolen my triumph.

'You lying piece of shit,' Brihtwold explodes on meeting my eyes.

He's found the time to don his byrnie and holds a seax in his right hand, a shield in the other – the one thing I don't have.

'I'll kill you,' he roars, face contorted with rage, jabbing towards me with the sharpened point of his seax. I swerve it, but only just, for the Wessex ealdorman isn't dead, and now he aims his seax at my exposed neck. 'I knew you were Mercian scum the moment I saw you.'

I've gone from nearly winning this to being entirely exposed.

I feel Brihtwold's blade bite deep. I growl low in my throat at the pain that shoots up my right arm.

'Kill him,' the Wessex ealdorman urges Brihtwold.

Brihtwold's shield jabs at my face, knocking me once more into the bleeding ealdorman. I stumble over my fallen seax. I'm down on my knees, lifting my arms to protect my head from Brihtwold's advancing shield.

'Garwulf,' I roar, hoping he, at least, has seen my predicament. But I can't rely on him. Instead, I fumble on the floor, trying to reclaim my seax, but there's so much slick gore, it's impossible. I can hardly see, either, as I bow low and then even lower, wanting to avoid the blow from Brihtwold's shield boss. Damn him. I thought he was my friend, or rather, he thought I was his friend. I healed Tyrhtil for him. I did what I could to assist him, even though we were enemies.

My rage continues to build as I'm knocked about, first one way and then another. If I'm forced any lower, I'll be lying on the floor, my clothes soaking up more and more of other men's blood.

'Kill him,' the ealdorman urges Brihtwold, the pain he's in showing in his shrill voice. It grows weaker and weaker, and yet his encouragements only grow wilder.

Damn him, and damn bloody Brihtwold.

Finally, my hand connects with my seax handle. I pull it to me. I still have my war axe, but it's little use to me at the moment. I need the seax. Its point will aid me as nothing else can. Being so low to the ground, I can't get any sort of momentum to swing the axe. It'll be different with the seax.

Yet, before I can do anything, I'm crushed even lower to the ground, my knees protesting beneath my chest as some great weight adds itself to the shield pressing me down. They mean to drown me in the blood of my enemies.

Abruptly, my thoughts return to my uncle. He fought until his strength deserted him. In fact, he fought the Wessex warriors beyond all endurance. I see his pallid face, the blood sheeting down his chest, and I know I'll not allow that to happen to me.

Gathering all of my strength, I shift my weight, fumble in the combined space to get my right booted foot beneath me. All sorts of pains make themselves known down both sides of my body. And it's such an effort, such a struggle, but once my foot is there, I have some leverage.

I pull up against the shield with my bowed head and neck, feeling the hard iron shield boss settling into the gap between my neck and my chin. I keep my hand tight around my seax and my war axe, but if I need to, I'll drop the war axe and rely on the seax, using the other hand to push as I try to regain my feet.

I feel the shield waver and know I'm prevailing against it. There's more force behind me than Brihtwold. He has only his body and his hands. I have the leverage of the floor as well. And then the room to move my other foot as well. But before I can do so, a weight rests on my heel, causing the back of my leg to pulse with pain. I try to move my foot, wiggle this new weight aside, but it stays firm. As it's coming from behind me, I can't push it away with my hands because I can't reach.

I know there's nothing for it but to use my war axe.

Frantically, I swing it behind me, knowing I'll have to release the well-worn wooden handle, but mindful that it's a risk as I can't see anything. I grunt around the pain. I'm not pinioned to the floor any more, but I've not made the progress I wanted.

Teeth gritted, eyes seeing little but legs and feet, my nose filled with the unmistakable scent of blood and piss, I swing the war axe. Immediately, I feel the weight move and hear someone else's agonised shriek.

I snatch my foot back beneath me and swing my knee upwards, my booted foot flat on the floor. Then, still bent almost as double as Wynflæd, I thrust upwards, all of my strength in my shoulders and my neck.

The shield presses on me even more firmly, and then it doesn't. I rear upwards, seax in my hand, the shield unwieldy in Brihtwold's. I hold my seax to his throat. It's all happened so quickly, I don't even realise that Garwulf hasn't abandoned me. He's there as well, driving his seax in and out of the Wessex ealdorman's body, time and time again, as shout after shout bursts from his mouth.

The noise is deafening. I can't hear what Brihtwold says to me, although I can well imagine. His lips open and close, his pink tongue visible, snot running from his nose and into his mouth. I hold my blade steady. I don't want to kill him, even if he meant to kill me. Tyrhtil aided the rest of the Mercians and me. If only for that reason, I'll spare Brihtwold if he'd just stop trying to bloody kill me.

Even now, he's swiping his seax blade close enough to my

byrnie that I can feel it tugging at the padded material, as though a bird pecking at the ground. It almost tickles.

'Put your bloody weapon down, and you'll live,' I bellow at him, unsure how loud my words are because of Garwulf's screaming but desperate to have them said and understood.

And Brihtwold must hear them because fury settles in his hard eyes. I know he'll fight me to the death, no matter that I don't wish to kill him.

With my war axe gone, I try to snatch his weapon, force it away from me, but it keeps coming closer. As it does so, the grip on my seax becomes even more erratic. I can see the blade raising spots of blood on Brihtwold's neck. I grit my teeth and try again.

'Put your weapon down.' But Brihtwold glowers once more.

'Fuck you,' he spits, only to still.

I gasp, seeing Frithwine's triumphant face from behind Briht-wold, his seax blade jabbed into and out of Brihtwold's body as blood burbles instead of words.

'No,' I cry. 'No, no, no.'

But it's too late. Brihtwold sags before me, and now he's down on one knee. I whip my seax blade aside, not wanting to add another wound to the ones he already has, traitor tears forming in my eyes. I didn't want this. I promised Tyrhtil. It brings me no consolation to know that I didn't kill him.

And then Brihtwold tumbles to the ground, a damp sound as he encounters the sopping floor.

'I finished him for you because you bloody couldn't,' Frithwine gloats, his face a haze of bruises, bleeding cuts and exulting triumph, no doubt keen to show me that he can kill a man just as easily as I can.

'No, no, no,' I moan once more, joining Brihtwold on the floor, reaching for his head to take one look at his face before it stills for evermore.

'What?' Garwulf has the sense to ask me. Around us, the sound of fighting has faded away. I can hear little but the ringing cry of Garwulf constantly repeating in my ears.

I gasp a sob, and then I'm on my feet, seax in my hand, going after Frithwine.

'You bastard.' I have him by the hair, my seax coming closer and closer.

'What?' he cries. 'Did you mean to let the Wessex scum live? Did you mean to save our foe ealdorman rather than kill him? It was certainly taking you long enough.'

'No,' I roar, only to feel a hand covering mine, forcing the seax away from Frithwine, even though I want nothing more than to kill him for what he's done.

'No.' Wulfheard's single word startles me. His body thrums as he holds me firm. I can feel the eyes of every single Mercian warrior on me. I can see what they think of me. But how can they know?

'It was a mistake.' Ealdorman Ælfstan's voice is remarkably calm. 'These things happen. It's a pity.'

I round on him, Wulfheard's grip releasing just enough to allow me to do so.

'He was my friend.'

'No, he wasn't. He was no Mercian.' The words echo through the hall's silence, which only moments ago was alive with the sound of conflict. Now, the only men who breathe are Mercian. 'But he was your ally, I'll allow that,' the ealdorman concedes.

I feel all the fight leave me. Now, if it weren't for Wulfheard, I'd be slumped on the floor, perhaps mistaken for one of the dead.

'We need to move fast, secure the rest of the Wessex warriors before any of them can make good their mistake.'

The ealdorman babbles to the rest of the men. I don't even note who yet lives. All I know is that I've let Tyrhtil down. I've broken my oath to him. I didn't protect Brihtwold as I said I would.

'Icel,' Wulfheard snaps at me.

'What?' I can feel my breath rasping too quickly through my dry mouth, and my heart thuds far too loudly.

'Can you help Oswy?'

'What?' I gasp once more. The words are incomprehensible to me.

'Help Oswy.' Wulfheard releases me and pushes me towards Oswy. He kneels on the floor, blood seeping from a wound high on his chest, his byrnie brown from lost blood, not from the leather of its construction. 'Can you help him?'

I nod. This then is something I can do.

I rip my gloves aside and press my fingers into the wound. It's deep but not very long. I suspect a seax has stabbed into him, hoping to find the byrnie less dense close to his collarbone.

'Help me,' I instruct Wulfheard. 'I need him lying flat.'

It's an effort. Oswy is as twisted as I was when crushed beneath the shield held by Brihtwold. The thought of him brings a hiccupping sob to the surface.

Somehow, we get Oswy onto his side, and his legs can be stretched out from there so that we can lie him flat.

I rip aside the rest of his byrnie, using my seax to stab through the material. Then I gasp. Oswy's chest is covered in a matt of fine blond hair, and I can easily see the long-healed scars of previous wounds. One runs all the way over where his heart beats, and I can see the pinpricks where his skin was pulled tight by a needle and pig's gut. But what concerns me more is the new wound. It's as long as my little finger, black with blood that seems to burst forth with every beat of his heart.

I move aside, bend and cut a tunic clear from one of the dead, not heeding whether they were Mercian or from Wessex, and thrust it against the wound.

'I need to stop the bleeding,' I confirm. 'Heat,' I pronounce. The wound is deep, I've no pig's gut to pull it tightly back together, but there are the remains of a fire glowing in the hearth. 'Here,' and I hand over my blade with the copper-etched design that already marks me permanently as a Mercian. 'Heat it in the fire,' I instruct Wulfheard.

He hurries to thrust the blade into the hottest part of the flames.

'Oswy,' I call to the warrior. His eyes are opening and closing rapidly. I fear he'll fall into a deep sleep and will never wake. 'Oswy,' I snap at him. His eyes startle and meet mine. 'Stay awake,' I instruct him, remembering all over again how frustrating it is to wait for the blade to become hot enough to seal such a wound. If it even will.

A bloodied hand fumbles for mine, where I hold the tunic tightly against the pale skin. I grip it, offering as much reassurance as I can. The returning grip is far too weak for a man such as Oswy.

'Hurry,' I call to Wulfheard. I can tell that the scrap of linen is quickly becoming sodden. I daren't risk moving it aside, thinking at least while I hold it the flow of blood is slightly contained.

'I'm coming,' Wulfheard shouts back to me.

'Give it to me,' I demand as soon as he's close enough for me to take the blade where fire seems to play over its edges.

'Move aside,' Wulfheard orders me. I think to do as he says, but the moment I move my hand, blood once more pumps from the wound. I crush the linen against it and hold my hand out impatiently for the blade.

'Give it to me,' I repeat.

'The handle is too hot,' Wulfheard retorts. He wears his gloves and has the handle wrapped in a piece of cloth.

'It hardly matters. I carry its marking anyway.'

I think he'll refuse, but then Wulfheard thrusts it towards me. I force his hand aside, and the cloth he holds it within, and all kinds of pain thrum through my scarred hand. I ignore it.

I pull the linen aside from the wound and hold the blade tight against the ruptured skin with one swift movement. Oswy screams in pain, bucking beneath me, and I join him, my cry of pain shriller than his. And still, I hold the blade there, even when it feels as though the handle of the seax is going to erupt through the other side of my hand.

The scent of burning hair and seared skin rushes into my nostrils. But slowly, slowly, the pulsing blood stops, trickles away to almost nothing, and then there's none. I fling the seax aside, Wulfheard skipping to avoid it as I fumble in my weapons belt. There are supplies there, and I need them. But it's impossible with only my left hand to respond to my commands.

Frustrated, I yank the small bag aside and upend it onto the still form of Oswy. The wad of moss is before me, and I hold it against the reddened and blackened side of Oswy's skin.

'I need something to hold this in place,' I announce, hoping someone will provide it. Back at the campsite, on Brute's saddlebags, I have more supplies of moss, of honey too and yarrow, wild carrot, woodruff and the leaves of a dandelion which I could grind into a paste and apply to the wound as well. But none of those things is here, with me now. And Ecgred's workshop is far away.

An almost clean piece of linen is flung into my hands by Frithwine. I assumed he'd gone with Ealdorman Ælfstan, but it seems not.

'Help me,' I demand from Wulfheard and Frithwine.

Between us, I manage to bind the moss to the wound, even as Oswy stirs and comes fully awake again, his eyes hazed with pain.

'What did you do to me?' he wheezes, his voice husky, tears showing in the corners of his eyes.

'I stopped the bleeding,' I announce, even now thinking of the woodruff, brooklime and lily I need to apply to my burn, and that's without considering the various cuts and bruises I can now feel as the heat of battle leaves me.

'He probably saved your life,' Wulfheard informs him, not without some sympathy.

'Bugger, you mean I'm indebted to the little shit?' Oswy glowers.

'Well, if you survive, then yes,' Wulfheard agrees, and now his voice is hard. 'Not, it seems, that he should have wasted his time and gained an injury for himself in the process.'

I'm unaware of Wulfheard turning my right hand, eyeing the singed flesh there, but I do feel it when someone else joins our small grouping, and nothing more sinister than a sliver of cool air ripples over my burn.

I stand then, purposefully avoiding the still body of Brihtwold on the floor, and reach for the nearest jug. I sniff its contents, and happy that it's only cool water, I thrust my singed hand into it, shrieking as my burned skin touches the coldness. The room spins around me, my mouth sour with vomit, and if it weren't for the stool that's hastily placed beneath my crumbling legs, I'd hit the floor.

Dazed, I glance around at the piles of bodies. There are many more than fifty dead Wessex warriors. Immediately, my thoughts turn to Tyrhtil. What will he think of me when he discovers Brihtwold is dead?

'Can you defend yourself?' I'm only just aware of the conversation taking place between Wulfheard and Oswy.

'Aye, I can.' Oswy's reply is terse with pain.

'Then we leave you here, for now. Icel, come on. Frithwine as well. We need to ensure none of the Wessex warriors manages to escape. There are too few of us to linger here.'

I turn my hand in the jug, feeling the sharpness of my pain dull, but not by much.

'I can't use my right hand,' I complain.

'Then use your bloody left one.' Wulfheard is as unrepentant as when he made me fight even while my uncle lay dying.

I stand, sway a little, and reach for another jug, sniff it, and then throw back what remains of the water in it. The sharpness of it restores me to some of my senses.

I don't flex my burned hand. It would be agony to do that now. It'll be agony whenever I do it, but I know not to do it now, specifically.

I scour the floor for my seax and bend to grip it. The vestiges of heat pool in my left hand, but I feel better holding it than leaving it behind. But I need something else as well, something that Brihtwold had and I didn't. I eye his staring face, and wince at his wounds, but there's nothing for it. I slide Brihtwold's body aside with my foot and reach for his shield. I can't do much with my burned hand, but I can wrap the leather thong around my wrist. At least I'll have something with which to fight. I turn my back on Brihtwold. He hated me, in the end. I need to remember that.

And then, with Wulfheard leading, I follow him into the heart of Londinium.

24

I expect there to be chaos outside the hall. After all, the Wessex warriors were called to protect Ealdorman Wassa. But it's eerily quiet.

'Which way?' Wulfheard demands.

'Where are we going?' I huff.

'Towards the rest of the Wessex scum.'

'Then I suggest we head towards the river.'

The rest of the Mercians under the ealdorman haven't waited for us. That leaves me feeling exposed.

'Where are they?' Frithwine gasps. I don't know if he means the Wessex warriors or the Mercians. 'We can't have killed them all.'

'No, they're no doubt running for their lives. Probably towards the fort,' Wulfheard confirms as he jogs in front of us. Each jolt sends a spike of pain through my throbbing hand.

'Shouldn't we go to the fort then?' I ask. Why else did we go to all the trouble of capturing it?

'No, the river, as you say. We can return to the fort once we've killed as many of them as we can.'

I swallow against a fresh wave of nausea. I'd like to believe my remorse causes it at the death of Brihtwold, but I know it's the pain of my hand.

Ahead, a blaze of leaping flames draws my eyes, almost blinding me so that I stumble and then trip, landing heavily, shield flat to the ground, a shriek erupting from my mouth before I can stop it.

'Don't look at the fire,' Wulfheard warns me as he helps me to my feet. Tears run from my eyes. Damn, it hurts.

Frithwine lets forth a bark of laughter. I turn, thinking to swing my other fist into his gloating face.

'Leave it,' Wulfheard cautions me. 'He doesn't have to be your friend to stand at your back and guard you. He merely needs to be a Mercian, and he is a Mercian. He's proved that.'

When I'm back on my feet, I purposefully keep my eyes away from the flames and ensure I keep pace with Wulfheard. My rage at Frithwine powers me onwards and won't allow me to stumble again. It allows me to smirk when I hear him kick a loose stone, followed quickly by the thud of his knees hitting the hard surface.

Wulfheard pulls up short. 'Can neither of you stay on your feet?' he glowers.

We've yet to encounter anyone, but suddenly, we're joined by others.

'What's happening?' one of them calls, his distinctive rolling accent marking him as the enemy.

'A fire, at the waterfront,' one of the others replies to him, as, in front, Wulfheard slows his steps and comes behind the first man. I know what he's about to do, but all the same, I wince as he lifts his seax and holds it against the man's throat before slicing it open.

Frithwine rushes to mirror the action. Just as he's about to loop his hand around the Wessex warrior's neck, the Wessex warrior himself stumbles, landing heavily on the floor, Frithwine unable to do anything other than fall with him.

Both land with a clatter of bones and blades. When Frithwine stands once more, he has half a smirk on his lips, and his blade is bloody. Lucky sod has managed to kill our foeman without injuring himself.

'Well done,' Wulfheard snaps, but he's moving as he speaks. I keep pace with him as more and more Wessex warriors tumble onto the roadway, their cries of outrage making it evident it's the fire that concerns them. Somehow, it's yet to be common knowledge that the Mercians are inside the walls. But it means there are too many of them to attempt the same tricks again.

Instead, Wulfheard slows his steps, allowing the eleven Wessex men to shamble onwards in front.

'We get them ahead of us, and then we take them,' he whispers to me, his words just audible above the jangle of footsteps and clanging iron. Ahead, the sky grows brighter and brighter. I appreciate that the fire is ripping through anything that's wooden close to the gate that leads out towards the quayside. I don't know if Ealdorman Ælfstan has started the blaze or if we're simply taking advantage of the conflagration for our own ends. I hope the rest of the Mercians are already there. If not, the three of us will be vastly outnumbered. Not that we aren't already.

'Hurry up,' a voice cries as one of the Wessex warriors powers his way through our slower progress.

Wulfheard speeds his steps a little, as though following his commands, and then hooks the man to the side, stabbing him with the seax at the same time. The man falls heavily. Wulfheard bends to heave him out of the way. Frithwine assists him because I can't, not with my shield tied to my throbbing hand.

And then we're before the fire. The Wessex warriors mill around unsure what to do. A handful have formed a chain, buckets in hand, as though to douse the fire, but only a bucket or two of water makes it onto the fiercely burning buildings.

'Mingle with them.' Wulfheard gathers us both close to him as he gives his instructions. 'Kill 'em, when you can. Try to do it quiet-ly,' is his parting shot as he moves away from us.

Sweat beads my face from the run and the pain in my hand. It takes me three breaths to realise that Frithwine has already obeyed Wulfheard.

Once more, I'm alone amongst a sea of the enemy. I even miss Frithwine's presence, for all I despise his mocking of me.

Outraged cries fill the air, the men looking for someone to take overall control, but the ealdorman is dead, and Lord Æthelwulf has fled by ship. There's no one unless someone else takes up the mantle.

'Help us,' someone bellows from the line of men trying to bring buckets filled with water to quench the flames.

'Bugger that,' a voice next to my right elbow opines.

I glance at his outline against the flickering of the orange light. I would kill him if I had the use of my right hand, but I don't. Instead, I step backwards, and as I do so, I lean towards the left, close to a man who smells of ale, and gouge him across his waist. His body judders, but he doesn't feel the pain, not yet.

I skirt around him, moving towards the left and where I antici-pate the rest of the Mercian warriors have gone. A crack, followed by a whoosh of hot air and the thatch roof of the burning building cascades inside the four stone walls, and the flames leap higher.

'Help us.' Again, a strangled cry, but no one rushes to help. The one person that does is easy enough to skewer with my blade through his back. He gargles, but no one hears the sound amongst the growing outrage.

'Why won't any of you damn bastards help us?' a Wessex voice growls.

'Who're you to tell us what to do?' another replies.

'Where's the ealdorman?' yet another demands to know.

'Too busy drinking and feasting his household warriors.' The reply echoes through the growling mob, and I know it's one of the Mercians because his accent is similar to mine.

'Sod the ealdorman. Help us,' the first voice begs.

A handful of men do move aside as though they'll assist them, but they quickly disappear, no doubt beneath Wulfheard's blades.

I'm not enjoying killing men unawares, and yet, as exposed as I am, there's little choice. My seax blade is busy, stabbing and slashing, even in my weaker left hand. One man even gets punched with my shield, where he hovers to the rear of the group. All of them go down with little or no sound. Until they don't.

'What you doing?' The outraged shriek reaches my ears. It's quickly followed by the clash of iron on iron, the action seeming to ripple outwards as though a pebble flung into a pond. It's followed by more cries.

'Æthelred is bloody dead. Who killed him?' And between one heartbeat and the next, the milling Wessex warriors realise they're under attack. Not that I know who Æthelred is, but it seems enough of the other men do, and they're immediately suspicious about what's unfolding.

Men reach for weapons and turn to one another, determining if they know each other. I do the same, mirroring their actions, working my way steadily from the rear of the group towards the gateway that opens on to the riverfront of the Thames, from where Tyrhtil went to face the Mercians only a few days ago.

Yet, much closer to the burning building, I glimpse the flashing blades of warriors fighting one another. I spare a thought for Frithwine as I duck out of the gateway.

Men lie prone on the floor, full buckets of water emptying into the mud and stones of the much-walked path, and there I encounter Ealdorman Ælfstan.

His face glistens with sweat, and his byrnie sags open at the front. He's been struck by something.

'Ah, Icel. About time? Where's Wulfheard?'

'Isn't he here?' I ask. There are also two figures on the quayside. They carry a small flame with them, and before my eyes, they set it against the hulk of the only ship I can see there, and then against the wood of the quayside as well. The dank smell of the river wafts towards me.

'No, he's not.'

'Then he's fighting out there.'

'What? Amongst that ruckus?' The ealdorman has a reasonable view of what's happening between where he stands and the burning building.

'Yes, with Frithwine.'

'Frithwine?' I'd not realised Garwulf stood shadowed by the ealdorman's frame, and now he darts forwards into the swell of fighting before Ælfstan can think to detain him.

'Arse,' the ealdorman complains.

More blades catch the gleam of the firelight, and any attempt to stop the fire has fizzled out. These men would rather kill each other because they're suddenly so distrustful of one another now that one of their own is dead. That makes what we're trying to accomplish so much easier.

'We can leave them to it and make our way back to the fort,' the ealdorman informs me. I wish we'd gone there first, but I can see some logic to the ealdorman's efforts. He wanted to kill Lord Æthel-wulf. When that option was taken from him, he determined on killing as many of the Wessex warriors as possible. That meant attacking Ealdorman Wassa, and ensuring no one else could escape through the river gate. Any Wessex men left alive after the fire and the slaughter in the building will have no option but to risk swimming for their lives, or surrender and risk the Mercian king's wrath.

'We need to get Oswy. We had to leave him behind. He was too wounded to go on,' I inform Ælfstan.

'Yes, we'll retrieve Oswy as well. It shouldn't be too difficult, not with the Wessex fools determined to kill one another.' There's disbelief in Ælfstan's voice at what he's witnessing.

'But we need to find Frithwine and Wulfheard.'

'Wulfheard can look after himself,' Ælfstan quickly interjects. 'But not the two young fools,' he concedes. 'Why are you carrying your shield like that?' Abruptly, the single ship catches fire, blazing high into the air. It must reveal what I'm doing.

'I burnt my hand, aiding Oswy.'

'How bad is it?' Ælfstan asks me.

'I can't hold a blade, so I have the shield.' I lift the Wessex shield to show him.

'It has the wyvern on it,' he spits, disgust on his face.

'Aye, well, we couldn't bring the Mercian ones, and I'd rather have something than nothing.'

'Be wary. The rest of my men won't know of this.'

'I'll just make sure I shout bloody loudly then.'

Ælfstan chuckles darkly at my aggrieved tone. 'Make sure you do.'

By now, Waldhere has joined us, Cenred as well. They must have been tasked with firing the ship and the quay. They've performed the task well.

'Where's Garwulf?' Cenred asks.

'He went to find his brother. Amongst that lot.'

'Stones,' Cenred exclaims. 'We need to get him.'

'If we can, yes, but if not, we'll have to leave him. His brother is there as well. But our priority, now the daft sods are all killing one another, is to get Oswy from the stone building and make it back to the fort.'

'What happened to Oswy?'

'He was wounded. I sealed the wound as best I could with heat. But he couldn't continue to fight.'

Unease settles around Waldhere's face at the news.

'We need to go,' he prompts Ealdorman Ælfstan, desperate to be gone.

'After we retrieve the others,' Cenred reiterates.

'Only if we can.'

But Cenred hasn't waited to listen to that. Instead, he sneaks back through the gate and quickly out of sight.

'Stay close, Icel,' Ælfstan cautions, following Cenred.

'I carry this because of a wound to my hand,' I try to appraise Waldhere, but he's gone before I can show him what I mean. 'Wonderful,' I huff to myself and then follow their steps as well.

All is chaos on the other side of the thick walls. The Wessex warriors are terrified, lashing out at anyone who gets too close to them. They fear they've been betrayed, even if they don't know by whom.

I step over a man desperately trying to pull himself clear of the fighting and then slip in the bloody gore of another. I regain my footing, only to be knocked backwards by two men engaged in fierce hand-to-hand combat. This time, I fall in the slick gore, the shield banging onto the floor. I shriek, the cry ripping from my mouth at the stab of pain that surpasses the throbbing of my burnt hand.

It's agony to scramble to my feet, keeping my seax in my left hand, for fear someone might attack me while I'm down. The borrowed shield is becoming a liability, or so I think until I move forward again and one of the Wessex warriors attempts to stab at me with his long-reaching sword. I use my shield to protect myself, braced for the throbbing pain from my hand.

My foe isn't expecting such an attack, and he drops the sword because his grip is too loose. Next, he rushes me, thinking to yank the shield from my arm, but I swing it behind me and lead with my seax. He dies as it stabs into his exposed Adam's apple, and I continue on my way.

If it weren't for the flames from the burning building, I wouldn't be able to see anything, but it gives just enough light for me to avoid the worst of the fighting. I dart out of the way of two men flinging stones at one another, lifting my shield to deflect a badly thrown one. The wet sound of one of the projectiles hitting home makes me flinch. I remember too well how effective a heavy projectile can be against an unprotected head.

It's impossible to determine how many Wessex warriors remain, but it can't be more than fifty. And even then, there are so many men mewing in pain, or silent in death, that in no time at all I believe there'll be even less of them.

Glimpsing Ealdorman Ælfstan ahead, I follow his path and then pause when he veers away from the road I know leads back to the stone building where we left Oswy. In front of the burning building is where the fighting is most violent. Men move as though the sea against the land, wave after wave taking down some, while others fight for breath and to keep on their feet, heads popping up before being sucked back down once more.

I could force myself to Ælfstan's side, but Cenred is already there, great, sweeping strokes of his seax ensuring no one bothers Ælfstan. If I do the same, my shield will be a hindrance, not a help, and anyway, if we're about to leave this spot and return to the fort, then surely I should retrieve Oswy?

My indecision nearly costs me my life, as another huge piece of stone lands just beside my foot, the leering face of the stone-slinging Wessex warrior illuminated by a patch of moonlight. That decides it for me.

Turning, I dash back the way we've come. I need to reach Oswy and Tyrhtil. I'm sure that the others will extract themselves from the antagonistic fight.

My eyes quickly adjust to the darkness, and I don't fall. My steps are faster this time.

Within sight of the stone building, a Wessex warrior lurches into my path. He startles on seeing me, hastily rearranging his trews from where he must have been relieving himself.

'What's happening over there?' he demands to know, his eyes touching on my shield, making him think I'm an ally, not an enemy.

'Big bloody fire, and a fight to boost. The ealdorman isn't here.'

'No.' He shakes his head and almost stumbles with the motion. I can't tell why. 'The poor bastard is dead, seemingly killed by his own warriors, or that's what the one who yet lived told me.' He must speak of Oswy, and I hope he's not dead despite our less than pleasant relationship.

'So, who's in charge?' I ask him, turning, as he does, to look at the raging fire.

'Buggered if I know. But I'm not getting involved in all that. I'm going to the fort. What are you doing? Running away from the fight?' Despite his intentions, his words ripple with derision.

'It's not my fault,' I counter, checking the grip on my seax by releasing it and then gripping it more firmly again.

'Where are you from, Kent?' he continues.

I don't have time for this, so I pivot quickly, swinging my body in the opposite direction to the one I usually employ, and thrust my seax up into his armpit.

'No, I'm a Mercian,' I spit back at him. 'And we're going to win this war and kill your bastard king.'

His eyes open wide with shock and pain, but his hand covers mine before I can pull it clear with my seax.

'You little shit,' he glowers at me. The gap between us is too small for me to bring my shield into action, but I can feel his blood flowing over my hand. He's dying; he just doesn't know it yet.

'Aye,' I allow and use my right foot to stamp on his. He hops back, and the seax comes free, bringing with it blood that flows so thickly it's as black as night.

Free from him, I redouble my efforts to get to Oswy. It's possible that the man I just killed isn't the only one to have discovered what happened in the building.

Then, just before the steps that lead into it, a voice cries out from the darkness.

'Who goes there?'

The voice is unmistakably from Wessex, and I can't see who speaks.

I hesitate, unsure what to do now. This new threat may have a spear to fling at me or even be hiding just out of sight. I wish then I'd not left Ealdorman Ælfstan and Waldhere behind me. I could do more if I weren't alone.

I raise my shield and hold it to the right side of my body, peering out into the gloom, with my seax ready for whatever attack might be sprung on me now. Only then do I resume my run. If I can get inside the building, I'll have walls at my back to protect me. Oswy might be able to help me as well.

I dash up the few steps, mindful of creeping shadows, and then someone steps into my way. He's wounded, that much is immediately apparent as he holds on to the low wall, and in his right hand, he swings a huge war axe towards me. Its blade doesn't shimmer but is matted with blood and filth. I'm impressed he can hold it, let alone menace me with it. I brace to thrust my damaged shield hand to counter the blow; only he must be weaker than he thinks. He overbalances, the war axe sending him falling forwards towards me, and he's on me before I can move aside.

The shield is between us, but his weight crushes me as we fall one step and then another, and I can hardly breathe. I think I'll die here, like this, unable to move. I try kicking and forcing all my weight behind the shield, but it's just too painful. Even with my burned hand turned against the wood of the shield, it's agony, and I've lost my seax in the fall.

Worse, the man doesn't even fight against me. It's clear he's knocked himself out, and so he'll kill me without even trying.

'Help,' I call, wishing I didn't feel so frail at uttering those words. 'Help me,' I try again, managing to suck in more air this time.

Yet, I can hear no one coming. I need to get out on my own. But how? My body is crushed into the stone path, loose stones with their sharp corners sticking into my back.

I get my legs beneath the man who crushes me, but it does me no favours. If anything, all I succeed in doing is forcing him further over my chest. I extend my shield as high as I can with my knees, and then I feel some easing, and a perplexed face peers down at me.

It's Oswy.

'What are you doing?' he queries, doing his best to pull one of the man's arms aside.

'Coming to rescue you,' I huff. It's good to see him standing, even if he shouldn't be.

As the man's body slides half clear from me, I'm able to buck my body away from him, the shield coming free last of all, bringing a fresh wave of pain from my burn. I have to stop concentrating on just breathing to drive back the dizziness that means to have me join him on the stone floor.

'Well, I thank you.' Oswy attempts to smirk, only to stagger as well.

'Bloody hell.' I move as quickly as possible, regaining my feet and forcing my right shoulder beneath him to keep him on his feet. 'We're going back to the fort,' I inform him.

'What of the others?'

'Causing a fight down at the riverside gate. The only ship is gone, the quayside as well, and now the Wessex fools fight amongst themselves.'

'Right,' Oswy replies, but I can tell he's confused. I'm not surprised. His half-torn tunic drips with blood, for all his seared wound does seem to be holding.

'Come on. We'll do it together,' I confirm, but Oswy swallows and shakes his head.

'No, kill him first, and then we'll go.' He nods towards the slumped shape before us.

I think I've killed enough defenceless men today, but I slip my seax through his fat neck all the same. His body judders and then stills.

25

It's slow-going with Oswy. But I'm amazed he can move at all. Another man would merely lie there and allow the Wessex warriors to come for him. But not Oswy.

I'm reminded of Oswy's knowing smirk when King Wiglaf's queen embarrassed Edwin on that long-ago day at Tamworth, when her son was able to beat Edwin in a fight, because Edwin was purposefully tripped by Eahric. Is Oswy the same man to laugh at a young lad, or has he changed since that happened? I can hardly tell, and I'm unsure if I much care. My childhood friend Edwin let me down, staying at Kingsholm when Cenfrith and I were forced out. Oswy, for all his humiliations, has fought at my side. Mind, he wasn't best pleased when he discovered I might have saved his life. But, for now, that remains to be seen. Oswy might still die.

Neither of us speaks as we labour, like some strange three-legged creature, towards the fort. I direct our steps to find Tyrhtil, but he's not where I last saw him. I think to call his name, but Oswy growls at me, and I move on, uneasy. Does Tyrhtil know that Briht-wold is dead? Does Tyrhtil even still live?

Overhead, I can tell that the night is moving on apace. The

moon emits the thinnest beams of light between the dark and fore-boding clouds, but for the time being, it doesn't rain, although water drips all around us. The ancient stone is pitted and filled with puddles.

I carry my seax in my hand, although my shield repeatedly bangs against Oswy's legs, and I'm tempted to disentangle it from my aching hand. I've either become used to the pain, or it's dimming. I suspect I've become used to it. No burn like that would heal without the correct treatment. Longingly, I think of the supplies in Ecgred's workshop, but I can't get to them at the moment. My priority is Oswy and ensuring he makes it back to the fort's safety.

To begin with, we're lucky. No Wessex warriors see us or question what we're doing. We pass buildings that have been pressed into use once more, thatch or canvas, stretched over where the roofs have long since collapsed. We even pass the shelter where I slept after the battle to cross the River Fleet. I try not to consider that, of the three of us beneath the half-roof, I might by the only who yet lives.

As I'm deep in thought, our luck finally runs out. The fort comes into view, a black-edged object against the blueish-black of the night sky, and abruptly, I can hear weapons and someone engaged in a loud and foul-mouthed argument.

'Let us in, you damn swine,' someone calls, fists pounding against the small wooden door.

'Over here,' I caution Oswy, moving him from the weed-tumbled road so that we can stand behind the remains of a building and try to work out what's happening. There's a group of our enemy.

'Bugger,' Oswy groans, leaning against the wall so that I can move without taking him with me.

I don't crouch down, but rather peer around the edges of the stone walls, trying to take a reckoning of the Wessex warriors there. There must be nearly twenty of them. At the same time, I endeavour to ensure the Mercians still hold the fort intact. I consider whether the ealdorman and the others have already made it safely inside. Are we the only ones stuck here? I wouldn't be surprised. It took me a long time to get Oswy this far.

'What should we do?' I turn to Oswy. He has his eyes closed, sweat beading down his face. He won't be able to fight in that state, and I'm also hampered.

'We have until the sun comes up to decide,' is his less than helpful response.

I'm unsure. Is Ealdorman Ælfstan already behind the wooden door and the thick stone walls, or will he appear and assist me? I wish I knew.

Oswy mumbles, the sound low in his chest. It speaks to me of a man in indescribable pain, and I've nothing to offer him. But, Ecgred's workshop is near. Dare I risk going there? I'm torn with indecision.

'We could go back to the wall?' Oswy whispers, as before the door of the fort, the Wessex warriors, finally realising that something is very, very wrong, begin to attack the wooden door in a concerted effort to get inside. The crashing sound makes it difficult to hear Oswy's quiet words.

'Bugger. They know the Mercians are in there.'

'But are they seeking out more Mercians?' Oswy makes a fair point.

'We should wait,' I decide, just as Oswy says the opposite.

'We should leave.'

'It's a long way, from here, and you can hardly walk, and neither of us can protect one another.'

'We can make it,' Oswy says through gritted teeth.

'What if the tunnel's blocked? Wulfgar might have forced

himself free, but we didn't remove the blockage altogether, and neither of us can do it alone.'

'So, what, you don't even want to try?' Oswy's fury is sharper than a blade.

'I didn't say that. The ealdorman might appear any moment now.'

'He might yes, or he might be inside the fort, and we can't get beyond our foemen. Listen to them?'

Our enemy is howling at the Mercians inside the fort. I hope Godeman has a firm hand on the Mercians he has command over. If not, they might just do something that would see us all die.

'We can go to the healer's workshop,' I offer as an alternative. 'At least from there, I can get some medicine to ease our pain. We can continue to the wall thereafter if we need to do so.'

Oswy's nose wrinkles in disgust at the suggestion, but then three more Wessex warriors run past us, on the way to joining their comrades, their weapons waving angrily, and he relents. 'Get me there, and get me something so that I can at least fight without feeling every bloody throb of agony through my chest.'

I open my mouth to tell him he's not the only one in pain, but I snap it shut again. I'm not about to argue with him about who's in the most pain. As Wynflæd told me, every man and woman feels it differently, and it's not for me to belittle the child who sobs from a broken leg while a man weeps and wails from a splinter in his finger.

'Let me help you.' Once more, we move as though a strange three-legged creature, and one that scuttles amongst the ancient ruins.

First, we need to cross the expanse where the Wessex warriors just ran. The movement reminds me too much of when we needed to evade our enemy when Edwin, Cenfrith and I were on the borderlands between Mercia and the Welsh kingdoms. A stab of sorrow for all I've lost since then almost makes me sob, distracting me from my throbbing hand.

While Oswy looks towards the fort, I gaze into the dark reaches of Londinium, and when we're both convinced no one will see us, we skitter across the road and hunker down behind a squat building. Thin tendrils of smoke escape through the roof, assuring me that it was recently occupied.

Our progress is painfully slow. I wish, more than once, that we could have made it inside the fort. I feel exposed from all sides, and I don't believe that Oswy and I can mount any sort of defence between the two of us. He's growing weaker and therefore heavier on my shoulder, and I try to urge him to move more quickly, but it only makes him go slower and slower.

I allow him to rest as frequently as I can so that I can recover.

Whatever is happening at the fort fades slowly into the background. I concentrate only on moving forwards, on reaching our destination. Then, when it's in sight, I realise my mistake. There's no one inside the workshop now. There's no fire for me to mix a potion to give us both strength. There's no one to help me grind and cut the herbs I need. And, there's no bloody great big door to ensure the Wessex warriors won't come for us to finish the job they've started on Oswy.

But Oswy is beyond caring by now.

I cry with relief when I can finally allow Oswy to lie down once more. His entire body shudders, and I can see that tendrils of blood are oozing from his wound. It must hurt like a bastard.

I turn to the empty hearth, noting that there are logs and pieces of kindle to start a fire but no means of doing so. I need hot water and heat, but I won't be getting any unless I run back towards one of the temporary shelters the Wessex warriors have used. And I'm not prepared to leave Oswy to fend for himself. It's too apparent, to my eyes at least, that he's a Mercian, and it's not just the weapons he holds with their eagle emblems on handle and hilt, pommel cap and sword buttons.

I lift my hand with the shield still attached to it and fiddle with the leather thong, but the damn thing has become twisted and holds my wrist in its grip. Wishing I had something better than my left hand to perform the delicate task, I cut away the leather ties and look at my burn. It's too dark to make out much detail, and I'm grateful for that.

'Here.' Oswy fumbles with something on his weapons belt and hands it to me. 'You do know how to use it, don't you?' he asks, and I nod. I do know how to use a striking stone, not that something made of iron should be termed a stone.

All the same, I eagerly bring forth a spark by rubbing the two ends one over another, and the flame quickly transfers from my hands to the kindling and then to the wood itself.

Ideally, I'd like to take the time to rest, but I feel too exposed. I turn to the supplies on display and reach for items I need for a healing wound and a healing pottage. I'm hungry and growing weaker the longer I delay eating.

I place oats and some water left in a jug on the side into one silvered cauldron. I sniff it and then swallow it. It's not fresh, but dead flies don't pollute it. It'll have to do. Then I reach for more items: garlic, nettles, yarrow and wild carrot. My hands skitter over the jars, opening lids with my left hand as I cradle the jars close to my chest with my right arm. It's slow and painful work, and that's before I've even thought to cut the herbs and leaves to the required size.

Oswy snores softly from the corner, and while he sleeps, I examine his wound. When he's still and unmoving, other than for breathing, the injury seems well enough, but I can see where blood leaks from a section I've not sealed shut with the heat of my seax. I could stitch it closed, but I can't thread the needle, not with my right hand so unresponsive.

I stir the cauldron with the oats and add garlic leaves, unchopped, and nettles. I can't cut them any smaller, so I add many more than I usually would. I hope the goodness will be released from the leaves as I purposefully try to crush them with the wooden spoon I use.

Next, I look for vinegar. It'll sting, but I need it to clean my hand and Oswy's wound. There's a whole host of jugs of assorted sizes, and, of course, the one I need is firmly sealed with a plug of moss, and no matter what I do, I can't pull the plug loose.

'Bugger,' I complain, foiled in my attempts while Oswy sleeps. If he were awake, he'd be able to pull the plug away, but I can't.

By now, and with some encouragement, for the wood doesn't wish to burn well, I have some warm water in another silvered cauldron, hanging over the fire thanks to the wooden and metal contraption above it, from which chains hold the pots in place. I move it aside and splash some of it into a wooden bowl. Returning the cauldron to the heat, I add the yarrow and woodruff and two fat dandelion leaves that are just starting to curl. Again, I can't cut the herbs as small as I want to. I opt for quantity over quality.

I crush woodruff, lily and brooklime into a paste with the spoon and only then, hesitantly, and knowing it will hurt, do I place my right hand into the wooden bowl of cooling water. I gasp at the shudder of pain and blink back tears. I might have thought I burned my hand badly last time when I endeavoured to heal Cenfrith, but this time, I've done far more damage. I judder, cold sweat breaking out on my forehead, and still, I hold my hand beneath the water. I need it to be as clean as possible before binding it with the poultice.

Using my left hand instead of my right, it's challenging to carry out all the tasks. I feel awkward and clumsy. Lifting my hand clear from the water, I move closer to the fire and examine the welts in the light of the flame. I gasp at the sight. Where before, the image of Mercia's eagle had transferred faintly from the copper wire twisted around the hilt of my seax, this time, it seems to have burned even deeper. It's easy to make out the beak, the single, staring eye. I try to clench my fist, but that makes me sweat once more.

I turn aside, keen to pack the wound with the poultice I've made. I coat the palm of my hand with the slick substance. I've no butter to use, but I've made use of something else in one of the jars, which I suspect to be the oil from crushed flowers. It almost does the same job as the butter.

Carefully, I bind my hand with a clean-looking piece of linen and only then do I stir the cauldron once more, my stomach growling as the rich smell of garlic washes over me.

I pull it away from the heat of the fire, leaving the other cauldron with the salve in it to bubble and boil. Once it's done, I'll also add some of the oil to it, and then I'll be able to apply it to Oswy's wound. All the time, I'm alert to any noise coming from outside. Surely, I think, someone will notice that the workshop is being used once more.

The flames from the fire concern me most, and it's a relief when the darkness of night gives way to the grey gloom of dawn. The fire will be less noticeable now.

All the same, I wake Oswy from his sleep.

He barely opens one eye as he batters aside my insistent hand.

'You need to wake up and eat, and I have a poultice for your wound.'

At those words, he groans, and his eyes open wide. He turns and vomits. I grimace at the stink. At least he wasn't sick on me, I decide.

'Bugger, it hurts.'

'Yes, it bloody will.' As much as I would appreciate some sympathy for my wound, I know better than to offer any. Wynflæd seemed as caring as a heated blade in her exchanges with her patients, and yet she cured them all the same.

I move to spoon the pottage into a bowl, held in the crook of my arm, and hand it awkwardly to Oswy, where he's managed to force himself into a sitting position.

'I need to drink,' he says.

'I only have one hand. Give me a moment.' If we stay here for much longer, I'll need to find water, which will mean leaving the workshop and Oswy.

I splash what little there is of the remaining water into a wooden beaker and hand it to Oswy.

'Slowly,' I caution him when he goes to gulp it back. 'You'll make yourself sick again if you drink too much.'

He slows his drinking and then picks at his pottage, wrinkling at his nose.

'Well, you're not much of a cook, are you?' he complains. It seems he expects a feast, even now.

'If you don't eat it, you won't start to heal,' I advise him and eagerly begin to eat my portion. I balance the bowl on my knee and eat with my left hand. I admit it doesn't have much taste to it, but it's warm and filling, and I swallow it all without complaint.

Oswy takes his time, his eyes peering into the recesses of the workshop as though seeking out our enemy. Now that he's awake, I can tell he's unsettled.

As soon as he's finished eating, I make him lie down and carefully examine his wound before applying the salve to his chest and once more binding it.

'It needs some stitches,' I inform him. 'But I can't do them now. I can't thread the needle, and I doubt you'd be able to either.' Oswy has enormous hands. The thought of asking him to pull a pig's gut through the eye of a needle is laughable.

He hisses and bucks beneath my ministrations.

'Keep as still as you can,' I advise him, but it seems that as gentle as I'm being, it's not gentle enough.

'What do we do next?' he asks me, distracting himself from what I'm doing.

'We need to escape or get to the fort.' I've not looked outside. I've certainly not gone to see what's happening in front of the fort. I would hope that the Mercians have prevailed, but I don't know the ealdorman's next intentions. Indeed, he must be considering fighting his way to the gates and opening them to allow the Mercians inside by now.

'Which is the quickest way out of this hellhole?' Oswy asks, the word ending on a gasp of pain as I secure the bandage more tightly.

'Neither. We're almost in the middle of both places, as far as I can tell.'

'Bloody wonderful.' Oswy sags back against the bed. I realise I'm burdened with someone too injured to move and yet whom I need to encourage anyway. I hope that, unlike Cenfrith, Oswy doesn't determine on saving others before himself.

Around his heavy breathing, I hear a noise and startle.

'Did you hear that?' I whisper, but Oswy shakes his head.

I reach for my seax with my right hand and then switch it to the left one when it's both too painful to grip and impossible with the poultice I've applied to it. The sound comes again. I can't determine if it's careful steps over gravel and stone or something else entirely.

I move to the side of the open door and peer out. My view is obscured. I can only see what might be coming at me from the right and in front. I've no idea if someone is coming from the left. But then I hear another grinding noise, and my head flicks to the back entrance.

'Stay here,' I caution Oswy. He's sitting upright, his hand fumbling for his seax where it still hangs on his weapons belt. He's heard the noise as well.

I scurry beyond the fire and then through into the shadowy recesses of what was a storeroom when Ecgred lived. It's gloomy in there, the roof almost touching the ground where it hangs low. But I'm sure the noise is coming from out there.

I rush to the doorway, looking out on to the ruins. The abandoned stone flashes beneath the sunlight, but I still can't see anyone. And then the noise comes once more, and I think I know what it is this time.

26

Someone else has had the same thought as me and means to make use of the abandoned supplies within the healer's workshop.

'Shit,' I grunt, trying again to grip my seax with my right hand. Even a wounded man might still prevail against my left hand if this comes down to a fight. And Oswy will be no use to me. He's more likely to fall over just by standing than confront one of our enemies.

Once more, my heartbeat thuds in my ears, making it almost impossible to hear, but I don't move. This doorway is squat. If a Wessex warrior is coming this way, it's better to encounter him here than anywhere else.

Now, I can hear the agonised groaning of a man. His words are too soft for me to make out, but he mutters under his breath, no doubt encouraging himself onwards. Just one more step. A little further now. I know the arguments well enough.

When the man is as close as possible without actually being inside the workshop, I step outside, seax returned to my left hand. But I'm not prepared, not at all, for the sight that greets me. Before I can stab down, using the seax to slice through the man's neck, where he slides, more than crawls along the roadway, I recognise him.

'Tyrhtil?' I gasp. I confess I'd thought him dead when I couldn't find him behind the forum.

'Icel.' He tilts his head up to see me, his voice less than a rasp. I can see where he's rested his cheek on the uneven road and forced an imprint of stones on to his blood-drenched cheek.

'I thought you were dead,' we both say at the same time. No doubt when I didn't return for Tyrhtil, he assumed the worse. Equally, when I couldn't find him, I presumed he too was dead.

I put my seax back on my weapons belt as I bend to help him stand.

'Where's Brihtwold?'

I swallow against the grief inside me that threatens to spill.

'He's dead,' Oswy calls without any sympathy. 'He tried to kill Icel.'

The words are like a blow to Tyrhtil. I see his body shudder.

'The lad was loyal to his homeland,' Tyrhtil moans.

I don't know what to say to that. Silence hangs between us, punctuated only by his groans of pain.

'You said you'd protect him.'

I close my eyes. I don't want to be reminded of this.

'And he tried to,' Oswy calls once more. He's made it to his feet and sways just as alarmingly as Tyrhtil. 'But the bastard tried to kill him, regardless.'

Understanding washes over Tyrhtil's face, and then he staggers again.

'Then it's all over.' His words are more an exhalation of thought than spoken.

'Not for you,' I urge him. I can heal him. I know I can.

'But there's nothing for me to live for if the boy is dead,' Tyrhtil persists.

'Yes, there is,' I huff, trying to get Tyrhtil to move into the main room of the workshop. 'Someone needs to mourn his death and tell his family, and that needs to be you.'

'No,' Tyrhtil insists.

I stop, stand my ground and look at him. 'My uncle died on the edge of a Wessex blade. I mourn him and honour him by living while he's dead. You'll do the same.' I'm surprised by the bite in my words and by how right they feel.

'But—' Tyrhtil tries to argue with me.

'Oh, shut the hell up,' Oswy interjects. 'Let the boy treat you, and then you're free to decide whether you want to live or die, but you crawled here, from the look of you. That speaks to me of a man who wants to live.'

Tyrhtil glowers. I anticipate him lashing out at Oswy, but instead, he nods his head.

'Aye, you might have the right of that. Come, Icel, show me what you can do to cure this old bugger, and then I'll decide what to do with the both of you.' The words are almost full of humour, but they still sting me, all the same.

'Has the fort fallen?' I ask him, manoeuvring him into position to get a good look at his wounds from where he perches on another of the cot beds.

'How would I know? I've spent the night crawling here, and I've seen no one.'

Tyrhtil grips my bandaged hand then, and I wince.

'What have you done to yourself?' There's fear in his words.

'A burn. It'll heal,' I advise him, snatching my hand back before he can squeeze it any tighter, my eyes flicking over the blistering on his chin. At some point, during his journey here, he's popped the blister, and now it oozes a disgusting yellow liquid, mixed with the remaining hair of his beard and the muck he's picked up along the way.

'Where are the slaves?' he demands to know.

'Not here. I'll do what I can, for now, and then when the Mercians hold Londinium once more, I'll ensure the slaves are allowed to tend to you.'

Tyrhtil looks uneasy at my words, but what choice does he have?

Quickly, I move to the fire and add more wood to it. The heat springs up immediately. My next concern is water, or rather, a lack of it.

'Stay here,' I order both Oswy and Tyrhtil. I have to hope that they don't attempt to kill one another while I'm gone. It might make it easier for me in the long run, but it'll be bloody messy and probably noisy as well.

I take both jugs with me as I exit through the rear of the workshop and quickly make my way to the nearest well. Glancing all around, I seek out other Mercians or Wessex warriors, but there's no one close. I also peer into the distance, but I can't see the fort well enough to determine what happens there. Unease makes my movements jagged. I almost drop the jug I cup with my right arm.

The water isn't the clearest when I dip the jug into the well, but I know of nowhere else. I'll just have to boil it all before we drink it. The jugs are heavy once they're full, and I have to clutch them against my body because I can't carry them both with the pain from my right hand. They were heavy even without the water added to the weight. I go carefully. I don't want to slop the water onto my hand or feet.

Entering the workshop with some caution, I can hear nothing but the dull rumble of the two men speaking.

'Here we go,' I interrupt them.

Adding more oats to the healing pottage, I also add a small amount of water. I'm not going to waste any of it. Next, I tip the contents of the remaining salve onto the wooden worktop and add more water to the pot. This I return to the fire while also hooking the other cauldron and splashing the contents of one of the jugs into it. That'll be to drink once it's boiled away the filth of the well. I add more yarrow and woodruff to the water and a generous amount of birthwort and agrimony. Only then do I turn to Tyrhtil.

He looks no better in the gloom of the workshop. If anything, it only makes his pale face even more apparent.

'Where are you wounded? Other than your face and the wound I first treated?'

'It's the same wound. It's opened again. I took a fresh cut to my belly.'

'Show me,' I demand, but I'm already fearful that I might have promised something I can't achieve.

Tyrhtil lifts his ruined tunic, hanging in strips of fabric over his chest, and I wince. The wound that I stitched is pink and angry. Some of the stitches have come apart on the left side of his body. Through the torn stitches, I can see where his innards attempt to escape once more. But that's not the end of Tyrhtil's wounds. He also has another deep cut running beneath his arm, lengthwise, on his chest so that it almost meets his belly wound.

'How many did you fight?' I demand from him, shaking my head. There's a lot here that needs treatment. I'm glad that I only have two patients, or I'd not be able to give either the attention they need.

'Enough,' Tyrhtil grunts.

'I'm going to clean away the grime on your face first.' It's not the priority, but it's the easiest of the three injuries to tend to, and it'll be easier for me to look at him without the yellow ooze on his chin.

As carefully as I can, I clear away the muck with a piece of linen. I've found a sack filled with torn rags hanging over one of the shelves in preparation for such treatments. Tyrhtil growls through tight lips as I work. Then, I smear in the same paste I've put on my hand, although I can't bind the paste there. In the end, I realise, replacing the yellow puss with the green paste doesn't make Tyrhtil look that much better.

Next, I tend to his belly wound.

'It hurts?' I ask him.

'Of course, it bloody hurts,' he grumbles.

'That's a good sign,' I inform him and start to explore the fresh wound by walking the finger of my left hand over it. 'There's a lot of bruising here.' I'm not sure if he did that with his crawling or in the heat of the battle.

'That's the least of my worries,' Tyrhtil retorts, but he winces as my fingers explore.

I'm convinced that the bruising is accounting for the majority of his pain. I also examine the other wound. It's at least as deep as the nail on my small finger, and it's bled a great deal, but now the crust of a scab is there.

'Open this for me.' I take the vinegar jar to Oswy. 'I can't do it with one hand. But be careful,' I caution him hurriedly when I fear the contents will pour all over the floor.

Oswy hands it back to me. His expression is inscrutable.

'This will hurt,' I inform Tyrhtil.

He snaps his teeth shut, gritting them against the pain. He bucks and twists as the vinegar slides over both wounds. I work quickly then to clean them and apply the healing salve. I add a covering of moss for the belly wound because it's easy to tie a bandage around. For the long, slicing cut, I merely pack it with the healing salve.

'I could bind it, but that would be your entire chest, and it would be difficult to move.' I leave unsaid my fear that both men will need to fight their way out of Londinium at some point. I can't see that they haven't realised that.

Although Tyrhtil is in pain, sweat streaking his chest, he doesn't complain, and I admire his resolve. I offer him a bowl of pottage when it's cooked and then cooled water to drink. Everything feels subdued, as though we're just waiting for the fighting to resume again. I'm pleased Tyrhtil doesn't ask me about Brihtwold again.

I sit on the floor, rest my head on the wood of one of the two beds and, even though I don't mean to, close my eyes.

When I wake, it's growing dark outside once more, and the rain has resumed. The fire is little more than embers. I can hear the snoring of the two injured men. I'm not sure what woke me, and then realise it's because I need to piss. I scramble to my feet and move to the rear of the workshop, slipping through the back door and standing just below the thatch, adding my water to that which thunders from the sky. I can see next to nothing. Everything is watery, and there's no sign of movement or flame light throughout Londinium. But that means nothing with the visibility so poor.

Returning inside, I flex my right hand, feel the ache and stabbing pain of the burn, and wish I'd not thought to use it just yet.

I move to where the front door should be and gaze towards the fort. I need to get Oswy and Tyrhtil to it, but I don't know if the Wessex warriors are still battling to get inside. If they are, there'll be no chance of escaping that way. Instead, I'll need to return to the drainage channel and hope Tyrhtil and Oswy can fit through the gap, despite their injuries.

'What is it, Icel?' It's Oswy who speaks.

'Nothing. Just checking, but it's impossible to see anything with the rain.'

'Then it's the ideal time to move on.' Oswy labours to a sitting position. 'No one will be expecting people to be out in such weather. I can feel the cold from here.'

I sigh with unhappiness because Oswy is right.

'But which way?' I ask.

'The wall, it's the safest option.'

'It might be, but it won't be easy and what if you can't make it through the gap?'

'Then I'll damn well climb it and take my chances.'

'Suit yourself.'

'What are you talking about?' Tyrhtil's words are slurred with sleep.

'Escaping.' I move to check on him as he wakes, adding the small amount of remaining wood to the fire as I go.

'I thought the Mercians held Londinium?' Tyrhtil winces as he speaks, and I can feel the heat from here. That isn't a good sign.

'They do, but as of yet, we can't get inside the fort.'

'So, what, you mean to escape back to the Mercian camp?'

'We need to do something. We can't stay here and wait for the Mercians. I'd have thought they'd be here by now. But it seems not.'

Tyrhtil leers at me. 'Perhaps the Mercians don't hold Londinium then, and I should hand you over to the Wessex warriors.'

My hand stills at his words. I snatch it back even though my intention has been to check on his bandage and healing salve.

I can sense Oswy struggling to his feet.

'Why would you do that?'

'You killed young Brihtwold. I can see you dead to repay the favour.' Tyrhtil's words are furious.

'You have a fever,' I snap at him. 'You're not thinking straight.'

'Oh, but I am, much more clearly than since I first encountered you and Brihtwold. If I hand you over to the ealdorman, then I can return to Wessex and live out the rest of my days in some peace and quiet.'

'There won't be any more living if you don't let the lad help you, and I won't allow him to do so unless you swear on your life to keep our presence secret.' Oswy's words are spoken with a thrum of fury. The speed of his movements assures me he must be feeling better. 'And the ealdorman is dead. Didn't you know that?'

'All I need to do,' Tyrhtil crows, 'is to shout, and the Wessex warriors will come running.'

I'm not sure of that, but all the same, I don't know how many warriors remain alive inside Londinium. Neither do I know Tyrhtil well enough to decipher if he means what he says or is just toying with us in his delirium.

'You won't kill me,' Tyrhtil glowers at Oswy, who holds his seax right in front of the other man's nose, menacing with it. 'Icel won't allow you to. His heart is too soft.'

I don't appreciate the taunt and the way he sneers at me. It transforms him from the jolly individual he'd been when he thought me a Wessex warrior.

'Look, he was sent behind the walls to kill all the Wessex warriors, and what did he do? Put his skills to work healing us all so that we could live to fight another day. He has no desire to kill, only to heal.' I've never considered my skills as something to be so openly derided. I glance to Oswy. I don't know him well enough to know how he'll react to Tyrhtil's hot words.

'Icel doesn't have a soft heart,' Oswy continues to glower. 'He killed Wessex warriors to keep our king alive. He sacrificed his uncle to ensure our king could reclaim his kingdom from your weak-willed fool of a king. He does have a keen desire to stay alive. He did what needed to be done inside Londinium. After all, the Mercians hold the fort, your ealdorman is dead, and Lord Æthelwulf has fled. There are no more than a handful of you Wessex scum left, and while he might have healed you or started the process, it's hardly kept you alive for much longer, has it?'

'Perhaps,' Tyrhtil continues to burble. 'But will you take that risk?'

I want to tell Oswy to stop, because his seax is now biting into Tyrhtil's skin close to his throat. I want to tell him that Tyrhtil is sick. But I'm equally astounded to hear him applauding me for what I've done. I was aware he knew of my actions in the fight with the Wessex warriors in the borderlands, but other than Wulfheard and Ealdorman Ælfstan, no one has praised me, apart from Lady Cynehild.

I'm also unsure about whether I want him to leave Tyrhtil alone. I did think I knew Tyrhtil, and had found someone I could count as a friend, even if he should have been my enemy. In his delirium, Tyrhtil has forgotten all that, and it's a problem. I can't defend Oswy and myself if someone does heed Tyrhtil's call for help. Unease fills me.

'Standing with Icel is no risk,' Oswy glowers, continuing to menace with his blade. Tyrhtil has no weapon. But he sucks in air, his chest expanding, as though to gather enough to shout to his fellow warriors. The two are like old, tired bears, trying to fight with their lost strength of youth, but Oswy is the strongest. He can stand without swaying, and he has a blade in his hand.

I want to turn aside, not watch Oswy make a ruin of Tyrhtil. After all, Tyrhtil has aided us, helped me. But before the Wessex warrior can open his mouth to shout of our existence, I watch as the thread of blood on Tyrhtil's neck grows longer and then wider, blood beginning to pool down his chest. I can't look away. I can't even close my eyes as Oswy cuts Tyrhtil's throat wide open.

And then Tyrhtil's body bucks and slides down onto the bed he's been resting on. Oswy turns to meet my gaze. I don't know what he sees in my eyes. It isn't horror, because his actions don't horrify me. He killed our enemy to ensure we lived. I'll miss Tyrhtil, I won't deny that, but at the end, he became my enemy just as Brihtwold did. And, there was never a guarantee that Tyrhtil would survive his wounds. I've done what I could, but would he have made it the Mercian camp? I really don't know. I can't forget that he was a Wessex warrior, not a Mercian one.

Oswy nods, and at that moment, I feel as though I've become his equal, not a lad just to tolerate because his lord demanded it from him.

'Come on, Icel. We need to escape.' I know he's right.

With a parting look at Tyrhtil's still form, I swallow around the stab of grief I feel, and move towards the back of the workshop.

The rain continues to fall, as though determined to drown out all sound, and that's both to our advantage and disadvantage.

'Follow me,' I caution Oswy. I've not spoken to him since he killed Tyrhtil, not even to thank him for protecting us from Tyrhtil's shrieks.

At the last moment, I turn back into the workshop, a memory tugging at me. I pull two cloaks from a peg where they've been abandoned. They're both woefully short for us, but they have hoods that might protect us from the worst of the rain. We've not had cloaks since we abandoned them at the fort.

I help Oswy swirl his cloak around his body, noting the massive gap from above his knee to his feet which isn't covered by the material. Then I do the same, and together, we leave the workshop, our steps slowed by Oswy's wounds.

I don't look back. I never want to see that place again, no matter the wealth of supplies it holds.

In no time at all, I'm drenched, despite my cloak, water dripping from the too-short hood to land on my chin and in my eyes when the wind blows the rain in a sudden squall. We quickly reach the well where I gathered the water, and I move us close to the exterior wall as soon as I can. It would be too easy not to see the gap in the wall through the watery torrent in front of us.

I don't pause or allow too much extra time for Oswy to mirror my movements. We're alone and exposed to whatever has happened between the rest of the Mercian warriors and the Wessex foemen. Oswy is wounded, although he's shown he can still kill a man quickly enough.

As the rain blows from the east, the wall provides some relief from the deluge when we're able to keep close to it. Still, in many places, we have to avoid the tangled ruins of broken-down walls and the reaching ruins of weeds and brambles that have enjoyed their day in the sun but are now slowly dying, if far from giving up the fight. I stumble and fall, elbow-deep in a thick patch of nettles, and immediately, both hands begin to itch uncomfortably, the irritating sting of them making me hunt for a dock leaf when I've regained my feet.

Not that I find one until the initial sting has become almost unbearable. Bad enough that my burn aches, throbs and itches, now the rest of my palm is as itchy.

Eagerly, I sniff and then rub my hands on three of the leaves, the relief immediate. I don't stop walking. Behind me, Oswy groans and heaves in breath, but doesn't complain, not once. And then finally, I'm sure we're in the very spot where we gained entry. I recognise the pile of rocks where we hid the dead Wessex warriors, but my heart stills when I can't see the gap in the stone wall.

'No,' I moan low in my throat, scurrying forwards to peer closer and closer in the gloom. It's easy enough to find the drainage ditch, but there's no more than a palm's-width gap below the stone, which had been loose enough to move aside. 'The stone's shifted,' I admit with defeat to Oswy. 'It'll be impossible to move it between the two of us.' I glance back towards where I know the blackness of the fort is.

'We're not giving up,' Oswy announces. 'I've not walked all the way here, just to give up. Come on, help me.'

But I shake my head. 'It took three of us the first time, and the gap was five times as big as it is now. It can't be done.'

'There is no can't, Icel. We have to do this, and you'll help me or, so help me, I'll hold a seax to your throat as well, and see how you like it.'

I turn to face him. In the gloom of the low-hanging cloud, the constant rainfall and with his face pale as a dead man, Oswy looks menacing. I fear him at that moment. I'm too terrified to argue with him.

'Help me, then,' I urge him, bending to the piece of stone. It's slick, and my hands slide painfully off its surface, so cold that it's as though they've been stabbed. 'Bugger.' I hop on the spot, hands throbbing from the cold, the contact with the stone, from the pinpricks of the nettles, from the burn that has cut me deeply, all coming to the fore. 'I can't bloody do this,' I roar at Oswy. All of my fury, grief and frustrations fill that moment in time as I shake my hands, trying to dispel the pain and the sickening sensations running through them and my body. 'I don't want to be here. I never wanted to be here. This isn't what I should be doing with my bloody life.'

Oswy rears back at my rage. His eyes are wary but implacable. 'Your uncle was a fool when he made you think there was a bloody choice, Icel. There's no choice. Not while Mercia is threatened and weak. Would you have Wynflæd cower in fear once more? Would you have Lady Cynehild torn from the monastery and raped? Would you allow that to happen just because you'd rather be sheltering in the skirts of Wynflæd? As much as healing is a skill, it's only needed because of Mercia's bloody enemies. Icel, listen to yourself. Do you need others to protect you because your hand hurts? Grow up and get on with it.'

Oswy bends to the task, the back of his cloak all that I can see, and my rage bubbles and burbles, and then abruptly drains away when I think of my uncle's sacrifice and of Wynflæd, even Lady

Cynehild. I can't abandon them to life under the yoke of another when I have it in me to prevent it.

I slide my hands beneath the stone, questing for a rough patch that I can grip more tightly with my fingers. I don't even look at Oswy.

'On three,' he huffs and then counts, and I strain. My hand screams in agony, my back cries out in pain, and still, I don't let go. I'll move the damn stone. I vow it. I breathe in through my nose, out through my mouth, repeating the action time and time again, and slowly, imperceptibly, I hear the groan of the stone grating against others.

It finally gives, and with it, Oswy tumbles to the floor. As the stone clears the longed-for gap in the drainage ditch, a surge of water trundles beneath the wall to thunder over the side of the high wall and then into the pit of murk which must be twice as deep by now.

'Get on your feet and through the damn gap.' There's no compassion in my voice. Oswy has forced me to face some uncomfortable truths. I'll show him no sympathy.

Oswy holds out his hand, and I wrench on it. He surges to his feet, lips curled over his teeth, so he snarls.

'If I get stuck,' he spits at me. 'Force me through, no matter what you have to do.'

'I'll do what needs to be done,' I assure him, and he lies down as soon as the worst of the water has drained away.

I see him shudder, the coldness of the rain immediately permeating through his cloak, trews, tunic and byrnie. And then he forces himself through, feet first, head the last thing to disappear. I can smell him when I crouch by his head, pushing it when he appears stuck, with my left hand. He holds, for what feels like an eternity, and then with a wet sound, he disappears. I snarl with laughter on hearing his exclamations of disgust for landing in the huge puddle on the other side.

I lie down, feet and legs as far under the wall as I can get them, and shuffle my way forward. The water once more surges around me, and for a moment, I fear it'll cover my mouth and nose, but the stone passes over my face. I all but shoot through the channel, landing with a cry of shock into the pool of water that's waist-high.

'Bugger,' I exclaim, finding my feet and wading clear of the mess. Oswy stands watching me, dripping wet, his cloak half off and half on, and the damn bastard is laughing at me. I consider punching him, but I shake myself and glance down at my shabby appearance. A smile plays around my lips as well.

'Come on, you daft sod,' he calls to me. 'Time to make our triumphant return to the Mercian camp.'

27

I've never shivered so much in my short life. By the time we stagger into the Mercian camp, having first argued with the watchman on duty, who's more stubborn than Oswy about allowing entry, I can't feel my body below the neck. Oswy's almost crawling.

'What happened to you two?' I look up from holding my hands towards a random campfire, pulling my clothes from my body at the same time, and catch sight of the perplexed expression of Ealdorman Tidwulf. He's dressed warmly. I envy him the thick fur-lined cloak he wears.

'We had to escape from inside Londinium.'

'But where's everyone else?' Naked to the waist, I glower at Tidwulf, teeth chattering.

'Haven't the Mercians opened the fort for you?' I feel sure that Ealdorman Ælfstan will have been successful in his endeavours by now.

'No.' The ealdorman watches me with unflinching eyes. I turn to look at Oswy, but he's shaking so violently that he doesn't hear the ealdorman. 'Where's Ealdorman Ælfstan?'

I'm finding it hard to think. I'm just too damn cold. 'They were fighting, by the riverside gate, two nights ago. Didn't you see the flames from here? The fire was huge.'

'Yes, we did.'

I'm not sure if Ealdorman Tidwulf is being purposefully obtuse with his answers.

'I went to get Oswy from where we'd left him, injured in the ealdorman's hall. We were to meet them at the fort, but by the time we reached the place, there was a host of Wessex warriors preventing us from getting inside.' By now, I've removed my trews, and someone has flung a dry cloak at me. They've clearly taken it from their shoulders. The heat is welcome, if not the smell. Theodore also appears alongside the ealdorman. He assists Oswy, who's beyond doing anything. He's pushed himself to the end of his endurance. I pity him, even as I try to understand what Ealdorman Tidwulf's saying to me. 'Has the Mercian banner not been flying from the fort?' I demand. I feel sure that's what had been agreed.

'No. The fort's been quiet. The gates haven't opened, and we've seen no one on guard duty. What have you done to Oswy?' Tidwulf queries, as both Theodore and Gaya bend to assist him. I'm shocked by the sight of Oswy's blue flesh, even as I'm pleased to see that Theodore and Gaya move with the surety of Ealdorman Tidwulf's protection.

'He was wounded. I did what I could for him. Look,' and I thrust out my burned hand to show Tidwulf that Oswy isn't the only one to carry a wound.

'Well. This is a mess, isn't it?' Tidwulf admits, peering into the distance. 'Come with me, and find some trews. The king will need to hear of this.'

I nod but pause and turn to Theodore and Gaya.

'I sealed the wound, but it needs more stitches. I also fed him a healing broth and bound both wounds with agrimony, birthwort and woodruff.' Tidwulf speaks, I must assume to repeat my words in their tongue. I'm grateful.

'And your hand?' Theodore asks me. Again, Tidwulf translates the words.

'Woodruff, brooklime and lily, but there was no butter to hand. I used an oil instead.' Theodore nods as he listens to Tidwulf. Once more, Tidwulf translates his reply.

'Come to me when you've spoken to the king,' Theodore insists, through Tidwulf. 'I've more salve for you. You'll need treatment for the cuts and bruises as well.'

Then, he dismisses me, beckoning for some of the Mercian warriors to help him with Oswy. I can see that Ealdorman Tidwulf no longer keeps Theodore and Gaya as slaves. That warms me, despite my intense cold. I doubt they should ever have been enslaved to Ecgred. Whatever happened there, I'm pleased to see them wearing better clothing, warmer clothing, and issuing commands in a similar way to Wynflæd which they expect to be obeyed, even if it's done through Tidwulf.

I stagger after Tidwulf, ducking into Wulfheard's tent to pull my only other pair of trews from my sack of possessions. They're almost colder than my legs.

'Did you attack the market settlement?' I hurry to keep up with the dark-skinned, long-legged ealdorman.

'Yes, it was successful. We hold more and more of it now. The Wessex king will have to decide whether he'll die in the mint or make peace with King Wiglaf.'

The news thrills me, even while I worry about Ealdorman Ælfstan. Of all of Wiglaf's warriors, it's been him who was first kind to me. I also fear for Wulfheard. If not for him, I'd not have been able to kill the men that I have. Where are they? Why do the gates remain closed? It makes no sense to me.

Ahead, I watch Tidwulf gain admission to the king's tent. I

follow on behind. The king's household warriors leer at me and Eahric, the commander of the king's warriors, startles upon recognising me. I give the men what I hope is a grin, but I still don't have complete control over my facial features. The rain might have stopped, but in its place a bitter wind has sprung up.

'My Lord King,' Tidwulf interrupts the king without apology.

Wiglaf turns to greet him, a question on his lips that dies away when he catches sight of me. 'Where's Ealdorman Ælfstan?' issues forth instead.

'My Lord King, I hope he has the fort, but Oswy and I had to escape a different way because we were barred from entering the fort.'

Consternation sweeps Wiglaf's face. 'I don't understand?'

'Me neither, my Lord King,' I mutter, looking down at my hand and grimacing at the paleness of the flesh and the redness of the burn.

'I understood that the ealdorman would open the fort for us once Lord Æthelwulf was secured. I told him it was unnecessary, but he insisted. We almost have Lundenwic back in our hands now.' Wiglaf's face clouds with unease.

I shake my head, trying to make sense of what's befallen the rest of the Mercians. 'My Lord King, we killed many of the Wessex foemen, the ealdorman amongst them, although Lord Æthelwulf had escaped. We burned the riverside gate and the one remaining ship and started an unholy argument amongst them all. There just can't be enough of them remaining to have taken back the fort. Oswy and I heard nothing to suggest the Mercians have been overrun.'

'Why couldn't you join them?'

'My Lord King, Oswy was badly wounded. He couldn't fight,' I offer quickly. 'And there were Wessex warriors in our way.'

'He's a mess, my Lord King,' Ealdorman Tidwulf confirms, as though my words are to be doubted.

'So, what, you escaped through the drainage channel, just as when you gained entry?'

I nod, but I can feel the edge of Wiglaf's words. I'm beginning to suspect that if I'd returned without Oswy I'd be strung up as a traitor.

'My Lord King. We need to make contact with the men inside the fort. Perhaps there was a fight and they're locked inside the fort, or too wounded to open the gates?' It's all I can suspect. I shrug my shoulders as I speak, hardly the actions of a warrior sure of what's happened to his fellow Mercians.

'It's too much of a risk, my Lord King,' Ealdorman Sigered glowers. He's sitting so close to the fire that it appears his legs are in the embers of the flames. I note the thick fur cloak covering him. 'We have news from Tamworth that the bastard king of the East Angles means to take advantage of your continued absence. We must return to Tamworth. The victory is ours. What happened to the fort is irrelevant.' I'm staggered by Sigered's callous regard for my allies.

'We need to take advantage of the momentum,' I counter immediately, almost pleading. 'We had a firm hold of the fort. Goðeman was in command. He won't have done anything stupid.'

At that moment, Uor and Wulfgar appear as well. Ealdorman Tidwulf has summoned them. Uor eyes me uneasy. Wulfgar has the good grace to look embarrassed. I note how he stands straighter, sucking in his belly. I can only imagine the abuse he's faced since returning to the encampment because he was too damn fat to assist the ealdorman.

'You said the Mercians had the fort?' This is directed to Wulfgar.

'Yes, my Lord King, I spoke to Goðeman and Æthelmod.'

'But not since two nights ago, when you returned?'

'Not since before the fire, no, my Lord King,' Wulfgar confirms.

I'm beginning to feel uncomfortable under all the scrutiny. It isn't just my hand that itches now.

'My Lord King, what are you thinking? That something has befallen Ealdorman Ælfstan?' It's Ealdorman Tidwulf who queries the king.

'No, I'm thinking that something has befallen all of the Mercians, and yet two of them have survived and tell me a strange tale that makes no sense.' King Wiglaf's gaze seems to slide over me, as though he doesn't want to acknowledge that I'm there. His words are angry.

I think back to Oswy's harsh comments at the wall and to what I've seen and endured while inside the walls.

'My Lord King, I didn't ask to be sent inside Londinium, not once, but twice. I didn't ask to be the one here, telling you what's happening. I've done what I could for Oswy. I brought him back alive.'

'Barely,' Ealdorman Tidwulf interjects, and I round on him.

'You may have more knowledge of healing than I do, but I did my best, and there are many here who would have simply left him there to die. I didn't risk getting inside the fort because then he'd most assuredly have perished in the fighting. Two men can't overpower ten times that number when they both carry injuries.'

'And you would have died with him.' Tidwulf is unrelenting in his softly spoken attack.

'More than likely, yes, and then what would you have? You wouldn't know of events inside Londinium. You'd be ignorant of the fact that Lord Æthelwulf's fled, that the ealdorman is dead.' I scour those in the room as I speak, trying to decipher what the ealdormen are thinking. I can't bring myself to meet the king's eyes.

'Perhaps, but we wouldn't have missing Mercians either,' King Wiglaf comments.

I sigh heavily. 'Then fine, my Lord King. I've done everything wrong, and your Mercians are missing. Now, why don't you go back to attacking Lundenwic and fighting with one hand tied behind your back?' I know I'm speaking too disrespectfully, but I'm at the end of my endurance. I need to eat, and sleep, drink even. And I'm the one standing here, half naked, while the other men are all dressed warmly. I begin to understand my uncle's weariness when trying to make his kings see sense.

'Then what would you suggest?' King Wiglaf's furious words arrest my flood of words and bring me up short.

'My Lord King, I'd tell you to go to the fort. The Mercians hold it and will either open the gate for you or, perhaps, you might even find them open already. Maybe that's what they managed to accomplish with their final breaths.' I doubt it, yet I can make no sense of what's happened. I've been inside the fort. I know what Godeman's capable of doing. I'm convinced it's still held by the Mercians.

'It's too much of a risk, my Lord King,' Ealdorman Sigered reiterates. 'We would lose good men when we've almost won anyway. What does it matter about Londinium when we have Lundenwic restored to us? And we must think of King Athelstan of the East Angles. He's preparing for war.'

I suck in air to call Sigered the coward that he is, but King Wiglaf beats me to it.

'Londonia consists of both Lundenwic and Londinium, of the trading settlement and the ancient fort with its vast walls. I want no Wessex warriors standing on Mercian land. Look how they use it against us. I won't have it.' Wiglaf thrusts his arm up high to indicate the fort. 'And it's nearly winter. King Athelstan of the East Angles will wait, now. He prefers to fight with the sun on his back.'

'Then, my Lord King,' and Sigered bows from his chair, showing the top of his bald pate as he draws out the word 'king', 'I believe you have your answer.'

I'm not alone in growling at the older ealdorman who manages

to avoid a fight even when he's encamped with the rest of the
Mercian force, on a battle line, with the enemy no more than a
spear throw in front of us.

* * *

I'm taken to where Theodore and Gaya have been allowed a tent to
offer the Mercian wounded assistance. As I move to the rear of the
camp, I appreciate how few Mercians are there.

'We hold the trading settlement. A good majority of the warriors
protect it,' Ealdorman Tidwulf informs me. 'King Ecgberht and a
handful of his warriors continue to hold the mint and have access
to the river in one location. I suspect they're anticipating reinforcements from his son.'

'So, why has their escape route not been blocked off?'

'Do you not think we've tried, lad? We have, and we lost thirty-
three men in the process. The cost was high. The king wants the
remainder of his men returned to him, including Ealdorman
Ælfstan and Wulfheard, before trying once more.'

'Theodore.' Ealdorman Tidwulf strides inside the small space,
warm with the press of bodies and with a comforting smell scenting
the air that reminds me of Wynflæd's hut. As Theodore meets his
eyes, he switches to their tongue and then repeats what he says so
that I understand as well. 'Assist Icel with his hand. He'll be needed
later. And what of Oswy?' I'm pushed, not unkindly, onto a small
wooden stool by the ealdorman's large hand while he goes to
Theodore's side.

Theodore responds quickly, his words a flood that Tidwulf
translates. 'Icel has done well with both wounds. What concerns
me most is how cold Oswy has become. We're doing our best to
thaw him out.' I sit forward and catch sight of a heavily swaddled

body lying on a squat bed. 'It would be a pity if the escape kills him rather than the initial wounds.'

'Do everything you can,' Tidwulf orders and hurries from the tent. I watch him go and shiver as a waft of cold wind jostles the canvas and the wooden struts which form the basis of the structure.

Gaya appears, smiles and gently places a wooden bowl into the crook of my right arm. I smell the warm pottage while my stomach rumbles and reach to take the spoon from her with my left hand.

Eagerly, I guzzle the warm food, grateful it isn't scolding, or I'd burn my tongue to go with my hand. Only when I'm finished does Theodore sit beside me.

'Show me,' he asks, reaching out with his wizened hands. He knows those few words and speaks them haltingly.

I uncurl my hand slowly, gasping as I do so. Theodore picks up my hand and moves it one way and then another beneath the light. I watch the wound change colour, from red to even redder, as he presses on the parts of my palm which haven't been burned.

'You truly mean to mark yourself as a warrior of Mercia,' he offers, Gaya translating his words this time, her tone not unkindly, her words slow and deliberate. Carefully, Theodore cleans away the residual from the poultice I've applied to my hand. Then he adds his own, binding it tightly with a long strip of linen, which he wraps around my hand three times before tying it off. 'Keep it clean and dry,' he orders me. 'No more sliding in drainage channels for you.' Gaya offers the words he speaks.

'I don't think that'll be possible,' I mutter unhappily before continuing. 'You seem well set up here.'

'Ealdorman Tidwulf has been good to us, for now. We've not had too many men to tend so far. The wounds are either scratches or mortal, and for those warriors, nothing can be done but a decent burial.' This time, it's Gaya who speaks without translating

Theodore's words. She must understand our tongue better than him.

'Here, drink this,' Theodore hands me a beaker, which I sniff before sipping. Again, Gaya offers me his words while Theodore stands, chuckling as I drink deeply. 'You'll be well,' he confirms, using her voice. 'Just try not to burn it again, and as I said, keep it clean and dry.'

Mindful that I still wear no tunic, I stand, stretch and make my way through the camp to where my sack of supplies has been left in Wulfheard's canvas. I slip a not so clean tunic over my head, add my spare cloak beneath the other one I've been given, and make my way to where the horses are stabled. I've a mind to check on Brute. It feels like I've not seen him for weeks, and knowing how difficult he can be, I fear all our good work together might have been undone in my absence.

I find the horses sheltering from the bitter wind behind a steep embankment at the camp's rear. The Mercian forces have laboured up the incline and have no intention of doing the same in reverse. For all the wind's bitter at the top of the slope, it's much milder lower down. I shiver into my two cloaks and immediately spy Brute amongst the other horses. It's easy, really. He's the only one looking at me.

Reluctantly, he makes his way towards me from between two other beasts. It appears that the steeds all stand closely together to mitigate the cold.

'Hello, boy.' I reach out my left hand to stroke his long nose, but he whiffles at my right hand, which I have to hold away from him. 'It'll be fine,' I console him. He lifts his head to appraise me. I laugh at the look in his eyes. I can't say that my damn horse believes my words. 'What have you been up to?' I ask him, running my eyes appraisingly along his body. To my untrained eye, he looks thinner than when we left Tamworth, but I feel hollower as well. Life on the march doesn't guarantee a full belly. 'I'm sure we'll be going back to Tamworth soon,' I console Brute and become aware of judging eyes watching me. I turn then and gasp.

'What are you doing here?' Edwin and I speak the words at the same time. He is, if possible, taller than last time we encountered one another inside Kingsholm before Lord Coenwulf had my uncle and me thrown out from his home. He's also grown even more muscles. I'm quite sure that he'd have been able to lift the stubborn stone inside Londinium on his own. I'm shocked to find my childhood friend here, on the front line of this war with Wessex.

'You haven't heard then?' Edwin replies cockily, hands on his weapons belt, which shows a full range of weapons.

'Heard what?' I'm too tired to bite at his tone.

'Ealdorman Coenwulf means to make an alliance with King Wiglaf. He says it's time to stand behind the king who'll reunite Mercia after all these years of strife. With his father's death, my new lord is amenable to reconciliation with the anointed king of Mercia.'

I startle at the words.

'And he's here, fighting beside the king?' I think to look behind me, to seek out Lord Coenwulf. I can't envisage the angry ealdorman as a warrior. He didn't strike me as the sort, but what do I know?

'No, he's not. But he's sent his warriors to fight on the king's behalf, to prove his loyalty to our king.' I can't tell from Edwin's words whether he approves of this development or not. Certainly, King Wiglaf and his son, in particular, have never been kind to Edwin when he resided at Tamworth.

'And you're one of Ealdorman Coenwulf's warriors?' I ask.

'Yes. Why? Does that surprise you?' Edwin's words are rimmed with fury.

'No, no, I'm pleased for you. That you've finally achieved what you always wanted.'

Edwin laughs then, the sound mocking. 'Unlike you, Icel. I know what you did. Everyone speaks of your heroics in saving the king's life. Not content with casting me aside, you take my position at the king's side as well.'

'Now, wait a moment,' I caution Edwin. 'You were only too eager to stay behind in Kingsholm when you were given the option by my uncle when Lord Coenwulf demanded we leave after his father's horse died. He blamed me for killing the horse even though everyone said I eased the animal's suffering with my ministrations.'

'An option? Your uncle made it clear I wasn't needed.' Edwin stresses the word 'I', and it hurts me to hear such fury directed at Cenfrith when he's no longer here to defend himself.

'That's not true. You could have come with us.'

'I could not,' Edwin seethes, his eyes bright beneath the hood he wears over his dark hair. 'But Lord Coenwulf saw my potential. He allowed me to stay and train with his warriors.'

I rub my forehead with my left hand. Edwin remembers everything incorrectly, and it infuriates me. I'm growing tired of people questioning me when I've done nothing wrong.

'So, you're here to fight for the king in reclaiming Londonia?'

'I am if the king agrees to Lord Coenwulf's requirements.'

'So, you haven't fought for the king?'

'Not yet, no. Why, is that what you've been doing? Carrying on your uncle's endeavours?' His words sting with sarcasm.

'I've been doing what my king commands of me, yes.'

Edwin laughs once more. The sound is long and bitter. How I want to punch him in the face and wipe the smirk from his red-faced cheeks that show no deprivations from being part of the Mercian force these past few weeks. He looks well fed, warm and his clothes are all clean and protect him from the biting weather.

'Then I'm pleased for you, Icel. You've everything I ever wanted, and still, you don't seem happy about it.'

His words strike me as weapons, but there's something else that fills my thoughts.

'What are Lord Coenwulf's "requirements"?'

Edwin looks confused at my question, and then his face clears.

'Money, a position of authority, an acceptance that Kingsholm remains his, and a wife.'

'Who does he wish to marry?' None of the rest of those demands surprises me. It's only what Ealdorman Sigered asks for every time Mercia proclaims a new king. Ealdorman Sigered demands a high price for his questionable loyalty.

'Lady Cynehild, I believe. You should be happy. She hated you for all those years that King Beornwulf was king.'

I stride away from him then, leaving the question he asks but doesn't ask, unspoken. Lady Cynehild didn't wish to remarry. She told me as much. Would King Wiglaf force her to it? And then I still. I know who'll force her to wed again, and my lips curl with unease. I thought I could speak for the lady, sway the king to her true desires to remain at the nunnery, but if it's King Wiglaf's wife, Lady Cynethryth, who thinks to profit from this union, then I know myself to be powerless. Women, as Lady Cynethryth knows only too well, are always pawns in the game of marriages and alliances.

28

'There you are.' A voice cracks through the air, arresting my stomping path, and I face Ealdorman Tidwulf once more. I would have thought the king had lesser men to send on his errands, but perhaps not.

'The king wishes to speak with you.'

'Good, that suits me,' I confirm, my thoughts consumed with Lady Cynehild. But before I can reach the king's tent, I'm aware of a ripple of unease rising through the camp. Tidwulf and I pause, looking around, trying to make sense of what's unsettled everyone. What my eyes fix on makes my heart beat too quickly.

Somehow, the Wessex force has reformed. They're striking out towards the Mercian encampment from inside the market settlement and also from along the eastern bank of the River Fleet, on the same side as the Mercian camp. Their intention is clear. They mean to attack us, now, while we're wholly unprepared.

'Defend your king,' Ealdorman Tidwulf roars at the confused mass of Mercian warriors.

Men, who moments before had been sleeping, eating, or

relieving themselves, spring to action, as they reach for weapons and pull on byrnies, and helms.

'You too, Icel,' Tidwulf orders me.

I rush to Wulfheard's tent, eager to dress appropriately. I have no byrnie, yet when I stoop inside the tent, there's one there, waiting for me. I don't know who brought it for me, but I'm not about to leave it behind.

I pull it over my head as quickly as I can with my bound right hand. It's an effort to fasten it around my body one-handed. Only then do I reach for my seax to slide it into space on my weapons belt, on the right side of my body. It feels uncomfortable, but there's no point having it in reach of my useless right hand. My Mercian shield also waits for me. I heft it awkwardly, wincing as a shudder of pain works its way along my hand. I realise it's the shield I'd been forced to abandon outside the imposing walls during the first battle. I also spy a war axe beneath the shield and take that as well.

I grumble with frustration, while my heart beats as though hooves over the stone roadway. Oswy won't be able to fight, and the king has left many of his warriors to hold the trading settlement, while King Ecgberht clings to the mint. Those men must be dead or overwhelmed, and Wiglaf will have to call on his newest ealdorman to supplement what warriors he has left to him. Edwin, the smug git, will be fighting in the shield wall. Lord Coenwulf will get his wishes, for the king won't be able to go back on a promise once the warriors from Kingsholm have fulfilled theirs. Of course, it all depends on the Mercians being victorious. I'm not sure that will happen.

As I emerge from inside the tent, a sense of panic shrouds me. I'm not alone. There's no order to the onward rush of armoured men. I watch as two men collide rounding a tent from opposite sides, the one only just missing the other with his drawn seax. This attack has come from nowhere. Has Lord Æthelwulf taken advantage of the Mercians' belief in their success, and now means to snatch it from them? I can think of no other means by which the Wessex warriors have managed to reform. I do find it interesting that they march north, close to the walls, but that they don't erupt from inside the fort itself. That gives me some hope that the men I left behind still live.

I thrust my helm onto my head and join the rush of men to where Ealdorman Tidwulf has taken command of the king's forces. I don't know where the king is.

'Form up, men,' Tidwulf orders from in front of the line of defences that the guards have been watching, and through which Oswy refused me admittance days ago.

Ahead, the ground lies hard and barren, the sun nothing more than a pale glimmer on the horizon. The only warmth to be found on this field of slaughter will be from the blood that's shed in a few short moments.

'Ealdorman Muca has the left, the king the right, and we fight in the middle. Now shield wall.' Tidwulf leaps back into the line of advancing men, his intention of joining the battle clear to see.

I cast a final, hopeful look at the grey-walled fort. Surely, if the Mercians inside live, they'll see what's happening and add their strength to the Mercian defence. But I see no sign of movement and the gate remains closed. Instead, I focus on not slipping or tripping over the rugged ground filled with dying tufted grasses.

I can see what Ealdorman Tidwulf hopes to accomplish. He wants to ensure that the advancing Wessex force on the eastern side of the river can't make it to the bridge. King Wiglaf made it clear he believed the Wessex king done for, unless he received reinforcements. Now, it seems, those reinforcements have arrived. If not exactly in the most helpful of places.

If we hold the Fleet bridge, then the two Wessex forces can only join together if the one risks the menacing surface of the dark river.

I don't know how deep it runs, but it'll mean a cold swim, of that I'm sure.

Risking a look towards the bridge, I fear we won't reach it in time. The Wessex force is advancing quickly from the open market settlement. I can't determine how large the force is, but there are enough to overpower the depleted Mercian force.

'Halt.' The cry comes just as we draw level with the bridge. We've made it before the Wessex warriors, surely a mistake on their part.

I listen to the sound of men filling the wooden bridge. I don't envy them such a task. If they hold the bridge but have to fight to do so, there's no guarantee they won't plunge into the icy waters below them. I can feel the cold of the water against my knees.

'Hold.' Ealdorman Tidwulf's words crack like thunder.

I ready myself. I'm not in the first line of the shield wall and not even the second. I've been too slow for that honour.

The fort is closer now, but I can't see more of Lundenwic than the smoke that scurries into the sky from fires burning there. They might be from hearths. I just don't know. Everything else is lost from my sight.

I turn to face the men who surround me. I recognise some of them, and it takes me a moment to remember where from because they aren't men who lived at Tamworth. Only then do I glimpse Edwin's pale, sweating face, and I remember. These are the warriors from Kingsholm. They seemed a fierce bunch when I was in Kingsholm, but that was before I fought the Raiders, the men of Wessex, and watched my uncle bleed before my eyes. Perhaps they aren't quite so fierce after all.

I look away. I don't want Edwin to know we fight so closely together. This is his first real engagement. I hope he lives through it, even though our conversation was less than friendly before.

'Hold.' Tidwulf's voice fractures the air one more time.

Although I'm not in the first two lines of the shield wall, I keep hold of my shield, having looped my hand through the strap. I have a spear, thrust into my hand by one of Tidwulf's warriors, distributing the equipment along the rear of the shield wall.

I know what I'm to do with it when the time comes, even if I lack all skill with the long, thin weapon. I suppose it takes little ability just to jab and stab with it, and that's all I'll be able to manage with my left hand.

No sooner have I checked my grip on the weapon, I hear a shriek from close by, and the Wessex warriors on the eastern side of the Fleet crash into the front of the shield wall.

I can hear little but dip low, keen to weave the spear through the legs of my fellow warriors and pierce one of the Wessex foemen with it.

The shield wall heaves forward, an initial success against the Wessex force, but it leaves me behind, crouching low. I rush to rejoin it, only for the whole thing to surge backwards. I'm forced to dash back or risk being crushed by my comrades.

I wait this time, eager to see what will happen now that some sort of middle ground has been reached. Will the Wessex warriors come at us once more or merely hold, hoping against hope that the bridge that divides them will quickly fall? Do they expect their king to tackle the Mercian warriors blocking the bridge?

I can hear the murmur of voices, the growl of a Wessex warrior, perhaps Lord Æthelwulf in overall command, the words rolling compared to mine.

Weapons clash, shields hammer one another. Now I risk bending again, as do others at the rear of the shield wall, and thread the wooden haft through the tangle of legs. I can see where others are doing the same on the Wessex side. I thrust and stab, aiming for what little I can see of feet and legs.

I draw my weapon back, relishing the slash of maroon that mars the blackened blade, and then I stab forwards with it once more. I can feel that the men at the front of the shield wall are doing well. Their movements are quick. Elbows rearing backwards and jabbing forwards. Blades flash. I begin to believe we'll win the fight easily.

Only then I feel something heavy hit the ground in front of me. A Mercian warrior, and then another. I rush forwards, desperately untangling my right hand as I go, throwing it to the ground and reaching for the shield held overhead by the second line of warriors. I drop my spear to grip the shield tightly with my left hand, allowing the man who's been holding it to fill the gaping void in the shield wall. Others hasten to do the same. One of the warriors from Kingsholm, his name evading me for now, stands beside me. He bends his head, arms thrust upwards to hold the shield, and I can tell he's done this many times before.

It gives me some much-needed confidence.

Beneath my feet, the wounded try to drag themselves away if they can. Hands reach out for them, and some of the men stand easily, angered to have been flattened in such a fashion. One fights his way back to the front, furiously surging through those who've taken his place. But the man beneath my feet is motionless. I fear for him, with the bloom of burgundy leaking beneath his belly.

'Move him,' I call, hoping someone from behind will hear me, but the body stays where it is, all eyes focused to the fore, as the same happens between the two shield walls somewhere else along the line. We hold this time, better prepared for it.

'Buggers,' a voice beside me cries.

I don't know what he means, but curiosity makes me look up and around the rim of the shield, and I see it. Atop some of the shields to my left, warriors stand. The Wessex men have run along their own side's shields and now stab down into the Mercian line with spears. As I watch, head extended to see in the small gap between my shield and the one over my head, one of the men falls backwards, tumbling into the mass of his allies. A Mercian must have stabbed upwards with his spear, skewering our foeman high on his thigh.

'Ware,' Ealdorman Tidwulf calls, his cry taken up by others, as our enemy redouble their efforts to get through our line. More and more of the Mercians are screaming now, shouting their denial.

The ground is rapidly turning sodden beneath my feet and so much blood.

And then the man before me staggers backwards, knocking aside my weak grip on the shield.

I rush into the gap as he vomits noisily behind me. A seax is embedded in his neck, and he won't live to continue the fight.

I brace my feet on the slick surface. They slide a little and then hold. Glancing to either side, I check the two men who support me. To my left is one of the men from Kingsholm, to my right, Wulfgar. He chuckles on meeting my surprised eyes.

'Sometimes, it's better to be fat,' he quips.

'It is,' I confirm, my thoughts turning to Ealdorman Ælfstan and Wulfheard. Where are they?

But I've no time for such thoughts. The shield pressing against mine seems to grow ever heavier. I feel the strain in my already tired arm. I meet the pressure, weight for weight, body tense, just in case the Wessex scum decides to play me for a fool. I refuse to fall beneath his shield. I can sense a blade coming towards me, but it's to the side of Wulfgar, and he spies it just as quickly as I do. Using his right hand, he drives down with his seax, and the gloved hand judders, flinging open so that the seax thuds to the floor. I kick it aside. I don't want to trip on it later.

'My thanks,' I call to Wulfgar, but there's no time. For now, the Kingsholm warrior is, in turn, threatened. The enemy hand is lower than the one that tried to stab me. I know I'll struggle to hit it if I do what Wulfgar has just done, instead jabbing my shield-holding elbow at the hand. But the grip only tightens, perhaps sensing victory. 'Arse,' I exclaim, knowing it hasn't been enough.

Luckily, the warrior behind me has seen the problem. He reaches out and grips our foeman's wrist, pulling him closer and closer. I feel the enemy shield butt up even more firmly against mine. I hold my place even though there's less and less room. As my fellow warrior forces the hand higher, I reach across and slice just below the elbow with my seax. Blood fountains into the air. I snap my mouth shut, closing my eyes as well so that his blood won't blind me.

When I open my eyes once more, the stubby arm's gone, but I feel fingers on my foot. I shout, thinking I'm under attack, only to see the gloved hand, gore flooding from the severed wrist. I boot it aside, grimacing at the sight of such a terrible wound.

The two sides seem to be in a stalemate. I worry the Wessex warriors are waiting for the bridge to fall, for King Ecgberht to reinforce them from the western side. If that happens, the Mercians will be outnumbered. I'm not sure by how many but, certainly, enough to make a victory possible. All these Mercians will have died, and King Ecgberht will still be in control of Londonia.

Wulfgar snarls beside me. I risk looking at him and see a seax blade perilously close to his belly, while at the same time, a long spear attempts to trip him. I stamp down, holding the spear in place, allowing him to focus on the seax. He stretches out once more, pulling the rest of the warrior towards him, and a crack of fracturing wood rings from behind his shield. He grimaces. I steady myself for what will come next. I hold my shield firm, not allowing the shoving and thrusting to dislodge my feet.

Wulfgar grins at me, blood dripping from his teeth. 'Ready, you little shit,' he taunts.

'Do it,' I explode.

Wulfgar lowers his shield, exposing the black and white wyvern shield that faces him. It's no longer flat but rather concave, held together more by the hand gripping the leather strap than anything else. Wulfgar slashes through the strap, and as I keep my enemy at bay, I jab my seax at the warrior there.

Defiant eyes glare at me from behind a helm, but as he tries to defend himself with half a shield, Wulfgar hacks open his throat, and he tumbles to the floor. Immediately, Wulfgar replaces his shield and presses home his advantage. I hear the enemy calling one to another, desperately trying to fill the space left by the broken shield. I'm reminded of what it felt like to fight on the wrong side of the shield wall. But Wulfgar doesn't stop applying his weight against the shield, and the warrior I face slowly tumbles backwards without the support of the warrior to his left.

Now I look to Wulfgar, and he dares me with his eyes.

I lower my shield and stab down with my seax into the man's exposed belly as his shield has fallen over his upper body. His legs buck, one of his knees clattering against my shield, but I keep my grip and return to my position in the shield wall as quickly as I can. My right hand throbs, but I've managed to wrap my hand through the strap. I can only hold it with the aid of my allies. Without them, I'll have to hold it with my left hand and have no other weapon, other than my helmed head to defend myself.

The Wessex shield wall is compromised now. The desperate cries of men to 'bring that bloody shield here' encouraging the Mercians.

'Attack,' Wulfgar roars. 'For Mercia,' he follows on with, and the cry is taken up by more and more voices, Ealdorman Tidwulf adding his command to the uproar.

I feel the Wessex shield wall warp. Any moment now, I'm sure we'll overwhelm them. I sense we've pushed them past where the bridge over the River Fleet stands, and so there'll be no help for them from there, provided the Mercians maintain their control over the bridge.

I apply my shoulder to the shield, sensing my arm growing weak. I don't want to be the reason why our offensive fails. We move forwards at a steady pace. The shield warriors Wulfgar and I have felled are eventually replaced, shields slapping into place, but it's too late. My speed increases, the entire shield wall moves quicker, and then the Wessex defence breaks entirely apart.

29

They run, those who can, and I follow on behind, howling at them, as the remainder of the Mercians do. Wessex men too wounded to move lie on the ground, desperately watching as they're entirely abandoned. A blond-haired man, his face streaked with blood, assesses my approach, but he's too slow. Before he can duck aside, I slice open his neck with my seax. I move on before I know he's dead, but I suspect he is. No man can live through such a cut.

Ahead, Ealdorman Tidwulf hollers for some semblance of order, but the Mercians have been cut loose, and the Wessex dead pile up. I watch as Tidwulf drives his curved blade into a fleeing man's back. He relishes in this victory just as much as the rest of us.

I see a helmed head crawling towards the riverbank, and I rush to it. The man is missing his right leg beneath the knee. In his wake, he trails blood and gore. I stab him through the neck, and he should thank me for the respite. I suck in much-needed air, gazing back towards the wooden bridge.

The fighting there's bloody and brutal. The Wessex host is driven mad by their comrades' destruction on this side of the river. The king's banner summons the Wessex warriors to their lords, and my lip curls as I see King Ecgberht, some distance from the fighting, astride his mount. It's impossible not to know him when he wears his elaborate warrior's helm, complete with horsehair. He has no intention of joining his men.

I think of Ealdorman Ælfstan, of Ealdorman Tidwulf and King Wiglaf and appreciate that these men will face their enemy with their men. King Wiglaf might not always have been the man to do so, but he's learned what's expected from him now. He's come to know the importance of being prepared to die for his kingdom.

But all is not well. As I watch, the bridge seems to shudder. Two Mercians are pitched over the side, their cries piercing, ringing out above the thundering commotion of the battle.

'My lord,' I shout, trying to recall Ealdorman Tidwulf to this new problem. But he doesn't hear.

I survey the scene before me. The ground dips as it nears the River Fleet, and there are few living men on the strip of scrubby grass before me. All the Mercians are long gone, following those of our enemy who hope to make it back to the ship I can now see dipping and rising on the River Thames. It seems that Lord Æthelwulf took the ship and used it to bring reinforcements. Why he chose this side of Londinium's walls, I don't know. Unless, of course... And I turn and gaze once more at the fort. Did Ealdorman Ælfstan and Wulfheard have to stop Lord Æthelwulf from claiming back the fort with increased numbers? Is that why they've not been seen and have been unable to open the gate? I hope so.

I hear another outraged cry, followed by a shriek of pain and the crash as a body hits the surface of the water, making me shudder at the thought of such a cold death.

'My lord,' I try once more, but no one heeds me, apart from one set of eyes that I know far too well.

Edwin is blood-splattered, his byrnie ripped beneath his left arm, his helm askew.

'The bridge,' I call to him all the same. I can only hope that the king will notice the problem, that he'll order his men back to the slaughter field. This isn't yet a victory.

'What can we do?' Edwin demands. His voice is weak. Perhaps he's winded from the fight.

'We can hold this end of the bridge,' I reply, not even considering whether we can or not.

I manipulate my right hand so that I can grip the shield a little tighter, biting down on a fresh surge of agony, and then bend and yank another Mercian shield from the lifeless hand of a man who lived that morning.

'Get another shield,' I order Edwin.

He does as I ask without thought, and then I'm shambling over the uneven ground, mindful of the dead and dying, the abandoned blades I could slice myself open on if I fall and trip.

The Mercians hold the bridge for now, but their numbers are dwindling. Where, I think, is Ealdorman Muca? He should be here, making sense of the chaos. I consider he might be dead, along with the Mercians who've fallen into the river.

'We hold, here, until the king or one of the ealdormen sees our plight.'

I've to hope that someone will come soon. The Wessex warriors are more than halfway along the bridge. I catch sight of the wyvern banner and know that their bastard king thinks to cross soon as well.

'Hold,' I call, wishing my voice sounded as firm as Wulfgar's or the ealdorman's, but it's a fragile thing after everything I've done today.

Three sets of eyes glare at me from their position on the bridge, shields in front of them, seaxes ready should one of the Wessex warriors make a run for it. They hold contempt for my feeble efforts.

'Do you see anyone else coming to help?' I demand from them. 'Anywhere?'

King Wiglaf has held back. He can't see what happens here. He must only be aware of the victory over the reinforcements.

'Do what you can,' one of them mutters to me, his expression fierce behind his helm. He turns back to face the seemingly unstoppable Wessex assault.

'Stand with me,' I inform Edwin. The bridge is only just wide enough for a horse to cross. Two of us can easily block it, provided we hold our position.

'It won't work,' Edwin argues. His face is twisted in fear.

'It bloody has to.' I broker no argument. 'If King Ecgberht reaches this side of the river, we'll never reclaim Londonia, not with the numbers we have.'

I think Edwin will argue with me, but instead, he nods, just the once, and kicks aside a muddy ball of grass to make room for his feet.

I can feel the bridge moving, the Wessex warriors no doubt making a run for it. I force my shoulder into the one shield, the other wedged beneath it. Edwin does the same, and the four shields just about cover the expanse. But, we have only one hand for weapons between us, and I can feel the coldness from the river wrapping itself around my feet. We're exposed.

And then the onslaught begins.

The first blow against my shield sees me waver, almost slip. Luckily, my foot digs deeply into the gravel left on this side of the pathway, no doubt forced there by a cart or some such. I hold my place. I can't risk looking around to see if any aid is coming. I must endure until it does.

Edwin jumps back from his shield, the force of the blow against him making his eyes open wide, and a roar of fear erupt from his throat.

'Let us through,' a voice begs, but I shake my head. The Mercians will have to give their lives to retain the bridge. If we yield, the Wessex warriors will be through and racing towards King Wiglaf.

'Hold,' I urge Edwin through tight lips.

He makes no reply.

I look upwards. A war axe appears over the shield rim, one I'm powerless to dislodge. If I reach up, the shields will give way. I hold my head lower, refusing to acknowledge the Wessex banner that flutters at the corner of my vision.

I'll not allow that banner to cross this bridge.

Another war axe crashes through the shields, through the one held in place by my other shield. It misses me, but there's space through which the Wessex warrior can see, and they can see nothing. Who then must they think prevents them from crossing? Do they realise it's no more than two boys?

I hold firm, the pressure on the shields to part so intense all of my body aches from the efforts. I feel ragged and broken, everything hurts, but that doesn't matter. I'm only one person, but I must do everything I can for Mercia. If my uncle gave his life to Mercia, then so can I.

Another war axe thunders into the shield held by Edwin. I catch a flash of the blade and then close my eyes as splinters of wood fly through the air. We might be holding them at the moment, but I know we can't do so indefinitely. Edwin must realise the same. His eyes lift to meet mine, and they say more than our angry words did earlier that day.

If we should die here, then we'll both have met our fate as warriors of Mercia. I hope that my uncle would be proud of me, that Lady Cynehild will not be too angry with me, that Wynflæd will not mourn for me too deeply.

Our temporary structure shudders, and although I can't see, I'm sure there must be horses on the bridge. No doubt they mean to use their horses as a battering ram to force Edwin and me aside.

A seax stabs through the shield. I feel it grating over my helm, and I'm grateful to have such protection on me. Now a spear slides between my legs, turning and twirling, and it's impossible not to fixate on it, even though I can't move my feet without fear of slipping.

A clang of iron on iron, and Edwin's helm falls backwards, exposing his forehead and his bewildered eyes, but still, he holds.

The spear hooks my foot, the hilt pulling on me, but I keep my place until the spear slices through the leather of my boot and leaves a scorching burn mark in its wake.

Tears fall down my cheeks now. I might want to be remembered as a warrior of Mercia, but I'm no more than a child. Wiser heads than mine should have realised what was happening. Why did they leave it to me?

'Stand aside.' Wulfgar's booming words startle me. His shield crashes into the place where the gap has formed. He stinks of blood and sweat, but at least he's seen the problem. 'Hold,' he informs me.

I feel more and more of Mercia's warriors falling into place behind me. One after another, after another, shields and seaxes ready in hands. And then I hear a sound I never thought to hear again.

'For Mercia.' Through the mass of men comes the command of Ealdorman Ælfstan, and he isn't far behind.

I meet his eyes, and he grins at me.

'Sorry it took us so long,' he bellows. 'We had some Wessex scum to hold at bay.' His words are filled with good cheer, and they embolden me. If Ealdorman Ælfstan can hold against so many of our enemy, then so can I. I redouble my effort to keep the shield in place.

And Ealdorman Ælfstan doesn't come alone. I catch sight of the other Mercians who braved the drainage channel and who I feared lost on the edge of a Wessex blade: Goðeman, Cenred, Osmod, Landwine, Waldhere, Kyre, Maneca and Æthelmod. Even Frithwine and Garwulf.

The Wessex warriors, no doubt aware that the Mercian shields have been reinforced, redouble their efforts to get across the bridge. I can hear the sound of spears being thrown, the whooshing loud in my ears. The cries from across the bridge suddenly increase in volume. While I expect hooves to be used against the shields, the sound of hooves on wood leads me to believe they're going the other way.

'Hold men, hold.' King Wiglaf's voice, joining Ealdorman Ælfstan's, renews the Mercians' resolve. We push, and we shove. At one moment, I think I'll fall beneath the crush of Mercian feet, only for Ealdorman Ælfstan to haul me upright, his grip fierce. His eyes rake me in, perhaps noting wounds I've gathered, while I watch him. His cheek is bloodied, although the blood is old and scabbed. I consider what other wounds he carries even as the remainder of the Mercians rushes across the bridge, chasing down the Wessex warriors. I gasp air into my tight chest and peer at where the Wessex banner is leading the retreat.

I think they'll retake Lundenwic, but then I catch sight of more warriors carrying the eagle banner and know that there's no means of escape that way, not through the tightly packed streets of the trading settlement.

Abruptly, five mounted Wessex warriors veer away from the rest of the men. Unheeding of the men they crush in their wake and eagerness to escape, they encourage the horses to move faster and faster. King Ecgberht means to flee by any means necessary.

'My lord.' I point and call to Ealdorman Ælfstan.

'My Lord King,' Ælfstan quickly shouts in turn, and Wiglaf

turns to face him, little more than his eyes visible beneath his shimmering warrior's helm.

He follows where Ælfstan indicates, and I see the distaste in his eyes. My uncle told me that King Wiglaf was craven, but he's since proved otherwise. Whether he fled the battlefield or not when first faced with King Ecgberht of Wessex no longer matters. He fights with his warriors now.

'Bastard.' The word echoes on the lips of us all.

'Catch him,' the king roars.

Now every eye is on the retreating figure of King Ecgberht, and the words have two effects. The Wessex warriors howl with fear. The Mercian warriors with outrage and derision.

'Get the horses,' Ælfstan calls to me.

I seek out Edwin before I dash away, but I can't see him amongst the carnage of the attack.

My lip sours when I race closer to the encampment and spy Ealdorman Sigered, sitting proudly on his black mount, his eyes on the action before him, even if his hand is nowhere near his seax or sword.

'The horses,' I puff, his horse walking backwards as I rear up before it.

'What?'

'The Wessex king means to escape,' I point, even as I rush onwards, crashing through the abandoned tents and canvases, skipping high to avoid hempen ropes keeping the temporary dwellings upright.

I spy Theodore, watching from the tent's doorway he now commands. His eyes are narrowed. Does he sense the victory or the impending doom? I wish I knew.

'He means to escape,' I bellow at him, the words drifting behind me, hanging still while I plough onwards.

Abruptly, I pull up, seeing the horses arranged before me. How many should I take? How will I know whose animal belongs to whom? And then Brute is before me, eyes blazing, and I smirk to see him, pawing the ground, ready and waiting.

Eagerly, I go to mount. I have no saddle or reins, they're in my tent, but one of the stablehands has seen me.

'My lord?' he calls, and I smile.

'I'm no one's lord. Bring me Ealdorman Ælfstan's horse and nine other beasts, saddled and ready to gallop.'

The youngster offers me a toothy grin and goes to release the reins of the horses who have been made ready. I realise the ealdorman's horse isn't amongst them, but another of the stablehands rushes through the herd of horseflesh and brings one animal towards us. I pause.

'I have time to get my saddle,' and I turn, thundering back to my canvas, breathless with my haste. Already I can imagine King Ecgberht being too far away to catch, and yet, we'll accomplish nothing without horses.

With my saddle held clumsily against my chest by my left hand, I rear up and dash back the way I came. Brute waits for me, head bowed, and he takes the saddle, the bit and the harness without argument, although the stablehand has to assist me with the more difficult task of cinching it in place as I have only one hand to do so. And now the other horses are ready as well.

'Come with me,' I urge the stablehand who helped me, but his face clouds with fear. 'Tie the horses' reins to their saddle. I'll not have them tripping,' I quickly rephrase. Only then do I allow Brute his head. I encourage him onwards, giving him the freedom to gallop as quickly as he dares, jumping over hempen ropes and even over one fire spitting feeble smoke into the air. Behind me, other hooves rumble.

I hear a voice cry. 'There's a ship to the west of Lundenwic.' Theodore stands, waiting for me to pass him, to tell me what I need to know. He shows no fear, neither does Gaya, who must have given him the words to shout. In fact, both of them have weapons in hand. They'll fight for Mercia, just as I will. They must hate the Wessex king just as much as I do.

'Thank you,' I call, racing past Ealdorman Sigered and his few men who still stand as his guard and do nothing. Brute shows no signs of slowing when he crests the rise and the slaughter field, with its host of carrion crows and groaning men, the stink worse than blood-month. I encourage him onwards, checking I don't rush alone. Eight of the other horses keep pace with me, Ealdorman Ælfstan's steed amongst them.

The bridge comes into focus quickly, King Wiglaf trying to clear a path to allow him access, while the fighting has dwindled to little more than two or three areas of fierce battling. But still, that path is blocked to us.

'Stay here,' Ealdorman Ælfstan cautions the king, mounting even before his horse has come to a complete stop. 'We'll get to him.'

Ealdorman Ælfstan steers his horse down the rise beside the river without pausing for an argument. I can see how deep the river is now. But Ealdorman Ælfstan believes it's the quickest path. That much is evident as he forces his horse into the water. The animal stands firm and then gives in to the vigorous demands from its rider. Together, they crash into the river, and I shiver, even as Brute follows on behind.

I don't know who else mounts the remaining horses, but my ears fill with the murmur of the river, and then Brute is released by the current and rushes up the embankment. No more than four Wessex warriors attempt to intercept us, but the ealdorman meets them with his blade. I slash one man with my seax, opening a thin line of blood across his forehead, even as I kick him, and he tumbles beneath the hooves of one of the horses coming on behind.

Ealdorman Ælfstan hasn't paused, and I encourage Brute to catch him. I need to share the information that Theodore ensured I knew.

'The west,' I huff when Brute catches up to the ealdorman. 'A ship, according to the healer.'

Ealdorman Ælfstan's lips narrow in a tight line, and he grimaces.

'Craven bastard,' he roars, his horse redoubling its speed beneath his feet.

I bend low over Brute's neck, allowing him the space he needs to bunch his powerful legs beneath his tight belly.

So quickly, I almost can't focus on anything, we skirt inside the boundaries of Lundenwic. I can see where a fierce battle has been fought. Collapsed buildings still smoulder, puffs of smoke rising into the cool air as though fog.

Ealdorman Ælfstan appears to know where he's going. With his eagle shield before him, people who reside inside Lundenwic skip out of the way of the advancing horses, turning weapons to face the ground as they realise he's Mercian.

I've never stepped foot inside Lundenwic before. Although there are clearly defined trackways, they're tight and twisty. The houses are built almost so close together that one holds up the roof of its neighbour. It's so unlike Londinium, I'm staggered, yet the most prominent difference explains everything. To my left, the River Thames churns darkly, an open expanse rushing along the banks of the trading settlement. The much-needed shore front where the market transacts all of its business, where there are wooden and thatched homes, where wattle and daub is the building material of choice. There's almost no grey stone to be seen.

No sooner have I seen this than Brute comes to an abrupt stop. I almost fall, just managing to stay in my seat by gripping the reins tighter and tighter, my knees coming together over Brute's neck.

'What?' I gasp, and then I realise what he's seen. Here there's a broken tree trunk, no doubt from one of the wattle and daub houses that once lined the roadway, now burned, so that little more than ash remains. And the sharpened stake of what's left of the post. If Brute hadn't stopped, he would have run onto that stake.

Around me, the other mounted warriors shriek their fear as they see the way barred and take evasive action. If not for Brute, more of the horses would be dead.

When everyone has rushed through the space behind the fallen post, Brute continues, now at the rear of the group.

I watch as the horses regain their speed, the ealdorman too far in front to catch unless he stops. And then I crest a hill and see the ship Theodore told me about. It's not a huge ship, but already small figures scamper over it. They ought to see their king coming towards it and must know that it's time to retreat.

I push Brute on. King Ecgberht can't be allowed to escape, not after all the carnage he's caused, and not when he's gone from commanding a force large enough to make Mercia and Northumbria kneel before him to little more than four men at his back. He's abandoned all of his warriors.

If King Ecgberht escapes back to Wessex, he'll only live to gather more men from his Carolingian allies and start the task of taking Mercia once more. If that happens, Mercia will never be safe from his pretensions.

Yet, no matter how fast Brute gallops, or Ealdorman Ælfstan, far in front, it seems that King Ecgberht is faster still. I watch him dismount, running alongside his horse because the animal only truly slows as it thunders into the murky depths of the River Thames. The other riders at his rear turn on seeing their king safely aboard. I appreciate that we must fight them before we can even get to their king. They dismount, slapping their horses to have them clear of the coming battle.

'Hurry,' I shout, but there's no one to hear me. Everyone else is in front of me, rushing towards the River Thames. I have a better view than all of them until I dip low, the river for once higher than I am, and now I can see nothing but the mud-splattered trackways that lead west towards Mercian settlements further inland.

Ahead of me, the other horses are keeping a good pace, apart from one of the animals, which has reared up and now limps onwards. The Mercian quickly dismounts, checks the animal for obvious signs of injury and rushes onwards himself, tangling the reins around the animal's saddle so it won't further hurt itself. I admire the warrior's dedication.

I pass the horse, head down, sweat-streaked. I wish one of the stablehands were ready to help the poor animal, but I can do nothing for it now.

Brute spurs onwards, surging past the running Mercian, and now I can see again.

Ealdorman Ælfstan has reached the four Wessex warriors. He, too, has jumped clear from his black mount and faces all four of our enemy.

The sound of weapons crashing together is loud enough to be heard from where I am. The ealdorman holds off the enemy with his shield and blade. The next mounted warriors attempt to go around the small skirmish, but one of the Wessex men detaches himself from the group and rushes against him. The same thing happens to the next Mercian as well. Ealdorman Ælfstan battles the remaining two so that the fourth and fifth Mercians can race on to the ship.

I can see where the Wessex king watches his warriors dispassionately while shipmen dig oars deep into the turgid River Thames, eager to get as much of a gap between themselves and the riverbank as possible. It's going to be close, my eyes wavering between the chasing horses and the ship, but I fear King Ecgberht might just have managed to escape.

But the Mercian – I recognise him now as Wulfgar – directs his horse into the river, and the animal hastens to obey, moving level with the ship. Wulfgar lifts his seax and war axe, flinging the one at the king, stabbing one of the shipmen with the other.

I hold my breath, but the war axe misses King Ecgberht by no more than a hair's breadth, while the shipman stabs down with his oar, battering Wulfgar and his horse so that Wulfgar slides free from his horse's back.

The next Mercian flings himself at the ship, legs circling in the air as his horse comes to a sudden stop, lending him some momentum. But the boat is too far away, and the warrior crashes into the River Thames. I hear a cry of pain, and unconsciously, I'm looking to Ealdorman Ælfstan once more.

One of the Mercian warriors has fallen. Ealdorman Ælfstan battles three of the Wessex men alone.

I spare a lingering look to King Ecgberht, but even Wulfgar has turned his horse back towards the shore, collecting the struggling Mercian as he goes, for fear he'll drown beneath the weight of his weapons and sodden byrnie. King Ecgberht must smirk beneath his warrior's helm, despite the fact this is no victory for him, other than that he still lives.

Dismayed, I aim Brute towards Ealdorman Ælfstan. I must save him from the three Wessex warriors. The remaining Mercians have ridden to the riverbank, and from there, they shout derisively at the king of Wessex. Now he truly is escaping with little more than the clothes on his back – such infamy. The Mercians will enjoy sharing the story of that. But, first, Ealdorman Ælfstan is under threat.

One of the Wessex men is already bleeding from a wound across his neck. But the other two are hale, despite Ealdorman Ælfstan's careful attack. He fights with precision, none of the rage I would expect to see in a man fighting for his life. I'm reminded of how similar his technique is to my uncle's.

I rush Brute at the bleeding man, kicking out with my right leg, and only then leaping from the saddle. I have a firm grip on my seax by the time I land on the churned earth. I twist my right hand through the strap on my Mercian shield. I ram it into the bleeding man's head where he tries to stand, having tumbled to the ground at the force of my kick. He falls backwards once more, spread before me, arms above his head, legs below my feet, and I stab down through his byrnie. His body judders as he draws his last breath.

But I don't have time to spare. Ealdorman Ælfstan is down on one knee, blood streaming from a wound on his exposed cheek, his helm knocked askew, or perhaps lost in the headlong dash. I don't know. And still, the rest of the Mercians are oblivious to what's happening.

I rush at the back of one of the men. Thick brown curls escape below his helm, and he has shoulders as broad as Wulfgar's. In one hand, he menaces Ealdorman Ælfstan with a seax, while he punches the side of his face with the other. The sound is unmistakably wet. I launch myself at him, desperate to get him off Ælfstan. Ælfstan is bleeding from his lip as well, one eye entirely bloodshot. I can see that he wavers.

The warrior must sense me, and when I'm in mid-flight and unable to move position, he turns. I meet his fist head-on. It crashes into my chest, driving the air from me, leaving me gasping but stabbing at the same time. I lash out at his arm, his shoulder, as he withdraws his hand from me, and blood arches into the sky.

'Little cock,' he growls at me, but I'm on top of him, punching with my left fist and jabbing with the right, each movement agony as the shield thuds into him. He moves his head from side to side, evading my blows, and I growl low in my throat. Beneath me, I can feel him forcing his knees higher to gain purchase on the ground. If he gets to his feet, I won't be able to stop him. Even now, it's akin to fighting a bear.

And still, Ealdorman Ælfstan isn't safe. I would wish Wulfheard were here, able to help Ealdorman Ælfstan, but I've not seen him, only the ealdorman.

'Keep still.' The words are snapped with authority.

I glance up to see the very man himself.

'I can't kill him while you crawl all over him.' His words are thick with displeasure and pain.

I slide from the Wessex warrior's body, tense, expecting him to jump up and continue his fight, but, instead, I'm greeted with the wet sound of iron through flesh. I choke, blood pouring from my nose just as it does from Ealdorman Ælfstan.

He's still on one knee, swaying from side to side, as though a tree in a storm, but the Wessex warrior is dead, his head just below Ælfstan's knee, a seax sticking out from his neck.

I take a deep breath, struggling to get enough air into my body, and collapse to the ground, violently coughing.

'Nice,' Wulfheard offers as I roll over and spit to clear my mouth, not realising my bloodied saliva lands on the dead man's face.

'Sorry,' I gasp, but Wulfheard shakes his head at me, a smile on his pain-etched face.

'How did you...' he begins but then stops. 'I don't need to know,' he confirms, surveying the scene before us. By now, the other Mercians have realised what's happening, and they've moved back to help Ealdorman Ælfstan. But it would have been too late if not for Wulfheard's arrival.

I eye him, noting that he has a bandage around the top of his left arm and can't stand straight, favouring his right foot.

'What happened?' I demand to know. 'Where have you been?'

'Lord Æthelwulf returned with reinforcements. We had to hold the fort and couldn't make it to the gate. Come, we need to return to the king, inform him that we failed and that King Ecgberht has escaped.'

'It's hardly a failure,' I retort, patting my body to check for other wounds the giant might have inflicted on me. 'His warriors are dead. Londonia is Mercia's once more.'

'Aye, but the bastard still lives,' Wulfheard growls, and he makes a good point.

'We'll get him next time,' I retort, tending to Ealdorman Ælfstan as I speak. I hold his head still, but his eyes can't focus on me. He's taken a knock to the head. I know what he needs to cure that.

'There better not be a bloody next time,' the ealdorman grumbles, and then he vomits all over my boots.

AUTHOR NOTES

Thank you for returning to the Eagles of Mercia Chronicles. I hope you've enjoyed this faster-paced, more violent second book. Icel is a wonderful character to write about.

And now for some history. The name of Londonia for Lundenwic and Londinium is taken from *Citadel of the Saxons* by Rory Naismith, an enticing idea of combining the two separate settlements that we now know as London at a specific period in time, and easy to distinguish from the more distinct entities of Saxon Lundenwic and Roman Londinium. It's long been accepted that London as we know it has changed significantly since the Roman and Saxon days. Londinium, the premier Roman site in England, was a vast sprawl behind substantial stone walls, although the walls weren't built first. They were constructed between the 180s and 220s, whereas the earliest timbers on the site so far found date to AD47. As such, Londinium was not initially built as a defensive settlement but rather as a place for the Roman occupation of Britain to showcase all that it had to offer to the often unruly and ungrateful tribes of Britain.

The ruin that was Londinium was not what the area's traders

needed when they came to redevelop the settlement in the seventh century. The walls of Londinium would have still been largely intact, making it difficult to get to the River Thames, which was crucial for their waterborne trading network, which extended over vast distances, to succeed. Instead, and skipping over the River Fleet (now subterranean, and therefore a 'lost' river of London), they made their home further west, and Lundenwic, the clue is in the ending of the name 'wic' meaning market, first came into prominence.

Of course, Londinium remained, as did much of its walls. So, at this period, it would have held an appeal for military conquerors, even if the true wealth was in the trading ambitions of those living in Lundenwic and, of course, in the status of holding it. Rory Naismith informs that Lundenwic was half as big as Roman Londinium in terms of area covered, at 60 ha, and at its height had 7,000 inhabitants, a far cry from the anticipated 25,000–30,000 who had occupied Roman Londinium at its peak. Interestingly, another factor that prevented Londinium from being reused during the Saxon period could have been the extent of stone remains – these would have hampered those who wished to build with wood, as the Saxons did.

The idea of having Icel walking through these ruins, which would have been ancient even in the 830s, was too good an opportunity to miss, although it's not as easy as I thought it might be to piece together what Londinium might have been like. It doesn't help that my geographical knowledge of London is poor.

Recent archaeological finds imply that Roman Londinium went through many phases of development, and it's intriguing to consider what might have remained visible in the 830s. The roads may have long since disappeared, the areas close to the river, the Walbrook, might have become boggy, and there would have been a general sense of abandonment. I can't help thinking it would have

been an eerie place – too vast for any Saxon force to hold compe-
tently and perhaps echoing with the sound of all those who once
lived there. What must the Saxons have thought of this settlement?
Did they genuinely believe, as it's written, that it was the 'ancient
works of giants'?

Both of these settlements were firmly Mercian holdings at this
point. The king of Wessex was making his ambitions clear by trying
to hold on to them once King Wiglaf was once more king of Mercia.
The settlement of Southwark, which would have been on Wessex
land, does not seem to be in use at this specific time – in fact, the
Roman bridge connecting Roman Londinium to Southwark might
have been gone by as early as the fourth century.

The Anglo-Saxon Chronicle (ASC) has little to say about what
happened during AD830, other than to praise King Ecgberht for his
success against the Welsh kingdoms, a success that I've made a
failure because I can't determine any change that shows these
Welsh kingdoms were subject to another. There was no love lost
between Mercia and Wessex, and their unease with one another
had endured for at least a century before these events occurred.

The word *toforans*. I was going to use the word 'toff', but wary of
it being a 1930s invention, I dug a little deeper and discovered that
while toff might be related to the word toffee-nosed, it could also be
much older. *Toforans* means superior in Old English.

For those who don't share my love of Saxon coinage and the
mints, the Saxons did have coinage. These were often stamped with
the king's head (and I do mean stamped). Finds of coins provide
much-needed information about what was happening in the Saxon
kingdoms at this time, which the written record has either glossed
over, or failed to mention. A recent discovery of a coin showing
Ludica's head (the king of Mercia before Wiglaf) has confirmed that
he did indeed rule Mercia for some time. These finds constantly
and consistently rewrite much that's known from the scanty written

record. But, at the time, the kings of Saxon kingdoms tended to have control over the mints. The fact that King Ecgberht was unwilling to relinquish his hold on the mint inside Lundenwic might reveal that he had no mint of his own, or that Mercian coinage was simply the most respected – perhaps like the British pound or the US dollar these days – it was deemed to be more stable. King Ecgberht also had coins produced there that proclaimed him as king of Mercia. I imagine that riled King Wiglaf no end.

My decision to have Icel escape and return through a drainage channel is based on a trip I made to Roman Corbridge nearly fifteen years ago, when my two small children (at the time) took great delight in crawling through the hypocaust system, much to the unease of many. If they could do it, then so too could Icel. And, in fact, if you visit the Roman Corbridge website, there is indeed a photo of a small child doing just that. Not much changes.

Icel will return, soon. Thank you for reading.

ACKNOWLEDGMENTS

I would like to thank the team at Boldwood Books for being so supportive, especially my editors, Jade Craddock and Ross Dickinson, and Caroline Ridding for allowing me to tell my story of Icel.

To my better half and adult children – thank you for trying to understand that 'headphones on' means I'm working. I know you all try to live with my sometimes bizarre behaviour.

I would also like to thank my beta readers, EP, CS, ST and AM, and pay a special tribute to Christine Hancock, who sadly passed away before she could meet the younger Icel. I will certainly miss her sharp observations about my writing, and our meanderings and musings about events in Saxon England. Every historical fiction writer needs someone who shares their passion in order to debate such matters.

I would also like to thank my father, MC, for his help, as always, in finding antique maps that allow me to piece together a time before maps even existed. Without such help, I wouldn't know my River Thames from my River Trent, and certainly, my reimagining of Londonia wouldn't have been possible. I must also give a shout-out to Shaun at Flintlock Covers for then turning those ideas into something that can be visualised on a page.

And, finally, a big thank you to my readers. You allow me to continually linger in Saxon England, and I'm so, so grateful.

MORE FROM MJ PORTER

We hope you enjoyed reading *Wolf of Mercia*. If you did, please leave a review.

If you'd like to gift a copy, this book is also available as an ebook, digital audio download and audiobook CD.

Sign up to MJ Porter's mailing list for news, competitions and updates on future books.

https://bit.ly/MJPorterNews

Son of Mercia, the next book in The Eagle of Mercia Chronicles, is available now.

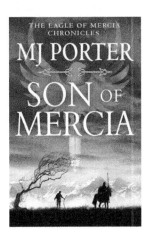

ABOUT THE AUTHOR

MJ Porter is the author of many historical novels set predominantly in Seventh to Eleventh-Century England, and in Viking Age Denmark. Raised in the shadow of a building that was believed to house the bones of long-dead Kings of Mercia, meant that the author's writing destiny was set.

Visit MJ's website: www.mjporterauthor.com

Follow MJ on social media:

 twitter.com/coloursofunison

 instagram.com/m_j_porter

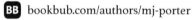 bookbub.com/authors/mj-porter

Boldwood

Boldwood Books is an award-winning fiction publishing company seeking out the best stories from around the world.

Find out more at www.boldwoodbooks.com

Join our reader community for brilliant books, competitions and offers!

Follow us
@BoldwoodBooks
@BookandTonic

Sign up to our weekly deals newsletter

https://bit.ly/BoldwoodBNewsletter

Made in United States
North Haven, CT
21 April 2023

35730130R00183